Charlotte Betts began her working life as a fashion designer in London. A career followed in interior design, property management and lettings.

The Apothecary's Daughter is her debut novel and won the YouWriteOn Book of the Year in 2010, the Romantic Novelists' Association Joan Hessayon Award for New Writers in 2011 and the RoNA's Historical Category award for 2013. The sequel, *The Painter's Apprentice* was published in 2012 and shortlisted for the Festival of Romance's Best Historical Read Award in 2012. *The Spice Merchant's Wife* was published in 2013 and won the Festival of Romance's Best Historical Read Award in 2013. *The Palace of Lost Dreams* was shortlisted for the Romantic Novelists' Association's Historical Romantic Novel RoNA award in 2019 and *The Fading of the Light* in 2022.

Visit Charlotte's website at www.charlottebetts.com

Also By Charlotte Betts

THE SPINDRIFT TRILOGY

The Light Within Us
The Fading of the Light
Letting in the Light

STANDALONES

The Apothecary's Daughter
The Painter's Apprentice
The Spice Merchant's Wife
The Milliner's Daughter*
The Chateau by the Lake
Christmas at Quill Court*
The House in Quill Court
The Dressmaker's Secret
The Palace of Lost Dreams
The Lost Daughter of Venice

*ebook only

The Italian Garden

CHARLOTTE BETTS

PIATKUS

PIATKUS

First published in Great Britain in 2024 by Piatkus

1 3 5 7 9 10 8 6 4 2

A CIP catalogue record for this book
is available from the British Library.

ISBN 978-0-349-43276-2

Typeset in Caslon by M Rules

Printed and bound in Great Britain by
Clays Ltd, Elcograf S.p.A.

Papers used by Piatkus are from well-managed forests
and other responsible sources.

Piatkus
An imprint of
Little, Brown Book Group
Carmelite House
50 Victoria Embankment
London EC4Y 0DZ

An Hachette UK Company
www.hachette.co.uk

www.littlebrown.co.uk

For Jane and Chris Mowforth,
with love and thanks.

Villa Marchesi, Bellagio, Lake Como

June 1862

There was the merest sliver of grey light between the shutters when Flora slipped out of her bed. She tiptoed across the rug and glanced through the half-open door into Umberto's dressing room. He lay facing her, his clenched fist resting on the pillow. Even in sleep, her husband still looked angry. Shivering in her nightgown, she turned away.

The floorboards creaked and she froze, her heartbeat thudding in her ears.

But he didn't stir and, after what felt like an eternity, she edged towards the other door. The handle turned noiselessly and then she was creeping barefoot along the landing.

The oil lamp on the high shelf in the nursery was turned down low to avert Isabella's night terrors and Flora leaned over to kiss her daughter's cheek. 'I love you more than life itself,' she murmured, breathing in the sweet scent of her child's skin, 'but I cannot endure any longer. If there was any other way ...'

Isabella slept on, her copper curls fanned out over the pillow.

Flora's face crumpled with the effort of holding back the tears but then a sound came from the corner of the nursery. Her breath lodged in her throat but it was only the baby whimpering in his cradle.

She went to him and stroked his forehead, hoping to soothe him back to sleep. 'I am so very sorry,' she whispered, 'but everything will be all right. Your Papà adores you and you will be happy.'

Orlando arched his back and let out a wail.

There was no more time. She must go before the wet-nurse came to tend to him.

Hastily, she pressed her lips to Isabella's forehead, her heart breaking. 'I promise you, we'll meet again in a better place,' she whispered. Tearing herself away, she edged out of the nursery and hurried down the stairs. In the hall, almost blinded by tears, she slid back the bolts and ran out into the misty dawn.

Sobbing, she raced through the garden and down towards the boathouse by the lake, heedless of the wet grass and sharp stones under her bare feet. Once, she had loved this place but now she was desperate to leave it.

She scrambled into the boat, shoved it away from the landing stage and rowed out onto the lake. The water was as flat as molten pewter with the night sky beginning to lighten in the east. All around her the mountains were veiled by low clouds. She rowed until she could no longer see the house through the mist that curled up off the lake. She shipped the oars and listened to the silence. Now, there was only herself in this vaporous grey world.

She dipped her hand in the water and held it there until it was numb with cold. Oh, if only she could numb her heartbreak as easily as her fingers!

But it was too late and she must act. She pulled her nightgown over her head and draped it over the side of the boat. Filled with dread, she stared into the depths of the lake.

It was time.

Chapter 1

Kew Gardens

October 1919

Muttering under my breath, I hacked off spent flower spikes and dying foliage until all that was left of the delphinium was sorry-looking stubble. I attacked the browning leaves of the next plant while I brooded over my latest encounter with Harold Naseby. Full of glee, he'd told me he'd just seen Sergeant Waring, in uniform, heading towards the office.

Most of Kew's gardeners had enlisted in 1914, but Naseby's flat feet had exempted him from military service. He'd been one of the few remaining men at Kew when I was recruited a year later, along with several other young women, from Swanley Horticultural College. Naseby made no secret of either his dislike of women in what he considered should be an all-male preserve or of his particular antagonism towards me. He'd borne a grudge ever since Mr Coutts, supervisor of the Herbaceous Grounds, the Rock Gardens and the Flower Gardens, had praised me for my diligence and expertise.

Raking up the clippings of dead foliage, I thrust them into the barrow.

'You can stop that now, Violet.'

Warily, I turned to see what Naseby wanted this time.

'Get yourself down to Coutts's office right away.'

As soon as I saw the smirk on his face, I knew what was going to happen. After all, I had been expecting it. I wiped my palms on my breeches and walked away without acknowledging him. I was damned if I'd let him see my despair.

I tapped on Mr Coutts's office door a few minutes later, and he looked up from an array of seed catalogues spread out over his desk.

'Ah, there you are, Mrs Honeywell.' He didn't invite me to sit, which I took to be a bad sign.

I clasped my hands together and tried to ignore my skipping heartbeat.

'Sergeant Waring has been released from military service at last,' said Mr Coutts, his gaze roaming all around the office but avoiding me. 'He returned from France last week and is ready to take up his former position in the Herbaceous Grounds. You'll remember that your employment here at Kew has only ever been a temporary situation. The arrangement must now come to an end with immediate effect.'

'Immediate?' I said. His words were like a kick to my stomach. 'Without notice?'

He pushed a brown envelope across the desk. 'Your pay up to the end of the week. Waring has been kicking his heels for months in France, waiting to be demobbed. It's important that the men who fought so bravely on our behalf should return to a normal life as soon as possible. Besides, Waring has a wife and child to support.'

'But I need employment. There isn't anyone to support me.'

'You have your widows' pension.'

The pension wasn't enough; everyone knew that. 'It's not only the salary. My work means everything to me, Mr Coutts. Couldn't you find me another position? In the glasshouses, perhaps?'

'I'm afraid that's impossible.' He peered over his spectacles at me. 'Working at Kew has been a splendid opportunity for you but you always knew it wouldn't be permanent. The war forced exceptional circumstances upon us. Life must now return to its natural order, and for a lady, that is not the workplace.'

A flash of anger made me glare at him. 'Women proved their worth in many different capacities during the war. Now it's over, are all those of us who found satisfaction in being useful to be discarded onto the compost heap?'

'Not at all; merely returned to your rightful place in the home. Perhaps you might find some charitable cause to keep you occupied?'

'Since my husband was sacrificed to the war machine,' I snapped, 'I don't have a proper home anymore. But I want, I *need*, to work.'

'Perhaps, but not at Kew.' Mr Coutts shuffled through the seed catalogues. 'A prestigious position such as this will be impossible to match,' he said, 'but from time to time, I receive enquiries about finding suitable applicants for gardening situations. One or two of the other young ladies surplus to current requirements have found employment in that way. Would you like me to put your name forward next time?'

Arguing with him would only destroy this fragile lifeline and I swallowed my pride. 'Yes please, Mr Coutts.'

'Very well. Don't forget to clean and oil your tools before you leave. You'll want Sergeant Waring to know you carried out your work in a professional manner, won't you?'

'Yes, Mr Coutts.' As I turned to leave, he spoke again.

'Your work has been exemplary, Mrs Honeywell. I shall write you a good reference.'

'Thank you.' I closed his office door behind me and walked

with heavy steps back towards the Herbaceous Grounds. I'd been waiting for the axe to fall ever since the Armistice, but now that it had actually happened, I was crushed. Working at Kew was my oasis of calm in a world that war had changed beyond recognition.

Although the country was now apparently at peace, I saw ruined lives all around me. We'd braved the privations and separations in the desperate hope of a reunion, but for some of us that never came. For others, there was the shock of discovering we didn't know each other anymore. My grieving heart still ached and sleep frequently eluded me. I pictured William's face and my steps faltered. After the misery of the recent years, gardening and the regular rhythm of the seasons had been the only way for me to find any tranquillity and sense of purpose.

Naseby was lurking in the Rock Garden by the Herbaceous Grounds. He stepped forward, blocking my path. 'Everything all right, Ginger?' he enquired, his innocent expression belied by the gleam of malice in his eyes.

I ignored his inaccurate reference to my auburn hair. 'You've got what you wished for,' I said. 'I'm leaving Kew. Sergeant Waring is returning from military service to take up his former position.' I gave a scornful laugh. 'I daresay you won't find him easy to trample over with those great flat feet of yours.'

'No doubt he'll command more respect than a mere woman.'

I snatched up my garden tools and dropped them into the wheelbarrow with a clatter. 'Well, good luck, Naseby,' I said, smiling sweetly. 'You'll probably need it, if you're going to be the only man working here who *isn't* a war hero.' Holding my head high, I set off down the path.

Ruminating over the situation as I cycled away from Kew, I failed to see a shattered beer bottle in the gutter and punctured a tyre.

I eased a shard of glass from the rubber with a groan and pushed the bicycle the rest of the way to my father's house in Richmond.

Dusk was falling as I walked up the path of Rosedene, the Victorian villa that had been my childhood home until my marriage. Even though I now lived in a bedsitting room in Twickenham, I visited Rosedene once a week to have dinner with my father and stepmother.

I shoved the bicycle into the garden shed. Since I wouldn't be going to work in the morning, I'd have time to repair the beastly puncture in daylight tomorrow.

Letting myself in by the kitchen door, I greeted Mrs Alleyn, the cook, who was paring potatoes at the kitchen table. Before the war, we'd also had a housekeeper, a parlour maid, a scullery maid and a gardener. Now, Mrs Alleyn managed the house with the aid of a twice-weekly charwoman and her husband who cut the lawn and planted potatoes in Mother's rose beds.

A pudding was steaming away on the gas, the condensation running down the window.

'Your favourite treacle sponge today,' said Mrs Alleyn.

'Lovely! I had a puncture so I'll stay tonight after dinner.'

'Your bed's still made up from last time.'

My stepmother's complaining tones emanated from the sitting room, followed by the rumble of my father's voice attempting to pacify her.

'Father's back early, too,' I said.

'About half an hour ago. Mrs Hall doesn't sound too happy, does she?' Mrs Alleyn, who'd known me since I was a little girl, gave me a conspiratorial glance. 'Probably best to go and tidy yourself before dinner until it's blown over.'

I came downstairs when I heard the dinner gong. My father and stepmother were already seated in the dining room and the atmosphere was choked with simmering resentment. Father's face was drawn and anxious and Mildred's mouth was pinched together, as if she'd swallowed a wasp. It wouldn't be a good time to tell them I'd lost my position at Kew.

'Good evening,' I said, taking into my place at the table.

'I have some news, Violet,' said Father, without preamble. 'I've received a letter confirming that Edmund is well enough to return from Cornwall.'

'But that's marvellous!' My younger brother had been recovering from shell shock in a nursing home for the past six months.

Mildred sat rigidly on her chair, her fingers tapping the table.

'Doctor Gillespie at Spindrift House writes that he's much improved,' said Father, 'though he isn't yet fit to work.'

Father and I had been distressed to see Edmund's pitiable condition when we visited him in the military hospital after he'd been brought back from France. 'When is he arriving?'

'Friday evening. I'm to meet his train at Paddington.'

'I'll come with you,' I said.

'And then what?' snapped my stepmother. 'Can he care for himself? As I've made perfectly plain to you, Gerald, I'm not prepared to nurse him.'

'I'm sure that won't be necessary, Mildred.'

Mrs Alleyn carried in the macaroni cheese.

Dinner was eaten in uneasy silence while I considered how to break the news that I was no longer required at Kew.

On Friday, I met Father at Paddington station. We waited on the crowded platform for Edmund's train, jostled by businessmen in suits and soldiers with kitbags. The shriek of guards' whistles echoed under the great glass roof and the air was thick with steam and cigarette smoke.

'I'm nervous,' I confessed.

'So am I,' said Father. 'When I saw him at Spindrift House two months ago, he'd almost stopped that terrible trembling, but he still wasn't his normal self.'

'Perhaps the sea air will have benefited him?' I said.

Father ran a hand over his thinning hair. 'The truth is, Violet, my income isn't sufficient to keep him in a nursing home any longer.'

'And Mildred doesn't want him at Rosedene.' It was hard to keep the resentment out of my voice.

'I know you and your stepmother haven't often seen eye to eye but she isn't always so contrary. She can't bear to be reminded of the war by your brother's continuing illness.'

Ten years ago, a mere six months after my mother died, I'd been distraught when Father married Mildred. She was a widow and a regular churchgoer at our Parish church. When she started weaselling her way into his affections even before the funeral, I couldn't help but see her as an interloper.

'I wish your dear mother . . .' Father pulled a handkerchief from his pocket and blew his nose.

'I understand now how lonely you must have been after she passed on,' I said. 'I felt the same after William was killed.' I no longer begrudged my father his choice of marrying again, only that it had been Mildred he'd chosen. As for myself, at twenty-seven, I had no expectation of another husband. Any unmarried men who returned from the war more-or-less undamaged would undoubtedly take their pick of the vast number of younger women available. No, my mission in life now was to safeguard Edmund from a cruel world and help him to be whole again.

A plume of smoke further up the line heralded the train's arrival, and those intending to travel gathered up their cases and kissed their friends goodbye.

The train chugged into the platform amidst a swirl of steam.

Brakes squealed and hissed. Carriage doors burst open, and a flood of passengers alighted.

Full of hope and trepidation, I scanned the milling throng for Edmund. After a few moments, I glanced at Father. 'Do you think he missed it?'

He squinted towards the end of the train. 'Isn't that him?'

A gangly young man was descending painfully slowly from a carriage further up the platform. A young woman with flaxen hair assisted him.

'There he is!' I ran helter-skelter along the platform and came to a halt before him. He didn't look at me.

'Edmund?' I said.

Still he didn't respond but stood stock still, his gaze firmly on the ground, his fingers clenching and unclenching. Cold dread settled in my chest. Edmund had returned to us but there was no flicker of recognition in his eyes.

'I'm Lily Gillespie,' said the young woman. 'Dr Gillespie's wife. I offered to accompany Edmund since the hustle and bustle of the world outside Spindrift House is still a bit much for him.'

'I'm grateful to you. I'm Violet Honeywell, Edmund's sister.'

Mrs Gillespie smiled. 'He's spoken of you.' She tapped Edmund on the arm, pointed at her ear and then at me.

His face lit up when he saw me and he pulled balls of cotton wool from his ears. I hugged him, my head barely reaching his shoulder. He gripped me as if he'd never let me go. 'It's going to be all right now,' I crooned.

Father, out of breath, hurried to join us. He clapped Edmund on the arm and grasped his hands. 'Welcome home, my boy.' The spark of joy in his eyes died when he saw how his son's gaze flitted nervously about.

Lily Gillespie handed me Edmund's case. 'The cotton wool in his ears is to dull any sudden noises,' she said. 'He'll need a very quiet environment and no excitement or it will set him back. Really, he'd have been better with a few more weeks in the nursing home so don't expect too much, too soon.' She rummaged in her bag and pulled out an envelope. 'Case notes for his doctor and a list of suggested medications. Peace, calm surroundings and plenty of time will be his best aids to recovery.'

Father shook her hand. 'We're so grateful for everything you've done.'

'It's a pleasure to see his improvement, but today has been long and challenging for him,' she said. 'A taxi home would be a good idea and some Horlicks at bedtime.'

Mrs Gillespie saw Edmund settled in a taxi before she said goodbye.

I sat beside my younger brother, holding his hand. His eyes were closed and small tufts of cotton wool poked out of his ears. When I'd seen him in the hospital, he'd had a military haircut, but now his dark hair curled onto his forehead, just as it had when he was small. It was painful to see him so diminished and unlike the happy, mischievous boy he'd once been. Ten years ago, when he was thirteen, I'd faithfully promised our dying mother that I would cherish and guide him after she'd gone.

Edmund had enlisted in 1914 as little more than a youth and returned to us as a broken man. I no longer had a husband to care for, but I would do everything in my power to restore my brother to health.

Chapter 2

I was writing a letter at the folding card table that served as desk, dressing and dining table in my bed-sitting room. It was originally the front basement room of the narrow terraced house in Twickenham, and the window faced north. Since I'd always worked outside, the lack of light hadn't previously bothered me, but now, the prospect of spending the winter cooped up in such a dark and cramped space was depressing.

I put down the pen, blotted the ink and reread my wording for the advertisement I'd toiled over, reducing it to as few words as possible to save money, while still conveying the essential information.

Experienced, trained horticulturalist, formerly of Kew Gardens, seeks employment. Herbaceous borders, rock gardens, rose gardens a speciality. References available. Apply to V Honeywell.

It would do. The newspaper would add the box number for any applicants to contact me. I'd received three responses from my two previous advertisements. One had been looking for assistance

12

in the garden for two hours a week, and another required me to relocate to Essex, which was too far away for me to visit Edmund. The third had sounded promising. A gentleman offered a full time situation working in his Chelsea garden and asked me to attend an interview. When I'd presented myself, the elderly man of the house took one look at me and shook his head. 'Not suitable for a woman,' he'd said and told the maid to show me out before I could argue my case.

I tucked the letter, together with a postal order to cover the cost of the advertisement, into an envelope. Spring was a better time to apply for a gardening vacancy, but perhaps someone might offer me temporary employment to put their garden to bed for the winter. There was also the chance Mr Coutts might hear about an opportunity for me.

I washed up my breakfast plate and tidied up before putting on my hat and coat. Looking on the bright side, the previous month's unemployment had allowed me the freedom to spend my days with Edmund. My bicycle leaned against the wall, and I wheeled it along the passage and through the front door.

A cold wind tugged at the brim of my felt hat as I cycled through the streets towards Richmond. I stopped only to post the letter and then hurried on, head down into the wind until I arrived at Rosedene.

Mrs Alleyn was ironing in the kitchen and the slightly scorched smell of clean laundry took me straight back to my childhood. 'How is he?' I asked.

'Same as yesterday. I've just taken him a custard cream and a cup of tea. Shall I pour one for you?'

'I'll do it.' I hung my hat and coat in the lobby. The old brown teapot in its knitted cosy sat on the table and I fetched myself a cup. 'I'll go straight up.'

'Righty-ho, dear.'

I was halfway up the stairs when I saw my stepmother standing at the top. 'Morning, Mildred.'

'Is it? That brother of yours kept me awake with his shouting last night.'

'Bad dreams again?'

'It's about time he showed some backbone and braced up.' She sniffed dismissively.

'How fortunate we are,' I said, through gritted teeth, 'that we didn't have to experience all the battlefield horrors that Edmund endured for our sakes.' I pushed past her and opened my brother's door.

'Violet!' Mildred called after me. 'Kindly ask Edmund to stay in his room when my friends are here this afternoon. I don't wish to be embarrassed by one of his scenes.'

I would have slammed the door behind me, but I knew that would distress Edmund. Instead, I closed it with exaggerated care. He was still in bed, and I put my cup of tea on the bedside table and bent to kiss his forehead. 'How are you today?' I murmured.

'I made a complete ass of myself last night,' he said. He looked up at me with shame in his hazel eyes. 'Father had to sit with me until one of the doctor's sleeping powders took effect.'

'It wasn't your fault,' I said, 'and you will get better.'

'Will I?'

I nodded decisively. 'Of course you will, though it might take a little time.'

'I *want* to be back to my old self. It's just that ... ' He lifted his hands helplessly. 'It's as if there's something inside my head that's determined to frighten me and make me behave like a fool. I keep praying, but I think God has abandoned me. How could He let such terrible things happen?' Perspiration beaded his forehead. 'Pictures of what I saw keep coming into my mind. There was a day when I was sheltering in a water-logged crater

14

with a comrade. A shell exploded, and once the dust had settled I saw his face . . .'

'Don't talk about it if it's too much,' I urged, worried it would make him feel worse.

He pressed his knuckles into his eye sockets. 'Perhaps if I can talk about it at last, maybe then I'll get the pictures of it out of my head?'

I stroked my brother's hair off his forehead, just as I had when he'd been a small boy waking from a nightmare. 'Tell me, then,' I murmured.

Edmund took a shuddering breath. 'Half his face had been blown away and his legs were just a mess of disintegrated bone and blood. I put my coat over them so he couldn't see the damage. Eventually his agonised screams turned to moans, but the shellfire went on and on until I was nearly mad. The soldier bled to death, but even after that he kept staring at me with his one eye and I couldn't stand it.' He looked up at me, his expression so bleak I shivered.

'It's all right,' I said, 'don't feel you have to go on.'

'I must,' he said. 'In a frenzy, I dug with my bare hands into the mud at the bottom of the shell hole to bury him. But then . . .'

'Yes?'

'My fingers plunged into the body of a soldier previously buried there. That was when I lost all reason.' He fell silent.

Sickened, I pressed my hand to my mouth.

Edmund's breathing was fast and shallow. 'Sometimes it feels as if I'm back there and it's all happening again and again and again.'

'But you aren't,' I said. 'You are here with me now, quite safe and the war is over.' But would he ever be able to forget? I clutched his hand. 'The Harpy isn't helping, is she? We must drown out those horrible memories and find something good to look forward to.'

'But what?'

'We'll start with small things. Perhaps we'll visit the library and choose a book to read together. Or we might write some poetry.' I hoped he might find that cathartic.

The ghost of a smile crept across Edmund's face. 'I like reading poetry, but you know I can't rhyme two words together to save my life.' He looked thoughtful. 'I might try sketching or painting. I was good at that during my schooldays.'

'I'll buy you a sketchbook and you can give it a go.'

Edmund stroked the back of my hand with his finger. 'You're the best sister I could ever have wished for.'

'I promised Mother I'd always look after you, didn't I?' I said, my voice breaking.

'And you do. I still miss her. Don't you?'

I nodded. 'I'd never have thought of taking up horticulture if it hadn't been for her love of the garden. Do you remember how she made our old gardener mutter under his breath whenever she sent away for a new variety of rosebush or tulips that weren't in a colour he approved of?'

Edmund smiled at the memory. 'And then there were the little flowerbeds she gave us. I grew sunflowers that were taller than me. It seemed incredible that such an enormous flower could grow from that little seed. I'd like to take up gardening again when the weather improves.'

'Well, that's another thing to look forward to, isn't it?'

The rest of the morning passed quietly, and I persuaded Edmund to dress and sit in the armchair.

Mrs Alleyn brought us lunch on a tray. 'Mrs Hall is expecting friends for tea,' she said, 'and she's rearranging the sitting room furniture, inspecting the best china for dust and wishing she had new curtains. I thought you'll be more comfortable having your lunch up here.'

'That was kind, Mrs Alleyn,' I said.

When the doorbell rang later Edmund started, his eyes wide and afraid.

I caught hold of his arm. 'It's all right. Look, put the cotton wool in your ears and you won't hear the bell ring next time.'

The bell rang several more times over the next fifteen minutes and, despite the cotton wool, Edmund became increasingly agitated.

Waves of laughter and the sound of high-pitched female voices rose up the stairs.

It made me anxious to watch Edmund's long fingers plucking restlessly at the skin on the back of his hand. 'Why don't we go out while Mildred is entertaining? We can go to the library and find you a book of poetry. It'll be lovely and quiet, and we can read in peace.'

A short while later we crept downstairs, told Mrs Alleyn where we were going and left by the back door.

I tucked Edmund's scarf around his neck against the wind and took his arm. We walked in silence towards the library.

On the pavement ahead of us, a black cat crouched by the gutter, its tail waving slowly from side to side as it prepared to pounce on a piece of crumpled paper. A gust of wind snatched up the litter and lifted it over the road.

A motor car sped along the street, and at the same moment it passed, the cat leaped into its path in pursuit of its prey. The vehicle skidded to a stop with an ear-piercing squeal of tyres and brakes, and the engine backfired with a series of loud bangs.

Edmund let out a cry and threw himself flat to the pavement, dragging me down with him.

The sudden impact of the pavement against my chest knocked my breath away. I lay unmoving for a few moments, and then pulled myself into a sitting position.

Edmund shuddered beside me, rolled into a ball with his hands over his ears and his eyes tightly shut.

The car door flung open and a man ran towards us as I attempted to calm Edmund. 'Good God! I thought that dratted cat was going to be the end of me. Are you all right?'

'It's my brother,' I stammered. 'The noise . . . it distressed him.'

He bent down to peer at Edmund. 'Shell shock, is it?' he asked. 'Saw it all the time in the trenches. Poor devil!' He took off his coat and put it over Edmund's head, rather like putting a cloth over a parrot's cage to make it go to sleep. 'I'm Captain Hamilton, by the way.'

A small crowd started to collect around us; a butcher's boy on a bicycle, an old lady with a shopping basket who offered us smelling salts and a young mother with a baby in a pram.

Captain Hamilton lifted Edmund up and carried him into the motor.

As we were driven away, I saw the black cat sat on a wall on the other side of the street, serenely washing its whiskers. Edmund clung to me, his whole body shaking and his complexion greenish-white.

The tea party was still in progress when we arrived at Rosedene. Edmund's legs gave way beneath him as Captain Hamilton and I tried to get him up the garden path, and Mildred came to see what was going on when our rescuer struggled to support Edmund up the stairs.

'Quietly!' she hissed when he stumbled against the banisters. 'You'll disturb my friends.'

Captain Hamilton raised his eyebrows and heaved Edmund onto the landing. 'He was badly frightened when my car backfired.'

Mildred turned her wrath on me. 'Whatever were you thinking of? Taking him outside, indeed! He's not fit to be seen in public.'

Downstairs, the sitting room door opened, and one of Mildred's friends peered out at us. 'Is everything all right?'

'Everything is perfectly fine, thank you,' trilled Mildred. 'Just a teeny mishap. My stepson is so clumsy!' She pushed past me. 'I'll speak to you later,' she said in an undertone. 'And I'll thank you to keep that brother of yours out of sight.'

Seething, I went into the bedroom where Captain Hamilton was removing Edmund's coat and shoes.

'I can't thank you enough,' I said. 'I'd never have managed to get him home without your help.'

Our rescuer pulled a face. 'It wouldn't have happened if that cat hadn't run into the road.' He glanced at Edmund. 'People seem to think shell shock can be cured by an effort of will, but your brother is as much a casualty of war as some poor chap who had his foot blown off.'

'I wish the government recognised that,' I said. 'Edmund doesn't receive a pension, though he might have if he'd lost a toe.'

'Shameful, isn't it?' He touched Edmund on the shoulder. 'I'll be off now, old chap. Good luck!'

I showed him to the front door and returned to Edmund's bedside.

Later, Father returned from the bank and the dinner gong sounded shortly afterwards.

When I came downstairs, I heard Mildred railing at Father through the dining room door. I paused outside and stiffened my spine as I listened.

'It simply can't go on,' said Mildred. 'Edmund's making no effort at all to brace up. I've made sacrifices for you, Gerald. I even converted to Roman Catholicism to marry you. And, against my better judgement, I took on your children and did my best for them. I never imagined they'd still be underfoot when they were adults. I could die of embarrassment at what the neighbours must think about Edmund making an exhibition of himself in the street like that. Try as I might, it's impossible to have him in the house any longer.'

'It can't be helped, Mildred—'

I shoved open the door. 'Don't you understand that Edmund is *ill*, Mildred? He's stuck in a terrifying world of his own and he can't escape his terrors.'

'Then he ought to be locked up in an asylum where he could get proper help.' Mildred cast a glance at her husband. 'I certainly shan't stay in this house a minute longer if I'm to be at the mercy of a dangerous lunatic.'

'Edmund's not mad!'

'Then it's time he showed more moral fibre. He pretended to be ill to wriggle out of active service, and now he's sponging off his family instead of going out and finding work. He's nothing more than a coward and a shirker!'

'That's not true,' I shouted.

'Well, you would stand up for him, wouldn't you, having married another coward.'

I drew in my breath sharply. 'William was a Conscientious Objector—'

'Exactly!' Fury contorted Mildred's normally pretty features. 'He was too cowardly to fight the enemy to save our country.'

'How *dare* you! William gave his life saving the wounded,' I said. 'As a member of the Friends' Ambulance Unit he was as brave as any soldier. He ran again and again into No Man's Land to fetch injured men to safety. And what did *you* ever do to help the war effort? Absolutely nothing!'

Father banged his fist on the table, rattling the glasses, and reared to his feet. 'Stop it, both of you!'

In the throbbing silence that followed, I stared at my normally mild-mannered father.

'I *will not* have this constant bickering,' he said.

'Quite right, Gerald,' said Mildred. 'Your daughter needs to learn some manners. I don't want her here anymore.'

'For goodness' sake!' I said. 'I'm looking after my brother so you don't have to. Not that you'd bother.'

'Violet, enough!' thundered Father. 'Mildred, go into the sitting room. You shall have your dinner on a tray tonight – out of my sight.'

Mildred burst into noisy tears and stumbled from the room.

Father sat down again and wiped his face with his palm.

'I'm sorry,' I whispered.

'So am I.' His complexion was ashen. 'It's an impossible situation and I don't know what to do.'

It shocked me to see Father so helpless. We sat in silence until a tentative knock came on the door and Mrs Alleyn entered with our dinner. 'Chicken pie,' she said, putting our plates on the table. Discreetly, she withdrew.

We both ate a few mouthfuls and then gave up before it choked us.

'I could sell the house and buy a flat. Perhaps then I could send Edmund back to Spindrift House.'

'Father, you mustn't!' I said. 'Rosedene is our last link with Mother. I can't bear to think of it being sold.'

'A significant proportion of my savings has gone to nursing home fees, and I can't think of any other way to raise the funds.'

He looked old and tired, and it worried me. 'Mildred is right in one way,' I said. 'Both Edmund and I should be self-sufficient.' I frowned while I thought it through.

Perhaps there was a way to solve the problem.

'If Edmund had lost a leg or been gassed, Mildred might have been more accommodating,' said Father. 'She could have boasted about having a war hero in the house. It's mental illness that upsets her.'

'Mildred will never give Edmund the love and care that I can,' I said, making up my mind. 'I'll take him home with me.'

'That's impossible. Your bed-sitting room is unsuitable for you both.'

'Now I'm out of work, I can't afford anything more spacious. Unless you could make a contribution, Father? It would still be less expensive than nursing home fees.'

'You'd really be prepared to care for your brother?'

'I promised Mother I would.' If I could mend this one fragment of the terrible damage caused by the war, perhaps I might find inner peace again.

'You shouldn't be put in such a position.' Father bounced his knuckles against his chin. 'But perhaps we might try it for a while and see how you get on. I could send Mildred to stay with her sister for the next month, and you'd need to give notice on your bed-sitting room. During that time, we could look for more suitable accommodation. I'll pay the difference in rent and provide an allowance for Edmund's food and so on. While Mildred's away, you and Edmund can stay here. How does that sound?'

I hugged him. 'It's the best answer to difficult circumstances. I imagine even Mildred will be relieved to agree.'

22

Chapter 3

Ten days later, I received a response to my advertisement.

Dear Mr Honeywell
 *I read your advertisement with interest and would like to
discuss a gardening project with you. If you are free on Tuesday
2nd November, perhaps you would meet me in the lobby of
Claridge's hotel in Brook Street at half past nine?*
 Yours sincerely
 Luca Marchese

Nonplussed, I read the note again. There was no address for me to
confirm or refuse the invitation, and the name sounded foreign. I
wasn't surprised the sender had addressed me as Mr Honeywell,
since I'd deliberately stated my name as ambiguous. How else
was I to have the opportunity of meeting a future employer and
persuading them I was capable of carrying out my duties as effi-
ciently as a man?

On Tuesday afternoon, I put on my myrtle-green coat and
matching hat. I made sure to pull it down to cover most of my

hair in case my potential employer held the same views as my stepmother about the character defects assigned to redheads.

Upon my arrival at Claridge's, I attempted not to be too intimidated by the quietly luxurious surroundings. I presented myself at the reception desk and asked if they would inform Mr Marchese I had arrived.

'Mr Marchese is over there, madam,' said the receptionist, 'by the window.'

A dark-haired man was lounging in an armchair, absorbed in a book. He was about the same age as myself, wearing a well-cut suit and darkly good-looking in an understated way.

I crossed the gleaming marble floor and went to stand beside him.

An omnibus rattled past the window and raindrops beaded the glass.

He gave no sign he'd noticed me, so I cleared my throat. 'Mr Marchese?'

He started and looked up at me with topaz eyes set beneath black, winged brows. He wore an unusually beautiful silk tie woven in subtle shades of olive and old gold.

'I'm Violet Honeywell,' I said. 'You answered my advertisement about a gardening situation.'

Rising to his feet, he smiled. 'I apologise, Mrs Honeywell. I was completely lost in my book.' I shook his proffered hand, curious that he hadn't been at all surprised I was a woman and that he had no foreign accent.

'Do sit down.' He held up his book. *The Four Horsemen of the Apocalypse*. Have you read it?'

'I have, actually. I thought the relationship between the stoical father Don Marcello and his passionate son Julio was extremely well written.'

'Excellent!' He ordered coffee from the waiter and then regarded me thoughtfully until I began to fidget. Since he didn't seem inclined to ask me any questions, I ventured to move the interview along. 'Shall I tell you about my horticultural qualifications and experience?' I asked.

'I went to Kew a few days ago and spoke to Mr Coutts. He told me quite a bit about you.'

'I see.' So, that explained how he knew I was Mrs Honeywell.

'Yes, your Mr Coutts gave you a glowing reference. In a nutshell, he told me you're not only conscientious but have an artistic eye for planning and planting herbaceous borders.'

'Flower borders are my particular interest,' I said, 'but I'm happy to work in all areas of horticulture.'

'In my letter to you, I mentioned I have a gardening project in mind. My grandmother designed and planted a flower garden many years ago.' He chuckled. 'Her name was Flora. Rather fitting, don't you think?'

I smiled. 'My friends have made the same comment about my name. I was christened Violet.'

'Violet,' he murmured. 'Yes indeed; how apt.'

The waiter brought coffee in a silver pot. He poured it into cups before silently placing a plate of shortbread biscuits beside us and discreetly withdrawing.

I sipped the delicious coffee and nudged the conversation back on track since Mr Marchese seemed in no hurry to do so himself. 'And is the project to maintain your grandmother's garden?'

'Not exactly.' He crossed his legs and leaned back. 'She drowned when my father was a baby.'

'How sad!'

'My grandfather was grief-stricken. After she died, he couldn't bear to see her garden still in glorious bloom when her body was lost somewhere at the bottom of the lake. Utterly distraught, he destroyed the garden and nailed the door shut. He forbade the family to mention it again. The garden is walled, and no one had been inside it for fifty-seven years until I forced my way in a few months ago. I'm afraid it's terribly overgrown.'

'What a poignant story,' I said.

'Isn't it? The crux of the matter is that I've been struggling to find a special gift for my wife as a surprise for her birthday next August. I'm in London for business reasons, but when I saw your advertisement it sparked the idea of restoring Grandmother Flora's garden for my wife Sylvana.'

'I can't imagine anything more romantic.' Mr Marchese's wife was an extremely fortunate lady. 'Of course, horticultural fashions change,' I continued, 'and flower gardens of over fifty years ago might not have the same appeal to our modern eyes. Colour choices were often rather garish, and the plants were regimented into neat rows. Nowadays, we prefer naturalistic planting in drifts of softer hues.'

'I've found my grandmother's gardening notebooks,' he said, 'and there's a sketch plan of the original layout. I wouldn't expect you to recreate it exactly as it was. Use your vision and expertise to make it a beautiful and quintessentially English flower garden for a woman of today.'

'Then you'll want perfumed roses, clouds of lavender, irises, peonies, night-scented jasmine and clematis scrambling over pergolas. What a very exciting project!' My pulse beat a tattoo at the thought of it.

'And I think, perhaps, you are just the person to undertake it?'

Was he offering me what sounded like my dream job?

'It's certainly an extremely interesting idea,' I said, 'but I'll need to know more about the budget and the location of the project. Since the garden has been neglected, it must be cleared before the new planting takes place. Depending upon its size, I may need assistance if it's to be ready for next August.' I was practically breathless with elation. I wanted, with all my being, to work on this garden.

He uncrossed his legs and leaned towards me. 'Let me tell you a little more. My family home is set on the shores of a lake, and the land was laid out as parkland and formal gardens several generations ago. There are currently two gardeners. We used to employ six men, but since the war ...' He shrugged. 'Well, you must know how difficult it is to find trained staff these days. Still, you will have any help you need to clear the land and lay paths and so on. You'll be in charge and have a free hand with the design.'

I could hardly believe I might be granted such an opportunity. 'And I'd report to you to discuss plans and budgets?'

'Yes, but all I ask is that the finished garden is so full of seductive perfume, colour and beauty that my wife will never want to leave it.'

'A garden takes time to mature into its full glory,' I said, 'and by August many flowers are beginning to fade; however, if the budget is large enough, I can achieve a creditable result in the time. By the following spring and summer it could be glorious and, with careful planting, the garden will continue to develop over time and produce blooms all year round.'

'You'll have whatever you need. There's also a library where you can study Flora's notebooks and plan the layout.'

I envisioned myself in a calm and spacious room with my research books spread around me.

'How would you feel about leaving London?' asked Mr Marchese.

'I'm happy to relocate anywhere, as long as it's quiet and I can rent suitable accommodation for myself and my brother.' If the house was beside a lake, perhaps it was in Scotland or the Lake District. Either would be peaceful.

'You will have rooms with glorious views of Lake Como,' said Mr Marchese. 'It's very beautiful.'

I blinked. 'Lake Como?'

'Didn't I say? Villa Marchese, my family home, is in Bellagio in Italy.'

My exhilaration evaporated in an instant. 'But I can't go to Italy!'

Mr Marchese's face fell. 'Why not? Are you worried about the language? My mother is British, just like my grandmother and I'm bilingual. The servants speak some English, and I would be there most of the time.'

'It's not that,' I said. Disappointment weighed on my chest like a brick. 'There's my brother, you see. The war was difficult for him. He suffers from neurasthenia, and my father and stepmother can't look after him. So, I promised . . .' There was a lump in my throat. I held out my hand. 'I'm sorry, but it won't do for Edmund. It would be impossible for him to travel that far.'

Mr Marchese rose to his feet, regret written across his face. He shook my hand. 'I'm sincerely sorry. I would have loved to see you bring my grandmother's garden to life again.'

'I apologise for wasting your time.' I turned and fled before I disgraced myself by shedding tears of bitter disappointment.

A few days later, I moved into Rosedene with my father and Edmund. Mildred had decamped to stay with her sister, and the house was blessedly calm again. We had a month to find new lodgings before she returned.

I resigned myself to remaining unemployed until the spring when it might be easier to find a new situation. It was hard not to feel resentful towards Mildred. If she'd been more sympathetic to Edmund's condition, I might have left him in her care for a few months while I went to Italy. But Edmund needed me, and I wouldn't abandon him now.

Over the following days, Edmund felt sufficiently well enough to sit in the morning room and use the sketchbook and paint box I bought for him. He found it an absorbing pursuit and produced some creditable watercolours. On the Sunday we attended mass at Our Lady of Sorrows without incident, and he appeared calmed by the familiar rituals. On the Monday I left him under Mrs Alleyn's watchful care while I went to see three flats. None were suitable, being either damp or adjacent to noisy neighbours or roads. I wished I could talk with William and ask his advice on what to do. I missed his quiet good sense so much. Dispirited, I returned to Rosedene.

Letting myself in through the kitchen door, I was greeted by the comforting smell of toast.

Mrs Alleyn was making pastry at the table. 'Edmund has a visitor,' she murmured. 'They're having tea in the sitting room. Shall I bring you a cup, too?'

I wondered if it might be one of my brother's soldier comrades. 'I'll take it in,' I said.

Opening the sitting room door, I caught my breath. Edmund sat beside the gas fire, buttering a tea cake while the visitor held the toasting fork up to the fire. Both turned to look at me.

'This one's nearly done,' said Mr Marchese. 'Come and eat it while it's hot, Mrs Honeywell, and I'll toast another.'

'Luca brought strawberry jam, too,' mumbled Edmund through a mouthful of tea cake.

My eyebrows rose, and I gave Mr Marchese a questioning look.

'I hope you'll excuse me dropping in like this without an invitation,' he said. 'I brought tea cakes as a peace offering.'

'But how did you know where we live?'

'I asked Mr Coutts. I wanted to meet your brother and tell him about my desire to bring Flora's garden back to life.'

'I do think you might have told me about it, Violet,' said Edmund. 'An English flower garden is an ideal project for you.'

I resisted saying it was perfect. 'But it's in *Italy*,' I said in a matter-of-fact tone. 'You know the train journey from Cornwall to London was utterly draining for you. Lake Como is much further away than that.'

'I'm no longer a child, Violet.' Edmund wiped butter from his mouth. 'I shall buy some rubber ear plugs and bury my face in a book while we travel. It may be a little difficult, but it's time I start to venture further afield. Besides, Luca has offered me work, too. It's a wonderful opportunity, and I must stop dwelling on the past and stand on my own feet again.'

'*Work?*' I turned to Mr Marchese. 'I'm not sure you understand—'

'I think I do,' he said. 'I've explained to Edmund how desperately we need gardeners at Villa Marchese, and he's willing to learn. If you will take control of Flora's garden, he could assist you. I'd pay him a decent wage. The situation is peaceful, and the air is very healthy. It's a perfect place for a soldier to convalesce.'

'I don't think—'

There was a stubborn set to Edmund's jaw that I remembered from his childhood. 'Violet, allow me some dignity, will you? I've explained to Luca about my nightmares and how sudden noises trouble me and he understands. I cannot live with the knowledge that I'm responsible for you sacrificing your own needs and desires. Please, Violet?'

I hesitated, unable to forget his panicked reaction to a motor car backfiring.

'I still have some business to attend to in London,' said Mr Marchese, 'but in a fortnight we could take the train from Victoria to Dover together. First class, of course,' he added, 'then stop at an hotel for the night before catching the early boat to Calais and then on to Paris by train. The Simplon Express leaves Paris in the evening and we'll arrive in Milan at noon the next day.'

Edmund's gaze was riveted on Mr Marchese's face, and I worried he'd been persuaded to attempt an impossible journey.

'I'll be meeting my wife in Milan,' continued Mr Marchese, 'so I'll settle you and your brother at a hotel near the station for a quiet evening. The following morning, my wife will travel with us by train to Varenna and then for a short steamer ride to Bellagio. We'll be at Villa Marchese in time for dinner.' He smiled triumphantly at us.

'It's such a long journey,' I said, hearing the doubt in my voice. Was there even a remote chance that Edmund might manage it?

'I'll be on hand if your brother becomes anxious, Mrs Honeywell. You're the perfect person to bring Flora's garden back to life, and Edmund deserves a chance to move on from what has been an undeniably dreadful war for him. Please, say you'll do it?'

I glanced from Mr Marchese to Edmund. Both wore identical, hopeful expressions. 'Well . . .'

'I won't let you down, Violet,' said my brother.

'You've *never* let me down, Edmund,' I said. 'Working in a tranquil garden might be very healing for you, but the journey will be too much. I couldn't bear it if it set you back.'

He jumped up and hugged me. 'I'll close my eyes and ears until we arrive,' he said. 'But we're going to Italy. Everything will be so different there, I promise you.'

He spoke with such confidence that he almost convinced me. If he believed it himself, perhaps he *was* right. If I didn't allow it, would he always blame me for making him miss the opportunity? And what an opportunity it was! I imagined having a free hand to design and create a glorious garden, as Flora had done so many years before, and pictured bees humming over swathes of perfumed flowers in the Italian sunshine. 'Well . . .'

Mr Marchese grinned. 'I'll make sure you don't regret it.'

I wanted to go so much that it hurt. I studied Edmund's expectant expression and a wave of carefree optimism swept over me, washing away my doubts and fears. 'Well then,' I said, 'let's go to Italy.'

32

Chapter 4

It was a long and nerve-wracking journey to Milan. At the hotel, I guided Edmund, white and shaking, straight to his room and promised to return after he'd had a nap.

Downstairs in the lobby, Mr Marchese had ordered me a coffee for me.

'How is your brother?' he asked.

'Resting.' Gratefully, I sipped the strong black brew and felt some of my tension drain away. 'I don't know how I'd have managed without your help,' I said. 'The train doors slamming, one after the other, must have sounded like gunfire to him, and when the guard's whistle blew ...' I shuddered. Edmund's hoarse cries of terror had frightened me.

'A whistle was the signal used to go over the top of the trench. It made me shiver, so it's not surprising if it transported Edmund back to the battlefield.'

'You've been very tolerant of his frailties.'

Mr Marchese put down his coffee cup, adjusting its position until it was in the exact centre of the saucer. 'There's something I haven't told you.'

'Oh?'

'My elder brother Teodore suffered from the same condition, so I do understand what you and Edmund are experiencing.'

So, that explained his kindness and understanding. 'I'm so sorry. How is your brother now?'

He was silent for a moment and then said, 'Shell shock is called "the wind of the howitzer" in Italy. Teodore and I were in the same regiment. I did everything I could to help him, but his mental state became too obvious to hide. They gave him electric shock treatment. He thought he was being tortured. Then, they sent him straight back into battle.'

I gasped. 'That's appalling!'

'There was worse to come.' The expression in his eyes was bleak. 'The Italian army endured a terrible defeat at Caporetto in the autumn of 1917. Teodore wasn't the only soldier to break under the strain. He sank down and became lost somewhere inside himself. Accused of cowardice and desertion, he was carried out and propped up before a firing squad, along with other men suffering from the same condition.'

I pressed my fingers to my lips, unable to find the right words to express my horror.

Mr Marchese drew in a ragged breath. 'So, you'll understand why I want – need – to help Edmund?' His eyes glistened. 'I know this journey is difficult, but once we get him to Villa Marchese and give him the time and tranquillity he needs to return to good health, it will assuage some of my guilt at being unable to save Teodore.'

I'd been astonished by the extent to which he'd put himself out to bring us to Italy, but it made sense to me now. 'I'm so very sorry about your brother,' I said, 'and I'm indebted to you for your care of mine.'

'Edmund is plucky and determined to recover. He deserves

the chance of a full and happy life, and I believe we can set him on the right path at Villa Marchese.' He gave me a crooked grin. 'And besides, I'm convinced you have the talent to restore my grandmother's garden.'

'I'm sure your wife will be thrilled.'

'I hope so.'

He glanced at his watch. 'She's staying here in Milan with her cousin. I'd better be on my way.'

I hoped I might be able to discreetly discover from his wife what colours and flowers she preferred. 'The garden is to be a surprise,' I said, 'so how will you explain to her what Edmund and I will be doing at Villa Marchese?'

'A simple sin of omission. I'll tell her you've come to assist our gardeners, Massimo and Beppe,' he said. 'If Edmund doesn't care to come down to the restaurant for dinner, ask room service to send whatever you choose up to his room.'

'Thank you.'

'Shall we meet for breakfast at nine? We'll catch the eleven o'clock train to Varenna.'

I slept badly that night. My dreams were haunted by a recurring vision of William carrying an injured soldier on his back, staggering across No Man's Land into a hail of machine gun fire. I couldn't free my mind of the picture of his broad-shouldered body halted by bullets and falling to the muddy ground.

The following morning, Edmund came down to the hotel dining room for breakfast and seemed almost his old self again; however, Mr Marchese was as subdued and distracted as I was.

'Did you have a pleasant dinner with your wife and her cousin last night?' I asked.

He nodded. 'Yes, but I'd expected Sylvana to come and stay at

Villa Marchese for a week or two before she returns to her home in Florence. It turns out she has various social commitments here in Milan.'

'What a shame,' I said, sorry because he looked so forlorn. And he'd said, "her home", as if they didn't share it. I was eaten up by curiosity as to why that might be, but it certainly wasn't my place to ask my employer about his marital arrangements.

After descending from the train at Varenna, a delightful small town built at the edge of Lake Como, we boarded a steamer. The trees on the steeply wooded hillside still held their autumn colours and, in the late afternoon sunshine, it looked as if they were ablaze. I caught my breath at the sight of misty blue mountains on either side of us as the steamer forged its way across the lake. I glanced at Edmund's profile while he studied the idyllic landscape with a half-smile. We were nearing our destination and the tightly wound spring under my breastbone began to loosen.

Mr Marchese leaned towards me to speak over the sound of the engine. 'Nearly there,' he said. He pointed at a town on the opposite shore of the lake. 'That's Bellagio, right at the point where the lake divides. Lake Como is shaped like an inverted Y and there is Villa Serbelloni. Pliny the Younger is thought to have lived near there. I find it fascinating that he saw what we can see now and that I may have walked in his footsteps.'

Bellagio was a collection of red-roofed, ochre and cream houses tumbling down the wooded hillside towards the lakefront. The steamer pulled up to a jetty, and Mr Marchese waved at a powerfully built man on the quayside. 'There's Massimo,' he said. 'He's come to assist with the luggage.'

Perhaps fifteen years older than myself, Massimo had lively brown eyes, a tanned complexion and unruly dark hair curling out from under his flat cap. The skin at the corner of his eyes crinkled when he smiled at Mr Marchese.

Edmund and I disembarked, and Mr Marchese and Massimo fetched the luggage. When it was safely stowed in the large rowing boat moored nearby, we climbed aboard.

Massimo rowed us along the shoreline, and once the steamer had departed in the opposite direction, the only sound was that of the creaking of the rowlocks and the startled flap of a heron's wings as it flew away. The water had a brackish smell that reminded me of the Thames at low tide.

'We must be almost there,' said Edmund. There was a hint of hopeful expectation in his voice.

I'd told him about Teodore before breakfast. He was silent for a moment and then said, 'I have so much to be grateful for – especially you.'

Now, he caught hold of my hand and looked at me intently. 'Everything's going to be all right, isn't it, Violet?'

'I do believe it is.' I breathed deeply of the cool, clean air and experienced a *frisson* of excitement as we neared our destination. 'Italy!' I said. 'A few weeks ago I would never have imagined we'd be on such an adventure as this.'

Edmund squeezed my hand and a boyhood hint of mischief shone in his eyes again. 'What a lark!' he said.

Mr Marchese and Massimo were speaking together, and it was fascinating to see how my new employer's manner appeared to have changed from that of an English businessman to someone entirely foreign. Even his lips moved differently as he enunciated the words in rapid-fire Italian, liberally illustrated with gestures.

Massimo noticed me watching them and gave me such a wide smile it was impossible not to smile back. After all, we'd be working together in the garden, and it was important we were on good terms.

A boathouse tucked into the shoreline came into view. Massimo rowed towards it, and the boat glided inside.

I stepped out onto the landing stage, and Massimo's hand, warm and calloused, gripped mine to steady me. He set about unloading the luggage and lifted my travelling trunk, half full of gardening reference books, onto the waiting handcart as if it weighed no more than thistledown. It was encouraging to know I'd be able to call on his strength if we undertook any hard land-scaping in Flora's garden.

We went through an opening at the rear of the boathouse, and Mr Marchese pushed open a wrought iron gate. A steep path, scattered with russet leaves, wound upwards ahead of us through mixed woodland. Soon, the trees thinned and gave way to parkland.

'There's the house,' said Mr Marchese, pointing to the hill-side above.

My eyes widened at the sight of the substantial villa, and Edmund's eyebrows rose.

Villa Marchese was painted apricot-yellow with sage green shutters and had a terracotta-tiled roof. At one end of the building was a stone tower. Two staircases built from the same type of stone curved up to the porticoed entrance in the centre of the first floor. A carriage drive led to the terrace in front of the house with a cir-cular turning area. There was a cold breeze, but the house glowed in the late afternoon sunshine.

'It's much grander than I expected,' I said.

'It's much less grand than it used to be,' said Mr Marchese. 'The house was built by my great-great grandfather who made his fortune in silk manufacturing. Unfortunately, there's been little call for silk during the war, and so we live in a far simpler way now than we used to. Actually, I prefer this new lack of formality.'

'Silk is your line of business?' asked Edmund.

Mr Marchese shrugged. 'It is now. After Teodore died, my father had a stroke and he's no longer able to manage the business himself. As the eldest son, Teodore had been raised with the expectation of taking Father's place in due course, but now there's nothing else to be done except to pick ourselves up and make the best of it.'

His expression was so bleak that I wondered if he carried other sorrows he hadn't mentioned.

We climbed some wide steps connecting a series of stone terraces edged with cypress trees and ascended one of the exterior staircases. The entrance door opened into a marble-floored hallway, where the air was perfumed by a bowl of potpourri on a gilt table.

'Night falls quickly at this time of year, and it's too late now to show you Flora's garden,' said Mr Marchese, 'but we'll take a look straight after breakfast tomorrow.'

An elderly woman appeared from a shadowy passage. Dressed in black with a white lace collar, she spoke to Mr Marchese in a voluble stream of Italian. I could only assume she was welcoming him home.

'This is our housekeeper, Lucrezia,' he said. 'She was my nurse when I was a child and my father's before that.'

Lucrezia studied me with shrewd, dark eyes and then smiled, her face creasing into a mass of wrinkles.

'Come,' she said to Edmund and me.

'I expect you'd like to rest after the journey,' said Mr Marchese. 'You have the tower to yourselves, so you won't be disturbed by the household. Massimo will bring your luggage. By the way, we no longer dress for dinner. Since my father's illness, he needs assistance with changing his clothes, and it's too exhausting for him. Besides, the world is a different place since the war.' He turned to Edmund. 'If you'd prefer dinner on a tray in your room, Lucrezia will see to it.'

'Come,' said Lucrezia again. She trotted across the hall and opened a door into a lobby and then another door to show us that it led to the garden. There was also a coat cupboard, a bathroom and separate lavatory.

Beckoning us to follow her, we climbed a narrow staircase and arrived at a landing. She opened a door with a flourish, and we entered a sitting-room filled with evening sunlight from pairs of narrow windows on all four sides. 'Is for you,' she said.

Worn but comfortable sofas and chairs were arranged in a semi-circle around a stone fireplace in a corner of the room. The fire was already lit for our arrival.

'Violet, just look at this view!' said Edmund. 'You can see right out over the lake to the mountains beyond.'

I went to stand beside him and peered out of the window. The sun was low, and the lake was a sheet of silver at the foothills of the blue mountains.

Lucrezia led us up another flight of stairs to two whitewashed bedrooms, each with colourful rugs on the rustic boards, dark ceiling beams and fires crackling in the grates.

'Thank you, Lucrezia,' I said. 'We'll be very comfortable here.'

She nodded. 'Dinner at seven.'

After she'd left us, Edmund and I grinned at each other.

'I'd say we've fallen on our feet here, wouldn't you?' he said. 'And I know, I just *know* I'm going to be well again in a place like this.'

I hoped he was right. Despite the journey, he looked quite different from the pale and trembling invalid who'd returned from Cornwall. 'Removing you from Mildred's compassionless presence was an important step towards your recovery,' I said. 'And this accommodation is much nicer than any flat we might have afforded to rent in England.'

I looked out of the tower's back windows to see what I could of the garden before darkness fell. There was a wide terrace with

40

parterres on either side of a gravel path, which led to an archway in a dense yew hedge. Behind that, grassy terraces rose up the hillside.

Heavy footsteps came clumping up the stairs.

'That must be Massimo with our luggage,' said Edmund.

By the time my watch neared seven, I'd unpacked and put on my best dress – pearl grey to match my eyes– and I felt ready to meet the Marchese family. I was relieved I wasn't expected to change into an evening dress since I no longer possessed such an item. William, as a Quaker, had preferred me to wear unostentatious clothes.

I knocked on Edmund's door and found him chewing his thumbnail and looking pensively out of the window.

'Are you sure you want to come down?' I said. 'I can tell them you're too tired, if you like.'

He shook his head. 'I don't want to set myself apart as an invalid right from the start. I'll ask Luca if I may be excused if it's all too much.'

I nodded. 'Better that than …' I saw the irritation in his expression and stopped. My stomach churned at the thought of us being sent away because the Marchese family weren't understanding about his illness. Perhaps I cosseted my brother too much, but could he really have overcome his mental distress in such a short time?

Chapter 5

Edmund and I went down together, and a pretty girl in a brown striped dress and an apron met us at the foot of the stairs. She smiled and led us across the hall.

I was confused. She wore an apron, indicating she was a maid but not the usual black 'afternoon' uniform or the starched cap worn by an English maid. I wondered if she might be a poor relation helping with the domestic duties.

She opened one of the heavy timber doors in the hall and waved us into a drawing room. The high ceiling, tall windows with elaborate silk drapes and sunshine yellow walls weren't at all what I'd expected after the rustic simplicity of our quarters. I didn't have time to take in anymore because Luca Marchese came forward to greet us.

'Will you be comfortable in the tower?' he asked.

'It's delightful.'

'I hoped you'd find it quiet there. Allow me to introduce you to my family.'

Three people sat beside the fire: a middle-aged man, a woman with fair hair and an elderly man with white hair hunched into an armchair.

'Mamma, Papà and Nonno, this is Mrs Violet Honeywell and her brother, Mr Edmund Hall,' said Mr Marchese. He smiled at Edmund and me. 'My parents, Helen and Orlando Marchese.'

Helen looked up at us with friendly blue eyes. 'I do hope your journey wasn't too exhausting.'

'Forgive me if I do not rise,' said Signor Marchese. 'Welcome to our home.' He spoke fluent English, but his speech was slow, as if he had to concentrate to utter each word. Deep lines were engraved around his eyes, but it was clear he'd passed on his good looks to his son.

I realised, just in time to save embarrassment, that his right arm was impaired by his stroke. We shook our left hands.

He clasped Edmund's hand and held it for a long moment. 'I am happy you have come,' he said. 'I trust you will find peace here.'

'Thank you, sir,' said Edmund.

'And this is my grandfather, Umberto Marchese,' said Luca.

Umberto's olive complexion was seamed with lines, and he wore an old-fashioned brown suit with a paisley silk tie. His face broke into a smile, and he shook my hand in a fierce grip that belied his frail frame. '*Benvenuti a Villa Marchese.*' He turned to Luca and made a comment in Italian.

'Nonno,' warned Luca Marchese, 'you promised to speak in English for our guests!'

He shrugged and gave me a mischievous look. 'I say you are a beautiful English rose.' He kissed his fingers. '*Bellissima!*'

'Thank you,' I said, trying not to laugh.

Edmund stepped up to my side. 'Good evening, sir,' he said.

'Come and sit by me, both of you,' said Helen Marchese. 'I was delighted when Luca wrote to tell me we were to have some English guests. I hope we'll have lovely chats about some of my memories of the country. I've lost touch with many of my girlhood friends in Oxford and I haven't visited England for some years now, what with the war and …' Her voice trailed away but her gaze lingered on her husband for a moment.

Edmund and I perched awkwardly either side of her on a brocade-upholstered sofa.

She put on a bright social smile, but her eyes glistened with tears. 'Luca wrote to tell us you worked at Kew Gardens during the war?'

'I was very fortunate to be offered that experience,' I said.

'And you and your brother have come to Villa Marchese to advise our gardeners for a few months.' Turning to Edmund, she said, 'I understand you've been unwell and need a quiet place to recuperate. You will find it very peaceful here.'

'I'm sure I shall,' said Edmund.

Luca Marchese fidgeted in his chair and crossed and uncrossed his legs. 'Actually, I've brought Mrs Honeywell and Mr Hall here for a particular reason. I've commissioned them to make an English flower garden as a surprise birthday present for Sylvana next year.'

'What a lovely idea!' said his mother. 'Where will you site it? Adjacent to the parterre, perhaps?'

He glanced at his grandfather. 'There's an ideal place. I've asked Mrs Honeywell to restore Grandmother Flora's flower garden.'

Orlando Marchese opened his mouth to speak but Luca's grandfather pushed himself to his feet, his brow thunderous. '*Assolutamente no!*'

'But why not, Nonno?' said Luca. 'The walled garden is the perfect location. I'm sure Sylvana will spend many happy hours there enjoying the flowers. It will be far more beautiful than any garden she might find in Florence.'

'It's still my beloved Flora's garden,' said Umberto, 'and I don't want anyone to go there. It was her special place.'

'It was so long ago, Nonno!' Luca rubbed his palm over his hair. 'Sylvana loves living in Florence, and it's hard for her to leave her

44

friends. It's very important to me that she has an absorbing hobby to make her happy and excited to live at Villa Marchese.'

'Happy? Your wife should be happy at your side, wherever you live.'

'I'm sure Sylvana will soon make new friends here,' said Helen. She smiled at her husband. 'When I came to Villa Marchese, I thought I was in Heaven.'

'And you made it Heaven for me,' murmured Orlando. He turned to his father. 'Please Papà. Allow Luca to do this, and let Sylvana have her garden. After the sadness of recent years, we must all live in harmony.'

'We will treat Flora's garden with respect,' I said, hoping to mollify the old man. 'It will become beautiful again, and you will be able to sit there in the sunshine and remember your wife.'

Umberto assessed me coolly from beneath his bushy white eyebrows before speaking to Luca. 'The signora is not strong enough to make a garden.'

'Signor Marchese,' I said, 'I assure you I am perfectly strong enough.'

He shrugged, a gleam of what looked like amusement in his eyes. 'It is hard work for a woman.'

'It always takes hard work to create a beautiful garden.'

He waved a hand in the air as if dismissing the subject and sat down again. 'We shall see.'

I wasn't sure if that meant he'd given his permission for the garden to go ahead or not.

Helen leaned towards me and spoke in an undertone. 'My father-in-law's manner can be rather forbidding, but his bark is worse than his bite. He's old-fashioned, and in his eyes, gardening is man's work.'

'His wife worked in her garden though, didn't she?' said Edmund.

'But she had the benefit of a full-time head gardener and his staff to do the heavy work.'

The exchange with Umberto had rattled me. I was annoyed Luca hadn't warned me his grandfather might be upset before I brought Edmund on such a journey. What if we had to return home? He should have broached the subject with his grandfather before placing me in the firing line.

'I'm a trained horticulturalist and passionate about my work,' I said. 'However, I'm conscious that in the eyes of some I'll always be merely a gardener, and a substandard one at that, because I'm not a man.'

'That attitude to working women is very common here in Italy, too,' said Helen. 'It's been gratifying to see women from all walks of life rise to the challenge of taking responsibility for men's work while their loved ones went to war.' She gave me a rueful smile. 'I daresay some men feel threatened upon discovering their women-folk managed so capably.'

The door opened, and the girl in the apron came in with a tray of drinks.

Luca rubbed his hands together. 'Excellent, Claudia, an *aperitivo* – just what we need to whet our appetites for dinner!'

I took a glass of the ruby-coloured drink and sipped it. It was slightly fizzy and tasted of bitter herbs, aromatic plants and some kind of fruit. I decided I liked it.

Helen asked Edmund about our journey, and I took the opportunity to study my surroundings. A fire blazed in the marble mantelpiece, and gilded mirrors and framed pictures were hung on the yellow walls. A vast gilt and crystal chandelier was suspended from the decorative plasterwork ceiling, but several of the candle sockets were empty. Before the deprivations of war, it must have been a fine sight ablaze with the full complement of candles.

An oil painting of a young woman perched on a garden swing

with a laughing toddler on her lap hung above the fireplace. It was a joyous image, and the woman's auburn hair had come loose and curled around her shoulders. I thought she looked a bit like me or how I might have looked if the war hadn't destroyed my dreams. The woman in the painting wore a green, full-skirted dress from an earlier era – somewhere around the middle of the last century, I imagined.

'I wondered if you'd notice that portrait, Mrs Honeywell,' said Luca. 'It's my Grandmother Flora in her garden. Unfortunately, the child on her knee, my father's sister Isabella, died of diphtheria when she was ten.'

'I don't remember her,' said Orlando. 'I was so young at the time and it saddens me that I never knew her.'

'How tragic! But it's such a happy picture.' I studied the portrait again. 'I shall think of your mother while I'm planning how to make her garden thrive again. Look at those glorious pink roses and the honeysuckle in the background! The perfume must have been exquisite.'

'And it will be again, one day soon,' said Luca.

Umberto Marchese lurched to his feet. '*Basta!* Enough!' He let fly a flood of Italian, stalked across the carpet and slammed the door behind him.

Edmund jumped and his fingers clutched the arm of the sofa so hard his knuckles turned white. I tensed, waiting for him to crack.

There was a strained silence until Luca broke it with a heavy sigh. 'I apologise, Mrs Honeywell. I was too hasty and should have spoken to my grandfather earlier about restoring Flora's garden.'

'If you had asked him, Luca,' said his father, 'you know he would have forbidden it.' He gave a lopsided grin. 'So, perhaps it is fortunate you only mentioned it tonight? Your nonno dislikes change, and he loved my mother passionately. There is time for him to see the garden being restored and become accustomed to the idea.'

'I had no intention of distressing your father, Signor Marchese,' I said.

'Of course not.'

'Don't look so dismayed, Mrs Honeywell!' said Helen. 'My father-in-law is set in his ways, but I daresay he'll come round.'

I was relieved Umberto had left the room and hoped Luca would make his peace with the old man before Edmund and I started work.

Lucrezia came to announce dinner.

'My father-in-law has retired early,' Helen said to her. 'Will you take him some supper on a tray?'

Orlando struggled to his feet, shrugging off Luca's helping hand. He grasped the two sticks that rested against the arm of his chair and, painfully slowly, made his way towards the door. 'Come,' he said, 'or dinner will be cold.'

In the spacious dining room, he took his seat at one end of the table, while Claudia discreetly removed a place setting at the other end. Helen and Luca sat on one side, opposite Edmund and me.

Willow-green silk curtains complemented the pink roses worked on the tapestry dining chair seats. There was a large rug on the polished floorboards and, like the drawing room, the dining room was elegant without being ostentatious.

'Meals seemed very strange to me when I arrived here thirty years ago,' said Helen, 'but now I've lost the taste for British food.'

'We had spaghetti in Milan,' said Edmund. 'It was rather good.'

'My husband once took me to an excellent Italian restaurant in Soho,' I said. It had been on our honeymoon, and I had precious memories of that evening. I couldn't recall what we ate but only the love that had shone in William's eyes.

The maid served us with little twists of pasta that Helen told me were called *trofie*. They were smothered in a delicious cream sauce with fresh herbs.

Lucrezia poured us white wine. Despite the apparent opulence of Villa Marchese, there was no butler or footman to serve our dinner. I assumed the lack of menservants in a house such as this was due to the war.

'It's too dark to see Flora's garden tonight,' I said, 'but I'm looking forward to making a start tomorrow.'

'Surely there isn't much you can do at this time of year?' asked Helen.

'The spring will be here before we know it,' I said. 'Edmund and I must clear the ground during the winter, and a design for the garden must be prepared before we can plant anything. Seeds and plants will need to be ordered in good time. I'll require some help with that since I don't speak Italian.'

'I'm happy to assist,' said Helen, 'but Massimo's English is pretty good and he'll know which nurseries to approach.'

'And for the design, there are Flora's notebooks to inspire you,' said Luca.

'I love the prospect of an English flower garden,' said Helen. 'Gardens in Italy can be a little too formal for my taste.'

'If I'd known that,' said Orlando, 'I would have asked Massimo to make you an English garden.'

'But would Massimo know how?' said Luca. 'I'm sure Sylvana will be happy to share her garden with you, Mamma.'

Lucrezia brought in a platter of little fried fish that Orlando said came from the lake. We ate them with a slice of something called polenta that resembled a savoury bread pudding. I wouldn't have minded if I never had it again.

'I have lived at Villa Marchese all my life,' said Orlando, 'but I have never seen my mother's garden.'

'Probably because Nonno forbade you,' said Luca.

Orlando nodded. 'I was always curious about my mother, and when I was about ten, I remember trying to open the door. It had been screwed shut. Beppe, Massimo's father, found me and threatened to tell Papà. I never tried again, and because the garden is hidden, I had almost forgotten about it.'

'I found it by chance,' said Luca. 'I was meandering through the shade of our rhododendron walk one hot day in September and thinking about Teodore. I remembered the secret den we'd made amongst the tangled shrubs when we were children. We'd woven branches together and spent a whole summer playing there. There was no sign of it anymore, but I found an ancient door in the wall behind the rhododendrons.'

'I told you boys never to enter the walled garden,' said Orlando.

'We didn't,' said Luca. 'But when I found the door recently the wood was so rotten that part of it crumbled off the hinges when I tried to open it.'

'The door had been shut for fifty-seven years,' said Orlando. 'It must be a jungle by now.'

Luca laughed. 'I couldn't see much through the gap in the door, but I doubt Grandmother Flora would recognise it today. I'm sure Mrs Honeywell, with Edmund's help, will bring it back to life.'

Edmund glanced at me.

Luca Marchese's faith in our abilities was flattering. I only hoped it was possible to live up to his expectations.

The sky was pale blue when I peered out of the tower window the following morning, and the lake sparkled in the sunshine. Anticipation bubbled inside me at the prospect of seeing Flora's lost garden at last. I plaited and pinned up my hair and put on the gardening uniform I'd worn at Kew: a beige shirt and tie with khaki breeches and a woollen waistcoat. My thorn-proof gardening coat, stout boots and beret were hanging in the lobby downstairs, ready to put on after breakfast. I gave a cursory look at my reflection in the mirror, decided I looked suitably workmanlike and then went to knock on Edmund's door.

He opened it straight away.

'Did you sleep well?' I asked.

'Better than I can remember for a long time. Shall we go down for breakfast?'

A young parlour maid was washing the floor in the lobby, but she scurried away when she heard us coming downstairs.

Luca and his mother were in the dining room, where she offered us coffee and pastries. 'I'm going to come with you to look at the secret garden,' she said. 'I'd never thought about it all the time I've lived here, but now I'm intrigued.'

'It's like a story out of a fairy tale, isn't it?' I said.

'"Sleeping Beauty"!' Helen smiled. 'Sadly, Flora isn't in there waiting for her prince to kiss her awake.'

I sipped my coffee. 'Has your father-in-law mentioned the garden this morning?'

'No. He's still in his room.'

After breakfast, Luca led us through the hall to a rear lobby. A glazed door opened into an arcaded loggia spanning the width of the ground floor of the house. The walls were decorated with trompe l'oeil columns of marble and faded frescoes of lakeside landscapes. Painted trellises smothered in vines adorned the vaulted ceiling.

'What a delightful way to transition between the villa and the garden,' I said.

'It's always been a favourite place of mine to sit and read,' said Helen. 'In the summer, we dine here.'

'Teodore and I used to race each other along the arcade on our tricycles,' said Luca. Abruptly, he turned away and led us out into the garden.

51

The once-splendid, but now unkempt, parterre I'd seen from the tower windows was laid out on either side of a gravel path. The walkway disappeared through an archway in a high yew hedge, where there was an intriguing glimpse of a large statue. Beyond that, the hillside rose steeply in terraced lawns punctuated with statuesque specimen trees.

Despite the pale sunshine, the air was cold, and I was glad to be wearing my thick gardening coat. Our boots crunched over the gravel as we walked through the archway. A stream cascaded over stone steps down the hillside behind, and a rill filled a circular pool. The marble fountain in the centre was a statue of Neptune entwined with naked water sprites and assorted sea serpents, all spouting water.

'It's a bit ostentatious, isn't it?' said Luca. 'Still, I have fond memories of paddling in the summer when we ...' he glanced away, 'when I was a child.'

Helen slipped her arm through the crook of her son's elbow, and we walked along a path that meandered over lawns dotted with mature trees. Above us, at the highest point of the grounds near the top of the cascade, was a Roman-style temple framed by cypress trees.

'The view from the temple over the gardens towards Lake Como and the mountains must be magnificent,' I said.

'I spent a great deal of time sitting there after Teodore died,' said Helen. 'In so far as anything could ever heal a mother's grief, that eased my pain.'

Luca kissed her cheek. 'He wouldn't have wanted you to grieve, Mamma,' he said, his voice choked, 'but only to remember the happy times.'

'I know.'

'Your son was treated cruelly,' said Edmund. 'I realise now how lucky I've been and how much I have to be grateful for. Not least that my mother didn't have to suffer like you.'

'No family should have to suffer the loss of a son,' said Helen.

My heart bled for the Marchese family's grief and for all the families whose lives had been devastated by the war.

'Come,' said Luca. He tucked his mother's hand into the crook of his elbow. 'Let's go and find what is left of Grandmother's garden.'

We passed the stable yard, silent and swept clean. I imagined the sound of horses' hooves on the cobbles while stable lads fed, watered and exercised their charges in earlier times.

'The horses went to aid the war effort,' said Luca, 'and since Papà cannot ride now, we keep our old mule Zizzo to take him to church or make any local visits in the pony trap. We catch a ferry or a train when we need to travel somewhere further afield.'

Beside the stables was a pair of cottages set amongst a small copse of trees.

'This is where Massimo and Beppe live,' said Luca. 'Massimo is coming with us to see how much help you're likely to need with clearing the garden.'

'Those trees,' I said. 'They're mulberries, aren't they?'

'Mulberries are, or were, grown all around Lake Como at one time. Silkworms are very fussy; they eat only mulberry leaves. Silkworm farming was a thriving cottage industry in this area. The whole family would be involved because it was a round-the-clock business. The worms grow at a phenomenal rate, but they're delicate and can be carried off very quickly if great attention isn't given to their welfare.'

'Were silkworms farmed here, at Villa Marchese?' asked Edmund.

Luca smiled. 'That's how my family made their fortune. More and more of the raw silk is coming from China now, but once upon a time, this plot of land was a simple farm. My great-great-grandfather Oreste had grandiose ideas. His wife brought a good dowry with her and, instead of selling the silk filaments they produced on the farm to a factory owner, he set up a small factory of his own.'

'How interesting!' I said.

Massimo must have been looking out for us because the door of one of the cottages opened, and he came out carrying an evil-looking curved billhook over his shoulder. He greeted us with a cheerful wave, and we set off together along the path until we came to two large glasshouses and a sizeable vegetable garden bounded on three sides by yew hedging. The fourth side was a stone wall, some ten feet high and covered by espaliered peach trees.

'Flora's garden is behind that wall,' said Luca.

'Where's the door? I asked.

'A little further on.'

'Many years ago, my grandfather was the head gardener at Villa Marchese,' said Massimo. 'He told me when Signora Marchese made her garden she wanted high walls, so her husband gave her the kitchen garden behind the Rhododendron Walk.'

I was surprised. Although his English was heavily accented, he spoke it fluently. 'And the vegetable garden was moved here?'

He nodded.

The stone wall disappeared behind a thicket of ancient rhododendrons with twisted limbs as thick as a man's thigh. The pathway skirted around the densest growth until Luca stopped and held out a hand to his mother. 'Through here,' he said.

We shoved our way between the undergrowth, stepping over and under contorted branches while brambles tore our clothes and tried to trip us up. Leaves and twigs made a roof above us, cutting out the light.

'We'll have to clear a proper path before we can do anything else,' I said.

'Heaven knows what the garden will be like,' murmured Edmund, 'if the approach to it is as overgrown as this.'

Massimo went on ahead, slashing at the brambles with his

billhook, like an intrepid explorer hacking through the jungle in some exotic land.

Under the canopy of rhododendrons, the ground smelled of leaf mould and damp earth, but I imagined a child might have found it an exciting place to build a camp away from prying adult eyes. I quickly pushed the thought away. Now William had gone, I would never have a child of my own to build secret dens.

At last, Luca stopped. 'Here's the wall again!' he said.

'Where's the door?' said Edmund.

Luca glanced both ways and then pointed a few yards further along the wall. 'Do you see that fallen tree? I'm sure it's near there.'

The men forged ahead, Massimo cutting through the undergrowth to make a path.

Helen smoothed back a lock of hair that had been snagged by a bramble and smiled at me. 'Men do love an adventure, don't they, Signora Honeywell?'

'This is turning out to be more of an adventure than I'd anticipated,' I said. In truth, I was as anxious as Edmund that if this was the 'civilised' part of the garden, what could we expect inside?

Luca shouted in triumph, and by the time Helen and I reached the men, he was putting his shoulder to the rotten wood. It groaned and splintered as flakes of green paint scattered onto the ground, but there was a gap wide enough for us to squeeze through.

One by one, we stepped inside the lost garden.

Chapter 6

Outside the garden, the rhododendron thicket overhead allowed for little light as we battled through the undergrowth. Now, I stood inside the garden doorway and blinked in the November sunshine. It wasn't only the sunlight that made me halt but the sight of a chest-high carpet of brushwood and intertwined brambles that spread out before us in all directions. Some of the bramble stems were at least an inch thick and, together with sprays of desiccated blackberries and colonies of rosebay willow herb smothered with downy seed heads, they formed an impenetrable mass. Swathes of ivy were festooned from saplings like maypoles, and mounds of vegetation scrambled over who knew what. There were also several self-seeded trees, one of them swamped by a mass of dead honeysuckle stems. The wall on the far side of the garden looked as impossible to reach as the moon.

'Oh, my!' said Helen.

I couldn't find the words to express my dismay. I'd been expecting the lost garden to be overgrown, but this . . .

Massimo sliced through a spiny stem with his billhook and then yanked at the severed end. It pulled free of the mass and whipped across his face like an angry snake. He uttered what sounded like a curse.

Luca, his brows drawn together, was watching me uneasily. 'I was reading a newspaper by the fire in London when your advertisement gave me the idea of recreating Flora's garden,' he said. 'Now I see it properly, I wonder if it's going to be more challenging than I'd imagined.'

Anger flared inside me as I glanced at the scratch across Massimo's cheek, now decorated with spots of blood like a string of rubies. Luca Marchese's privileged background probably meant he'd never lifted a garden spade in his life. Still, how could he have been so naive as to imagine that I, alone, could battle against the power of Mother Nature to clear a wilderness like this? After all, when he interviewed me he didn't know about Edmund or have any idea of whether he would be well enough to share the physical effort. I opened my mouth to tell Luca he'd entirely misrepresented the situation and it was ludicrous for me to even contemplate undertaking such a project.

Edmund pulled me to his side and whispered urgently in my ear. '*Please* don't say it, Violet! I absolutely cannot face returning to London.'

'But—'

'Luca, this is an utterly hare-brained idea,' said Helen. 'You cannot possibly expect Mrs Honeywell and Mr Hall to make this ... this *wasteland* into a garden in time for Sylvana's birthday next August. It might take ten men ten years. Whatever were you thinking of?'

Luca bowed his head. 'Perhaps I didn't think it through properly. All I wanted was to find the perfect present for Sylvana.'

'You always were impetuous, Luca,' said his mother, 'but this is madness.' She folded her arms, her cheeks pink with anger.

'Please, Violet!' murmured Edmund. 'I promise to put in the effort, but do let us stay.'

His expression was strained, and he gripped my shoulder as if it were a lifeline. Bringing him to Italy had been hard enough, even with assistance, but how could I ever get him back to London on my own?

'Don't you see?' Edmund said, his eyes pleading with me. 'This place is good for me. I *know* it will help me to be well again.'

Could he be right? I remembered my promise to our mother to look after him and hesitated while I weighed up the risks of conveying him safely home.

'Mrs Honeywell?' Luca was waiting for me to speak.

'It would be unprofessional of me,' I said, 'to work on this project without telling you that I agree with your mother, Mr Marchese. With the best will in the world, we'd never clear the land in time to plant it and make the garden bloom for August. At least, not without considerable additional help.'

'I can see that now.' He turned to Massimo. 'Would Beppe be able to manage the rest of the garden if you worked here until the land is cleared?'

Massimo pursed his lips in thought. 'He suffers with *reumatismi* – how do you say? Ah, yes, pain in his hips, when it is cold. And there is too much work here for only three people.'

'I suppose we might manage it with a temporary gang of labourers,' I said. 'They wouldn't need any special horticultural training to tear up the undergrowth and burn it.'

'No,' said Luca. Thoughtfully, he scanned the overgrown jungle. 'Labourers might collect the leaves in the main garden and undertake other tasks under Beppe's direction, too, leaving Massimo free to work here.'

'But can you find labourers?' I asked. 'You said there weren't any gardeners to employ.'

'There must be men in the village who would be glad of short-term employment,' he said. 'And, as you pointed out, they don't need to be skilled.'

'I suggest we see if you can employ a temporary workforce over the next couple of weeks. If not . . .' I shrugged, 'it will be too late to clear the ground for the spring, and we'll have to abandon the idea.' My heart was heavy at the thought of turning my back on a project I so badly wanted to complete. If nothing else, bed and board were being provided, and we could save our salary to contribute to our train tickets back to London.

'Meanwhile,' said Edmund, 'since you're already paying us and time is of the essence, we shall make a start.' His voice was determined.

A movement in the rhododendrons behind me caught my eye. Umberto was looking out from behind the bushes to peer through the garden doorway. No doubt he was looking at the state of the garden, jubilant that it would be too much for me. That decided it. 'Will you find us some tools, Massimo?' I asked.

He grinned at me. 'We have many tools but no men to use them.'

'Luca,' said Signora Marchese, 'you'd better return to the house. Your father will be waiting to speak to you about your business trip.' Shaking her head, she went through the doorway and the others followed.

I stood still for a moment, taking it all in, before pushing past the rotten door and leaving Flora's garden alone with its ghosts again.

Massimo, Edmund and I returned later with two wheelbarrows full of scythes, saws, axes, billhooks, shears and secateurs and set about clearing a direct path to the walled garden through the rhododendron thicket. My experience at Kew Gardens certainly hadn't prepared me for the amount of physical effort involved.

Massimo brought the mule, Zizzo, to drag away the heavy boughs to be stacked elsewhere until there was time to cut them up for firewood. Edmund gathered up the twiggy debris to be burned.

In the walled garden, I hacked my way into the undergrowth inside the doorway until I'd made a clearing large enough for a bonfire. Once the new path was passable, Edmund and Massimo wheeled barrowload after barrowload of brushwood and brambles into the garden for me to feed into the fire. The plume of black smoke that rose from it made me cough and my eyes run. I could see that we might need to keep it burning for weeks to dispose of the vast amount of vegetation.

In the middle of the day, the maid Claudia brought us bread, cheese, olives and a billycan of coffee. We retreated from the smoke and she sat on the ground with us to eat our simple repast. She warmed the coffee, black and strong, on the bonfire and poured it into tin mugs for us when it was ready. She and Massimo chatted easily together in Italian as if they'd known each other all their lives.

'I will go to the town tomorrow,' said Massimo as we finished our coffee, 'and see who wants work. I think six men will be enough.'

'It's hard to say,' I said. 'We don't know what we'll find after we clear the vegetation. We need more hands on deck as soon as possible, but we should discuss with Mr Marchese how much he's prepared to spend.'

'I will speak to him before I go to the town,' said Massimo.

Claudia collected our mugs and plates into her basket. 'I must go,' she said. 'Lucrezia will be waiting.' She bent forwards and kissed Massimo's forehead, then walked away.

Massimo laughed when he saw my surprise. 'Claudia is my daughter.'

'Oh! I didn't realise.'

'She is the jewel of my heart,' he said, pressing a hand to his chest. 'My wife died when Claudia was only ten years old.'

'Our mother died when I was thirteen,' said Edmund. 'It's hard for a child to lose a mother.'

Massimo nodded.

He looked sad, so I changed the subject. 'How is it that you speak such excellent English?'

'English has been spoken at Villa Marchese for a long time.' He smiled. 'You British ladies capture the hearts of the men here and bring your English ways with you. My grandfather married Flora Marchese's maid, who came from Sussex. She sang me songs like "London's Burning" and "The Grand Old Duke of York" when I was a little boy.'

'So, you have British blood then?'

'Some, but I have never been to see England.'

'And then Luca's mother came here?'

'She didn't speak Italian at first, but her husband wanted her to feel at home, so he arranged for a tutor to come every week to teach her Italian and to teach the servants English.'

'How fortunate for us,' said Edmund, 'that Villa Marchese is an Anglo-Italian household since neither of us speak a word of Italian.'

Massimo grinned. 'Who knows,' he said, 'perhaps you will learn.'

As dusk fell, Massimo and Edmund went to clean and oil the tools before putting them away, leaving me to watch the bonfire until it died down.

The garden within the walls was a large rectangle with the doorway in the centre of one of the longer sides. I half closed my eyes, imagining a path leading straight ahead to a special feature on the opposite wall. A gazebo or an arbour, perhaps?

Flames and a shower of orange sparks suddenly erupted from

the bonfire with a noise like a volley of bullets. I stepped backwards hastily, thankful Edmund wasn't nearby. The fire illuminated the sight of a dumpy little man in the garden doorway. His legs were bowed, and he wore stout gardening boots. Lifting a hand, he waved at me. I waved back, and he hobbled towards me.

'*Buonasera*, Signora Honeywell,' he said. 'I am Beppe.' His gap-toothed smile, brown eyes and weathered complexion were friendly.

'You're Massimo's father?' I asked.

He laughed. 'You are saying, how can this little man be the father of such a big strong fellow as Massimo?'

I hoped he couldn't see my blush, for that was exactly what I had been thinking.

The smile faded from his face as his gaze wandered around the garden. 'The last time I was here I was eleven years old. It was so beautiful then.' He shook his head. 'After Flora Marchese drowned, I was sad and came here to weep. Then I saw her husband come into the garden with an axe. Like a madman at full moon, he shouted and screamed at God. He smashed everything: the roses, the statues in the grotto, the benches, the pergolas, the pots of lemons. I hid behind the tool shed, frightened for my life.'

I shuddered at the vision of so much violence. Umberto's mind must have been turned by his grief. No wonder he didn't want anyone to see, though there would be precious little sign now of the damage he'd caused. 'What a shock for you,' I said, 'but over the years Mother Nature has hidden the destruction. I hope to work with her to make the garden bloom again.'

Beppe puffed out his breath. 'It will be hard.'

'What was it was like before it was destroyed?'

'So many flowers! And the bees. I remember the bees. And the pond with lilies and . . . ' He screwed up his eyes in concentration. 'Green with four wings.'

'A dragonfly?'

'Yes, yes!'

'Where was the pond?'

'In the centre of the garden.'

A flaming branch tumbled off the top of the bonfire, and I prodded it back into the blaze with a stick. 'What else can you remember?'

'A few minutes ago, I met Massimo taking the tools back to the shed. Now I see why he laughed when I told him there was a tool shed in the garden already.' His brow furrowed. 'I think ... Yes! Over there!' He pointed to one of the mounds of vegetation against a wall. 'I remember because Isabella made a little house inside it for Luna.'

'Luna?'

'The kitchen cat. The cook wanted to drown her kittens.' His eyes almost disappeared when he smiled. 'I said I would take them to the lake.' He leaned forwards to whisper. 'Instead, I gave them to Isabella.'

'I saw the painting of Isabella with her mother on the swing.'

Beppe nodded. 'I was the son of the head gardener and Isabella was the daughter of the house, but we were good friends. We played together in this garden.' His face broke into a smile. 'She wrote to me after she went away to school.'

'She must have missed you,' I said.

'I've kept her letters.' He banked up the fire again. 'The mistress, Signora Flora Marchese, worked beside my father. Isabella's nursemaid watched us, but the mistress said we were safe inside the walls of her garden.'

'How sad that she and Isabella didn't stay there,' I said. A scimitar of moon hung above us in the darkening sky and, despite the fire, I shivered.

'Go to the house,' said Beppe. 'I will make the fire safe.'

'That's kind of you but—'

'You are tired, and I would like to stay here, remembering happy days.'

'Then, thank you.'

Once back at the house, I entered the tower by the garden door, leaving my boots on the rack in the lobby. I strip-washed in the bathroom and changed into clean clothes, but my hair still reeked of smoke. I suspected this would be the state of affairs for some time since my hair was long and thick and it wasn't practical to wash and dry it at the end of every day.

I went downstairs again and found Signora Marchese sitting by the fire in the drawing room.

'Excuse me for interrupting you,' I said. 'I hoped to have a few words with your son.'

'He's still discussing business matters with his father,' she said. 'Will you join me for tea until he's free? Claudia brought the pot to me only five minutes ago with an extra cup for my husband, but he's still busy.'

'Tea would be very welcome. It's hot and thirsty work tending the bonfire.'

She smiled. 'I thought I detected a hint of woodsmoke.'

'I apologise; it's dreadful, isn't it? I did wash when I came in, but there isn't time to dry my hair tonight. I'll be back tending the fire again at first light.'

'It's hard to do a man's work and still be obliged to conform to the normal dictates of femininity.' She handed me a cup of tea and offered a plate of shortbread.

'I'm not sure anything will ever be normal again. Many women's lives have changed out of all recognition. So many of us had to step into a man's shoes during the war. It was an opportunity to show we're made of sterner stuff than most men imagined and also, for some, to find fulfilment. Of course, the war was far worse for the men.'

'But the women suffered, too.'

'I hardly know a woman who isn't grieving.'

'Including us.' Helen's mouth quivered and she took a bracing breath. 'I'm astonished by your courage at even contemplating the renovation of Flora's garden.'

'What else can I do? Edmund seems so much better, but if your son hadn't been there to help us, I fear he'd have had a mental collapse on the journey here. If we have to return before he's ready, I don't know how I'll get him home safely.'

'Poor boy! But please, don't worry,' said Helen. 'Luca travels to London now and again for business reasons, so you shall stay here until his next trip.'

'That's very kind of you and it eases my mind, Signora Marchese. And, of course, Edmund and I would earn our keep by working in the grounds, even if Flora's garden is too difficult a project for us to complete.'

Helen frowned while she sipped her tea. 'I'm afraid my son has always been impulsive. Sometimes, I despair. He really should have considered the state of the walled garden more carefully before asking you to come all this way.'

I gave her a rueful smile.

'Nevertheless,' she said, 'I'm delighted you are here to remind me of the land of my birth.'

'I hadn't expected to be eating shortbread and drinking proper English tea with milk in Italy.'

Helen laughed. 'I love Italy, but I will always be an Englishwoman.'

The door opened and Luca came in. 'What are you two laughing about?'

'Oh, this and that,' said Helen. 'Have you finished talking to your father?'

'For today.' He raked his fingers through his hair. 'He has a great deal to teach me about the business.'

'If you're free, Mrs Honeywell wishes to speak with you.'

He turned to look at me, his expression taut. 'I'm sure today must have been very hard work, but please don't tell me you've had enough already and you're returning to London?'

'I don't give up so easily,' I said. 'You mentioned that you have your grandmother's gardening notebooks. I'd very much like to see them.'

His face cleared. 'Of course. Will you come with me to the library?'

Chapter 7

The shutters were closed and a lamp on a side table cast a gentle glow over the library. Luca lit several more lamps, which revealed a room lined with mahogany bookcases and cupboards. Leather armchairs, softened with velvet cushions, were arranged in a crescent around the marble fireplace. There was a pedestal desk and a splendid eighteenth century drawing table before the window – a vast improvement on my battered, second-hand drawing board.

Luca set a match to the fire. 'If you want to work in here at any time, let Claudia know. She'll make sure the fire is lit and bring you tea.'

'It's too dark to work outside now, so it's a good opportunity to look at Flora's notebooks for inspiration for the new garden.'

He opened one of the cupboards, took out a pile of leather bound books and placed them on the table. 'So, you haven't completely given up on the idea then?'

'I really do want to make this garden, Mr Marchese, but it will depend on how much help is available.'

'I understand,' he said, 'and I must apologise. As my mother pointed out, I can be impulsive, but when I saw your advertisement, an English flower garden seemed such a perfect idea for Sylvana. I'd only seen a glimpse into the walled garden, and I hadn't appreciated quite how wild it is.'

'Does your wife like flowers?'

'Like them?' There was puzzlement in his tone. 'All women like flowers, don't they? I needed to find a very special present for her because ...' His voice trailed away.

'Because?' I prompted.

'The truth is, we'd planned to continue living in Florence, but since my father became incapacitated, I'm the only one left to keep the family business going. My grandfather has been forced out of retirement to advise me, but he is too old to work all the time.' He frowned. 'It's impossible for me to live in Florence and visit the factory in Como several times a week.'

'The silk business wasn't what you'd wanted?'

He shook his head. 'Not at all. I'd always known Teodore would step into my father's shoes. From when he was a small boy, he loved to visit the factory, knowing that one day it would be his. I was a bookworm and read English at Oxford, like my father, and had dreams of becoming an author. When I graduated, I found work with a publishing house in Florence and intended to write in my spare time but ...' He turned his palms to the ceiling and shrugged.

'War was declared.'

'I suppose I'm lucky. I had to give up my dreams, but I must be thankful I returned unharmed.'

I reflected for a moment on what he'd said. 'And your wife?' I was itching to know why she remained – alone –in Florence while her new husband was here.

'We met before the war. She and her first husband, an art dealer, attended the same literary and artistic salons in Florence as I did. Sylvana speaks several languages, and she's a wonderful hostess. She is so full of life. I ran into her again this summer, after my discharge from the army. She'd been widowed early in the war and, after all the misery, there didn't seem any point in us having a long engagement. We married three weeks later.'

How lucky for her to find another husband, I thought. 'But she remains in Florence?'

'Until August.'

I couldn't press him any further. 'And you don't mind me looking at these?' I asked, drawing the pile of journals towards me. Four were bound in green leather and had the year embossed in gold on the spine: 1856 to 1859. Then there were three linen-covered notebooks covering the years from 1860 to 1863, each with a watercolour flower painted on the cover – a pansy, a rose and a sweet pea.

'I found them tucked into the back of one of the library cupboards when I was searching for Amores, Ovid's first volume of poetry. Have you read it?'

I shook my head.

'Pity. I glanced at a couple of the journals and they don't seem to be particularly personal,' said Luca. 'The entries are mostly notes of how well certain plants grew and when they flowered and were pruned, and so on.'

'That will certainly be useful,' I said. 'The seasons will be a little different from at home.'

'The only thing I ask is that the journals remain here in the library and you return them to the cupboard after you've looked at them.' He folded his arms. 'It would be wise not to let my grandfather know I found these. He can be a bit touchy about Flora.'

'I quite understand,' I said.

'I'll leave you to it, then.' He grimaced. 'My father has asked me to look at the business accounts.'

The door closed behind him, and I opened the first journal, dated 1856. The flyleaf was inscribed with bold, black script:

To my dearly beloved Wife, Flora, and the flowering of her Eden. May it bloom as gloriously as our love.

I was nonplussed. Umberto was an old man, but he didn't give the impression that he'd once been such a romantic. I opened the first page of the notebook to find it densely covered with neat copperplate writing.

January 1856. I am filled with excitement that my dearest husband has indulged my whim to make an English flower garden amongst the Italianate parkland of Villa Marchese. He has given me the walled kitchen garden, and I shall fill it with beautiful and sweetly fragrant blooms. It will be my secret haven from the world and especially from my husband's vile stepmother.

I frowned at this reference to Umberto's stepmother. Luca had never mentioned her, but I wondered if an unhappy relationship with his stepmother troubled Umberto's childhood. I had personal experience of how awful that could be and felt some sympathy for him.

I remember my mother's country garden in Sussex with great fondness. We spent many happy times there together when I was a child. She gave me seeds and a flowerbed of my own, and it seemed to be a special sort of magic when, with the application of regular watering, Granny's bonnets or marigolds appeared a few weeks later. I hope my little Isabella will find the same joy as I do in watching plants grow.

Flora's words echoed my own feelings, almost as if she were speaking directly to me, and I experienced a strong sense of affinity with her. Why, we even had the same colour hair! I longed to be able to tell her that I'd found exactly that same magic in a sprinkling of seeds. I didn't have a little Isabella to toddle along beside me while I was gardening, however and there was sadness in the knowledge that neither mother nor child had gone on to enjoy long and happy lives. I turned back to the journal to read on.

> *Poor Mama! I think perhaps that I hope to recreate my fond memories of that sunny garden of my childhood. I still mourn her, but her benevolent spirit will walk beside me, gently prompting me to grow her favourite flowers. It's too early in the year to sow seeds, but until then, I shall plan my garden. Meanwhile, Signor Bernardi and his men are digging over the walled garden and removing the last of the cabbages.*

I guessed Flora's mother hadn't lived into old age. In any case, she and I had both been imbued with a love of gardening by our respective mothers. I turned back to the journal and read pages and pages of notes on which seeds had been sown and when, either in the greenhouses or straight into the ground, and how the different varieties of plants performed. Additional notes had been added in the margins with comments such as:

> *Next year add more well-rotted manure* and *Stake dahlias against the wind!* And later, *Gabriele helped me prune the roses.*

I fanned through the journal, reading short extracts here and there, and was delighted to find the sketch of Flora's garden that Luca had mentioned. Beautifully watercoloured, it was spread over two pages with tiny notes describing the planned planting. The drawing showed a rectangular walled garden divided evenly into four sections by intersecting brick paths. Each of the large squares thus formed was further subdivided into four with an obelisk of climbing roses at the junction of the paths. Diagonal paths fanned out from a central pool surrounded by a rose garden. The main axis path leading from the entrance doorway culminated in a rockery and a grotto against the opposite wall, just where I'd imagined adding a feature such as gazebo or a shady arbour.

I sat back in the desk chair and drummed my fingers on the table while my mind worked feverishly. Flora's design was very attractive, though the Victorian ideal of carpet bedding wasn't at all to my taste. Most of the flower colours were too bright, even garish when planted closely together in regimented rows: scarlet pelargoniums, azure blue trailing lobelia, purple petunias, asters, begonias and marigolds.

I squinted at the garden layout and imagined wandering along lavender-lined paths, brushing my fingers over clouds of gypsophila and reaching up to pull a rose towards me to breathe in its perfume. I wanted the garden to feel as if I were immersing myself in an impressionist painting; soft and naturalistic cottage garden planting set within the geometric framework of the paths. I pictured the long borders against the walls densely planted with drifts of herbaceous flowers in shades of white, mauve and blue, moving through the colour spectrum to pinks, reds, oranges and yellow and then back to white.

I don't know how long I was lost in my reverie, but I blinked when the door opened and Luca came in.

'I came to tell you dinner will be ready in five minutes,' he said.

'So soon! I was so absorbed in the journals that I didn't realise the time.'

'Have you found anything interesting?'

'Your grandmother's watercolour sketch of her garden is fascinating. Whilst the planting isn't in tune with modern taste, the layout is charming.'

'Do you think you might use it?'

'I can't see any reason not to, but it may depend on what we

72

find when we clear the brambles and weeds. I'd prefer to make changes to the planting, though,' I said. 'Apart from anything else, changing the carpet bedding three or four times a year, as they used to do during the old queen's reign, requires manymore gardeners than are available these days. Thousands of bedding plants would need to be grown from seed each year to maintain the flowerbeds.'

Luca frowned. 'That would be a problem. Without sufficient manpower, the garden would soon look unkempt. And the glasshouses are needed for the kitchen garden.'

'What I propose is that, although we will concentrate on a good display for your wife's birthday, we should also plan for the rest of the year. We could plant roses, honeysuckle and clematis to clothe the walls and form scented tunnels over some of the paths. Then we'll use herbaceous plants that are dormant in the winter but that reshoot annually. We'll underplant them with annual spring bulbs to begin the floral display early in the year.'

'What about the winter?'

'It's more difficult to maintain the show in the colder months; however, some shrubs like camellias flower very early with beautifully exotic and colourful blooms.' I was warming to the theme now, and my voice was full of enthusiasm. 'There's also winter flowering jasmine, aconites and snowdrops, Christmas roses and scented Daphne. The garden won't be as vibrant in the winter, but there will always be something of interest to see.'

'You conjure up a delightful picture.' Luca paced over to the fireplace, stirred the flames with the poker and then turned abruptly to face me. 'Somehow, we *have* to create this garden. Sylvana enjoys being surrounded by beautiful things. She's sure to fall in love with it. She's lived in the town all her life, but this garden must surely open her eyes to the charm of the countryside.'

'It would be the perfect place to sit and read a book, to paint or to wander amongst the flowers with her friends,' I said, 'but without additional assistance, it simply won't be possible to finish it by August.'

'I've spoken to Massimo, and he's gone into the town to see what he can do.'

'If he's successful, I'll start work on my own planting plan for Flora's garden.'

A bell rang in the hall, and Luca glanced at his watch. 'Time for dinner.'

'I'd better go and find Edmund. He went to rest.'

'He's already having a chat and an *aperitivo* with my father.' Luca smiled and offered me his arm. 'Shall we?'

In the drawing room, Edmund's complexion was pale with fatigue after a day of hard physical work, but I was delighted to see him talking freely with Orlando.

Later, as we took our places for dinner, I tensed when Umberto Marchese came into the dining room and sat down beside me.

'Good evening, Papà,' said Orlando. 'Will you spare me a few minutes after dinner to discuss the purchase of a new loom for the factory? Luca and I have selected the one we believe is most suitable, but I'd like your opinion.'

Umberto inclined his head to his son. 'The question must be whether a new loom is required at all.'

'Now the hostilities are over,' said Luca, 'there's sure to be a resurgence in demand for high quality silk—'

'Luca,' said Helen, 'you know I don't care for business talk at the dinner table, if you please.'

'I apologise, Mamma.'

Lucrezia carried in the soup tureen. She ladled it into bowls, and Claudia handed them around.

Umberto tasted his soup before turning his dark gaze to me. 'How did you find my wife's garden, Signora Honeywell?'

'It's an almost impenetrable jungle of saplings, brambles, weeds and ivy,' I said.

The tension in his posture relaxed. 'So, your long journey has been for nothing,' he said, 'and you and your brother must return home.'

'It's too soon to decide that, Nonno,' protested Luca.

Umberto's comment stiffened my resolve to remain and annoyance made me speak more sharply than I should have to an old man. 'I haven't decided yet what we'll do. If additional labour can be found to help clear the land, we'll stay.'

'The past is finished and must stay in the past!' Umberto slapped his palm on the table, making me jump and the silver and crystal rattle.

Edmund gasped and leaped to his feet, his eyes wide with fear.

Before I could go to him, Orlando caught his arm. 'All is well, Edmund,' he murmured. 'Sit down beside me again. It was only my father losing his temper.'

Helen turned to her father-in-law. 'How thoughtless to upset Edmund like that.'

'*Mi scuso.*' Umberto had the grace to look apologetic and he heaved a sigh. 'My wife's death is the great sorrow of my life. It is painful to think of opening her garden again.'

My brother remained standing, his body rigid while Orlando continued a flow of calming words. Eventually, Edmund swallowed and sat down.

It wouldn't help matters if I argued with Umberto. 'Perhaps,' I said tentatively, 'after all these years of grieving for your wife, it's time to remember the happiness you shared?'

'Every day, in my thoughts, I speak to her. I ask what I could have done to save her.' He shook his head. 'But she never answers me.'

I couldn't help but feel sorry for this sad old man, so trapped in

75

mourning for a wife who had been dead for nearly sixty years. 'If the garden is restored, perhaps you'll find solace there and be able to hear her voice in your mind again.'

He shrugged and turned to his grandson. 'Why do you spend money on a garden, Luca? If you believe there will be a demand for silk again, then you must invest your money in the business.'

'My wife wouldn't find that an interesting birthday present, Nonno.' Luca's voice was calm, but there were lines of strain around his eyes.

'But a wife must support her husband.' He continued in Italian.

Luca flushed and responded. I couldn't understand the words, but his manner conveyed his discomfort as he attempted to pacify his grandfather.

Edmund sat with his head bowed, a sheen of perspiration on his top lip and his fingers restlessly twisting his napkin.

Helen glanced at him with compassion and asked me about my favourite parks and gardens in London. Orlando made a valiant effort to talk of his happy times time at Oxford.

I barely noticed what I ate during the rest of dinner, and the conversation was muted and careful. Edmund ate nothing but stared at his plate.

When the rest of us had finished, Umberto went with Orlando to his study to discuss the new loom.

Edmund excused himself and retired upstairs.

'Luca,' said Helen, 'since you weren't asked to join your father and grandfather, will you sit with us?'

Claudia brought us a tray of coffee in the drawing room, where Luca stood before the fireplace and gazed into the flames.

'Take no notice of your grandfather,' said Helen. 'You know he can be quick-tempered, even with your father.'

'Am I wrong,' he asked, 'to want to give Sylvana something special to mark her thirtieth birthday?'

'Not at all, darling. The garden will be a delightfully unusual present but you must consider your grandfather's feelings.'

Luca nodded. 'I'll talk to him and tell him how the restored garden will keep Grandmother Flora's memory alive for all of us.'

I sipped my coffee. How lucky Sylvana Marchese was to be married to such a kind and thoughtful man. The question now was whether she'd be able to have her present or if Edmund and I would retreat back to some dreary basement flat on the Bayswater Road until I could find a new situation. I could hardly bear the thought.

Helen turned to me. 'I am sorry my father-in law gave Edmund a fright. If you'd like to go and see if he's all right, we quite understand.'

I stood up. 'Thank you. It would set my mind at rest.' I said goodnight and hurried back to the tower.

Chapter 8

Edmund's sleep was filled with harrowing night terrors. Several times, he yelled and sprang out of bed, his eyes wild. He didn't recognise me then, and it took all my strength to calm him and put him back to bed. All the while, he stared over my shoulder at something I couldn't see, as if he were watching a film showing unbearable horrors over and over again.

I sat beside him until morning, holding his trembling hand and soothing his cries of anguish. It distressed me that such a small shock as a fist banged on a table by an old man in a temper had plummeted Edmund back into his nightmarish wartime experiences. He was trying so hard to overcome his anxieties, but I feared he might never be his old, cheerful self again.

In the morning, he lay poker straight in bed with his fists clenched against the sheets to still the trembling of his hands.

'You must stay in bed today,' I said. 'I'll come and see you at lunch time, and I'll ask Claudia if she'd be kind enough to look in on you with some elevenses.'

'You're too good to me, Violet.' Edmund's voice quavered. 'I'm sorry. Last night, I simply couldn't rid my mind of the things I saw and heard . . .'

I kissed his forehead. 'Try to rest.'

Edmund nodded and pulled the eiderdown over his head.

I closed the door quietly behind me. Downstairs in the bathroom mirror, my face looked ghastly, and I was so tired I didn't know how I would get through a day of backbreaking physical work. Giving myself a mental shake, I went to find some breakfast.

Luca was alone in the dining room.

'I'm afraid Edmund is indisposed this morning,' I said, helping myself to a roll and a cup of coffee.

'I apologise for my grandfather,' he said. 'He doesn't like it if anyone disagrees with him, but he can also be very kind. Papà told me Nonno was a loving and indulgent father to him when he was a boy.'

'After all this time, he still mourns your grandmother,' I said.

Luca drained his coffee cup. 'Massimo came to see me early this morning and tells me he expects several men to arrive here for work today.'

'That is good news!' I breathed a sigh of relief; it looked as if Edmund and I would be able to stay a while longer.

It was grey and damp outside as I walked through the gardens. I could glimpse the mist-wreathed lake through the trees, but the mountains were obscured by low-lying cloud.

When I passed the stables, Zizzo whickered at me over the door to his stall. I went into the deserted yard to rub his velvety nose, and we were making friends when he threw up his head at the sound of voices. A group of men, led by Massimo, tramped past the yard with mattocks and scythes over their shoulders. My spirits lifted, and I hurried after them.

The men were entering the newly cleared path through the rhododendron thicket by the time I caught up with them. One of them gave me a curious look and spoke to his companion in an undertone.

Ahead, Massimo pushed aside the splintered door, lifting what was left of it to prevent any scraping over the threshold. The labourers followed him into the garden except for one, a middle-aged man, who moved the door back and forth to test the rusty hinges.

'*Buongiorno*,' I said.

He nodded in acknowledgement and answered in Italian.

I shrugged. 'I'm sorry, I don't understand.'

He pointed to his chest. 'Vincenzo Rossi.'

Smiling, I held out my hand. 'Signora Honeywell.'

He shook my hand firmly and then stood aside to allow me to enter the garden.

The air was still acrid from the previous night's bonfire. The men gathered around Massimo, who beckoned to me to join them. He spoke to the workers and, slightly intimidated by seven pairs of eyes studying me, I straightened my back and managed to meet their curious stares without blushing.

One of the men burst out laughing, nudged the man next to him and nodded at my breeches. I knew that look on the man's face: it was one Naseby had perfected during my time at Kew Gardens. I guessed he didn't care to work with – or for – a mere woman.

Massimo took a step forward, expression serious, and whatever it was he said the man instantly became quiet. Massimo pointed at his chest and then at the men one by one, asking them each a question.

Each one nodded and said, '*Si*, Massimo.'

He turned to me. 'I have told them that within these walls you are the boss. You will decide what they must do, and I will tell them your orders. If there is any troublemaking, there will be no more work for them – for any of them.'

'Thank you,' I murmured. The men were watching me with sullen, unnerving faces. I had to nip it in the bud or working with them would be impossible. I stepped forward and gave my most confident smile to the man who had laughed. I pointed at myself. 'Signora Honeywell,' I said and held out my hand.

Our eyes locked, but I refused to be the first to look away. I waited.

At last he gave a small sigh and took my hand. 'Raimondo.'

'It's a pleasure to meet you, Raimondo.' My tone was dry, but I was relieved to see a flicker of amusement in his otherwise stony expression. After that, it was easier. I went around the group and introduced myself to Tito, Paolo, Andrea, Sandro and Nero. Vincenzo, I had already met and acknowledged by name.

'Massimo,' I said, 'please will you tell the men I'd like them to divide into two work parties and clear a pathway alongside the garden walls. They'll need to use pickaxes to dig out the stumps of the brambles and scrub, and they can stack the debris near the bonfire. One of them can feed the fire, but they need to make a clearing in each corner of the garden for new bonfires. We must rid ourselves of all the undergrowth before we can even think of digging over the soil.'

He spoke to the men, and there was some light-hearted jostling as they formed two teams before setting to work.

'I don't think some of them are happy to work with a woman,' I said to Massimo.

He laughed. 'They don't know that you work as hard as any man. Shall I cut down that sycamore sapling?'

'If you can reach it through the tangle of brambles and ivy.' I looked across the garden and wondered how we could possibly make sufficient progress to plant in the spring, even with the additional labour.

'Do not worry,' he said, as if he knew what I'd been thinking. 'The men will clear the land, and you will create a beautiful garden.'

'I shall make every effort to do so,' I said. 'Meanwhile, I'll start on the central path. I want to find Flora's pond.' I knew I must make significant progress, despite my weariness, if I were to prove my worth to the men.

Massimo picked up his bow saw and set off to hack his way through the undergrowth towards a young sycamore tree reaching for the sky from beneath its cloak of brambles.

Over the following days, there was no time to think about our exhaustion or the blisters on our hands as we sliced back overgrown vegetation from dawn to dusk. Bonfires were set at intervals around the perimeter of the walled garden. It soon began to feel like Dante's seventh circle of Hell, surrounded with a river of boiling blood and fire. Little by little, we cleared areas of the garden, and vast knots of bramble roots and tangles of ivy and brushwood crackled and twisted in the leaping flames. The air was so thick with smoke that we tied moistened handkerchiefs over our faces and mopped our streaming eyes.

Late one morning, Luca came to see what progress was being made, and I showed him the original herringbone brick path I'd revealed.

'Most of it has crumbled,' I said. 'There won't be time to replace it, so I suggest we use gravel as a less expensive alternative. In time, gravel could be replaced with stone or brick, as the budget allows.'

'I like brick paths,' he said, 'but the important thing is to finish the garden for next August. And, who knows, perhaps you'll stay on to maintain the flower garden afterwards?'

It hadn't occurred to me that there might be longer-term employment for me at Villa Marchese. The prospect was certainly interesting, depending upon my brother's health, of course. Edmund's nights were still disturbed by bad dreams, and he hadn't felt well enough to work. It worried me that he'd remained in his room for several days, his eyes shadowed and his face pale.

The following morning, I was dragging a buddleia bush towards one of the bonfires when I saw Edmund. My heart lifted, and I waved.

'I'm sorry I let you down,' he said, his gaze on the ground.

'You didn't let me down, Edmund. How are you feeling now?'

'Embarrassed. I want to work.'

'Are you sure you're ready?'

'Don't mollycoddle me, Violet! The men will laugh. What would you like me to do?'

'You can put this buddleia on the bonfire. And mind your footing; the brick path is disintegrating.' I watched him drag the shrub away, desperately wanting to believe he was getting better. I turned back to the tangle of chest-high brambles between me and where I hoped we'd find the pond and began to slash at the thorny stems.

At midday, we downed our tools and walked back to the villa. Helen had instructed the cook to provide lunch for the workers every day, so a trestle table had been set up under the shelter of the arcaded loggia. I sat at the head of the table between Edmund and Massimo. The men chattered amongst themselves, making short work of the bowls of hearty bean soup, crusty bread, slabs of cheese and a basket of apples. Once everyone finished, I used the opportunity to ask the men if they had any problems or suggestions before we returned to the garden.

Vincenzo raised his hand and spoke briefly.

'What did he say?' I asked.

'He is a carpenter by trade,' said Massimo. 'He offered to make a new door for the garden.'

'*Grazie*,' I said to Vincenzo. He grinned and touched a finger to his forehead.

Claudia and the young maid I'd seen before came to clear the dishes, and we rose from the table to return to work. Massimo and I followed behind the others to discuss the progress made that morning. As we walked through the archway in the yew hedge, I glanced back and saw that Edmund had lingered to chat with Claudia.

Massimo followed my line of sight. 'My daughter is worried for your brother,' he said. 'She took him food while he was ill and sat with him while he ate it.'

'He mentioned she'd been kind to him. It embarrassed him that she had to see him when he was so agitated. He believed she'd think him a coward.'

'Any soldier who has endured bombardment knows that isn't true,' said Massimo, 'and my Claudia has much ... how do you say it, *compassione*.'

'Compassion.'

'Yes. Even as a little girl, she nursed birds with broken wings and kept house for her grandfather. And me, too.'

Edmund lifted his hand in a wave to Claudia and then hurried towards us.

It was dusk when we finished work. The bonfires had been damped down, and it was a relief to leave the walled garden and breathe clean air again. Edmund ambled beside me through the trees towards the house and we stopped to look across the lake. Lights twinkled in the towns fringing the opposite shore.

'There was a time I thought we'd never see such a pretty sight again,' I said. 'The blackout in London made it so difficult to cycle home at the end of a day's work.'

'But those days are over now,' said Edmund, 'and we must look to the future.'

It was encouraging to hear him sound so optimistic, but would he be able to put the war behind him? I linked my arm through his as we set off again. 'I saw you chatting with Claudia.'

'Hardly chatting,' he said, with a hint of laughter in his voice. 'It's very frustrating not speaking the language, isn't it? Claudia has some English, and she's agreed to teach me Italian.'

'It's a useful skill to speak another language,' I said, 'even if we're only planning to be here for a few months. It's a nuisance to have to speak to the men through Massimo and it's hard to know if they take me seriously.'

'I haven't seen any signs that they don't,' he said. 'They ought to respect you for how hard you work. I'm certainly impressed with how strong you are, even though you'd fit into a pint pot.'

I gave him a playful punch on the arm and he laughed, rubbing his bicep good-naturedly. 'It's good to hear you laugh again,' I said.

'I told you this place would be good for me, didn't I?'

When we arrived back at the villa, Edmund retired to his room to rest while I washed and changed to go and look at Flora's journals again. Lucrezia came to light the fire in the library and bring me tea. I made myself comfortable in one of the wing chairs beside the fire with my notebook on the side table and opened the second of the journals, dated 1857. The flyleaf was inscribed in the same bold hand as before.

To my beloved Flora from her devoted husband.

I know a bank where the wild thyme blows,
Where oxlips and the nodding violet grows,

85

Quite over-canopied with luscious woodbine,
With sweet musk-roses and with eglantine,
There sleeps Titania sometime of the night,
Lull'd in these flowers with dances and delight.

It disconcerted me that Umberto had ever been possessed by such a romantic streak that he'd felt moved to quote Shakespeare to Flora. I immersed myself in the journal again and read with interest of her plan to make a grotto, complete with a small waterfall and pool.

A couple of hours later, I'd made several pages of planting notes. Flora did not fill all the flowerbeds with regimented rows of salvia and lobelia, and it was useful to read about which plants and climbers fared well against the walls and the decorative ironwork tunnels over some of the paths. And then I read:

What could be more satisfying to my soul than passing spring and summer days in my garden with my fingers buried in the dark, rich soil? Isabella has her own small garden now, which she shares with the gardener's boy, young Beppe Bernardi. A year older than Isabella, the two children have become fast friends, just as I have with his father, Signor Bernardi. Within these walls, the common interest of a garden is a great leveller!

I smiled at this account, which corroborated Beppe's story of his friendship with Isabella. I read on and then caught my breath at something that disturbed me. Hoping I'd misunderstood, I read the passage again.

Gabriele and I walked together in the garden again late last night. There was a scimitar moon in a sky of black velvet, and the perfume of jasmine and honeysuckle was so intoxicating that, when he took me in his arms and kissed me, I cast aside all thoughts of propriety. He laid me down on his coat upon a mattress of flowers, and we became one.

I felt slightly sick. I'd imagined Flora and I might have been friends if we'd known each other, but it shocked me deeply that she'd been unfaithful to her loving husband. If Umberto had discovered her infidelity and she'd drowned running away to meet her lover, might that have been why he destroyed her garden?

Most of all, I wondered, who was Gabriele?

Chapter 9

On Saturday morning, I washed my hair. Oh, the luxury of sufficient hot water from the geyser and the time to bathe away the pungent smell of smoke that had clung to my person all week! Mildred had always rapped on the door if I was in the bathroom for more than five minutes, and I fully intended to have a good soak without such interference.

I lay in the bath with my hair floating around my shoulders, ruminating in a melancholy mood about Flora's meeting with her lover in the garden. She'd disappointed me by her infidelity to a husband who clearly loved her; you only had to read his inscriptions at the front of her journals to see that.

Suddenly, I sat up in the bath, sloshing water onto the tiled floor. What was it she'd written?

Within these walls, the common interest of a garden is a great leveller!

That must be it! She'd become friends with the gardener, Signor Bernardi. Was he Gabriele? I could hardly speak to Luca about what I'd discovered, but I could ask Beppe if his father's name was Gabriele. Whoever he was, he certainly hadn't been an angel. I sank back into the water. When my hair was dry, I'd return to the library and have another look at Flora's journals to see if she mentioned her lover again.

When the bathwater cooled, I put on my dressing gown, wrapped my hair in a towel and went upstairs to the tower's sitting room.

Edmund was painting in his sketchbook by one of the windows.

I peered over his shoulder and smiled. 'What delightful vignettes.'

'I'm less intimidated by starting with small watercolours,' he said. 'There are such wonderful views out of all the windows here, and I want to capture the different blues of the mountain ranges around the lake.'

'I shan't disturb you,' I said. 'I'm going to write a letter to Father and then read my new book while my hair dries.'

I sat on the floor in front of the fire and combed out my damp curls, which reached almost to my waist. It would be more practical for gardening to have my hair bobbed, but I couldn't help recollecting how William had loved to brush it for me. I gazed into the flames, remembering how gentle he'd been for such a big man. Our love was never hot-blooded but more of a comfortable friendship that warmed our hearts. He'd had the stoical strength of an oak, and I still mourned the loss, not only of his tranquil presence but of our lost future.

I wrote to Father to tell him how we were going on and to wish him and Mildred a happy Christmas. We wouldn't be together for the festivities, and I felt a pang of homesickness; nevertheless, it would be a relief not to suffer Mildred's sharp comments. Once I'd sealed my letter, I opened *Night and Day* by Virginia Woolf, which I'd purchased in Foyles before we left London. I was soon absorbed in Katharine Hilbery's difficult choice of becoming engaged to lacklustre poet William Rodney and her dangerous attraction to the passionate Ralph Denham.

I was reclining on the floor with my back to the fire and my head propped on my hand when there was a tap on the door, and Luca came straight in. My dressing gown had fallen open, displaying my naked knees and more décolletage than would be deemed decent at a party. Scarlet-faced, I snatched up the damp towel to cover myself.

My employer remained motionless in the doorway, staring at me. He blinked and hastily turned his back. 'I'm awfully sorry to intrude! I came to ask . . .' Retreating behind the door, he spoke to us from the landing. 'I came to see if you'd like to take a walk into Bellagio? Both of you, of course.'

'I'm afraid my hair will take another hour or so to dry.' I caught sight of Edmund's shoulders shaking as he sniggered behind his hand. 'It's too cold to go outside with wet hair.'

'But I'd very much like to see all the sights,' said my brother, his eyes full of mirth.

'I don't care to be responsible for making you catch a chill, Mrs Honeywell,' said Luca. 'Perhaps in an hour or two? Or whenever is convenient for you?'

I ran a hand through my damp curls to assess how long they would take to dry. 'Thank you, Mr Marchese. Shall we say an hour and a half?'

'Very good. I'll meet you then in the hall.' His footsteps hurried away down the stairs and the lobby door closed behind him.

'You should have seen his face, Violet!' Edmund slapped his thigh. 'He went as red as a baboon's bottom!'

I was still flustered and snapped, 'Don't be vulgar, Edmund; you're not in the playground now.'

'Well, don't look so cross. It doesn't suit you.'

Luca had wrong-footed me, and I was embarrassed. No man outside my family, apart from William, had ever seen my naked legs before. I added another piece of wood to the fire and tugged a comb through my damp tresses.

Precisely an hour and a half later, Edmund and I went down to the hall where Luca waited for us. I wore my myrtle-green hat and the matching coat, buttoned all the way up.

Luca gave me a tentative smile. 'I wasn't sure if you'd come after the way I barged in on you.'

'That's perfectly all right,' I said and changed the subject. 'I've written to my father and I'm hoping to post the letter while we're out.'

He glanced at my hair, now neatly coiled and mostly hidden under my sensible felt hat. 'I'll take you to the post office. We could walk into town, if you like, but the boat is quicker.'

We agreed to go by boat and walked down the steep path through the woodland until we reached the boathouse. Luca handed me into the boat and Edmund sat beside me.

I watched Luca covertly as he rowed and how he managed the boat with practised ease. He looked as if his thoughts were elsewhere as he gazed over my shoulder at the distant mountains.

A number of small watercraft were making their way across the lake and a ferry steamed by, making our boat rock from side to side in its wake. The lake was the colour of a Tommy's uniform today, and now that we'd pulled away from the pebbly shore, it was too murky to see down into the depths.

Edmund nudged me. 'Look at that little temple by the edge of the lake, Violet. Arabic in style, don't you think? Now that would be a marvellous place to sit and paint.'

'I should imagine there are enough breathtaking views around here to keep you busy for a lifetime.'

There was an avenue of plane trees along the edge of the lake, and then an imposing white villa came into view. Neoclassical in style, it had a double staircase leading up to the house from the lakeshore's lawn.

'Villa Melzi,' said Luca. 'It was built as the summer residence for the vice-president of the Italian republic in Napoleon's time. The gardens are enchanting with classical statuary, exotic planting and magnificent azaleas and rhododendrons in the spring. I might be able to arrange for you to visit the gardens when they're in bloom.'

'I'd enjoy that,' I said,' and it would be useful to see which plants grow well in this soil and climate.'

'There are several properties and gardens around the lake with notable owners,' said Luca, 'and they in turn have attracted many distinguished and famous visitors. Franz Liszt was staying at the Villa Melzi when he wrote his Dante Symphony; in fact, it was written in the temple we passed a moment ago, and Emperor Ferdinand I of Austria and the author Stendhal were once guests there.'

'What illustrious neighbours you have!'

'Bellagio is known as "the pearl of the lake". Visitors still come here and fall in love with its serenity. Many of them, including several British families over the years, have bought land and built grand summer residences here.'

'I can understand why,' said Edmund.

'It didn't please my great-grandfather Pietro, though,' said Luca. 'His father, Oreste, had set up a successful silk weaving factory, and Pietro went on to expand the business and make his fortune. He tore down the old farmhouse and built Villa Marchese, but the one thing he couldn't do was to buy more land adjacent to our boathouse. It always irked him that the gardens of Villa Melzi had such wide lake frontage that he couldn't make a more imposing approach for his own villa.'

'It impressed me,' I said.

Luca grinned. 'I'm rather fond of it myself. And we do have lake views from the villa and gardens.' He glanced back over his shoulder and changed course to row us towards several small boats bobbing up and down by some waterfront steps. 'We'll moor up here and walk along the lakeside promenade into the town.'

The clouds had cleared, and the sun came out. On the outskirts of the town was a large hotel, the Gran Bretagne. I could only imagine how busy the promenade might be in the summer months. Even in late autumn, the lake and the mountains were beautiful. It was no wonder visitors loved the place.

At the ferry station, a crowd of chattering passengers was disembarking from the boat, so we lingered to watch the waiting group embark. The ferry let out a blast of steam and then chugged off towards Varenna on the opposite shore.

Ambling into the town, we passed several elegant hotels along the cobbled streets before wandering up one of the stone 'stair-cases', steep and narrow alleys lined with little shops, to the highest level of the village. Further up the mountainside, interspersed with cypress groves, some of the trees still clung to the last of their autumn colours.

We stopped at the Romanesque church of San Giacomo in the market square with its triptych depicting a Madonna of the Graces with Saints Roch and Sebastian.

'My family worships here,' said Luca. 'If either of you would care to accompany us to mass tomorrow morning, you'd be very wel-come. But perhaps you might not wish to participate in a Roman Catholic service?'

'We were brought up in the Roman Catholic faith,' said Edmund. 'I'd like to attend the service.'

'I'm afraid I've lapsed,' I said. 'My husband was a Quaker, and I used to go to the Meeting House with him.'

'I've often thought that the Quakers' silent contemplation must be very calming,' said Luca, 'instead of being threatened with hell and damnation for your transgressions.'

'Silence can be calming,' I said, 'but after William died, I was too angry with God to listen to Him, either in the Meeting House or a Catholic church. But perhaps it's time I tried again.'

After we left the basilica, I posted my letter and enjoyed peering through the garden gates of the village houses with their terracotta roofs and green shutters. The clouds covered the sun again, and a sharp gust of wind made me shiver.

'We ought to go back,' said Luca, glancing up at the dark clouds rolling across the sky.

Descending one of the stone staircases was quicker than it had been going up, though I took care not to go too fast in case I tripped and bounced all the way down.

It was raining by the time we reached the boat, and Luca wasted no time in casting off. He strained against the oars as the cross-wind grew stronger, threatening to snatch my hat away. 'Stupidly, I forgot to bring the tarpaulin cover,' said Luca. 'I'm afraid we're going to get wet.'

'Look at the mountains!' said Edmund.

Thick cloud had descended from the mountaintops and rolled towards us across the lake like a grey wall. The water was the colour of slate topped with choppy, white-crested waves. 'The weather is very changeable here,' said Luca. 'A storm can blow up in a short space of time.'

Shivering in the cold wind, I stared across the wide expanse of the lake into the driving rain and wondered whereabouts Flora had drowned. Did her bones lie scattered on the lake bed beneath us?

'Don't look so worried, Mrs Honeywell,' said Luca. 'I promise we'll be quite safe and back at Villa Marchese before you know it.'

'I was thinking about your grandmother,' I said. 'You mentioned she drowned. Did it happen in a sudden storm?'

He looked behind him to get his bearings. 'It's a mystery. There wasn't a storm, and the lake was calm. Apparently, she left the house at dawn and a fisherman found the boat drifting in the middle of the lake that afternoon. Her nightgown was floating on the water.'

I stared at him. If she'd gone out in her nightgown and then left it near the boat, surely that could mean only one thing? But she had two small children. Surely she wouldn't have drowned herself? I couldn't ask him such a question.

Luca shot a worried glance at the glowering sky and concentrated on rowing.

And then, I thought, Isabella died from diphtheria only a few years later. I felt a pang of guilt for judging Umberto. It wasn't surprising if his manner could be dour after losing both his wife and daughter within a short space of time.

⁂

Later that afternoon, I walked through the drizzle to Beppe's cottage. There was no response to my knock, and I was about to leave when he opened the door, yawning. His white hair was ruffled and his cheeks flushed, but he smiled widely when he saw me. 'Signora Honeywell!'

'I'm sorry,' I said, 'did I disturb you?'

'Come in, come in!' He stood back to welcome me. 'I am an old man. Sometimes, I fall asleep in the afternoon.'

I followed him in to his beamed and whitewashed sitting room. There were two comfortable rocking chairs by the hearth and a table under the window. Colourful rag rugs softened the terracotta tiled floor.

'Sit,' he said, 'and we will share a drink.'

I unbuttoned my coat, still damp from being caught in the rain on the lake, and warmed my hands by the fire.

Beppe fetched a bottle and two glasses from a sideboard. 'Peach wine,' he said, opening the bottle. 'I make it with the peaches from the kitchen garden. It isn't every day I have a beautiful woman come to visit me.' His eyes twinkled as he filled the glasses.

I sipped the wine. 'It's delicious!'

'Tell me what I can do for you.'

'It was interesting to hear you talking about your childhood memories of the walled garden,' I said. 'I'd like to recreate the original layout of Flora's garden, though the planting will be different.'

Beppe nodded slowly. 'My father grew many thousands of seedlings in the glasshouses, but he had an army of under-gardeners. It would be very bad if you leave here when the garden is finished and Massimo and I are left alone to do this.'

'The old ways cannot continue,' I agreed. 'The garden will need gardeners to tend it, but I'm hopeful the new Signora Marchese will enjoy working in her garden, just as Flora did. And shrubs and herbaceous plants don't need to be grown from seed every year.'

'But with the rest of the garden, it is too much work for Massimo and me. I am sixty-seven and will not be able to work forever.' He shrugged. 'There have been Bernardi gardeners here for four generations, but Massimo has no son.'

Beppe had given me the perfect opening to ask him my question. 'Tell me about your father,' I said, 'I've been reading Flora's journals, and she mentioned him several times.'

'Papà was strong. Very strong and *bello*.' He frowned. 'Yes, handsome. He never said many words but he see everything.'

I pictured Massimo's laughing eyes and powerful strength. If his grandfather was anything like Massimo, I could understand why Flora might have found him so attractive. 'And what was his name?' I held my breath. Was this strong, silent and handsome gardener who captured Flora's treacherous heart called Gabriele?

'His name was Guido,' said Beppe. 'Guido Ettore Bernardi.'

Chapter 10

I blew a loose strand of hair out of my eyes and wiped blood from a scratch on my wrist. Massimo was watching me from the other side of the garden. Determined he wouldn't guess how exhausted I was, I picked up the billhook again and continued to hack at the thicket of brambles and bindweed. I couldn't be far away from the centre of the garden now.

I collected up another load of tangled brushwood and trundled the barrow to the bonfire. I was forking the last of it onto the flames when I heard a shrill scream behind me.

Edmund had tripped and fallen into a bramble patch, and he was shrieking and flailing his arms in terror.

I dropped the garden fork and ran. I pushed through the spiny stems and caught him in my arms. 'It's all right,' I crooned. 'I've got you safe.' His coat was snagged on the thorns, and the brambles became entwined around his legs as he thrashed about, trapping him on the ground.

'Get me out! Get me out!' he screamed. He was oblivious to my soothing words, and I couldn't hold him still enough to free him.

Massimo ran up and sliced through the brambles with his knife. Together we pulled Edmund to his feet as he shook and sobbed.

I held his face between my palms. 'It's all right now, Edmund,' I said again and again. Eventually, he gulped and blinked as if he now saw it was me.

'I was caught on the barbed wire in No Man's Land again.' He trembled, and the corner of his eye twitched. 'The Germans were shooting, and there were men dying on the wire. There was blood, so much blood, and machine gun fire—'

'It's all in the past.' I hugged him fiercely, anger boiling up in me at what the war had done to him – to us all.

'Take him inside,' said Massimo. 'I'll watch the fire.'

Indoors, I removed Edmund's torn trousers and snagged coat and put him to bed with hot milk and a sleeping powder.

'I'm sorry, Violet,' he murmured.

'It's not your fault,' I said, kissing his forehead. Once he was asleep, I returned to the garden.

'Are you all right?' asked Massimo.

I nodded. 'Thank you for your help. He's sleeping now, and I must get back to work.'

The sun was low in the sky when the men came to say goodnight, nodding or giving me a mock salute. Massimo had taught me a few phrases, and I thanked them in faltering Italian. Laughing and chattering, they set off towards the garden door. Their boat was moored in the boathouse, and they needed to return to the village before darkness fell.

As I thwacked at a thick clump of nettles, my billhook struck something so hard the blow shuddered up my arm. Rubbing my shoulder, I bent down to take a look. Pulling away the nettles and brambles, it became clear that there was something built of stone beneath. Had I found the pond? In an instant, my weariness lifted with the excitement of discovery, and I set to work with my billhook again. Once I'd cleared the undergrowth away from about six feet of the obstruction, it was clear that it was a section of a low stone wall, heavily encrusted with moss.

'Mrs Honeywell!'

I turned and shaded my eyes from the setting sun to see Luca walking along the pathway I'd cleared. He wore one of his beautifully tailored suits, and I was suddenly conscious of my untidy appearance at the end of a day's heavy gardening. I shoved some stray curls back under my beret and smiled. He'd been in Milan on business matters for over a week, and I hoped he would be impressed with what had been achieved in his absence.

'Hello,' he said. 'I wanted to come and see how you're getting on before darkness descends. Have you found something?'

'The pond at the centre of Flora's garden,' I said. 'Do you remember I showed it to you on her drawing? I wasn't certain that the design and the reality would be the same, but here it is in the middle of what was once the rose garden. All the paths lead to this point. Isn't it thrilling?' I stopped, aware that I was babbling.

Luca laughed. 'It is. Have you told Massimo?' I shook my head. He cupped his hands around his mouth and shouted for him.

Massimo, engulfed in smoke as he tended one of the bonfires, lifted a hand in acknowledgement and navigated his way through the clearings towards us.

'Look!' I said. 'I've found what I believe must be the pond.'

Massimo used my billhook to lift up a tangle of brambles and nettles on the other side of the mossy wall. He peered underneath and recoiled. 'It smells bad.'

There was still some water at the bottom of the pond; black, foul-smelling and clogged with fibrous vegetation. I put my hand over my nose. 'I wonder where the water comes from?'

'It is piped from the stream down the mountain,' said Massimo.

'There must be a pipe to this pool. I'll ask Beppe if he knows where it is.'

Luca put his hands on his hips and scanned the garden. 'What a difference you've made since I was last here! You must have worked like Trojans.'

I glowed with pleasure. 'We have. It's been hard, but there's a wonderful sense of achievement; however, there's still a great deal to do if the garden is to be ready for planting in the spring.'

'Paolo has his own building company,' said Massimo. 'He could make the paths.'

'And Vincenzo is a carpenter,' I said. 'Did you see the new garden door he made? Perhaps he might make the pergolas and obelisks for the climbing plants? Of course, we can't know how much these works will cost, and I can't finish designing the garden until I know if there's anything of the original hard landscaping that can be saved.'

Luca scratched his head. 'I hope I haven't underestimated the cost of the project. I hadn't realised there would need to be so much work.'

My high spirits plummeted. 'Then we must discuss it in more detail. If it's going to be too expensive, we'll have to change the design or fence off a smaller garden.'

He looked around with a frown on his face. 'I do want to do it all, not only as a gift to welcome my wife to her new home but in my grandmother's memory. I hope it might help Nonno come to terms with his grief for her.'

'It is nearly dark,' said Massimo. 'I will check that all the fires have been smothered.'

'Shall we go in, Mrs Honeywell?' asked Luca.

I gathered up the garden tools and put them in the wheelbarrow. We walked through the gloaming in reflective silence to the accompaniment of the barrow's squeaky wheel. Luca waited for me while I put the tools away in the shed, and then we set off again.

'I'll look at Flora's journals again before dinner,' I said, 'and ponder on how we might best reduce the size of the garden, if we must.'

'I hope that won't be necessary.'

'It would be a great shame,' I said, 'but as my father would say, "*We must cut our coat according to our cloth.*"'

After I'd washed and changed, I went into the tower and looked in to see Edmund still sleeping. I was distressed by the setback to his nerves. He had been sleeping better, perhaps due to all the unaccustomed physical work, and I'd only had to sit with him for one night in the past week. I tiptoed out of the room and went through the main house into the kitchen.

The cook, a large woman with a loud voice, was scolding the scullery maid while Claudia stood over the stove stirring a pan. 'I'd like a pot of tea, please,' I said. 'I'm going to work in the library.'

'I will light the fire for you,' said Claudia.

'Don't worry. I can set a match to it.'

'And Signor Edmund? Will he like tea?'

'He's asleep at the moment.'

'I will take him tea in half an hour.' Claudia smiled. 'If he rests too long, he will not sleep tonight.' She lifted the kettle onto the stove.

'That's thoughtful of you.'

I went to the library and lit the fire, thinking about how fortunate Edmund and I were to have found such a good place in which to work and live. Temporarily, at least. I didn't care to think beyond the following summer.

I collected Flora's journals from the cupboard and opened

the first one again, searching for entries where Flora had mentioned the pond.

> Gabriele and I measured and found the exact centre of the garden where
> I want the pond to be. Signor Bernardi hammered a post into the ground
> to mark the point, then tied a long piece of twine to it. He stepped two
> paces away from the post, but Gabriele shook his head and said the pond
> would be too small. He stole a kiss from me while Signor Bernardi's back
> was turned!

I caught my breath. So Gabriele, whoever he was, must surely have been a close friend of the Marchese family if he was able to come to the garden when he wished. And then steal a kiss from Umberto's wife.

> We settled on making the pond eight paces in diameter and a metre and
> a half deep in the centre, gently shelving with stepped sides for planting. I
> walked slowly around the central post, holding the end of the twine taut to
> measure the circle. Signor Bernardi pushed a peg into the ground wherever
> I stopped. When we were happy with the pond's size and symmetry, he
> sprinkled a line of sand between the pegs where we want the retaining wall
> to be built.
>   I can imagine my pond clearly now, with goldfish darting between
> the lily pads and a fountain in the centre. What could be more peaceful
> than to while away an hour or two surrounded by perfumed roses and with
> the gentle music of a fountain plashing into a pool? I am overcome with
> a sense of exhilaration that my garden is no longer only a sketch but is
> coming to life!

Yet again, I experienced a bond with Flora as if we were gardening companions travelling along parallel paths to creating a garden together; however, I couldn't overcome my disappointment in her that she hadn't been a faithful wife. But then, I had never been tested. It had been easy for me to be a faithful wife to dear William. Flora had been married to Umberto, who definitely wasn't always calm or patient like my husband. Although Umberto's dedication to Flora, written on the flyleaf of the journal, was so loving, I had seen another side to his character. I opened the next journal and read a passage at random from May 1857.

The landscaping has continued most of the winter months, and the brick paths are finished. The little cascade to the grotto is working now, and I have commissioned a large marble bench seat to place before it and a bronze statue of Cupid. Gabriele presented me with a statue of Flora for the rose garden pool, and water is now merrily spouting from her cornucopia. I am honoured to share my name with a Roman goddess. Even my dear friend Caroline is excited about my project now!

I wondered who Caroline was. Her name sounded English, but Luca had mentioned English people had bought properties around the lake. I was saddened to see the next entry.

I watch Isabella playing with young Beppe and only wish I was as fruitful as Flora the goddess of flowers. Isabella is four now. How I wish I could give her a little brother and my husband an heir! Why does God not see fit to bless us again with another little one?

Distress at my own childlessness, hidden deep within me, made my heart ache. But Flora's wish had come true eventually, and she'd given birth to Orlando, although not until several years later. I flicked over a few pages to August.

The lavender and rosemary is thriving in this exceptionally hot summer. It's distressing to see many other plants withering and turning brown.

*Most of the plants I grew from seed, either in the greenhouses or straight
into the ground, have suffered and some of the roses, too. The fig tree thrives,
however. It was here from the time my garden was the kitchen garden, and
it has very deep roots. My flowers would have died completely if Gabriele
hadn't come every evening and early morning to help water the plants.
Signor Bernardi and I have decided we must install more water tanks for
next year. Meanwhile, Umberto sits in the shade, glowering at us, despite
Gabriele's exhortations to him to assist. I'm sorry to say there are times I
cannot like Umberto.*

So there it was: the first sign I'd seen that there might be a crack
in Flora and Umberto's marriage significant enough to make her
disloyal. I flicked through the journal to late September until I
came to a sentence that had been underlined.

*The grotto is finished! The final fern was planted today, and the marble
bench carried in by six strong men. The little statue of Cupid has been
placed in the alcove prepared for him, and a marble basin installed under
the cascade. The grotto is the perfect place to sit out of the heat of the
midday sun. Or perhaps, for a lovers' tryst!*

The library door opened and Luca peered around it. 'I guessed you
might be here,' he said. 'Did you find anything interesting?'

'I've been reading about Flora's grotto, and I'm going to look
for it tomorrow. If it's more or less intact and we do need to plan
a smaller garden, we might retain it as one of the main features.'

'You sound as happy as a child with her hand in a box of
chocolates.'

I laughed. 'I suppose I am. Which delicious treat shall I
choose next?'

He smiled. 'Don't spoil your appetite; it's almost time for dinner.'

The following morning, I went to the walled garden at first light. I stood in the doorway, my gaze falling first upon where I now knew the pond to be and then on to the wall opposite me. There was a great mound of brambles and ivy there which was certainly large enough to conceal a grotto.

The men had cleared a wide path around the bordering walls of the garden but hadn't yet reached the place where I thought the grotto was situated. I calculated the shortest route to it through the remaining thicket and set to work with my billhook and shears.

I'd made good progress when Edmund arrived carrying a small basket. 'You weren't at breakfast,' he said, 'so I asked Claudia to give me a pastry for you. And there's some coffee, too.' He opened a flask, poured coffee into the cup and held it out to me.

'Bless you! I couldn't wait to come out here this morning, but I'm famished now.'

'You're looking for the grotto you mentioned last night?' He'd come down for dinner the previous evening, still pale but determined to return to work the following day.

I nodded, my mouth full of sweet pastry. 'It must be there – do you see that mountain of ivy against the centre of the wall?'

'I'll fetch my billhook,' said Edmund.

'We'll clear a narrow pathway to the wall through the tangled thicket,' I said.

An hour later, beneath a shroud of ivy, we uncovered the twisted trunk and bare stems of an ancient – but living – fig tree against the wall.

'What luxury!' said Edmund. 'We shall have ripe figs at the end of the summer.'

When Massimo and the men arrived, we were only about six feet away from where we hoped we'd find the grotto. The men finished clearing the pathway in a few minutes, but then Massimo stopped them. He grinned at me. 'It is your discovery, so you must cut away the last pieces.' He handed me a set of shears.

The men began to clap rhythmically as I pulled away the last of the brambles and swathes of ivy. I glimpsed stonework beneath and a shadowed opening.

I laughed as the clapping became louder and faster while I frenziedly tore the vegetation away. There was a huge overhanging branch of tree ivy forming a thick curtain over what I hoped to find. I grasped it and pulled with all my might. Pebbles rained down on my shoulders and dust showered my upturned face until suddenly, the branch came free and I staggered back. There was a loud clattering noise and then a tremendous thump on my head.

Edmund yelled my name.

The lights went out.

I came back to consciousness to discover myself on the ground and reclining in Massimo's arms. His face hovered over mine with a concerned expression as he wiped my forehead with a damp handkerchief. I struggled to sit up, but he gently pushed me down. 'What happened?' I asked.

'A rock fall.'

Edmund came into view. 'Are you all right, Violet?' His face was greenish-white. I saw his Adam's apple bob up and down as he swallowed. 'We couldn't wake you. I thought you were dead.'

'It would take more than a tap on the head to kill me,' I said with more bravado than I felt. 'Help me up, if you please, Massimo.'

'You should rest—'

'Later,' I said. Edmund looked so shaken, and I couldn't bear to see him descend into one of his panics. I was grateful for Massimo's strong arms again because I was decidedly wobbly. I touched a hand to my forehead and felt a lump already swelling. My fingers were smeared with blood.

'Let me take you inside,' said Edmund.

'I'm perfectly fine,' I lied. 'What did we uncover?' I turned to look at my handiwork. 'How marvellous; it *is* the grotto!' There was a man-made cave about nine feet wide and six feet deep made out of jagged, moss-covered rock. A lump of rock had crumbled away from the summit of the arch and lay now by my feet. A rather lovely marble bench with scrolled ends was situated in the centre and draped in a blanket of ivy. There was a marble trough against the back wall that was stained green and full of rotting leaves. Above it was an empty alcove.

'Where's Cupid?' I asked. My temples were pounding and my voice resounded painfully in my ears.

Massimo gave me a questioning look. 'Cupid?'

Something stirred at the edge of my vision, and I thought someone whispered in my ear. I couldn't hear the words, but then my attention was caught by something else. I stepped closer, ignoring my increasing dizziness. Set into the rough-hewn rock was a stone slab about a foot square, incised with letters. There was a diagonal fissure running across the plaque and several dents scattered over the surface. I rubbed some of the dirt and moss away with my fingertip and read:

IN MEMORY OF
GABRIELE PIETRO MARCHESE
1831–1859
LOST ON THE BATTLEFIELD OF SOLFERINO
BELOVED HUSBAND OF FLORA AND FATHER OF ISABELLA
FOREVER ALIVE IN OUR HEARTS

The memorial plaque wavered before my eyes, and then a black mist clouded my vision. Echoing voices came from very far away, and my knees buckled beneath me.

Chapter 11

Massimo carried me back to the house where I lay in bed, drifting in and out of consciousness for the rest of the day. A doctor was called, and after questioning me and shining a light in my eyes I was pronounced concussed. Helen came to sit by my bed, and it was reassuring to know she was watching over me. She applied damp compresses to a lump the size of a pigeon's egg on my forehead and encouraged me to take sips of water.

That night, Edmund dozed in the armchair in my bedroom, waking me briefly every hour to ensure I hadn't fallen into a coma. It was odd to have our roles reversed in this way.

The following morning, Helen insisted I stay in bed. Reading made my head ache, but by mid-afternoon, I couldn't bear to languish any longer. I intended to go to work in the garden, but when I stood up, my legs felt like India rubber. Hanging onto the handrail, I went downstairs. I looked in the bathroom mirror to discover I had two black eyes, as well as the bruising and cut on my forehead.

After I'd washed and dressed, I closed the bathroom door behind me and found Helen in the lobby.

'I was coming to see you,' she said. 'What are you doing out of bed? And why are you wearing your gardening clothes?'

'I must go back to work.'

'Absolutely not! The doctor said you need to rest, and Edmund tells me Massimo has everything under control. If you'd like a change of scene, come and sit with me for a while.'

I didn't argue with her since simply dressing myself had been draining. A short while later, we were in the drawing room with a pot of tea and a plate of small cakes.

'Luca's been so worried about you,' said Helen. 'He's had to go to the factory and stay in Como for a few days, but he sends his best wishes. And Massimo came to ask me how you were this morning.'

'Once the dizziness is gone, I'll be fine,' I said. 'Mind you, the men may laugh at me when they see my face.'

'I'm sure they'll be concerned for you. Massimo said that after their initial disquiet at working for a woman, they've grown to respect you.'

'That's good to hear,' I said. 'It is hard, physical work for a woman, though I won't admit that to the men, but I hope the worst will be over soon.' I nibbled one of the little cakes. 'That may be sooner than we thought if we have to reduce the size of the garden.'

'Reduce it?'

'It's a much bigger project than your son originally thought, and to realise the whole plan is bound to incur significant costs.'

Shaking her head, Helen said, 'I do wish Luca would take more time to consider the consequences of his hasty decisions. It's not the first time he . . .' Frowning, she delved into the workbag beside her chair. 'Do you mind if I sew while we chat? I have some shirts to finish for the orphanage. Poor little mites! The war has left so many children without fathers and mothers with insufficient means of support.'

'It's the same at home. I can't imagine how dreadful it would be to have to give up your children.'

Helen threaded her needle. 'Luca will be desperately disappointed if he has to curb his plans for the flower garden. He's set his heart on it.'

'It was a shame I didn't meet your daughter-in-law when we travelled through Milan. It might have given me a better understanding of what her favourite flowers might be.'

Helen laughed. 'Orchids or something exotic from a hothouse, I expect. You'll meet her next week when she comes for Christmas. Luca had a letter from her this morning confirming it.'

My head throbbed abominably again, and I pressed my fingers to my temples. 'Have you met her many times?'

'Only once. She's very beautiful and ...' Helen nipped off a thread from the small shirt she was working on. 'I suppose "vivacious" is the word.'

All at once I felt exhausted.

'You're looking very pale,' said Helen. 'Shouldn't you lie down again?'

'Perhaps I should. There's something I wanted to ask you.' I hesitated. 'It's a little delicate.'

'Go on.'

'When I uncovered the grotto, there was a memorial plaque inside for Flora's husband. I read the inscription, and it led me to believe she was married to someone called Gabriele.'

Helen nodded. 'My father-in-law won't speak of it.' She gave a tight little smile. 'There are quite a few things he won't talk about.'

'But you knew?'

'When Orlando brought me to Villa Marchese as his bride, he recorded our marriage in the family Bible. It's kept in the library as a family record. I was surprised to see Flora's first husband's name crossed out. He told me Gabriele was his father's stepbrother. You see, when Gabriele's father married his second wife, Magdalena, he adopted her son, Umberto.'

My head ached as I re-ordered my thoughts. So Umberto, although he bore the Marchese name, wasn't of the Marchese bloodline. 'What did Gabriele do to be obliterated from such an important family record?' I asked.

Helen shrugged. 'I don't know, but he died at the Battle of Solferino in ...' she frowned, '1859 I think it was. The war for Italian independence. Flora married Umberto two years later, but it was as if he wanted to eradicate Gabriele's memory.'

'I see.' It pleased me a great deal that Flora hadn't been an adulterous wife, after all. 'But Flora and Umberto couldn't have been married for long before she died?'

'Orlando was only a babe.'

'How desperately sad not to have his mother with him while he was growing up,' I said, thinking of my own mother.

'He never knew anything different,' said Helen. 'And he had Lucrezia.'

'Lucrezia?'

'She was seventeen when she was employed as Orlando's nursemaid. To all intents and purposes, she became his mother, and she remains here to this day. Orlando will ensure she always has a home with us. And Umberto was a good father to Orlando. He adored his baby son.'

I struggled – and failed – to picture Umberto being patient with a child.

'The only times Umberto was angry with Orlando was when he was older and became curious about his mother.'

'No doubt your father-in-law didn't want to talk about it?'

Helen chuckled. 'Exactly. Nevertheless, Orlando developed a passion for anything British, perhaps because it was forbidden. Eventually, he persuaded his father to let him have an English tutor once he'd pointed out that if he spoke the language fluently, he'd be able to increase company sales in London.' She smiled. 'And that was how we met. Orlando went up to Oxford in 1880, and my father was one of the professors there. We married five years later.'

'I wonder how Flora, another Englishwoman, met Gabriele?' I said. 'Recreating her garden has made me very curious about her, but I don't dare ask your father-in-law. Surely Flora wasn't the daughter of a professor at Oxford, too?'

Helen shook her head. 'Although, there is an interesting story about how she came to Italy.'

'Oh?'

'You look utterly drained, Violet, so that's a story for another day. You don't mind if I call you Violet, do you?'

'I'd be delighted.'

'And please call me Helen, of course. There's an old friend of mine I'd like you to meet. She'll tell you about how Flora came to Bellagio. I'll send her a note. Meanwhile, go and lie down until dinner.'

I left the drawing room but paused in the hall outside the library. Luca had asked me not to remove Flora's journals from the library, but surely, if I took one to my room to read while I was resting, it wouldn't hurt as long as I put it back? A few moments later, I hurried upstairs clutching the journal dated 1859 – the year Gabriele Marchese had fallen in battle.

I returned to bed and made myself a cosy nest of pillows and eiderdowns before opening the journal. Skimming through neat lists of the varieties of bulbs that had flowered especially well and the seeds that Flora had sown in the glasshouses for summer bedding, I came to several densely written pages that made me read faster.

113

April 1859

The seething arguments about Gabriele's intention to join Guiseppe
Garibaldi and the Hunters of the Alps boiled up into a hideous crescendo
during breakfast today. I had resolved not to allow myself to weep until
after Gabriele had gone, but I was so consumed by shockingly violent
feelings towards his stepmother that I forgot my imminent tears. I gripped
my knife while Madre Marchese's vitriolic words reverberated around the
dining room and imagined sliding it between the wretched woman's ribs. I
put the knife down and stayed silent. The last thing my dearest husband
needed was for me to fuel this pulsing animosity and make it the last
memory of home that he would carry into battle.

Gabriele tried once more to persuade Umberto to volunteer with him
and his friends Domenico Pierucci and Adriano Conti. He said every
single man must fight to free the northern Italian states from the yoke
of Austrian oppression. When Umberto refused, Gabriele called him
a coward and told him to stop hiding behind his mother's skirts. 'If my
father were still alive, he would have told you in no uncertain terms to do
your duty.'

'Do not dare to speak to my son of duty,' spat Madre Marchese. 'It
is you who fails in his duty by abandoning the business and your family to
go off and play foolish games with brigands.'

Ignoring her insults, Gabriele strode from the dining room. I hurried
upstairs after him to his dressing room where he was stuffing shirts and a
Bible into his kitbag. When I slid my arms around his waist his skin
was hot and his muscles hard with rage. I said that we had so little time
that we mustn't waste it on anger at Umberto and his mother. The tension
drained from him, and he kissed my forehead before taking a purse of gold
coins out of his chest of drawers. He told me that if he didn't return, it was
for me and Isabella. If he didn't return! Sharp claws of fear dug into
my stomach.

We fetched Isabella from the nursery and took her with us to say our goodbyes in the walled garden. I'll never forget the picture of Gabriele swinging Isabella's hand as she skipped along beside him in the sunshine, her copper curls bouncing on her shoulders. My dread grew with every step closer to the moment I must say goodbye to the man I will love forever.

The door to the walled garden was ajar, and Signor Bernardi and Beppe were weeding a bed of cheerful scarlet and yellow tulips. The gardener wished Gabriele God's speed.

Isabella showed her father the hyacinth bulbs she had grown, and they sniffed the sweet scent together. 'I wish you didn't have to go away, Papà,' she said. 'Promise me you will come back?'

My heart nearly broke as Gabriele fought to hold back his emotions. He never made a promise he couldn't keep. Lifting her into his arms, he hugged her and said he hoped to return in the autumn. He told her to go and play with Beppe, and as she skipped away he clutched my hand so tightly that his signet ring pressed into my palm. I thought it must have marked my skin with his initials almost as deeply as his love was engraved on my heart.

While Cupid watched over us in the grotto, we sat on the marble bench with the sound of water trickling over the cascade and splashing on the fresh green foliage of the ferns. I rested my head in the hollow of his shoulder, listening to his heartbeat; too rapid, but in perfect rhythm with my own.

'I shall picture you and Isabella here in our Paradise garden,' he murmured into my hair, 'whenever I am marching into action or lonely and afraid.'

'We will be here waiting for you,' I replied. 'Like our marriage, this garden has been created out of love. I will tend it faithfully until you return.'

We sat in silence, wrapped in each other's arms, while I tried not to think about what might be or what would be, but only to be present in the moment and to lock it in my memory.

He sighed and kissed me; not passionately as he had during the night, but with infinite tenderness. 'Until we meet again, my love, on Earth or in Heaven.' He stood up and my throat constricted. 'I love you more than life itself,' he said. Then, he released my hand and walked away.

A wave of nausea swept over me, and I was seized by an awful trembling, my gaze fixed upon him as he crossed the garden.

Isabella ran to him for a final hug. And then he picked up his kitbag from where he'd left it by the garden door and stood, framed in the opening as he turned to take a last look at me.

I mouthed the words, 'I love you'.

And then he was gone.

I put the diary down and wiped away the tears that wet my cheeks. For a while, I'd felt as if I was an observer in Flora's world. I knew well that feeling of sick dread because I, too, had experienced the pain of parting from a beloved husband. And for both of us, our worst fears had been realised.

I returned to the garden two days later. Massimo and Vincenzo came to greet me and shook my hand warmly.

Massimo winced at the sight of my colourful bruises. 'Your poor head!'

Vincenzo let out his breath in a long whistle, boxed the air in front of me, and then said something in Italian.

'What did he say, Massimo?' I asked.

'He says you must stop going to bars and fighting.'

I smiled. 'Tell him I have only a few bruises, but the man who tried to fight me is still in the hospital.'

Both men roared with laughter, and Vincenzo went back to his work still chuckling.

'Come and see,' said Massimo.

'You've made excellent progress while I wasn't here,' I said, following him. Two thirds of the garden were now free of under-growth, and the remaining saplings had been cut down.

'Beppe came to help. He is so happy to see the garden being cared for again.'

'That was kind of him.'

'He remembered that there was once a glasshouse in the garden, and we found it beneath the brambles. The wood had rotted and the glass was broken, but perhaps it could be made again in the future. And Vincenzo has built a toolshed so we can leave the tools here every night. But come now, I want to show you something.'

Massimo took me to the grotto, and I caught my breath in delight. The rock that had fallen on me was cemented firmly back in place. The dead leaves and ivy had been cleared away, and the white marble bench and basin gleamed after a good scrub. Even the memorial plaque to Gabriele had been washed with the moss scraped out of the lettering and the dividing crack.

'You have worked hard,' I said. 'It's marvellous.'

'We put fresh earth in the planting pockets ready for the ferns,' he said. 'Beppe will search for the pipework and stopcock to the cascade.'

'Oh, wouldn't it be wonderful if the cascade worked again?'

He nodded and then shuffled his feet and looked away from me. 'When I saw the rock fall on you, I thought my heart would stop.' He pressed a hand to his chest. 'It could have killed you.'

'But it didn't.' I smiled. 'We British are tougher than that.'

'*Per grazia di Dio.*'

'By the grace of God,' I echoed.

On his return from Como, Luca came to find me as I was about to finish work for the day.

'How are you feeling?' he asked.

'Much better, thank you.'

'Let me look at you.' He lifted my chin with his forefinger and turned me towards the light.

His eyes were topaz under his dark, winged brows, and I couldn't look away, mesmerised by the gold flecks around his irises.

'You still have bruises,' he said.

His touch disturbed me, although I knew he couldn't mean anything by it. I'd noticed how the Italians frequently touched each other, and the men would often sling an arm around one of his comrade's shoulders when they left the garden. 'The bruises aren't pretty,' I said, stepping back, 'but they're fading now. Come and see the grotto.'

We walked across the garden, and it was impossible for me not to glow with pleasure at Luca's enthusiastic response when he saw what we had uncovered.

'The grotto is made from volcanic rock,' I said. 'Do you see the bubbly texture? It's like cinder toffee.'

'There are still live volcanoes in Italy,' he said. He traced his finger over the fracture in the stone of the memorial plaque. "Mamma told me about this after you found the plaque. I had no idea that my grandmother had been married before or that Nonno has been adopted into the family, but it was all so long ago.'

'I was relieved to discover the truth about Gabriele.' I related my unease on reading Flora's journal notes and her romantic liaison with a man I hadn't known was her husband. 'It's odd,' I said, 'but I feel as if Flora and I are kindred spirits. I was horribly disappointed in her when I imagined she was having an affair.'

'I understand,' said Luca, 'because when I first met you at Claridge's, I was struck by how much you look like her portrait. It's your beautiful auburn hair, I suppose.'

I turned away to hide my blush.

'And then,' he continued, 'there are your names: Flora and Violet. And your common interest in horticulture.' He laughed. 'I knew immediately when I met you that you were the only person who could realise my hazy dream for recreating Grandmother Flora's flower garden.'

'I certainly knew it was a project I dearly wanted to undertake.'

'Mrs Honeywell ...' he hesitated, 'I hope we have become friends? I already address your brother by his first name, and I wondered if you'd be offended if I call you Violet?'

'Not at all,' I said.

He smiled. 'And I am Luca, of course.'

A shout came from behind us, and Massimo strode into view. 'You're back then, Luca?' The two men shook hands and clapped each other on the back. 'So, what do you think of the grotto?'

'It's remarkably preserved, isn't it?'

'And this,' said Massimo, thumping his fist on the newly cemented lump of stone at the apex of the arch, 'is the rock that fell on Signora Honeywell.'

Luca winced. 'You were lucky your injuries weren't worse.'

I shivered to think how it would have affected Edmund if I'd been killed. 'Very lucky.'

'And brave,' said Massimo.

'Do you see the planting pockets?' I said, embarrassed by the attention. 'We're going to order some ferns for them.'

Luca pointed to the rocky alcove.'And what is this?' he asked.

'It's for a statue of Cupid,' I said. 'I read about it in the journals.'

Massimo laughed. 'A statue? I wondered what you were talking about.' He turned to Luca. 'After the rock fell on Signora Honeywell's head, she said to me, "Where is Cupid?" I thought the blow to her head ...' He twisted his forefinger to his temple and rolled his eyes.

'Thank you very much,' I said with mock indignation,' but I

119

wasn't out of my mind. Flora's husband gave her a little statue of Cupid to put there.'

'So, where is it?' asked Luca.

'I've looked for it,' I said, 'but it isn't in the immediate vicinity. Perhaps we'll find it when we finish clearing the rest of the garden.'

Massimo glanced up at the sky. 'We must go in. It will soon be dark.'

Chapter 12

At dinner that evening, Luca confirmed he'd bring his wife to Villa Marchese for Christmas. 'We'll stay a few days,' he said, 'and then I'll accompany her back to Florence for a friend's New Year's Eve party.'

'A few days?' said Helen, her expression dismayed. 'But I hoped she'd stay for a fortnight so we'd have a chance to become properly acquainted. I've arranged for extra servants to help out and invited our friends to a luncheon party on New Year's day to meet her.'

'I'm sorry, Mamma.' Luca pulled at his starched shirt collar as if it were too tight. 'I hoped she would stay longer, but Sylvana has various social commitments in Florence.'

'I do not understand' said Umberto, 'why you wait until August to bring your wife to live at Villa Marchese.'

I paused in the act of lifting a piece of bread to my mouth. I didn't understand that, either.

'You forget,' said Luca, 'that Sylvana and I had planned a very different life. Leaving Florence will be a big change for her, and I need time to concentrate on learning how to manage the business.'

'I apologise, Luca,' said Orlando, 'that my illness and your brother's passing has caused you to change your life in a way you did not want.'

'Papà, no! That isn't *at all* what I meant.' His expression was stricken. 'Of course I want to support my family and the business in the same way as Teodore would have done. It's only that Sylvana and I need a little time to become used to the change in our circumstances.'

'I was twenty-two when I learned the business,' said Umberto. 'You are twenty-nine. It is your duty to your family to provide a son. Your wife will be thirty soon. Thirty!'

Luca held up a hand. 'When Sylvana and I choose to have children is a private matter between ourselves.'

'You think I am an interfering old man,' said Umberto, 'but I *know* you, Luca. You are not happy. I see this in your eyes. I love my family, and I want to see my great-grandson growing up at Via Marchese before I die.' His face had flushed a dull red, and his eyes glittered with emotion.

'And you will,' said Luca. His knuckles gleamed white as he gripped his hands together. 'Believe me, I do know my duty, and when the time is right ...' His voice trailed away and he blinked several times

'Sylvana will be sad to leave her friends when she comes to live here,' said Helen. 'I hoped coming here for Christmas would allow her to meet those who will become her new friends.'

'Thank you, Mamma,' said Luca. 'I'm not concerned that she'll mope, but I promised to give her until her next birthday to enjoy her time in Florence before she moves into Villa Marchese. I plan to host a party here to celebrate her birthday since we didn't have a large wedding. But for now, I must have time to concentrate on what Papà and Nonno are teaching me about the business.'

'You learn quickly,' said Orlando. 'I was pleased with the new contacts you made in London. We have received good orders. Now, that's enough talk of business for tonight.'

Claudia came to clear the dishes as Helen turned to Edmund and me. 'You'll find Christmas traditions a little different here from those in England,' she said. 'We celebrate Christmas Eve, or *La Vigilia*, as we call it. There will be no meat during the day, but there will be at least five different fish dishes for dinner.'

'Including local lake fish,' said Luca.

'I shall look forward to that,' said Edmund.

'And after we've eaten,' continued Luca, 'we'll go into the town to see the schoolchildren put on a Nativity scene in the market square before attending Christmas mass at the Basilica.'

'It will be fun to learn about how you celebrate the festive season,' I said.

Umberto clicked his tongue in irritation. He rose to his feet and dropped his napkin on the table. 'I will leave you to plan your Christmas entertainment while I inspect the account books.'

The door shut behind him.

'Well,' said Luca, 'that effectively takes the shine off Christmas, doesn't it?'

At breakfast the following day, Helen said, 'Massimo is bringing us a Christmas tree down from the mountainside this morning. I wondered if you would help me decorate it after you finish in the garden, Violet? Luca said he'd be home in time to assist.'

'I'd love to,' I said, pleased she'd asked me.

'It's not a tradition here to have a Christmas tree, but when I first came to Villa Marchese, I told Orlando it didn't feel like a proper Christmas without a tree.' She smiled fondly at her husband. 'That afternoon he returned from the mountainside, dragging a vast fir behind him. We've had a Christmas tree every year since.'

'We made it our tradition, didn't we, *cara*?' said Orlando.

Helen reached for his hand. 'We did.'

It was heart-warming to see the very real affection between Luca's parents.

'Violet, can you spare me this morning?' asked Edmund. 'If I go with Massimo to fetch the tree, it will be quicker and easier with two of us.'

'I don't see why not,' I said, 'but don't tarry too long. We must finish clearing the garden by January so we can prepare the ground for planting.'

We went to the garden after breakfast, and I told Massimo what I wanted the men to tackle next. Once he'd given them my orders, he and Edmund disappeared to fetch the tree, while I set to work digging out the stump of an ancient felled birch.

Edmund and Massimo returned after lunch, very pleased with themselves at having procured a splendid fir tree.

'We fixed it into a wooden stand, ready for you and Signora Marchese to decorate,' said Edmund, 'and we fetched the boxes of decorations down from the attic. She asked if you could bring some ivy to make a garland for the stairs, too.'

I pointed at a heap of recently cut foliage. 'There's more than enough ivy here for a dozen garlands.' It made me happy to see Edmund looking so cheerful with his cheeks flushed pink from working in the fresh air. It was too soon to count my chickens, but there was no doubt his health had improved since we'd arrived in Bellagio.

'I'll bundle the ivy into a barrow,' he said.

'Give me a hand to put this tree stump onto the bonfire first, will you?'

Edmund fetched the wheelbarrow and helped me to lift the

stump. 'Massimo is a decent chap, isn't he?' he said. 'He assumes I can do whatever is required of me, and that makes me feel more confident.' His eyes met mine as we heaved the stump into the barrow. 'You know, he thinks a lot of you. Never known a woman like you, he said.'

'The women he knows probably don't have earth under their fingernails.'

Edmund laughed. 'I daresay that's true!'

We worked until the light was fading, and then the men hurried off to the boathouse to row themselves back to the village.

Edmund pushed the wheelbarrow full of ivy while I closed the garden door behind us. We walked through the rising mist with Massimo, chatting about our day.

When we reached his cottage, Massimo nodded at Edmund. 'After dinner then?'

Edmund glanced at me. 'I'll wait for Claudia to finish work and escort her home.'

'Straight here and no stopping.'

'Yes, Massimo.'

Massimo pretended to punch him on the arm and turned to me. 'Goodnight, Signora Honeywell.' He walked up the path to his cottage.

'What was all that about, Edmund?' I asked.

'Claudia is going to teach me Italian.'

'I see. Under Massimo's watchful eye?'

'Absolutely. He's made me very aware of his daughter's purity and that he will skin me alive and throw me to the dogs should I touch even a hair of her head.'

'You'd better be careful, then.'

'I can assure you, there will be no chance of me taking any liberties with the young lady in question.' He sighed. 'Unfortunately.'

'It's a good idea to learn some of the language,' I said, 'but for goodness' sake, don't jeopardise our position here with a flirtation that can have no future.'

Edmund came to an abrupt halt and put down the wheelbarrow. 'What do you mean by that?'

'Only that Claudia is the apple of Massimo's eye. And this is Italy, where girls are chaperoned even more carefully than at home.'

'I have every intention of behaving like a perfect gentleman. As I said, Claudia will teach me Italian.'

'Since I hope we'll be here for the best part of a year, that's an excellent idea. Actually, I thought I might speak to Helen about where I can take lessons, too.'

Edmund pursed his lips. 'Perhaps Claudia will help you.'

'You'll learn faster on your own.' His smile of relief worried me. He might be interested in an attractive young woman, but Claudia's father surely wouldn't wish her to be romantically involved with a man who suffered with fragile nerves. I didn't want him to be hurt and risk him sinking back into his former mental condition.

We walked back to Villa Marchese in contemplative silence.

Edmund retired to his room to rest, and after I'd changed out of my work clothes, I went into the hall. The Christmas tree was at least eight feet high and had been placed in one corner. It filled the air with a fresh resinous scent. There were several wooden crates and a pair of steps nearby. I knocked on the sitting room door, and Helen bid me to enter.

'Ah, there you are, Violet!' Luca's father was sitting beside her.

'I've come to help decorate the tree,' I said.

'I'll be glad of your help.' Helen stood up and passed her husband his walking sticks. 'I had hoped Luca would be back by now, but I daresay he's been held up.'

I was disappointed he'd been delayed.

We went into the hall, and Luca's father followed us with faltering steps. Helen helped him into an armchair beside the fire.

'Edmund said you wanted some ivy to make wreaths? There's certainly no shortage of ivy in the walled garden, so I've left a barrowful outside.'

'Splendid!' said Orlando.

Helen fetched the portable gramophone from the drawing room, and we listened to Italian opera while we unwrapped the decorations in the crates. There were rolls of scarlet satin ribbon, tin candle holders and glittering glass baubles shaped to look like fruit.

'These are so beautiful!' I said, lifting up a pale green pear and a red apple.

'I brought them back from England some years ago,' said Helen, 'but they were handmade in Germany. I doubt we could replace them now since the war.'

'What's in here?' I asked, holding out a biscuit tin.

'Candles. I put them in there so the mice don't eat them while they're in storage. And look: I made these felt decorations when Teodore and Luca were small.' She held out her upturned palm.

One was shaped like a miniature Christmas pudding and another like a plump little robin. They had loops of black thread sewn at the top so they could be hung on the tree. 'These traditions bring back memories of Christmases past, don't they?' I said.

She nodded, and her eyes glittered with tears as she hung up a tiny red and green felt stocking with the initial T embroidered on it.

'Christmas was a magical time when we saw it through the eyes of our sons,' said Orlando.

I clipped the candle holders onto the spiky branches, remembering what a happy time Christmas had been when my mother was alive. There had always been the aroma of oranges and mince pies in the air, and Mama and Father had sung carols together as they pinned up the paperchains Edmund and I had made. Father, his pipe clamped between his teeth, would climb a rickety pair of steps to hang Chinese lanterns and arrange sprigs of holly on the tops of the pictures. Edmund, as the youngest, had always been held up to add the finishing touch to the tree: a glittering silver star.

A sudden cold draught from behind brought me back to the present.

'Sorry, I'm later than expected,' said Luca, closing the front door behind him. 'My last meeting went on for too long, and I missed the ferry. Well, that's a very fine tree!'

'Take your coat off, Luca, and assist the ladies,' said Orlando.

Claudia came from the kitchen to bring us a tray of dried orange slices and star-shaped biscuits.

I watched her covertly as she helped Helen thread them onto red ribbon to drape over the tree. She was certainly a pretty girl, and it wasn't hard to understand why Edmund had been charmed by her ready smile and quietly friendly manner.

A little while later, the tree was adorned with scarlet bows, biscuit stars and orange slice garlands. The candles were lit, and the glass ornaments shimmered in the candlelight.

'And now the *finale*,' said Luca's father.

Helen rummaged in a crate and unwrapped a small cradle with the Holy Child asleep inside. She removed the baby. 'We don't put the infant Jesus into his crib until Christmas Eve.' She held the cradle out to me with a smile. 'I'd like you to place this on the top of the tree.'

'Me?'

She nodded. 'I would have asked Sylvana, but since she hasn't arrived yet, I'd like you to do it.'

I glanced at Luca, wondering if Helen's comment was an implied criticism of his bride. 'I'm honoured,' I said.

Luca's smile was strained. 'I'll hold the steps for you.'

I took the little wicker cradle from Helen and secured it to the topmost branch with the attached wire. 'Is that straight?'

Luca looked up at me.

He was so close I could see the sweep of his dark eyelashes and smell the outdoor air on his skin. His proximity unnerved me. 'Is it straight?' I repeated.

'Absolutely perfect!' he said. He held out his hand to me as I descended the steps.

The touch of his hand sent a *frisson* up my arm, and I looked away when he smiled at me. There had been something in his expression that convinced me he hadn't only been speaking about the cradle. I was already uncomfortably aware of harbouring inappropriate feelings for my employer; especially since his wife was arriving the following day.

It rained heavily on Christmas Eve, and as the morning went on, the bonfires in the walled garden smouldered while the ground turned to mud.

Rain dripped off my sodden beret and ran down the back of my neck. 'We'll have to call it a day, Massimo,' I said. 'It's time for lunch, anyway. I'll pay the men and send them home early afterwards.'

We all trooped back to the house where lunch was waiting for us, warmed by two glowing braziers. The previous evening I'd made some extra garlands of ivy, and Claudia had arranged them down the centre of the table along with little bowls of *mandolate* and sugared almonds. Carafes of wine were placed alongside the water.

The men sat at the table under the shelter of the loggia, chattering noisily above the sound of the teeming rain splashing onto the grass.

Helen had asked the cook to make a large platter of spaghetti with clams for the workers' Christmas Eve lunch, and they cheered when Claudia carried it to the table. Filomena, the little scullery maid, brought baskets of bread before scurrying back to the kitchen.

The men ate their spaghetti with every sign of enjoyment. Afterwards, there was the local speciality of a *pan mataloch*: a sweet bread made with raisins, candied lemon and orange peel, figs and hazelnuts. It was fragrant with the aroma of fennel seeds.

'Do you like it?' asked Massimo.

I nodded, my mouth too full of the delicious sweet treat to answer properly.

His eyes gleamed with amusement. 'It originates from the time of Spanish domination in Lombardy. They left the recipe behind, so that was some consolation.' He leaned towards me and whispered, 'You should say a few words to the men before they leave. I will translate for you.'

I stood up and tapped a fork against my wine glass. One by one, the men stopped talking and turned to face me. I smiled to hide my nervousness. 'Thank you all for your hard work over the past weeks and for making what seemed to be impossible actually begin to happen.' I summed up all that we had achieved, and Massimo translated as I went along. I finished by asking them to come and collect their pay packets, which I had in a locked cashbox by my feet. I knew that Luca had added a Christmas bonus to each envelope.

The men came to take their pay, and I wished them a Happy Christmas.

'*Buon Natale*,' said Raimondo, shaking my hand.

'*Buon Natale*,' I echoed. He laughed at my accent and nudged Vincenzo, but this time, he was laughing with me, not at me.

The men set off into the rain with a chorus of goodbyes. I could hear them singing at the tops of their voices as they disappeared towards the boathouse.

'They are happy to have wages in their pockets and half a day off to be with their families,' said Massimo.

I glanced at Edmund talking to Claudia as she cleared the table. 'How did the Italian lesson go last night?'

'Your brother worked hard.' Massimo's eyes lit with mischief. 'My daughter is a strict teacher.'

'And I daresay you are a diligent chaperone?'

He shrugged. 'She is my only child, and I will guard her until it is time to hand her into the care of a suitable husband.'

'And that is as it should be,' I said.

'Your brother is a good man, but he is damaged by the war.'

'He is.' I hesitated. 'His health is much improved since we came here, but he still has bad dreams. I worry that—'

Massimo laid his hand on my forearm. 'You are worried he wants a romantic friendship with Claudia, and that he might be ill again if she will not have the same feelings for him?'

I nodded, grateful he'd put my fears into words.

'I understand. Claudia is attracted to your brother, but I do not want her to mistake compassion for love.'

That comment made me bristle, but it was undeniable that Edmund's state of mind was still delicate.

'If we try to keep them apart,' continued Massimo, 'the attraction may become greater. We will both watch them and wait to see what happens.'

'Thank you, Massimo.' I was relieved we shared our concerns.

'I would like you to know Claudia as herself and not a maid,' he said. 'Perhaps you and Edmund will come to share our dinner on New Year's Eve?'

William had always said it was the essence of a person that mattered, whether they were honourable and true, not whether they lived in a castle or a cottage. 'Thank you, Massimo,' I said, 'we'd like that very much.'

Chapter 13

Edmund and I walked into Bellagio during the afternoon to buy small gifts for the Marchese family: boxes of marzipan fruits for the ladies and bottles of wine for the men. Then we read and chatted together in the tower sitting room until it was time to change for dinner.

I dressed in my dove grey dress with the lace collar. I was mindful that I was to meet Luca's bride, so I took particular care to dress my hair in a flattering chignon. I dabbed rose water on my wrists and put on my mother's seed pearl earrings.

Edmund and I went downstairs together.

'You look well tonight, Violet,' he said.

'Thank you. And you're looking pretty dapper yourself.' It pleased me that he had more colour in his complexion than of late.

'I'm curious to meet Luca's bride,' he said.

'Do you think it might be awkward for us? I wonder if we should have had our Christmas Eve dinner in our rooms so Luca and his wife could have a family-only evening?'

'I'm sure Luca or his mother would have said so, if that were the case,' said Edmund.

Crossing the hall, we paused to look at the candles flickering on the Christmas tree and the glass baubles gently turning in the draught.

'It reminds me of the trees we had while Mother was still alive,' said Edmund with a wistful expression on his face.

'Mildred always threw out the Christmas tree on the day after Boxing Day because it dropped needles on the floor. Poor Father. Perhaps things will be easier between them now we aren't there,' I said.

We went into the drawing room where Helen and Orlando were chatting over pre-dinner drinks. Umberto acknowledged us by raising his glass. There was no sign of Luca or his wife.

'Come in, come in!' said Orlando.

'Edmund, I was just telling my husband that you paint,' said Helen.

'Very badly, sir, but it's an interesting new hobby for me.'

'Sit here, and tell me about it.'

Helen rang the handbell on the table beside her. 'Claudia will bring you both an *aperitivo*,' she said.

'We wondered if you might prefer us to have dinner in the tower tonight,' I asked, 'since your son and his wife will be here?'

'Not at all!' She leaned towards me and murmured, 'In fact, I'm a little nervous. The more the merrier tonight.'

I wondered why she was nervous. 'Edmund and I will be happy to make ourselves scarce if you prefer some quiet time together as a family over Christmas.'

'That's considerate of you, but it won't be necessary. I'm sure my new daughter-in-law will be pleased to have the benefit of some younger company.'

I glanced at Umberto, lost in thought over his drink, and then at Orlando, whose eyes took in everything but whose speech was slow and hesitant.

'Luca asked us not to mention to Sylvana that you and Edmund are here to restore the walled garden,' said Helen. 'He doesn't want to spoil the surprise. I suggested we say that I was friends with your mother and you're visiting me from London.'

'A white lie might save awkward questions,' I said. 'Are your son and his wife expected to arrive soon?'

Helen pinched her lips together. 'They arrived two hours ago. Luca knows his grandfather will be irritated if they're late. I can't think what they're doing — Oh!' Her complexion turned crimson.

'Perhaps young Signora Marchese wished to rest after her journey from Florence,' I said diplomatically. I preferred not to think about what else the recently married couple might be doing after being apart for a while.

Claudia opened the door and carried in two glasses of Campari and soda on a silver tray. I took one of the glasses, and Edmund's gaze was fixed on her as she turned to him. '*Grazie*,' he said, taking his drink. He was rewarded with her smile.

'Claudia is teaching Edmund some Italian,' I said to Helen after Claudia had returned to the kitchen. 'Since I'm hoping we'll remain in Italy for a while, I'd like to take language lessons, too. It's uncomfortable to rely on others so much.'

'Claudia is a sweet girl,' said Helen, 'but I'm not sure if her command of English is good enough to help you or your brother.' She glanced at Umberto and lowered her voice. 'Do you remember I sent a note to my friend, Signora Pierucci, who would tell you about how Flora came to Italy?'

I nodded.

'Well, she's invited us to visit her next week, so you can find out more then. She's elderly, but she knows everyone in Bellagio and might know who could help you with Italian lessons. And then, once you have a grounding in the language, we can all speak Italian here to help you practice. None of us will mind if you make mistakes, and immersing yourself among Italian speakers is the fastest way to become fluent.'

'I'm sure you're right, but it is a little daunting.'

She patted my wrist. 'I remember how it was when I arrived here.'

The sound of a woman's laughter drifted from the hall, and the door opened.

Luca, holding his wife's hand, ushered her into the room.

Sylvana stood framed in the doorway. She wore a ruby red dress that skimmed her willowy figure and perfectly matched her daringly bright lipstick. Her shiny black hair was bobbed in the latest fashion, and the string of pearls draped around her swan-like neck was casually tied in a knot and reached to her waist.

I immediately felt like a dowdy country mouse in my grey dress when placed beside this exotic and sultry beauty.

Luca's gaze was fixed on his wife. His eyes shone, and a smile played upon his lips.

'*Mia cara suocera!*' Sylvana stepped daintily across the drawing room carpet in a cloud of expensive perfume and pecked Helen on her cheek before repeating the exercise with Orlando and Umberto.

'But Luca says we must speak English for your guests.' She smiled at Edmund, who had stood up when she appeared, before finally turning to me. Her gaze raked me up and down. Then, as if dismissing me as no threat to her own allure, she drew Luca to one of the sofas where they sat close together. Her skirt was short and her legs and ankles slender.

'Yes,' said Helen, 'do let me introduce Signora Violet Honeywell and her brother, Edmund Hall. Their mother was my very dear friend while we were at school in England.'

I noticed she managed to utter this story without even blinking.

She smiled at Edmund and me. 'And this, of course, is my son's wife, Sylvana Marchese.'

Edmund and I murmured the usual polite responses, and Sylvana inclined her head with the briefest of smiles. I noticed there was a small beauty spot next to the corner of her carmine lips.

Claudia arrived with two more glasses of Campari and soda and offered the tray to Sylvana.

She waved it away. 'I'll have a Negroni.'

'A Negroni?' said Helen.

'You've never tried it?' said her daughter-in-law. 'But you must! It's all the rage. Count Camillo Negroni invented it at the Caffè Casoni in Florence. It is equal parts of gin, vermouth rosso and Campari with a twist of orange.'

Luca spoke to Claudia. 'Would you make my wife a Negroni, please? I'll have one, too. Anyone else?'

Umberto made a sound of disgust. 'What is wrong with young people today that they must always have something new?'

'Perhaps another time, Luca,' said Helen, ignoring her father-in-law.

'Unfortunately, my doctor does not allow me more than one drink a day,' said Orlando.

'Poor you!' Sylvana pouted in sympathy for her father-in-law.

'I daresay, you and Luca have had a great deal to talk about,' said Helen. 'The weeks have flown by, and you've spent so little time together.'

'We both have busy lives,' said Sylvana.

Umberto cleared his throat noisily. 'But what kind of a marriage is this, where a wife is not at her husband's side?'

'A modern marriage, Nonno,' said Luca. 'Life is different now from how it was when you were young.'

'Is that so? Important things are exactly the same.' He leaned forward, his dark eyes glittering beneath bushy white brows. 'I tell you this truth. *You cannot make a son when you do not share a bed!*'

I heard Helen's gasp and barely supressed my own.

Sylvana raised her eyebrows and fixed him with a baleful stare. 'As Luca said, we have a modern marriage.'

'Unlike in the old days,' said Luca, 'where a wife was a mere chattel, our marriage is a partnership.' His cheeks flushed as he addressed his grandfather. 'We respect each other's wishes.'

Perhaps it was uncharitable of me to wonder if Sylvana respected Luca's wishes to the same extent that he respected hers.

'Pah!' Umberto pointed a finger at his grandson. 'A wife must know her husband is her master, and she must do as she is bid. If not, I warn you, there will be trouble for you!'

'Nonno—'

'Enough, Papà!' chided Orlando. 'What will our guests think of us?'

'Please, don't apologise for him,' said Sylvana. She gave Umberto a pitying glance. 'I'm sure he didn't intend to be so ill-mannered. Old people have such narrow lives and are rarely aware of how the world has changed since they were young.'

Edmund glanced at me and widened his eyes in mock horror.

Clearly, Sylvana was perfectly able to look after herself, but I felt embarrassed for Luca. His loyalty must surely be divided between his wife and his family.

Helen hurried to change the subject and asked after the health of her daughter-in-law's parents. 'It was such a shame we didn't know you and Luca were planning to marry or we might have had the opportunity to meet them.'

Sylvana laughed. 'We didn't plan the wedding at all. I showed the priest my first husband's death certificate, and he gave us dispensation to marry straightaway. It was so romantic! As to my parents, I rarely see them, and they never travel to Florence. Besides, I had a large wedding the first time. It was no fun at all since every last one of my husband's dreariest and most ancient relatives had been invited.'

'We would have treasured an invitation to our only son's wedding,' murmured Helen.

'I'm so sorry, Mamma,' said Luca, his expression mortified. 'I know now how disappointed you were.' He raked his fingers through his hair. 'We wanted to put the heartbreak of the war behind us and snatch the chance of happiness straightaway. And after all, it's the marriage that matters, not the wedding, isn't it?'

'What is a marriage when the husband and wife choose to live apart?' snapped Umberto. 'My Flora was always by my side.'

Thankfully, Claudia arrived with the Negronis and announced that dinner would be served in five minutes.

'On Sylvana's birthday in August we shall hold a big party to celebrate her move to Villa Marchese,' said Luca. 'And you can invite all your friends then, Mamma.' He reached for his wife's hand and kissed it.

Sylvana gave him a sideways glance and a secret smile hovered on her full lips. Raising her Negroni to him, she said, 'To passion and prosperity,' then drained the glass in one.

Luca raised his own glass. 'Passion and prosperity!'

I looked away, feeling as if I was intruding upon a private moment. I'd lost my appetite, but it was still a relief when Helen rose to her feet and led us in to dinner.

Sylvana's manner towards Luca, and indeed even Orlando and Edmund, was flirtatious. I watched her brushing Luca's cheek with her finger and smiling up at him in apparent adoration. His eyes shone, and he glowed in the sunshine of her attention.

There were several courses of different fish dishes: a soup, crisp fillets of fried lake fish, clams with pasta in a spicy sauce, marinated anchovies with lemon and salt cod with potatoes. We finished our feast with black coffee, nougat and tiny glasses of a dark liqueur.

Orlando saw me make a face when I sipped the bitter, medicinal-tasting drink. 'Drink it,' he said, the light of amusement in his eyes. 'It's Fernet Branca —an acquired taste, but it will help your digestion after a large meal.'

I swallowed the liqueur quickly.

'Good girl!' he said.

'We'd better get ready to go into the town,' said Helen. 'It would be a shame to miss the children's Nativity tableau.'

'Massimo said he'll be waiting at the front of the house for you with the *timonèlla*,' said Luca, 'but the rest of us will take the boat and meet you there.'

'A *timonèlla*?' asked Edmund.

'It's the local name for a small horse-drawn – or in this case, *mule*-drawn –carriage.'

'Unfortunately, I can no longer walk far,' said Orlando, 'and certainly not up the stone staircases from the lakeside to the basilica at the top of the town.'

'You must buy a motorcar,' said Sylvana. 'Several of my friends have them in Florence. It's such fun to speed along the road with the wind in your hair.' She placed her hand on Luca's arm. 'We shall have a motorcar when I come here in August, *caro*!'

'I'm not sure the roads around Bellagio are good enough for speed,' said Helen. 'We use the ferries or the trains.'

'We're very much looking forward to taking the ferries to explore the pretty little villages around the lake, aren't we, Edmund?' I said.

'But Bellagio is so far from any place of interest,' protested Sylvana.

'There are lots of attractive places nearby,' said Luca. 'And it's glorious here in the summer.'

'It's such a shame you have to rush back to Florence, Sylvana.' Helen's voice was carefully void of disapproval. 'We had arranged several luncheons and visits for you to meet our friends. They will be disappointed not to see you.' She glanced at her watch. 'Now hurry along, everyone, or we'll be late for midnight mass. Go and fetch your coats, all of you.'

Chapter 14

The night was clear but cool as Edmund and I followed Luca and his wife down the hillside. Both the men carried lamps to illuminate the path to the boathouse. The rain had ceased, but the trees still dripped moisture and the ground smelled damp and earthy.

Sylvana, wearing a beautiful, chocolate brown coat with a huge fur collar, squealed when she missed her footing stepping into the boat. Laughing, Luca caught her in his arms and kissed her.

I felt slightly bilious and reflected that the Fernet Branca *digestivo* didn't help at all, at least, not when my nausea was caused by a degree of envy. I wished I possessed Sylvana's self-confidence and beauty.

Edmund handed me into the boat, and Luca hung the lamps from the prow before casting off and rowing us out onto the lake.

A waxing moon cast a silvery luminescence over the rippling black water. The lanterns on a myriad of other small boats glimmered like stars all around us.

There was a chill breeze, and I pulled up the collar of my old tweed coat and wished it was made of fur like Sylvana's. Luca's wife was beautiful and lively, and it was perfectly natural that he was entranced by her. She made me feel very dull, and I wasn't proud of myself for suffering pangs of jealousy. When William died, I knew it would be unlikely I'd find another husband to love; there simply weren't enough men left after the carnage of the battlefields. I thought I had been pragmatic enough to accept that hard fact and to build a new life on my own but secretly, I hadn't accepted it at all. I still wanted a man who would love me as much as I loved him. And I wanted children.

There was a smile in Luca's voice as he and Sylvana chattered about their Florentine friends and all the parties, concerts and galleries she'd attended since she'd seen him last.

'Rafaele and Serafina keep asking me why you haven't returned to Florence yet,' she said, 'but I promised I'd drag you away from your family for the new year celebrations.'

'I'm looking forward to seeing everyone again,' said Luca.

'All our friends are going to Emilio and Francesca's party,' said Sylvana, 'and we've been invited to a luncheon at Nico's palazzo on New Year's eve. There's a new exhibition at the Uffizi Gallery, and then six of us plan to take a boat out on the Arno for a champagne breakfast.'

'What a very glamorous life you lead!' said Edmund.

'We must always choose how we want to live our lives, don't you think?' she said. 'Unless you grasp opportunities, nothing exciting will ever happen.'

'That's true,' I said, 'but not everyone has exciting opportunities, do they?'

Sylvana shrugged. 'If you look for them, there are always chances to rise above the dreariness of an ordinary life.'

I reflected that I'd never expected to be working on a fascinating garden project in such a beautiful corner of Italy. And, if it hadn't been for Edmund's urging, I might never have grasped the opportunity of such a call to adventure.

It wasn't long before we arrived at the public mooring. We tied up the boat and set off along the promenade towards the town centre. The cobbled streets were lit by strings of suspended lanterns, and it seemed as if every light inside the shops and smart hotels were turned on, where snatches of music and laughter drifted from within. Groups of people processed through the streets, children ran about with their friends and there was a feeling of anticipation and excitement in the air.

We climbed one of the stone staircases to the top of the town and met Luca's parents and grandfather waiting in the *timonèlla* in the market square. Helen waved to us as she tied the mule's reins to a ring in the wall beside the basilica.

Luca helped his father down to the ground and handed him his sticks. Umberto waved away his grandson's offer of a supporting hand.

'Shall we go and see the *tableau vivant*?' said Helen. 'The children will have been making their costumes for weeks.' She laughed. 'But that's the easy part. They have to remain silent and stock still for over an hour.'

'That must take some practice,' I said.

We walked at Orlando's pace to where a crowd had gathered around an awning set up against the basilica wall. The inside was arranged to look like a stable. The floor was spread with straw, and a donkey and five sheep were tethered near the manger. Several costumed children represented the Holy Family, the inn keeper, shepherds and, at the edge of the stable, the three Magi. Mary and Joseph looked adoringly into the manger at a real baby that I imagined must be a little brother or sister of one of the children.

'Most churches and many homes display a *presepe* – a nativity scene – at Christmastime,' said Luca, 'but it's also common to see a living nativity scene like this in the towns and villages.'

Umberto came to stand beside me.

'Isn't this a charming tradition?' I said.

He glanced at me and nodded his head approvingly. 'I like to see the old customs followed.' His expression softened. 'As a child many years ago I played the part of one of the Magi bearing gold, then twenty-five years later Orlando was Joseph. Teodore . . .' His voice cracked, and he composed himself again. 'Then both my grandsons had parts as shepherds when they were small.'

I felt sympathetic towards him then. Despite his authoritarian manner, he was only an old man who loved his family. 'I imagine you're hoping to see your great-grandson standing there in a few years?' I said.

Umberto sighed heavily. 'If I live long enough, and if Luca and his wife remember their responsibilities before too long.'

We watched the school children, none of them older than about eight, struggling to keep as still as statues. The sheep chewed their cud and stared back at us. Then, the baby in the manger mewled and waved his tiny fist in the air. The girl dressed as Mary made a shushing noise to him.

'I think the Virgin is about to have some problems with Baby Jesus,' said Sylvana.

The words were barely uttered before the infant let out a loud wail. Mary glanced over her shoulder, her expression tragic. Joseph nudged his elbow into her ribs and murmured to her. The baby yelled again, and the donkey began to bray, making some of the children laugh and others cry.

Mary pushed Joseph out of her way and lifted the shrieking infant from his manger. The other children abandoned their poses and crowded around Mary, patting the baby's scarlet cheeks and trying to prise him from her arms. The tighter she held him, the louder he screamed in competition with the braying donkey.

A woman in the crowd hurried forward and spoke to Mary, who thrust the baby into her arms.

'What a hideous noise!' said Sylvana, her hands cupped over her ears. '*Prega Dio che non abbia mai bambini che urlano!*'

The children's school teacher frowned at her, and then tried to coax the children back into their positions.

Helen stood rigidly at Sylvana's side, and I wondered what it was that Sylvana had said to upset her.

At last, the babe's frantic cries subsided into sobs.

I smiled at Sylvana. 'Weren't the children adorable?'

'Enchanting, except when they were screaming.' She shuddered. 'Preserve me from ever having any mewling babies.' Slipping her hand through the crook of Luca's arm, she said, 'Isn't it time to go into the basilica for the Midnight Mass?'

He nodded and glanced at Orlando, who was leaning heavily on his sticks as he exchanged greetings with another man. 'My father needs to sit down now.'

Edmund and I followed the Marchese family into the basilica. I followed suit when they dipped their fingers in the Holy Water inside the door and crossed themselves. It had been some while since I'd made that simple demonstration of faith, but now the time felt right.

The candlelit interior of the basilica was decorated with evergreen garlands for the festive service. The musty air was ripe with incense, beeswax and the acrid odour of mothballs emanating from the congregation's Sunday-best clothes. The nave was already crowded, and progress to our seats was slow because people stopped frequently to greet one another. Luca smiled charmingly as he determinedly parted the throng to usher his father to a seat. The rest of us followed, and Edmund and I sat together in the pew behind the Marchese family.

After we'd knelt to pray, Edmund nudged me and nodded his head to where Massimo, Beppe and Claudia sat on the other side of the church.

I stared at the back of Luca's head. I wondered idly if the lock of dark hair that curled onto his collar would be silky or springy if I touched it.

Sylvana fluttered her eyelashes at her husband, and I saw his slow smile in response. A bitter yearning rose up in me. I wanted so much to love and be loved again, but if only for my own inner peace, I knew I must never let my longings focus on another woman's husband.

Edmund leaned towards me and whispered, 'I'm so thankful we came to Villa Marchese, Violet. It isn't very long since I wished I could close my eyes and never wake up. I feel so different now.'

'I'm glad,' I murmured. 'All I want is for you to forget the painful events of the past.'

'We both need to do that.'

I gripped his hand while the scene before me wavered through a mist of tears.

On Christmas Day, Helen made every effort to ensure Luca's new wife enjoyed the festivities. Edmund and I, too, felt very welcome. Stefano and Rosa, friends of Luca's who lived in Bellagio, joined the party for Christmas Day. Their English was better than my Italian, and we got by with gesticulations and good humour. There was an excellent lunch of several courses, including roast capon, with each dish acccompanied by a different wine. We finished with panettone and coffee.

Afterwards, Umberto and Orlando dozed by the fire while the rest of us played charades, engendering a great deal of merriment. Sylvana was very quick and clever, and she frequently won, clapping her hands in self-congratulation each time. The game began to pall for me.

'Perhaps we should take a walk in the fresh air before it grows dark?' I said.

Sylvana stared at me. 'Outside? It's cold and wet.'

'It's a British custom to take a walk after Christmas lunch, *tesoro*,' said Luca.

She shrugged. 'But I am Italian.'

'I'm used to cold, damp weather,' I said, 'and I'd like to take a turn around the garden. Does anybody else want to come?'

Edmund nodded.

'I will, Violet,' said Helen.

Luca stood up. 'I'll join you. A tramp around outside will stop me dozing off after all that rich food. Sylvana?'

She shuddered theatrically. 'It must be your English blood that makes you want to go out in the cold.' She turned to Stefano and Rosa and rattled off a stream of Italian.

Luca smiled. 'She said she'll teach them to shimmy. It's the latest dance craze from America.'

Ten minutes later, the 'English Contingent', as Luca named us, set off into the rain-soaked garden in our boots and mackintoshes. Neptune, together with his sprites and sea serpents, were busily spouting water in the fountain. The Roman-style temple set between cypress trees at the top of the cascade caught my eye.

'May we go to the temple?' I asked. 'I'm sure there must be a wonderful view from there.'

'There certainly is,' said Luca.

The rain was gentle on my face as we took the path that zig-zagged up the hillside beside the cascade, and it wasn't long until the four of us arrived at the temple steps. Water dripped from the carved stone pediment supported on four columns, and we ducked inside to sit on the bench.

'It's too misty today to see the lake,' said Luca.

'It doesn't matter,' said Helen. 'I still like looking down the hillside at the trees and the villa below. It reminds me of the earlier generations of the Marchese family and how hard they had to work to raise themselves up from simple farmers to business owners.'

Luca sighed. 'Nonno never lets me forget that, or how much he finds me lacking in the skills and character to take over the business.'

'Will it be such a hardship?' asked Edmund. 'Taking your brother's place may not be how you planned your life, but it's still a good life.'

'No one can ever take Teodore's place.' Luca brushed a raindrop from his cheek. Helen put her arm around his shoulder. 'Your father doesn't want you to be unhappy. All he asks is that you give the business a fair trial. If you are really unhappy, then it must be sold.'

'I'd never get over the guilt of being the one to let it go,' he said. 'It worries me that the factory is less profitable since the war, and I don't know how to turn it around. Every time I have an idea, Nonno tells me it's no good.'

'Your grandfather is very set in his ways,' said Helen. 'Of course you must listen to his advice, but the time will come when you'll be confident enough to know what is, or isn't, a profitable idea. And your father has confidence in you and the fresh ideas you will bring to the business.'

'I suppose so.'

My heart went out to Luca. 'You'll have Sylvana at your side to support you before too long,' I said.

His face lit up. 'Once she's settled in here and becomes part of the community, I'm sure everything will be different.'

Helen opened her mouth as if to speak, and then pressed her lips together.

'Shall we walk again?' I said.

Luca and Edmund stood up but Helen said, 'You go on. I'll sit here for a while and remember Teodore.'

When we returned from our rainy post-luncheon walk, the carpet had been rolled back in the drawing room and the gramophone was turned to its loudest setting. Sylvana was teaching the others to dance to rumba rhythm. I watched in astonishment as she shimmied over to Umberto and caught his hands to pull him up to join them on the dance floor. Even more astonishingly, he moved his hips and his face cracked into a smile before he sank back into his seat.

Despite my unchristian envy of Luca's wife, I was forced to acknowledge that she was a vivacious and seductive force of nature.

Chapter 15

Villa Marchese seemed very quiet once Luca and Sylvana returned to Florence. My mood was melancholy, and rich food and insufficient exercise had rendered me lethargic. I gave myself a mental shake and went to the walled garden to dig over a patch of earth beside the grotto.

The fresh air, together with some pale sunshine, soon dispelled my gloom. The earth was rich and dark, and once all the weeds were removed, it would make fertile flowerbeds. I was pondering on which seeds I might plant when my spade scraped against something hard. Half-buried, it was an irregularly shaped lump of dark brown metal. I brushed off the loose earth and revealed what appeared to be a baby's bare bottom, liberally covered in bluish-green verdigris. I realised it must be a statue and, excited by my find, worked the spade underneath and levered it out of the earth.

I knew at once what it was. Made of bronze, it had to be Flora's statuette of Cupid from the niche in the grotto. Sadly, one of his wings was bent and part of his bow was missing. As I lifted it into a wheelbarrow, Massimo walked into the garden.

'I've brought you a flask of coffee and a slice of panettone,' he said. 'Claudia said she'd seen you pass our cottage earlier and guessed you were on your way here.' He frowned at the statue. 'What is this?'

'It must be Flora's Cupid. Unfortunately, it's slightly damaged.'

'The statue you talked about when the rock from the grotto fell on you?'

'The very same.'

Massimo wiped off some more of the earth and scraped at the verdigris with his nail. 'I wonder if we can find the missing part?' He took the spade from me and turned over the earth where I'd been digging. After a few minutes, he let out a crow of triumph and bent to pick up the lost piece of Cupid's bow. 'I'll ask the blacksmith if he can repair it.'

'Meanwhile, let's put Cupid back in his niche,' I said.

Afterwards, Massimo poured me some coffee from the flask and we studied the new find.

'It looks perfect there, doesn't it?' I said. 'I can't wait to show Luca.'

Massimo gave me a sideways glance. 'I wasn't expecting you in the garden so soon,' he said.

'I was anxious about how much there is to do before we can begin planting.'

'I have an idea,' he said.

'What's that?'

He grinned and touched a finger to his nose. 'You'll have to wait and see.' He handed me the slice of panettone wrapped in a napkin. 'Meanwhile, don't forget to come and share our dinner tomorrow evening. Claudia is cooking the *cotechino* already.'

'*Cotechino*?'

'A special rich sausage made with pork and spices. Very good. Come at ten o'clock. Is the custom to eat at midnight to welcome the new year.'

'We're looking forward to it.'

The light was fading when I returned to the villa. I found Edmund in our tower sitting room painting again. I peered over his shoulder. 'You're becoming rather good at this.'

'Painting quietens my mind,' he murmured, absorbed in mixing a new colour. 'I want to finish this before I lose the light.'

'I shan't disturb you, then. I'm going to change out of my gardening clothes and work in the library until it's time for dinner.'

He nodded without answering, and I crept away.

In the library, I laid out Flora's gardening diaries on the table, including the one I'd taken to my room when I'd been concussed. I turned to her entries for August. I wanted to see if she'd mentioned any particular flowers that had bloomed in her garden in that month.

Sometime later, I felt a draught on the back of my neck and turned to see that Helen had come into the library.

Smiling, she said, 'I wondered if I might find you here. If you're free tomorrow morning, I wondered if you'd like to come with me to visit Flora's friend, Signora Pierucci?'

'I'd like that very much.' I held up one of the diaries. 'As you see, I'm reading Flora's notebooks, and I'm curious to find out more about her.'

Helen opened one of the bookcases and lifted down a large book bound in black leather with the title tooled in gold. She laid it carefully on the table beside me. 'The Marchese family Bible.' Opening it, she ran her finger down a list of names inscribed inside the front cover. 'Here is Oreste and his son Pietro, Gabriele Marchese's father. Gabriele's mother died in 1846, and Pietro then married Magdalena a year later. My father-in-law Umberto was her son. He was ten at the time and Pietro adopted him.'

'How old was Gabriele then?'

'Let me see. He was born in 1831 so he must have been

seventeen. He married Flora in 1852,' said Helen, studying the dates. 'So, he was twenty-two and Flora eighteen. Isabella was born the following year. And here is the record of Gabriele's death after the Battle of Solferino.'

I peered at the page and frowned at the thick, black line Umberto had scored through Gabriele's name. The date of Gabriele's death was noted as 24 June 1859. 'I see Flora married Umberto on the 7th of July in 1861, and Orlando was born the following April. It was a cruel thing that Flora drowned only two months later.'

'Perhaps it was better that he was so young,' said Helen. 'He had Lucrezia to love him, and he was Umberto's pride and joy.' She ran her finger down the list of names. 'Isabella died on the 14th July 1863 when she was only ten years old. Poor child!'

'The anniversary of Bastille Day,' I said. 'What stories there are to be told from the flyleaves of family Bibles.'

'Indeed there are.' Helen closed the Bible and replaced it in the bookcase. 'I'll leave you to finish making your notes.'

The following morning, Helen and I walked into Bellagio. We climbed halfway up one of the stone staircases towards the upper part of the town until reaching a decorative iron gate across a passageway. She pressed a brass bell push set into the wall beside the gate. Then we waited.

'Signora Pierucci is in her late eighties,' said Helen, 'but her mind is as sharp as a knife. She took me under her wing when I first came to Bellagio. She's a widow, and her children live far away so I visit her as often as I can.'

An elderly servant came to unlock the gate, her footsteps tapping across the cobbles. Her face creased into a smile when she saw Helen.

The gate creaked open and then clanged shut behind us. We were escorted into a house painted saffron yellow with pots of bay trees to either side of the front door.

An elderly lady, her back ramrod straight, waited for us in the drawing room. She held out her hands to Helen, who kissed her cheeks.

'I've brought my new friend from London to meet you,' said Helen. 'May I present Mrs Honeywell?'

I stepped forward to shake Signora Pierucci's hand and blinked when I saw she had an unmistakably English complexion with eyes of a faded cornflower blue.

'As you see,' she said, 'I'm not a native Italian – I was born in Kent.'

'Signora Marchese didn't mention that.'

'My husband was Italian. I've lived in Bellagio for seventy years, but part of my heart will always remain in England. Please, sit down both of you. Giovanna will bring us tea in a moment.'

'As I mentioned in my note, Caroline,' said Helen, 'I wondered if you know of anyone who might give Mrs Honeywell Italian lessons?'

'I've given this some thought,' she said. 'The best person would be Signor Romano, who teaches English at the school. I've approached him, and his fees are very reasonable. He would be pleased to come to Villa Marchese on Tuesdays after school.'

'That's excellent,' I said. 'Thank you so much for arranging it.'

'Not at all.'

'It will be so much easier for Mrs Honeywell if she can speak some of the language,' said Helen. 'As I told you, Luca brought her to Villa Marchese to restore Flora's garden.'

Signora Pierucci turned to me. 'I'm delighted for Flora's sake. How was the garden after being closed up for so long?'

'A complete jungle,' I said. 'It's astonishing how much havoc Mother Nature can achieve in a carefully tended garden when left to her own devices for nearly sixty years.'

'Dear Flora, how she loved that garden! She was never afraid to get soil under her fingernails, and she even roped me in to help her with the weeding and dead-heading. I spent many a happy hour there with my two sons and my goddaughter, Isabella.'

'I've been studying Flora's gardening notebooks,' I said. 'When I'm reading her words, it almost feels as if she's beside me, explaining how she planned the planting and designed the pond and the grotto. I'm trying to piece her notes together, with the aid of her sketch plan, to recreate the garden, although the planting will be more in tune with contemporary taste and resources.'

'Flora always brimmed with enthusiasm,' said Signora Pierucci. 'She and Gabriele, her husband, loved to work side-by-side in the garden whenever he was free. They called it their Eden.'

'Gabriele is the reason for our visit, Caroline,' said Helen. 'I had hoped you might explain to Mrs Honeywell how you and Flora came to Italy.'

'I confess it was pure curiosity to discover how and why a young English girl left her home to marry into an Italian family,' I said. 'But while reading Flora's notebooks, Gabriele's name was frequently mentioned. It confused me because I knew her husband was called Umberto.'

Signora Pierucci laughed. 'Don't tell me: you imagined Flora had secret yearnings for another man?'

I dropped my gaze. 'I'm afraid I did wonder.'

'Flora was the most loyal person I ever met,' she said. 'She adored Gabriele, and although I knew her well enough to see she never recovered from his death, she never complained. Umberto was four years younger than she, but he was smitten by her from the very first. Flora and I used to giggle about his school-boy crush on her. He proposed to her exactly a year after Gabriele fell on the battlefield, but she refused him.' Shaking her head, she said, 'Knowing how she'd loved Gabriele, I was surprised when she agreed to marry Umberto a year later.'

154

'I suppose she wanted a father for Isabella,' said Helen.

I was left waiting to hear more about Flora's relationships when a maid brought in the tea tray. After Signora Pierucci had poured the tea, she said, 'It was a long time ago, but it's still so clear in my mind. If you have time, I'll start at the beginning.'

I glanced questioningly at Helen, and she nodded encouragingly.

Signora Pierucci smiled. 'Well, then, Flora and I became close friends when we were eleven, very soon after we arrived at our boarding school. She was a quiet little thing to begin with and told me her mother had died the year before. Her father was a busy doctor, and he'd decided Flora would be happier in the company of school friends rather than at home with her elderly governess.'

'Spending all her time with a governess must have been very dull for her,' I said.

'It was. When we were seventeen and ready to leave school, my parents planned to take me with them on an extended visit to Italy. They had rented a villa in Bellagio for that summer. Then, Flora's father contracted tuberculosis. She was forbidden to see him in case she caught it, too, so my parents offered to take her with us to Italy. Her father was relieved she'd be cared for while he was ill.'

'What a marvellous opportunity for her!' I said.

'Papa had visited Italy several times and fallen under its spell. He was a wholesale draper with a thriving business; his speciality was decorative silk. Como and nearby Milan were the best places to find it.' She leaned forward, her eyes sparkling with amusement. 'What I didn't know at the time was that he and Mama had a particular reason for taking me with them. Papa had forged strong business links with a mill owner called Pietro and over the years they'd wondered if Pietro's son and I might make a suitable match. Naturally, Mama insisted on vetting the young man, and once I'd left school, the summer visit was a convenient way to find out.'

'And was this young man your future husband?'

'No,' Caroline Pierucci laughed. 'Gabriele – for he was the young man in question – and Flora took one look at each other, and it was as if Cupid's arrows had pierced both their hearts. It was obvious to everyone that the two had fallen deeply in love at first sight.' Her expression sobered. 'She never ceased to love him, even after he died.'

'Your father must have been disappointed that his plans were dashed.'

'At first, but Gabriele introduced me to his wealthy friend Domenico Pierucci, and Papa was delighted when we became engaged shortly afterwards. For Flora and me, it was marvellous that we'd both found husbands we loved and that we would be able to continue our friendship and support each other in a strange country.'

'Quite the romantic dream for a pair of young ladies!' said Helen.

'Indeed,' said Signora Pierucci. 'At least, it was until the Battle of Solferino in 1859. Gabriele died, and Domenico lost his arm during the conflict for independence.'

'I was widowed during the recent conflicts, so I can imagine what a dark time that must have been for you both,' I said.

She bowed her head. 'I'm sorry about your loss. I was lucky because my husband returned, albeit damaged in mind and body. I'm still troubled by nightmares of his descriptions of hundreds upon thousands of soldiers slaughtering each other in the bright spring sunshine.' She closed her eyes. 'One by one, the Austrians abandoned their positions, but by nightfall, the battlefield rang with the screams of the wounded soldiers scattered amongst the dead men. The French and Sardinian armies had few doctors and almost no medical supplies. Domenico said it was a scene of Hell on Earth.'

We sat in contemplative silence for a few minutes.

'The Battle of Solferino was a turning point in the struggle for Italian unification,' Helen said to me. 'The Franco-Sardinian Alliance, including the Hunters of the Alps led by Garibaldi, defeated the Austrians. Finally, in 1861, the unified Kingdom of Italy was created.'

'After the carnage on the battlefield,' said Signora Pierucci, 'Flora and I had no means of knowing if our husbands were alive or dead. We clung to each other while we waited for news. In the end, I was the lucky one, even if it would be weeks before Domenico was well enough to return home. Later, he said the worst part of his suffering was when he had to bring the news of Gabriele's death to Flora. She fell into a dead faint and then grieved in silence, becoming a pale shadow of my blithe and beautiful friend. It was made even harder for her because little Isabella refused to believe her father was dead.'

'Most of us feel a sense of total disbelief when a loved one dies,' murmured Helen.

'But life goes on,' said Signora Pierucci.

'Yes,' I said. I drew a calming breath and pictured William's smiling face, the pain of our lost future still sharp in my breast. 'I wish I'd known Flora. I would have loved to talk to her about her garden.'

Signor Pierucci smiled. 'She would have loved that, too.'

Chapter 16

It had already gone ten o'clock when Edmund and I left Villa Marchese for Massimo's cottage. He was in high spirits as he swung a torch to light our way through the garden, clearly excited to be with Claudia for New Year's Eve. I tried to ignore my disquiet. He deserved the usual pleasures of any young man's life, but I didn't believe him stable enough yet to cope with any disappointment in affairs of the heart.

Drifts of mist curled across the path, and Edmund teased me by growling loudly and telling me there were bears hiding behind the trees. I lunged at him with a fierce growl, and we were still laughing at our silliness when we arrived at the cottage.

The front path was edged with a row of flickering nightlights in jam jars. A lamp illuminated the porch, and there was a welcoming glow from the windows.

The door opened before we reached it, and Massimo came out to greet us, his arms held wide. He kissed me on both cheeks and shook Edmund's hand. 'We left the shutters open to help you see your way,' he said.

I was amazed by Massimo's appearance. Instead of his usual

shabby brown coat, waistcoat and thick-soled gardening boots, he wore a smart suit and tie with a white shirt. His unruly locks were brushed, his shoes shone and his healthy complexion and broad smile made him look unexpectedly young and handsome.

'Come in by the fire,' he said.

The interior of the cottage was a mirror image of Beppe's. It had a good-sized living room with a dining table in one corner. Beppe sat in one of the armchairs circling the black-leaded range where a fire crackled in the grate. A large saucepan sat on top of one of the ovens, and a copper kettle kept warm on a trivet. The room was fragrant with woodsmoke and something deliciously savoury.

Claudia came from the kitchen, wiping her hands on a tea towel. 'Welcome!' she said. She was pretty in a green skirt with a cream lace blouse. Edmund clearly thought so, too, since he could hardly take his eyes off her. I handed her a bottle of wine and a large box of *torrone*, a kind of nougat, as a contribution to our dinner.

Massimo ushered us to sit by the fire and brought us glasses of mulled wine, aromatic with cinnamon, cloves and curls of orange zest.

'So, the family up at the villa have gone away for New Year's Eve?' said Beppe.

'To Tremmezo,' I said.

Beppe nodded. 'That will be Signor and Signora Esposito. The two families have been friends for several generations. One of Pietro Marchese's sisters married in to the Esposito family.'

'I do not work tonight,' said Claudia, 'and I am happy to be with my family.' She smiled at Edmund. 'And our new friends.'

'It was so kind of you to invite us,' I said.

'You are far away from your family and should not be alone on New Year's Eve.'

She was a kind girl, as Massimo had told me

'And so, at midnight we begin a new decade,' said Massimo.

I doubted any of us would be sorry to say goodbye to the current one. I wondered what the 1920s would bring.

'We have survived,' said Massimo, just as if he'd heard my thoughts, 'and now we look forward to happier times.'

Beppe raised his glass. 'To happier times.'

We raised our glasses and echoed his toast.

'Another toast,' said Massimo. 'To the flowering of Flora's garden!'

'Flora's garden!'

Claudia offered us olives, walnuts and small pieces of toast brushed with olive oil, garlic and fresh herbs. 'Eat,' she said. 'Dinner is late on New Year's Eve.'

The toast, or *bruschetta* as she called it, was delicious. I'd learned to enjoy garlic, herbs and olive oil in the meals served at Villa Marchese and smiled at the idea of Mildred eating what I was sure she would describe as peasant food, unfit for a decent Englishwoman. I wondered if Father and Mildred had found peace between themselves, now Edmund and I had left. I hoped so – Father deserved some serenity

The clock on the wall struck eleven, and I felt a quiver of anticipation that soon it would be the new year. Conversation was easy between us, and we drank more mulled wine while we chatted.

'Will you sing for us, Claudia? asked Massimo. He turned to Edmund and me. 'My daughter has a beautiful voice.'

She stood by the fireside and sang a ballad, unaccompanied by any instrument. Her voice was clear and true, and Edmund gazed at her without moving until the end when he clapped loudly.

Claudia curtseyed and blushed. 'I must see if the dinner is ready,' she said, glancing at the clock.

It was ten minutes to midnight. I put my drink down. 'May I help you?' She looked at me askance, and I laughed. 'During the war I lived alone, so I'm used to cooking for myself.'

Her smile lit up her face. 'No servants?'

'None.'

'Come with me.' She lifted the pan off the range, and I followed her to the kitchen. A large table stood in the centre, and Claudia placed the saucepan onto a waiting trivet before taking off the lid. '*Cotechino con lenticchie*,' she said.

I sniffed appreciatively at the spicy aroma and thought I detected nutmeg, pepper and cloves. 'It smells delicious.'

She lifted a plump pork sausage from the lentil stew and laid it on a chopping board. She cut the first two slices to show me how thick each disc should be and watched me while I sliced the rest. 'Good. And now the *lenticchie*. It's traditional.'

We arranged the sausage slices in a spiral on each plate over a bed of lentils and then carried them to the living room.

Massimo lit the candles on the table, then clapped his hands and invited Edmund and Beppe to sit down to eat. 'We must wait until midnight,' he said. As he spoke, the clock began to strike.

Beppe scooped up a spoonful of lentils to show me. 'You see? Little coins. They bring wealth and plenty for the new year.' He popped it in his mouth and rolled his eyes with pleasure. 'My granddaughter is a very good cook.'

'She certainly is,' said Edmund.

We drank a full-bodied red wine with our dinner to complement the richness of the sausage and talked about our New Year resolutions.

'I will live every day of my life as if it is the last,' said Beppe and raised his wine glass. 'A toast to sitting in the sun and drinking good wine with my family and friends.'

'That is a good promise,' said Massimo. 'Mine is the same.' He looked at me.

'I'm going to learn Italian,' I said. 'Signor Romano from the school is coming to teach me on Tuesday afternoons.'

Massimo cheered. 'Will you stay in Italy?'

'I don't know about that,' I said, 'but I shall be here for some months.'

'When you know a little of the language, then we will speak to you only in Italian,' said Massimo. 'You will learn more quickly.' The expression in his eyes was warm. 'I hope you will stay here.'

'Already I am beginning to understand a little just by listening.'

He beamed. '*Molto bene!* That means—'

'Very good,' I said.

'See! You are a quick learner just like your brother.' Massimo gave Edmund a playful cuff to his arm.

'*Mi piace parlare Italiano*,' said Edmund with a flourish of his hand. 'I like to speak Italian,' he translated for my benefit.

'You're even learning the gestures to go with the words!' I said.

'*Molto bene*, Edmund!' said Claudia and kissed his cheek.

Beppe cheered and I caught Massimo's eye.

He shrugged and raised his glass. 'To the New Year!'

Blushing, Claudia rose from the table.

After we'd washed the dishes, she set me to work cutting slices of panettone and filling small bowls with dried fruits and nuts.

Massimo opened a bottle of dessert wine. 'The seven different kinds of dried fruits and nuts are traditionally eaten to ensure wealth and fertility in the coming year,' he said.

I sipped my wine and nibbled at walnuts. If William had returned safely from the war, would I now have a baby in my arms? How different life would have been if only ... I started at a touch on my hand.

'Violet?' Massimo's brown eyes were watching me. 'Are you sad?'

'No, of course not,' I said, pushing away my melancholy thoughts and forcing a smile. 'How could I be after such a lovely evening?'

'Your brother is happy.'

I glanced at Edmund, laughing at something Claudia had said.

Her face was tipped up to look at him, and her eyes were shining. My unease returned. 'Yes,' I said, 'but it's late and we should go. I must work in the garden tomorrow.'

'Not too early,' said Massimo. 'The men will be late to bed tonight after the celebrations.'

A short while later, Edmund and I put on our coats and thanked our hosts. They came to the door with us, and I kissed Beppe and Claudia while Edmund shook Massimo's hand.

Then Massimo kissed my cheeks and held my hands while he looked into my eyes. 'Be happy this year.'

I nodded. 'And you, too.' Over his shoulder I saw Edmund kiss Claudia's cheek and noticed how she hugged him back. 'Come Edmund. It's time to leave.'

Reluctantly, he released Claudia, and we went out into the night.

Chapter 17

Edmund and I slept late the following morning and breakfasted alone since the Marchese family remained in Tremezzo until the afternoon. Claudia appeared with our coffee, and we thanked her for the previous evening.

After breakfast, we put on our boots and headed for the garden. I carried a surveyor's tape to take measurements and a notebook for drawing up the plans.

We heard voices from inside the walled garden even before we opened the door.

'Good heavens!' said Edmund. 'What's that doing here?'

A great, brown carthorse stood beside Massimo together with a stocky man in an ancient coat tied around the waist with a piece of string.

'*Buongiorno,*' I said. I stroked the horse's neck and laughed when he nuzzled my hand, searching for a treat.

Massimo smiled, looking like his old self in his shabby gardening clothes again. I rather missed the handsome version I'd seen the night before.

164

'This is Signor Russo,' he said, and I exchanged nods with the man. 'He works a farm nearby and agreed to plough the garden.'

'But what a good idea! It will be so much quicker than digging the roots out by hand.'

'It will save much work,' said Massimo.

Edmund and I left them to it and retreated to look at the pond in the centre of the garden. The undergrowth had been torn away and revealed that the stonework beneath was almost intact.

'It won't take much to repair those loose capping stones,' I said.

Edmund grimaced as he peered into the pond. It was clogged with black mud, brushwood and brambles. 'It's going to be quite a job to clean this out.'

'Later,' I said. 'Time is marching on, and I must measure the garden.'

Edmund stood against one of the garden walls and held the end of the linen measuring tape while I walked away from him, unrolling from its steel drum as I went. I'd prepared an outline of Flora's garden into my notebook and began to note down the dimensions between the salient points onto the sketch plan.

At last, satisfied I'd captured the necessary information, I closed my notebook.

'While I have the tape measure in my hand,' I said, 'I'd like us to decide on the width of the seating area around the pond.'

We set to work marking out the area with pegs and string. Mindful that Luca hadn't yet made a decision as to whether he could cover the cost of restoring the whole garden, I made the seating area considerably wider than originally intended. More hard landscaping and fewer flowerbeds would reduce future maintenance costs and provide a delightful sitting place.

Later, we stood back to study what we'd achieved.

'I'm happy with that,' I said, 'but I'll have to discuss the budget again with Luca before we set out the rest of the paths. Since Luca may not be able to afford to do the whole garden, I must draw up alternative plans.'

'We may be ready for that sooner than we expected,' said Edmund with a nod towards Signor Russo as he guided his horse and plough back and forth across the garden. Massimo was digging and raking the freshly turned earth in the farmer's wake.

'We also need to start ordering materials, so Luca will have to make up his mind fairly quickly.' As Helen had pointed out, Luca had made another of his impetuous decisions when he chose to restore the garden for Sylvana.

'Shall we go and see what progress Massimo is making?' said Edmund.

The plough had turned the earth over in great clods, and I anticipated there was still a great deal of work required to break the soil down to the fine tilth necessary for sowing seeds. It would be a huge task, and I was more than a little relieved when the gardening workforce pushed open the garden door, filling the air with their cheerful chatter.

After wishing them a happy New Year, I returned to Massimo. 'I'm going back to the house to draw up the plans so we can work out the costs.'

He nodded, and there was a smile in his eyes when he looked at me.

'Edmund and I had such a good evening with your family last night,' I said. 'Thank you for making us so welcome.'

'It was our pleasure.' He lifted my hand and pressed it briefly to his lips.

I took a tiny step backwards, embarrassed by his effusive gesture, and he immediately released my hand.

'Will you ask the men to dig over the soil in this central section of the garden?' I said. 'There's plenty for them to do here until we know how much of the garden is to be restored.'

'Of course.'

As I walked away, I could feel his gaze upon my back until I closed the garden door behind me.

I lifted the desk top of the library's antique drawing table. It was beautifully made from rosewood, and I propped it up on the notched timber supports beneath until it was at a comfortable angle for drawing. I'd brought board clips to hold the paper securely onto the drawing surface and rested my T-square, pencil, scale rule and protractor on the timber lip along the lower edge of the board before turning on the brass desk lamp.

I'd always loved drawing up a new plan. When ordering quantities of landscaping materials or plants, it was important to take accurate measurements to avoid expensive mistakes. I scaled down the actual measurements of the walled garden to fit onto a piece of cartridge paper only 21 by 26 inches. It always seemed to me to be some kind of magic to represent something so large as a garden on such a small piece of paper.

I set out the perimeter walls first, carefully checking the measurements of the diagonals since a plot of land was rarely perfectly square. I was so involved in my task that I was oblivious to time and only briefly noted the sounds of the Marchese family's return when I heard Helen's voice in the hall.

Much later, the library door opened behind me, and I glanced up from the pool of light on my drawing to realise it was ink-black outside.

'Violet?'

Luca appeared by my side wearing his overcoat, and I couldn't contain my smile. 'Did you have a good journey from Florence?'

He nodded. 'What are you doing here in almost complete darkness?' he said.

'I hadn't noticed the daylight fading. Too busy working on the garden plan.' He looked tired, I thought. Perhaps there had been too many parties to attend and too many friends to see.

He peered over my shoulder to study the drawing. I closed my eyes momentarily at the scent of fresh air on his clothes and the pleasant hint of his rosemary hair pomade.

'It isn't finished,' I said. 'This is simply the survey drawing of the garden as it exists. As you can see, I've included the pond and the grotto because those features will remain. Next, I'll lay tracing paper over the survey drawing and sketch alternative layouts.'

'Alternative?'

'You mentioned your budget may be insufficient to restore the whole garden, so I'll demonstrate how we might screen part of it off to make a more modest layout.'

He grimaced and raked his fingers through his hair. 'It all depends how much it's going to cost. I really didn't think this through properly before I dragged you and Edmund away from your home, did I?'

I gripped my pencil, fearful he might be going to say he was going to abandon Flora's garden. 'I wanted very much to work on this project,' I said, 'and once I knew you understood about Edmund's difficulties, I was thrilled to come here.' I glanced away from his penetrating gaze. 'Anyway, there's no home waiting for us in England.'

'That's very sad for you.'

There was such compassion in his voice that I had to take a bracing breath. 'If we must reduce the scope of the design, then additional work could be carried out in the future, if funds allow. Perhaps you could spare me a little time to discuss the features that are the most important for you?

'I'd be happy to. After dinner perhaps?' He frowned. 'Or will that make your working day too long?'

'Not at all. I'm anxious to settle the final design.'

'I must go and speak to my father now,' he said. 'I may have pulled off a most satisfactory piece of business while I was in Florence.' He smiled. 'And if that happens, then I'll have more funds to spend.'

'Your wife is sure to be delighted, whatever size we make the garden. What woman could fail to adore such a glorious gift?'

'I'm sure it will become her special place.'

When I entered the drawing room for our *aperitivo* that evening, Luca ushered me to sit between Helen and himself on the sofa.

'Happy New Year to you all,' I said, 'or perhaps I should say *Buon Anno*?'

Orlando smiled at me from his chair and then returned to his conversation with Edmund. I felt a rush of affection for this family that had made us so welcome.

Claudia brought us our pre-dinner drink: Campari and soda, I noticed, not a Negroni now that Sylvana had gone.

'Did you enjoy your visit to Tremezzo, Helen?' I sipped my drink.

'It was very pleasant,' she said, 'but it's good to be home again. I hope it wasn't too lonely for you and Edmund here?'

'Not at all. Massimo invited us to dinner, and we had a jolly evening with Claudia and Beppe.' I smiled. 'It was quite a surprise to see Massimo resplendent in a smart suit.'

'So, he dressed up for you, did he?' teased Luca.

'We all dressed for the occasion,' I said.

'I remember he was very handsome as a young man,' said Helen, 'but he only ever had eyes for his wife. After she died he directed his energies into bringing up Claudia. Perhaps it's time he looked for a new wife now Claudia is grown – someone who shares his love of horticulture maybe?'

Luca's eyes widened, but then dinner was announced, and I was saved from responding to what I assumed was Helen's unsubtle attempt at matchmaking.

Umberto, sitting opposite me at the table, caught my eye. 'How is the work in my wife's garden, Signora Honeywell?'

After his previous reluctance to discuss this, I was surprised he'd raised the subject. 'We're making excellent progress,' I said.

'It is too hard and dirty for a woman. You must be exhausted.' He gave me a sympathetic smile.

'Women are often stronger and tougher than they look,' I said. 'Besides, our male workforce cut down much of the undergrowth, and a farmer came with his horse to plough the soil. It will be easier to dig and rake now to make it ready to sow the seeds.'

'I saw the garden when Luca broke the door down, but I did not imagine you could clear the land.'

I smiled at him. 'I'm not sure I believed it either.'

'And Luca thinks the garden will draw his wife to Villa Marchese?' Umberto bit at his thumbnail and then let out a sigh. 'So, perhaps some good will come from my wife's garden.'

We'd barely been served our soup before Umberto began carping at Luca again. 'So, you didn't manage to persuade your wife to return to Villa Marchese with you?'

'Sylvana has a very full diary at present.'

'Too full to be at her husband's side?'

'She's involved in fundraising events for children left in poverty since the war,' said Luca. 'I support her efforts for such a worthy cause.'

Umberto clasped his forehead. 'Your wife's first duty is to come home and give you an heir. She can learn from your mother how to knit and sew clothes for impoverished children while she waits for a son of her own.'

I put down my soup spoon, all at once unable to swallow while listening to this diatribe.

'I told you, Nonno,' said Lucca, 'Sylvana and I have an agreement—'

'What kind of man are you that allows an agreement that encourages his wife to run wild? I'll tell you what kind of a man: worthless, inadequate and impotent.'

'Papà—' began Orlando.

Umberto pointed a finger at his son. 'And you are no better if you support him.'

'I'm not staying to listen to this.' Luca flung his napkin down and strode from the room.

'That woman laughs in your face!' shouted Umberto after his grandson's retreating back.

There was a hushed silence and I glanced at Edmund. He was pale and his eyes were squeezed shut.

Umberto puffed out his breath in disgust and tore his bread into pieces to dip in his soup. Helen pushed back her chair to go after Luca, but Orlando shook his head.

The rest of us sat in silence until Claudia came to clear the plates and bring the next course.

Picking at the plate of pasta that was placed before me, I wondered how Orlando could have allowed his father to make such a verbal attack on Luca.

At last the seemingly interminable meal was over. Orlando and Umberto remained at the table with a glass of brandy, but Helen went straight upstairs and Edmund murmured that he was going to his room. I escaped into the library.

After that scene over dinner, the last thing I expected to find was Luca sitting in one of the wing chairs by the library fire, nursing a glass of whisky.

He looked up at me with such desolation in his eyes that I had to stop myself running to him. 'Would you like me to leave you in peace?' I said.

'Good heavens, no! The last thing I want it to be left alone with my miserable thoughts. I will never match up to Teodore in my grandfather's eyes, and it's made worse because Sylvana . . .' He forced a smile. 'I'm relying on you to distract me from that unpleasant scene. Come and sit by the fire with me for a while. Whisky?'

'Perhaps just a taste.'

He poured it from the crystal decanter at his side and handed it to me.

I sat down in the wing chair opposite him. I judged it best not to try and discuss what had happened. 'Have you read any good books lately?'

'When I was last in London, I picked up a first edition of *Lays of Ancient Rome* by Thomas Babington Macaulay. It's a collection of poems recounting heroic stories from early Roman history. It's background reading for the novel I'm writing.'

'How exciting! You mentioned before that you'd intended to write in your spare time when you were working for a publisher in Florence before the war.'

'I decided that if I could write while working for a publisher, there's nothing to stop me writing while I'm working in the family business. I write during the ferry journey to and from Como. Sometimes, I manage an hour or so before breakfast or after I've retired to my room in the evening.' A slow smile spread across his face. 'It's surprising how the words mount up in these brief periods of time. The story bubbles away in the back of my mind. I jot down notes in the middle of the night, and sometimes, even during meetings.' He leaned forward and whispered, 'Don't tell Nonno!'

I laughed. 'It's the same for me when I'm designing a garden. The creative process becomes obsessive. What is your story about?'

'I'm fascinated by ancient Rome. I mentioned before that it's believed Pliny the Younger once lived near here, where Villa Serbelloni now stands. It was so long ago, but people from that time must have experienced the same feelings of joy and grief that we do, and that's what I'm attempting to capture in my novel.

It's a love story set during the turbulent years of the fall of the Roman Empire.'

'Well, I shall look forward to reading it in due course.'

'Meanwhile, shall we discuss your plans for the garden?'

I fetched my notebook from the drawing table 'Think of the garden design like a shopping list.' I frowned. 'Have you ever written a shopping list?'

The corner of his mouth twitched. 'Cook usually does that, but I'm willing to learn.'

'We start with the essentials; in this case, paths, plants and boundaries. We've already decided to use gravel for the paths with a view to replacing it in the future with brick or stone. Paths not only reduce the quantity of plants, and therefore the maintenance required, but they define the flowerbeds and allow us to form pleasant seating areas where they intersect.' I stopped speaking when I saw one of his eyebrows lift in amusement. 'What is it?'

'Most women aren't so pragmatic about cutting costs.'

'I'm not most women,' I said. 'I have a duty to both you as my client and to myself as a professional horticulturist to arrive at practical solutions.'

Luca let out a low whistle. 'You should have been a general in the army. You'd have whipped the lot of them into shape in no time.'

'I daresay,' I said, trying not to smile. 'Of course, even gravel paths will be more expensive than sowing seeds, so my suggestion is that I plan the entire network of paths, but we don't lay them all to begin with.'

'That's very sensible,' said Luca.

'Plants will be the next item on our list, but I propose we approach that separately after I've drawn up the border and flowerbed plans. We must decide where to add pergolas and trellises to give height at various focal points. Finally, you may wish to add benches, statues, bird baths or other ornaments.'

'You mentioned you had an idea for reducing the size of the garden?'

'I can show you more easily if we go over to the drawing table.'

I laid a piece of tracing paper over the survey plan and hastily traced the outline. 'As you see, the existing plot is a rectangle with the door in the centre of one of the longer walls. The pond and the grotto are such attractive features that it would be a shame not to include them in the design.

'We must have them,' said Luca.

'The entrance is on the opposite wall to the grotto, and the pond is halfway between them. By erecting two trellises, we can divide the rectangular plot into three. The central section, a square, becomes the flower garden.'

'So the new garden would have walls on only two sides: behind the grotto and the opposite wall with the entrance?'

'Exactly. Trellis screens could be planted with fast growing climbers, or we might make a pergola on each new boundary. Better still, both. Then, for the time being, the areas on either side of the newly formed flower garden might be used for making compost, raising seeds or an additional kitchen garden. There would be nothing to stop the other areas from being developed later.'

'I'd set my heart on restoring the whole garden,' said Luca. He sighed. 'But there's a great deal of merit in this idea. I had no idea before how much work was involved.

'I'd love to do all of it, but it's more sensible to direct our energies into making a smaller garden initially.'

'Once Sylvana sees how lovely it is,' said Luca, 'she may want to decide herself how the remaining areas are developed. I'll commission a plaque with the words "Sylvana's Garden" inscribed upon it.' His eyes shone with enthusiasm.

'I'll draw up the new sketch design,' I said, 'and we can measure out the plot in the morning.'

'Thank you so much for your willingness to work late, Violet, and to make these changes.' He stood up.

After he'd closed the door behind him, I turned back to the drawing table and placed a fresh piece of tracing paper over the plan. Sylvana's Garden, he'd called it. Once, it had been Flora's Garden. But how I wished it could be called Violet's Garden.

Chapter 18

Anticipation put a spring in my step as I sauntered down the woodland path towards the lake. It was March and the buds on the trees were fattening, the birds were singing and the ground was bejewelled with daffodils. I opened the wrought iron gate and walked past the boathouse to wait on the lakeside. Snow still capped the mountains, but the bright afternoon sunshine scattered twinkling stars over the surface of the water. Boats and ferries sailed by, their wash slapping at the jetty, but there was no sign of the boat I was looking for.

I'd missed Luca while he was away. In the evenings, we'd discuss the planting plans, and he'd fallen into the habit of coming to the garden whenever he could to see what progress had been made. One weekend, we caught the ferry to Varenna where he'd arranged for the head gardener at Villa Cipressi to show us the gardens. I couldn't have asked for a better employer, and that was my secret heartache. Not only was he my employer, but he was married and could never be more than a friend.

I shaded my eyes against the sun, and my heart lifted when I saw Massimo rowing Luca towards the jetty.

'Welcome back!' I called.

Luca waved to me as he disembarked, his face breaking into a wide smile when I hurried to greet him.

Massimo heaved Luca's suitcase from the boat and up onto the jetty. 'This is heavier than when you left,' he said.

'Did you get them, Luca?' I asked.

'I certainly did – and some new books.' He slung his overcoat over his shoulder and kissed my cheeks. 'Charming fellow, your Mr Coutts. He sends his kind regards.'

In January, I'd written to Kew Gardens to ask Mr Coutts if he would order packets of seeds and summer bulbs for Flora's garden. I'd enclosed a list and asked him to suggest other annuals that flowered in August. He'd been very obliging and interested in the project, and he even offered some additional planting ideas. Luca had arranged to spend a fortnight in London on business, so I'd asked him to call on Mr Coutts to collect the goods and settle the bill.

Luca glanced up at the blue sky. 'It's much warmer here than in London, where it rained every day.'

'Here, too,' said Massimo.

'We were worried the ground might be too waterlogged to sow the seeds,' I said, 'but it's been fine for three days now. We've managed to plant quite a lot of the flowering shrubs and climbers that we ordered. I can't wait to show you.'

Walking up the hill, the three of us chatted easily about what had been happening while Luca was away. When we arrived at the house, Massimo carried the suitcase upstairs, leaving me in the hall with Luca.

'I'll bring the seeds and bulbs to you in the library after I've spoken to my parents and grandfather,' he said.

'Shall we wait until after dinner? I must hurry back to the garden now to finish planting the lavender hedge before it gets dark. Will you have time in the morning to come and see what's happened since you left?'

He laughed. 'You couldn't keep me away. I've missed my visits to the garden,' he said. 'And I love to see your passion for it.'

I couldn't say that my passion for the garden was a replacement for the lack of passion in my private life. 'I love not only the exercise and being in the fresh air, but the thrill of seeing my planning and sketches come to life. It's a miracle that something as tiny as a seed can grow to make a beautiful flower, don't you think?'

There was a half-smile on Luca's face. 'A miracle,' he agreed.

'Edmund and Massimo are going to make a start on dredging the dead vegetation out of the pond tomorrow. It smells awful.'

There was a movement in the shadows of the hall, and Umberto appeared. 'I remember there were many beautiful white waterlilies covering the pond,' he said. 'You must not disturb the mud at the bottom of the pond, Signora Honeywell, or the lilies and the fish will not thrive.' He turned to Luca. 'Come and tell me if your meetings in London were successful. Did you make good sales?'

'We'll talk later, Luca,' I said. I left him with his grandfather and returned to the garden.

I walked along the central path towards the pond close to where Edmund was planting roses.

'Did Luca bring the seeds and bulbs?' he asked.

'He'll give them to me when he's unpacked.'

Edmund leaned on his spade. 'We've come such a long way from that day we first opened the door to an overgrown garden buried by over fifty years of neglect.'

I looked around. 'Where's Massimo?'

'In the potting shed washing seed trays.'

I left Edmund tending the rose bushes and returned to the path under one of the pergolas to finish setting out the lavender walk.

Vincenzo and Raimondo came to say goodnight before they left for the day. They clapped when I uttered a few well-rehearsed sentences in Italian. My comprehension was considerably better than my conversation, but I spent much of my free time working on the Italian grammar exercises Signor Romano set for me and pored over Italian newspapers and books in the library. Edmund joined me on Tuesday afternoons for Signor Romano's excellent lessons, and Luca and his parents provided us with conversation practice. I was even learning to animate my speech with the hand and body gestures that were an integral part of the Italian manner of communicating.

Dusk was falling when Edmund came to tell me he'd planted the last of the roses. 'I want to finish painting the flower border plans,' he said. 'We can show the watercolours to Luca after dinner.'

I sat back on my heels and watched him walk towards the garden door. How very different he was now from the traumatised young man who had returned from the battlefront. The physical exercise helped him sleep better, and working with his hands in peaceful surroundings had brought him contentment – though I had no doubt that the close proximity of Claudia also had something to do with that.

I was kneeling on the ground planting lavender when I heard measured footsteps crunching over the gravel. I looked up, expecting to see Massimo, but it was someone quite different: Umberto was walking along the path from the garden door.

He stopped to look at the newly planted rose bushes and peered into the pond. There couldn't have been much for him to see since it was still clogged with mud, brambles and weeds. He stood there in the gloaming for several minutes, and then continued along the path leading to the grotto. He sat down on the marble bench, covered his face with his hands and wept.

I remained very still in the shadow of the pergola, fearful of embarrassing us both by attracting his attention. Eventually, my knees were so uncomfortable I rose to my feet and tiptoed away.

'Flora!' Umberto's hoarse cry came from behind me. '*Sei tornato da me!*'

I glanced over my shoulder. He thought I was Flora and that I had returned to him.

He reached out to me. '*Non andare!*' he begged. '*Ritorno!*'

I fled, and Umberto's desperate cries echoed after me.

After all these years, it seemed that Umberto still mourned his beloved Flora and distress had caused him to imagine he'd seen her ghost.

After an early breakfast the following morning, I stowed the seed packets in a wicker basket and Luca accompanied me to Flora's garden. We paused in the doorway to survey the changes made while Luca was away. Paolo had nearly finished the paths and was raking the last load of gravel. The sound of Vincenzo and Raimondo sawing and hammering had punctuated the days from morning to night for the past weeks. Two new boundaries in the form of pergolas backed with trellis screens, divided the garden into three, as I'd suggested, with the flower garden in the central section.

'You've planted the azaleas since I was last here,' said Luca.

'They'll flower next month,' I said. 'Of course, they'll be over before your wife's birthday, but she'll be here next year to see them when they're established. We'll underplant them with colourful annuals that bloom in August. We've also planted camellias and hydrangeas, so there will be a succession of flowering shrubs next year. I've included bougainvillea. It's not grown in English gardens, but it's suited to this climate and flowers all summer.'

'The new timber obelisks are attractive, aren't they?' he said.

'I'm expecting a delivery of wisteria, roses, honeysuckle and clematis to climb over them. I've selected scented varieties where possible.'

'The garden is really taking shape now.' Luca's eyes shone. 'The perfume will be marvellous. And Edmund and Massimo are going to start clearing the pond today?'

'I want it to be ready for when the specialist nursery sends us the waterlilies and pond margin plants.'

'We must have fish, too.' Luca sighed. 'How I wish I could stay here all day, but I mustn't miss the ferry. I have meetings at the factory.'

'The garden will develop quickly with the advent of warmer weather, so there will be more to see before very long,' I promised.

'Then I leave it in your capable hands.' His gaze swept over the garden. 'I'm so thankful I found you, Violet. You bring the essence of an English cottage garden to the planting that will be very special here. In Italy, a formal garden replete with cascades and classical statuary is considered a work of art but it has little to do with a passion for flowers.

I laughed. 'I'm not sure that's a compliment.'

'Believe me, it is.' He glanced at his watch. 'I must hurry, but I'll see you at dinner.'

I watched him sprint along the path with his words still echoing in my mind. *I'm so thankful I found you, Violet.* Of course, he was only referring to my usefulness as a garden designer and not to any womanly charms I might have. My heart ached, conscious I would spend the rest of my days without the comfort of a man's love.

Massimo was waiting for me in the kitchen garden glasshouse. 'I've cleared this side of the staging for you.' He shrugged. 'I don't use it all these days. The household is smaller than before the war when there were many servants to feed.'

'One day, the greenhouse we discovered in the flower garden will be restored,' I said. 'In the interim, perhaps Luca might make funds available for Vincenzo to construct some cold frames behind the pergolas in the part of the garden we aren't using yet.'

'Come to the potting shed,' said Massimo, 'and I'll show you the seed trays and the sacks of well-rotted potting compost for your use.' He grinned. 'Beppe always takes great pride in his compost heap.'

After he'd made sure I had everything I needed, Massimo returned to Flora's garden to work with Edmund to clear the pond.

I hummed to myself as I selected the packets of seeds that needed to be sown first, imagining the colour and fragrance to come in the summer. I set out the trays and began to fill and level them with the rich dark compost.

Later, the glasshouse door creaked open and Beppe hobbled in to see me.

'What good compost this is,' I said.

'Black gold.' He ran his fingers through the crumbly soil in the sack. 'We have many fallen leaves and barrow loads of lawn cuttings at Villa Marchese. Nothing is wasted, not even the peelings from the vegetables in the kitchen. The trick is to turn the compost every two weeks.'

'We must have a permanent place for a compost heap in the flower garden,' I said. 'Perhaps behind the pergola near to where we'll have the cold frames? In fact, I should decide now exactly where it's to be. Massimo and Edmund are clearing the pond, and the rotting vegetation will make a good starter for the heap.'

'I will come with you and say the best place.'

I could decide this for myself, but it would do no harm to listen to his advice. 'Let me write a label for these antirrhinum seeds, and then we'll take a look.'

A few minutes later, we went to the flower garden where Massimo and Edmund were busy dragging a fallen sapling out of the pond.

I opened the discreet new gate in the trellis under the pergola, and we entered the utility area.

Beppe clicked his tongue while he thought. 'There must be sun to warm the compost and it must be near to the gate, but not too close to the flower garden in case it smells.' He caught hold of my sleeve and drew me to one corner of the garden. 'Here, by the wall,' he said. His face broke into a gap-toothed smile. 'Vincenzo will make wooden sides, and I will bring you a present of manure from the stable to make it rot more quickly.'

I fluttered my eyelashes and simpered. 'A beautiful present from a handsome man. What more could a girl desire?'

Beppe roared with laughter.

The air was suddenly rent by terrible screams. Beppe and I froze, staring at each other.

'Edmund!' I knew he needed my help and raced helter-skelter back to the walled garden.

There was no sign of Massimo, but my brother was floundering chest-deep in the pond. Smothered in black mud and caught in tangled brambles and brushwood, he was in a frenzy, fighting to free himself.

Beppe shouted for Massimo.

I quickly climbed over the pond wall and plunged into the water. Thick mud oozed unpleasantly over the top of my boots. Tripping and stumbling, I thrust my body through brushwood and the accumulated sediment of decades of decaying vegetation. The sides of the pond sloped, and I lost my footing on the edge of a step, falling onto my front. Every inch of me was covered in stinking mud as I pushed myself to my feet, ignoring the thorns and twigs snagged in my hair and tearing at my coat.

'Edmund!' I yelled, but his fear rendered him unable to hear me. Screams faded to guttural moans as he flailed his arms to fight off some unknown threat, lost in the terrifying world of his war memories.

He wasn't far from me, and I tried not to panic as I shoved my way through the tangled mess of roots and stems enmeshing my ankles and impeding my progress. At the very moment despair paralysed me in its grip, I glimpsed Massimo clambering into the pond.

'Stay still, Violet,' he called. 'I am coming to help.'

I fought through the entanglements with renewed vigour until, at last, I reached Edmund. I wrapped my arms tightly around him and rocked him against my chest.

He tried to fight me off but then shuddered violently and went limp and silent. I staggered to keep my balance under his weight.

Massimo heaved Edmund onto his back and struggled to the side of the pond with my brother across his shoulders.

Close to tears, I stood motionless to catch my breath. Something rounded and pale lay half-buried in the black mud before me. I pushed it out of my way and it turned over. My breath stopped when I realised what it was.

A human skull stared back at me from empty eye sockets.

Chapter 19

Helen was marvellous. She took one look at Edmund's wild eyes and shaking limbs and instructed Lucrezia and Claudia to make up a camp bed by the fire in the library. 'He's too heavy to carry upstairs to the tower bedroom, Massimo.'

I'd shed my muddy coat and boots outside before we entered the hall, but I was still shivering and filthy from head to toe with sodden socks and my hair hanging down my back in rat's tails. 'We must inform the police,' I said.

'Nonsense!' said Helen. 'That skull must have been there for years and it can wait perfectly well until after Edmund is in bed. Massimo, will you rest Edmund on the hall bench until his bed is ready?'

'I'll fetch a basin and wash him,' I said. I stroked the hair from my brother's muddy forehead, hoping to still his incessant trembling, but he was still lost somewhere in his nightmare world.

Helen shook her head. 'Go and take a bath, Violet. Massimo can help me undress your brother. I'll wash him.'

'Oh but—'

'Violet, I was never able to help my Teodore before he died so,

185

please, don't deprive me of a chance to care for Edmund.' Her chin quivered and tears welled in her eyes.

I nodded and went to bathe.

Later, clean again with hair still wet, I found Helen sitting beside Edmund's camp bed in the library. He lay curled up on his side with his hands over his ears and his eyes tight shut.

'Massimo has gone home to change,' murmured Helen. 'He'll fetch the doctor from Bellagio and inform the authorities of what has been found.'

I rested my hand on Edmund's trembling shoulder, and it brought tears to my eyes to see him flinch at my touch. 'He's been so much better. Until this . . .'

'Was it the skull that terrified him so?'

'I imagine so. During the war, he was trapped in a shell hole along with the dead and horrifically maimed body of a comrade-in-arms. The shelling was relentless, and he couldn't escape.' I swallowed. 'When he tried to bury the dead man, he dug into the waterlogged soil with his bare hands and uncovered the putrid body of another soldier. That was when he lost his reason.'

Helen gasped.

'So, I imagine wading through the heavy mud in the pond today brought it all back – especially if he saw the skull.'

'The poor boy!' She shook her head. 'What puzzles me is where the skull came from. Did a person drown in the pond, and if so, where is the rest of the body? Or did someone throw it in there?'

'Why would they do that, and where would they have found a skull?'

Shrugging, Helen said, 'A medical student, perhaps? I don't ever remember hearing of anyone going missing from the house or even from the town.'

The door handle rattled, and Claudia carried in a tea tray. 'There is sugar in the tea to help the shock.' All the time she spoke, her gaze was fixed on Edmund.

'That was thoughtful, Claudia,' said Helen.

'I brought three cups. I wasn't sure if Edmund wanted tea.' She flicked a glance at my brother again.

'He couldn't manage it at the moment,' I said.

Claudia looked at Edmund's fingers, ceaselessly twitching, and nodded her head. Tears in her eyes, she closed the door quietly behind her.

Sometime later, the doctor arrived and Helen explained what had happened.

He examined Edmund but couldn't persuade him to speak. Taking a small bottle out of his bag, he handed it to Helen and, as far as I could understand, gave her instructions on the dosage. He was just closing his bag when loud voices came from the hall.

Helen tipped her head to listen and then asked the doctor to wait while she went to see what was happening. A moment later, I heard her arguing with a man.

The door opened, and a policeman entered the library with Helen a step behind. He strode over to Edmund and looked down at his shaking body before questioning the doctor. They had an animated conversation, and eventually, the policeman gave a heavy sigh and then gestured to me to follow him.

Massimo was waiting for us in the hall with another uniformed officer, and he explained to me that I was to go with them to give my version of events. 'Don't worry,' he said. 'I will translate the questions.'

The four of us trooped back to the pond in the walled garden, and Massimo described what he'd seen.

My eyes were fixed upon the skull I'd placed at the edge of the pond when I'd climbed out of it earlier. There was a large crack across the back, and I couldn't help but wonder if it had been the cause of death.

Then, with Massimo to translate, the uniformed officer asked me for my version of events. Afterwards, he dismissed me, but I heard him questioning Massimo again as I left the garden.

Walking past the gardeners' cottages, Beppe hurried outside. 'How is Edmund?' he asked. His deep-set eyes were full of concern.

'Very shocked,' I said.

'And you?'

I ran a hand wearily over my face and shrugged. 'I'm worried for Edmund. His mental state had improved so much, but I don't know what damage this incident will have caused to his peace of mind.'

Beppe patted my hand. 'He is young and strong, and you will make him well again.'

I hoped he was right, but at the moment Edmund didn't even know when I was near him. My heart ached as I returned to the house to sit beside him.

That evening, Luca returned from Como. He came with Helen to the library to see Edmund. He bent over my brother's recumbent form and murmured a few words, but Edmund didn't stir.

'You've been here all afternoon, Violet,' said Helen. 'I'll take your place for a while, and you can go outside for some fresh air.'

'Come,' said Luca. 'We'll walk round the garden together.'

We went out from the loggia and followed the path between the parterre and through the archway in the yew hedge.

Water gushed from the statue of Neptune entwined with his water sprites, and the glorious flamboyance of the ensemble lifted my spirits a little. We climbed the steep path beside the cascade to the highest point of the garden, and the air was cool now that the sun was dipping in the sky.

Luca led me to the Roman-style temple, and we sat on the bench inside.

'The *carabinieri* have cordoned off the flower garden while they search the pond,' said Luca. 'I suppose they think they might find a skeleton buried in the mud.'

I shuddered at the thought.

'Poor Edmund has had a dreadful setback,' he said, 'but we'll all do what we can to help him recover.'

'Your mother has been very kind to him. To both of us.'

'Edmund is sensitive, just as Teodore was. Mamma is still grieving and angry at the manner of my brother's death.' Luca rubbed at his eyes as if he was deeply exhausted. 'We're *all* angry that he was taken from us in such a way and believe it was a gross injustice. He was ill and needed care and compassion but instead . . .' Unable to continue, he blinked rapidly and stared at the view of the lake and mountains beyond the villa.

The setting sun suffused the sky with pink and apricot light and washed the lake with a copper glow. The silhouetted mountain ranges were slate-blue, and as we watched, pinpoints of glimmering lights appeared on the opposite shoreline and in the villages on the mountainside.

'I loved the excitement of living in Florence,' he said, 'but sometimes, I would picture this view of the lake and experience a deep longing to be sitting here.'

'If Villa Marchese was my family home,' I said, 'I'd never want to leave.'

'I never expected to take Teodore's place in the business, so I'd concentrated my efforts on making a life for myself elsewhere. When he died, I was completely unprepared to step into his role. I was angry and resentful that the life I'd been building for myself had been snatched away.' Dead leaves rustled as he moved his feet. 'I'm aware of how selfish that sounds when I escaped injury while my brother suffered and died. He'd been trained from boyhood to manage the estate and business, and so far, I've fallen short of what my grandfather requires of me. I feel so guilty that I wasn't the one who died.'

'You must not think like that,' I said. 'I'm sure many of us who survived the war find it difficult to rebuild our lives and have to learn to live under quite different circumstances. Myself included.'

Luca turned to face me. 'How did you expect your life would be?'

It hurt to think about it. 'I wanted to be a good wife for William.' I pictured him in my mind for a moment: sturdily built, calm and kind. 'My father and stepmother decried his lack of ambition, but he was good with his hands – a cabinet maker – and a steadfast Quaker. His religion meant that he was a conscientious objector. Others despised him for it, but he died a hero on the battlefield. We would have had a little house with a garden – and children. A simple life, but we would have been happy.'

'Oh, Violet!' Luca took my hands and held them between his own. 'You didn't ask for much, and it's cruel that even that has been denied to you. I wish—'

I couldn't bear him to pity me. I pulled my hands away and gave him a brittle smile. 'I've lost my husband, and there's no going back. Now, I've dedicated my life to Edmund's health and welfare. And to gardening, which brings me contentment.'

We sat in pensive silence watching the sky turn ultramarine while the sun sank behind the mountains.

I stood up. 'I must go to Edmund.'

'Of course,' said Luca. We set off down the hillside to the villa.

The following morning, Helen crept into the library where I'd dozed in a chair beside Edmund all night.

'How is he?' she whispered.

'He had bad dreams during the night,' I said, 'but he knew me when I shook him awake. I managed to settle him back to sleep.'

'Go and have some breakfast, Violet. You look exhausted. I'll stay with him for a couple of hours.'

I glanced at Edmund, and since he was sleeping soundly, I went to wash and change my clothes. The face that looked back at me from the bathroom mirror was pale and hollow-eyed.

In the dining room, I sipped at a cup of strong coffee and ate the hot roll Claudia brought to me.

'How is Edmund?' she asked.

'Perhaps a little better,' I said.

'May I see him?'

I hesitated. Edmund was vulnerable, and I didn't care to have him become reliant on Claudia. It would be too dreadful if he fell in love with her and she didn't have the same depth of feeling for him. 'Signora Marchese is with him,' I said. 'He's asleep, but you could look in on him for a few minutes, if you like.'

'Thank you.'

Luca came into the dining room and sat beside me to eat his breakfast. 'Shall we go and take a look at what the *carabinieri* are doing?'

It was good to be out in the spring sunshine as we walked to the flower garden. We weren't allowed in but peered over the shoulder of the police officer guarding the entrance. Their men had dredged several heaps of reeking mud, brushwood and vegetation out of the pond. I didn't envy them the task.

'What a foul job,' said Luca. He smiled mischievously. 'At least they're saving Massimo and Edmund the trouble.'

I shuddered. 'I'll finish the job myself. I couldn't possibly ask Edmund to do it.'

Luca's expression sobered. 'No, of course not. None of us would ask that of him, and I wouldn't subject you to it again either, not after what happened. Massimo can ask a couple of the men to come back and help him.'

We returned to the house and found Edmund was still sleeping. Helen volunteered to stay with him while she read her book. 'I'll send for you if he wakes,' she said, 'but you should get some fresh air if you intend to spend the night beside him again.'

I was anxious about sowing the rest of the seeds before it was too late, so I returned to the potting shed in the vegetable garden.

It was late afternoon when Massimo came to find me in the glasshouse, where I had laid out the seed trays on the staging.

'They've found something,' he said. 'We are all to wait in the house.'

'What was it?'

He shook his head. 'They did not say. Perhaps more bones.'

Subdued by that grisly thought, we walked back to the house.

The servants huddled together at one side of the hall, and Massimo went to speak to Claudia and Beppe. Luca and Orlando came out of the study with Umberto, and I went to see Edmund in the library.

'How is he?' I asked.

Helen rose to her feet from the chair at my brother's bedside. 'He woke for a few minutes and drank some water. He started to shake again, but I stroked his forehead and he went back to sleep so I didn't send for you. I haven't needed to give him the sedative the doctor left.'

'I can't thank you enough for your kindness,' I said.

We joined the others in the hall.

The police officer who had questioned me earlier called us into the dining room. Once we were gathered together, he started to speak. I couldn't follow it all, but the group let out a murmur of consternation.

'They've found some bones,' Helen whispered to me. 'Ongoing work will determine if there's a whole skeleton in the pond.'

Umberto pointed a finger at Luca. '*È colpa tua!*'

'It isn't my fault, Nonno—'

Umberto interrupted him with a flood of Italian, and his accusatory tone made Helen catch her breath.

'What is it?' I asked.

'Umberto says he locked Flora's garden all those years ago to be a shrine to his wife's memory, and Luca has brought disgrace on this house through his meddling.'

'But that's completely unfair!'

Luca entered into a heated argument with Umberto, their voices rising and their hands gesticulating wildly as each attempted to make their point.

The police officer banged his fist on the dining table. '*Silenzio!*'

An uneasy silence fell.

The police officer took a small object from his pocket. It was a gold ring with initials incised into a carnelian. He placed it on a sheet of paper on the dining table beside a stick of sealing wax and a box of matches. Lighting the wick of the sealing wax, he dripped it into a red puddle on the paper. He pressed the ring into the wax and gently lifted it away, leaving an imprint of the initials behind. He beckoned at us all to come closer and then asked a question.

'It was on a finger bone they found in the pond,' said Helen. 'He wants to know if anyone recognises the ring.'

I peered at it, but of course, I'd never seen it before. I shook my head and stepped back.

Orlando lifted the paper up to read the initials on the wax impression. 'GM.' He turned to Umberto and posed him a question in Italian.

'What is he saying?' I whispered to Helen.

'My husband is asking if these are the same initials as he's seen on some old documents in the safe.'

Umberto pulled at one of his bushy eyebrows and nodded.

Orlando spoke to the police officer, who nodded at Luca.

Luca left the room.

Umberto cleared his throat noisily and held up his hand to catch the officer's attention.

He spoke too quickly for me to understand it all, but I gathered he knew something about the ring.

Helen listened intently and then frowned. 'He thinks the ring belonged to Gabriele Marchese – his stepbrother.'

'Flora's first husband?' I said. 'But he died in the Battle of Solferino, didn't he?'

Helen frowned. 'Perhaps he left the ring behind when he joined Garibaldi's volunteers? Someone else might have been wearing it when they drowned in the pond.'

Beppe threw his hands up in the air and let out a torrent of Italian. Lucrezia nodded her head several times and added another comment.

Helen pressed a hand to her chest.

'What is it?'

'Beppe said Isabella believed she saw her father in the garden two years after he died. Lucrezia said Isabella told her the same story, but no one believed the little girl.'

'And now,' I said slowly, 'Isabella is dead, and there's no way of finding out the truth.'

'Unless someone confesses to murdering him,' said Helen.

Chapter 20

At six o'clock on a May morning, it was barely light when I opened the door to the glasshouse in the kitchen garden. I walked along the rows of seed trays, prodding the compost beneath the seedlings to see if it needed watering and examining leaves for signs of pests or disease. Satisfied all was in order, I carried selected trays, two at a time, to the waiting handcart outside. When it was fully loaded, I trundled off with my delicate cargo down the Rhododendron Walk.

Listening to the dawn chorus was a glorious way to start the day, despite the shrill accompaniment of the cartwheels grinding along the path. It surprised me to find the door to Flora's garden ajar, but then I saw Beppe inside leaning over the pond.

'*Buon giorno*, Beppe!' I called, and he turned to wave at me. I left the cart and went to speak to him.

'Do you see?' he said, pointing into the water.

I repressed a shudder at the memory of what had previously been concealed in the black mud; but now, two months after the bones had been discovered, the pond was restored. The water was clear, and flat saucers of waterlily leaves floated on the surface. 'The lilies are growing well,' I said.

'Look!'

And then I saw it: a flash of orange, followed by another.

Beppe laughed. 'A present for you. Twenty goldfish.'

'How lovely!' I said. 'Oh, wouldn't Flora have loved to see them here again?'

'And Isabella. She was so excited when her mamma bought fish for the pond.'

We watched the goldfish gliding around in their new home and a water boatman sculling across the water. I smiled at how the fish and insects brought the pond to life again.

'I have something else to show you,' said Beppe. 'Would you like to see the letters Isabella wrote to me after she was sent away to school?'

'You kept them all this time?'

Shrugging, he said, 'She was my friend. I will bring them to you later.'

'I'd love to see them,' I said, 'but now I'd better get on with the planting.'

I pushed the handcart into the part of the garden we'd screened off. Vincenzo had made three wooden compost bins against the wall and also several cold frames, which were full of seed trays and pots of plants. The risk of night frosts had passed now, so the glazed lids were propped open to allow the young plants to harden off. I lifted all the antirrhinums out of the frame and replaced them with seedlings I'd brought from the glasshouse.

Returning to the flower garden, I planted out the antirrhinums in the areas I'd allocated for them.

An hour or so later, Beppe returned with Isabella's letters. We sat on the marble bench, and he squinted at one of the envelopes. 'The first one,' he said. 'It is a mystery because I never discovered how the letters arrived. Each time, I found them on the doorstep.'

I wiped my hands on my breeches and carefully unfolded the first letter. It had been read and refolded so many times that it had separated in places along the creases. 'I may need some help,' I said. I began to read the letter aloud, translating it into English as I went. Beppe obliged with any words I didn't understand.

October 1862

Dear Beppe

I am sorry I didn't say goodbye to you, but I didn't know I was being sent away to school until the moment Madre Marchese pushed me in the carriage. I am trying to remember the sunny days and our joyful times together in the garden before Mamma drowned and my stepfather locked the garden door. Everything is so different now.

I faltered as I struggled to read the next sentence where the faded ink was smudged; by tears, I imagined.

This school is a horrible place. I cry myself to sleep every night. I'm so homesick, but without Mamma, there is no home for me.

I miss you Beppe.

Isabella

I folded the paper and returned it to Beppe. 'My heart aches for that sad little girl,' I said. 'She died so long ago, but her pain lives on in that letter.'

Beppe nodded. 'It upset me until she wrote again.' He handed me the second missive, which was little more than a hastily scribbled note.

August 1863

Dear Beppe

*I wanted you to know I am no longer homesick, and I am
happy in my new home. I shall not see you again, but I will never
forget you. I picture us sitting together under the fig tree, waving
away the wasps and cramming our mouths with the juicy fruit.
Those were good days, weren't they?*

Isabella

'There were no more letters,' said Beppe. 'She didn't come home
from school for the summer, but perhaps she was happy again
because she had a new friend there.' He tucked the letters into his
waistcoat pocket. 'But it always troubled me. Did she have a vision
that she was to die? She was so certain we would never meet again.'

After Beppe left me to work in the kitchen garden, I imagined
him running through the garden with Isabella and laughing
together all those years ago. At least she'd finally settled into her
school and was contented for what was left of her short life.

I picked up my trowel again and daydreamed about how beautiful the garden would be once the flowers bloomed. By the time I
firmed the earth over the roots of the last antirrhinum, the sun was
hot on my shoulders. Behind me, I heard footsteps on the gravel,
and I looked up to see Edmund and Luca approaching.

'Edmund!' I said. 'I didn't expect to see you here.' It had taken
my brother two weeks to recover sufficiently from the shock of
finding the skull before he could rise from his bed. Claudia had sat
with him whenever she could escape her duties, and I'd frequently
heard her singing to him. It had been several more weeks until he
was able to leave his room in the tower to sit in the shelter of the
loggia on sunny spring days.

'Luca persuaded me to take a walk,' he said.

'Perhaps you'd like to sit on the bench in the grotto for a while?' said Luca. 'The garden is so peaceful, and I'm sure it will do you good.'

'It will.' Edmund looked around. 'So much has happened since I was last here. I'm sorry I haven't been able to assist you, Violet.'

'Massimo and Beppe helped when they could spare some time from working in the villa's grounds,' I said. 'And Helen picked out and watered some of the seedlings.' I smiled at Luca. 'Your mother has discovered she enjoys gardening.'

'So she told me. Raising plants from seed fascinates her. Apparently, it's far more interesting than managing the lawns, shrubs and trees in the grounds.'

'I can't help but agree.'

'The roses, honeysuckle, jasmine and clematis on the pergola are looking good,' said Edmund, 'but they're still quite small.'

'They'll fill out with the passing of the years,' I said. I decided to risk drawing my brother's attention to the pond. 'Come and look at the goldfish.' I took his hand when he hesitated. 'The pond has been completely emptied, cleaned and planted with waterlilies. The water is beautifully clear, and Beppe brought the fish this morning as a surprise for me.' Gently, I led him to the pond.

He stood very still looking into the depths of the water. 'It looks ...' he blinked rapidly, '... quite different from how I remember it.'

'It is,' I said. 'Now it's teeming with life.'

He nodded and wandered off towards the grotto.

I watched him until he sat down on the bench. My tension drained away.

Luca cast his eye over the borders and flowerbeds. 'You've worked tirelessly, Violet,' he said, 'but there are still large areas unplanted. I know it's been difficult to complete as much as you intended without Edmund and Massimo's full-time help.'

'The borders aren't as empty as they look,' I said, hearing the defensive tone in my voice. 'Let me show you.'

We walked along the paths, and I pointed out where swathes of the rich, dark soil were hazed with green from emerging seedlings. 'To begin with, we have poppies, nasturtiums, gillyflowers, Love-in-a Mist and, just for fun, sunflowers. Then, those large pots near the back of the border are planted with lilies in pink, white and sunset yellow.'

'I remember those from my English grandmother's garden in Oxford,' said Luca. 'They have a wonderful fragrance.'

'I've selected perfumed plants wherever possible,' I said. 'There are night scented stock, which have insignificant blooms but an intense perfume. I've planted them amongst stock with colourful but unscented blooms in magenta, white, mauve and purple. And come and look at this! Do you see the sweet peas twining up this obelisk? The perfume will be breath-taking.'

'But will these tiny seedlings fill the borders?' asked Luca.

'The first season in this garden is challenging,' I admitted. 'I've relied heavily on flowering shrubs, climbers and annual seeds to keep within budget. It's labour intensive to grow so much from seed, so as far as the funds allow, I've planted bulbs and rhizomes, like irises, that will come back year after year. The dahlias, for example, will grow into big bushy plants by midsummer and provide large flowers right through to the first frosts.'

'So, if you planted more perennial plants into the garden each year, in time, fewer seeds would be needed?'

I nodded.

'If you remember, I made a useful business contact in Florence after Christmas. Well, I've recently signed a lucrative contract with this new client, so I can fund some extra plants. Perhaps you could go to the nursery with Massimo to buy what you think will make the most impact here?'

200

'That's marvellous, Luca. Congratulations!'

He laughed. 'I admit I'm relieved, and I hope that will keep Nonno happy for a while.'

I wondered if anything would ever make Luca's grandfather happy. 'I've concentrated on flowers that will bloom in August for your wife's birthday, but some perennial plants will make the garden look more established this year and give a head start for next ...' My voice trailed away. 'Oh, do look, Luca!'

On the other side of the garden, Edmund was kneeling beside a flowerbed and pulling up weeds.

Luca grinned at me. 'It seems the garden is working its magic on him. He barely flinched when you took him to see the pond.'

'It was a risk, but he seems to have faced his fears. I confess, what happened gave me some nightmares, too.'

'The police appear to have closed the file,' he said, 'but I wish we knew for sure if the bones belonged to Gabriele Marchese or to someone who came into possession of his ring before coming to an unfortunate end. I want to know what happened to Gabriele. There are so many unanswered questions and I hope the police can find the answers. Besides, if the bones belong to my grandmother's first husband, I'd like to ensure they have a proper burial in the family plot.'

'Meanwhile,' I said, 'there's so much to do in the garden I hardly know where to begin.'

'The evenings are growing longer each day,' said Luca. 'I'll finish work early whenever I can, and you can teach me how to prick out seedlings.'

The following morning, Helen brought Caroline Pierucci to visit and see how the work was progressing in Flora's garden.

'Oh my!' she said as she took it all in. 'It's smaller than I remembered, but it's going to be so beautiful. I'm pleased you've kept the pond and the grotto.'

'Mrs Honeywell uncovered the grotto,' said Helen. 'It nearly killed her when a piece of rock crashed down upon her head. And you heard what happened when her brother started to clear the pond.'

'How is he now?' Signora Pierucci asked me.

'Thankfully, he's recovering,' I said. 'He's over there tying the wisteria to the pergola; do you see?'

'I remember how difficult it was for my husband to return to a normal life after he came back from the fighting,' she said. 'Did the police discover how a skeleton came to be in the pond?'

Helen shook her head. 'There's no confirmation on whether it was Gabriele Marchese, either.'

'I'm going on my annual visit to the Conti family next week,' said Signora Pierucci. She turned to me. 'Adriano Conti, Gabriele Marchese and my husband Domenico were all local men who joined the Hunters of the Alps together to fight against the Austrians. Adriano was the only one of the three who walked away from the Battle of Solferino unscathed. Later, he moved to Turin and married Liliana, a local girl there. Domenico and I visited them every year. I still do.'

'Might Adriano shed any light on what could have happened to Gabriele?' asked Helen.

'I doubt it. There was such confusion. Besides, Domenico saw Gabriele's body. He said it was impossible anyone could have survived such a dreadful injury, especially since there were so few doctors.' Signora Pierucci shuddered. 'Enough of sad memories! Will you walk me round your garden, Mrs Honeywell?'

'Gladly,' I said. 'Perhaps you might remember if Flora had any favourite flowers? I'd love to plant them in her memory.'

She thought for a moment and then said, 'There was one that

was particularly special to her. It was a *Dicentra Spectabilis*. She planted it by the grotto in memory of her husband.'

'*Dicentra Spectabilis*,' I echoed. 'Of course! Its other name is Bleeding Heart because it has heart-shaped rose pink flowers hanging from arched stems.'

'An appropriate choice for a grieving widow.'

It pleased me a great deal that, as Flora's close friend, Signora Pierucci showed interest in the garden. I was delighted when she asked if she might visit again after she returned from her visit to the Conti family.

Helen and Signora Pierucci returned to the house, and I went to find Massimo, who was cutting the grass on the steep hillside beside the temple.

He put down his scythe and smiled widely when he saw me approaching. '*Ciao*, Violet.'

'Hot work?' His shirtsleeves were rolled up to expose his muscular forearms, and dark hair curled out of the open neck of his shirt. I found myself blushing in the face of such vigorous masculinity.

'It will be hotter next month,' he said, mopping his forehead.

'Do you have time to accompany me to the nursery? Luca has given me the funds for some additional plants.'

'When shall we go? I will need half an hour to make myself fit to accompany a lady.'

In the afternoon, we took a ferry to Lenno and then walked to the edge of the town where a nursery, specialising in herbaceous plants, was located. Signor Cocci, the owner of the nursery, showed us his extensive stock and, using my faltering Italian with Massimo to assist, I chose some hardy and drought-tolerant salvias with spires of purple flowers, agapanthus in both blue and white, purple sage and Michaelmas daisies in pink, purple and mauve.

'I'm planning a rainbow border,' I said, and Signor Cocci seemed interested in my idea of planting drifts of herbaceous flowers in shades of white, violet and indigo blue, moving from the cool colours to pink, orange, red and yellow and then back to white.

'Then you will need plants with warmer colours, too,' said Massimo.

Signor Cocci picked out some canna lilies, red hot pokers and daylilies.

'And you have already sown marigolds and nasturtiums,' said Massimo.

'There's one last plant I'm looking for,' I said. 'A *Dicentra Spectabilis.*'

Signor Cocci selected a fine specimen, and I examined it carefully before he placed it with my other purchases.

He nodded in approval, and I was flattered when he said that if ever I wanted to work in a plant nursery, I should come and speak to him first.

I thanked him, and Massimo nudged me as we left. 'You've made a friend,' he said, a twinkle in his eye.

An hour later we were waiting to board the steamer back to Bellagio. Massimo carried the pot planted with the Bleeding Heart.

'That was a very successful expedition,' I said. 'I'm so pleased the rest of the plants will be delivered as soon as tomorrow. They'll make such an improvement to the rainbow border.'

The small crowd waiting to embark moved forward and, since we didn't have far to go, we found a place to stand on deck. The boat steamed away from the jetty, and we rested our forearms on the ship's rail with the potted plant wedged firmly between Massimo's feet. The sky was blue, the lake shimmered and glittered in the sunshine and a warm breeze stirred my hair. I let out a sigh of contentment.

Massimo's eyes were smiling as he watched me tuck a loose strand of hair back under the brim of my hat. 'What a pity we must return to work now,' he said. 'Perhaps once the garden is finished, we might have a day's holiday? We could take Edmund and Claudia in the rowing boat for a picnic along the lakeshore.'

'I'd like that,' I said. It would be something to look forward to once the garden was no longer mine but belonged to Luca's wife.

Luca was as good as his word and came as often as he could in the evenings to help me with the watering, planting and tying in of the climbers. I loved those hours of quiet companionship, talking while we worked side by side. We never ran out of things to say and discussed books, philosophy, gardening history and Roman civilisation – one of Luca's passions.

'And how is your book coming along?' I asked.

'I'm more than halfway through the first draft,' he said. 'It's an absorbing hobby.'

'Will you allow me to read it?'

He hesitated. 'It's a story of unrequited love. I want to finish the first draft but then, I'll welcome comments.'

Cocooned in the warmth of the glasshouse while the sun set, we lit the oil lamps to give us more time when it became too dark to see what we were doing. Luca insisted I practise my Italian and helped me with my pronunciation. There were moments of merriment when I made mistakes. He explained that the importance of the Italian hand gestures had come about through a long history of being invaded by many other nationalities. 'They imposed their own language and customs on our people, and hand gestures were developed as a means of communication amongst those with no common language,' he said.

As each day passed, time spent in Luca's company grew more and more precious to me, Sometimes I would look up from my work and see that he was watching me so intently that I was covered in confusion, but also secretly pleased. I was forced to acknowledge to myself that I'd made the ill-advised mistake of falling in love with my employer. I clung to my fragile happiness although I knew it couldn't – mustn't – last. In three months' time, Sylvana would come to Villa Marchese to take her rightful place at her husband's side – and in his bed.

Chapter 21

The July sun was at its zenith and my back was roasting as I rooted out bindweed in the rose garden. Cursing under my breath, I disentangled the tendrils that had twined so tightly around the stems of the hybrid teas and threw them in a bucket to be burned. The rose bushes needed to be dead-headed again, too, if we were to have new blooms for mid-August. I thrust my border fork into the earth and wiped perspiration from my brow.

Edmund was pushing a wheelbarrow heaped with weeds along the path towards the compost heap. 'Hot, isn't it?' he called out. He wore a battered straw hat, and he looked healthy and strong again.

'Much hotter than it usually is in London in July,' I said. I joined him in the shade under the fig tree.

'I'm so glad I'm not stuck in some poky, little back office in Father's bank.' He laughed, his teeth white against his now tanned complexion. 'I'm never going to work indoors again, if I can help it. I never dreamed I'd ever become a gardener, but I'm so glad I've had this opportunity to learn.'

'And just look at what we've achieved!' I waved a hand at the burgeoning blooms set against the backdrop of swathes of purple bougainvillea scrambling over the trellises. 'All the hard work was worthwhile; don't you think?'

'Luca will be pleased with our progress when he returns on Monday.'

'Yes,' I said. I didn't want to think about Luca's visit to Florence. Although he'd gone there for a business meeting, it tormented me to imagine him sharing a romantic dinner afterwards with Sylvana.

'I've worked up an appetite,' said Edmund. 'I wonder if the figs are ready yet?' He plucked a fruit from the tree above us and bit into it.

I laughed when he spat it out again in disgust. 'They're still green, aren't they? I tried them myself a few days ago.'

'Come on, then. It's time to go in for lunch.' He lifted the handles of the wheelbarrow and set off again.

I picked up my bucket of bindweed and followed him.

After lunch, we returned to our rooms to rest. We'd fallen into the continental habit of starting work early, while it was still cool, and then taking a nap in the heat of the day before returning to the garden and working on until dusk. I removed the loose linen dress I wore for gardening when the weather was hot and dispensed with my bust bodice and corset. I decided not to put them on again when I returned to work and lay on the bed in only my petticoat. The shutters were closed to keep out the heat, and I drifted off almost immediately.

I awoke an hour later and sat drowsily on the edge of the bed, listening to a fly butting its head against the window. The room was stuffy, and while I was buttoning my dress, I thought how lovely it would be to go down to the lake and paddle in cool water before returning to work.

Picking up my sunhat, I went to tap on Edmund's door. 'Are you awake?' I called. There was no answer. I opened the door gently so as not to startle him, but the room was empty with the bed neatly made. I assumed he'd returned to work already and went down the tower stairs and outside.

It was too hot to hurry, but I was soon in the dappled shade of the woodland path that took me down to the lake and the boat-house. I removed my shoes and unrolled my stockings, leaving them both on the stony beach. The water was deliciously cool and clear where it lapped around my ankles. A ferryboat steamed by, and a moment later, its wash undulated over the surface of the lake. I had to lift my skirt as the water rose to my knees.

The overheated air was stirred by an onshore breeze, but the sun still beat down on my shoulders, and the back of my neck was damp with perspiration. I longed to float on the cool water, but I hadn't brought my ancient bathing costume to Italy with me. In the distance, a sailing boat tacked across the water and another ferry docked on the opposite side of the lake.

All at once, I couldn't stand the heat any longer. Unbuttoning my dress, I pulled it over my head and threw it on top of my hat and shoes at the water's edge. Wearing only my petticoat, I walked out into the lake. Mud squelched between my toes, but the water was clear enough to see the lake bed underfoot. Small fish came to investigate and then drifted away again. I waded up to my thighs, then my waist and chest, gasping as the water became deeper and colder. I ducked down until it covered my shoulders and laughed aloud with the sheer joy of feeling cool again.

I floated on my back for a while, eyes closed and drifting gently. My thoughts turned to Luca, as they so often did when I was on the cusp of wakefulness and sleep. I pictured the laughter that frequently lurked in his clear topaz eyes when we spoke together and the way he listened so intently when I described my plans for Flora's garden. Except, of course, that it was no longer Flora's; and it certainly wasn't mine. Very soon, it would be Sylvana's garden.

Abruptly, I turned onto my front and swam towards the shore until I reached shallower water. It was then that I saw Claudia and Edmund, hand-in-hand, emerge from the boathouse and stand on the jetty. Edmund took the girl in his arms and kissed her passionately. All my pleasure in the day drained away. I'd warned him several times not to get romantically involved, but here he was, kissing her. If Claudia tired of him, he could take it very hard and, in his mentally fragile state, who knew what harm that might do? Didn't he understand that I was trying to protect him?

Fear seethed up inside me, and I rose up out of the water to go and put a halt to it. I took a few steps but saw how my sodden petticoat clung to the contours of my breasts, leaving nothing to the imagination. I couldn't possibly confront them in this state. I sank back into the lake and waited until, after a last lingering kiss, they walked back to the woodland path and disappeared into the trees.

I paced up and down the jetty in the sunshine, brooding on Edmund's foolishness, until I was dry enough to dress again and hurry off to Flora's garden.

Edmund was crouched beside one of the flowerbeds, pulling up weeds. Hot and agitated, I marched straight up to him.

'Did you oversleep?' His smile was indulgent.

'I did not.' I rested my hands on my hips. 'I *saw* you,' I said.

'Saw me?'

'Kissing Claudia.'

His smile faded and he stood up. 'It's not your business, Violet.'

'Not my—' I drew a breath. 'Of course it's my business, Edmund. If she tires of you, or cannot cope with your illness, who do you think will be the one who has to look after you when you fall into a pit of despair? Claudia is too young to understand the implications of your nervous disposition.'

Edmund's complexion paled and a muscle flickered in his cheek. 'Claudia isn't a child. She's a compassionate and sensible young woman who isn't frightened off by my temporary indisposition. And, you must agree, I'm already so much better. Finding a skull like that wasn't an everyday occurrence.'

'Of course not, and you've suffered such terrible experiences—'

'Time heals. Apart from that recent setback, I'm quite different now from when I was invalided back from France. I understand that I must be grateful to you, Violet, and I truly am; however, I'm doing my best to build a new life for myself where I won't be a constant drain on you.'

I caught hold of his hand and held it to my cheek. 'You're *not* a drain on me. You're my little brother, and you know I promised Mother I'd always look after you.'

'I'm not unappreciative – how could I be after you've done so much for me – but Mother wouldn't have wanted you to give up your own life to look after me for all time. And I don't want you to, either. I want to lead a normal life again.'

'I'm happy to look after you,' I said, a note of desperation in my voice. 'The two of us must look after each other. After all, I have no one else but you since William was killed.'

Edmund sighed. 'Yes, and that's the root cause of your distress. Perhaps that's why you mollycoddle me so? It's time you found yourself another husband to care for.'

'And perhaps you haven't noticed that the options for that are extremely limited?' I spoke sharply; he'd touched an ever-painful nerve.

'Massimo likes you.'

I let out a snort of derision. 'And I like him, but he's older than me. Besides, he hasn't shown the slightest romantic interest in me.'

Raising his eyebrows, Edmund said, 'Are you quite sure about that? He seemed very keen on you when we went to his house for dinner.'

I hesitated. There'd been a definite spark of interest in Massimo's eye when we'd travelled to Lenno to visit the nursery. 'This isn't about me,' I said in firm tones.

'Actually, I think it is.'

'What do you mean? It's *you* I'm concerned for.'

'Please, I beg you, don't be. Look, I love Claudia and she loves me, but we aren't about to rush into any hasty decisions.' He turned away and knelt down beside the flowerbed again.

I stared at his profile. His stubborn expression was only too familiar to me, and I knew it might make his infatuation for Claudia even stronger if I argued my point any further at this moment. I made a strategic withdrawal to the other side of the garden.

Luca was expected to return from Florence in time for dinner on Tuesday. After I finished work, I changed into a clean skirt and a pretty lace-trimmed blouse I'd found in a shop in Bellagio. Twisting my hair into a loose knot at the nape of my neck, I secured it with pins. Leaning towards the mirror, I scrutinised my reflection. Despite my sunhat, new freckles were scattered across my nose and cheekbones. My stepmother would have been appalled and insist I bleach them with lemon juice and stay indoors until they'd faded. That simply wasn't possible for me. Besides, my lightly tanned complexion had the pleasing effect of making my grey eyes look brighter.

Downstairs in the drawing room, Edmund was laughing at something Orlando had said as they sipped their drinks.

'*Buona serata*,' I said. My brother rose to his feet, but he didn't smile at me. Orlando lifted his left hand to wave.

'Come and sit here,' said Helen, patting the adjacent seat on the sofa. 'I'm planning Sylvana's birthday party, and I'd welcome your advice on the flower arrangements.'

We chatted while I strained my ears listening for Luca's arrival.

'I hope you don't mind me asking,' said Helen, 'but I wondered if you'd given any thought to what you will wear for the party?'

'I wasn't sure if I'd be invited to attend.'

'Of course you must come! Edmund, too. The garden is a wonderful present for Sylvana, and you must be there when Luca shows it to her. So, do you have anything to wear?'

'Well, there's my dove grey dress with the lace collar.' I knew it wasn't the right outfit for a party, but I didn't have anything else.

'It's charming, but I think you should have something a little less restrained and more appropriate for a party,' said Helen. 'Before the war, Orlando gave me a length of green shot silk from the factory. Although it's beautiful, it isn't the right shade for me, but it will be perfect for you with your striking auburn hair. I'd love you to have it, Violet, and I have a very good dressmaker who could make it up for you.'

'Oh, but I couldn't—'

'Of course you can!'

The door opened, but it was Umberto who shuffled in. He muttered '*Buona serata*' and plumped down in his usual armchair. 'Luca is late tonight,' he said.

'His train was delayed,' said Helen, 'but he arrived a short while ago.'

Soon, footsteps clipped across the hall and Luca opened the door. His hair was wet but neatly combed. 'I apologise,' he said to the assembled gathering. 'It was a hot train journey from Florence, and I had to change.'

'After dinner . . .' said Orlando in faltering tones, 'we will talk about your meetings.'

He looked pale, and it was sad to see how difficult it was for him to speak sometimes.

'Of course, Papà,' said Luca, 'unless you're tired and you'd rather wait until morning?'

'We will see. The heat exhausts me.'

Lucrezia came to announce dinner, and we all removed to the dining room.

It was still sunny outside, but the sun was low and the shutters had been opened again. An evening breeze stirred the silk curtains, bringing some relief from the sultry air.

Claudia carried in platters of antipasti, and I watched her and Edmund covertly, but they demonstrated no inappropriate signs of affection for each other.

We sipped chilled white wine while we ate our *antipasti*. Orlando explained to Edmund that the wine was made from the local Verdese grapes. 'I have ordered several cases for my daughter-in-law's party next month.'

'That reminds me, Luca,' said Helen, 'I have the proposed luncheon and supper menus for you to approve, and I've been making enquiries about the music. I wanted to wait until you returned to make the booking so you can have the final choice. There's an accordionist and a violinist who would provide music for the dancing but an excellent harpist has also been recommended, if you'd prefer that?'

Luca put down his fork. 'Mamma, that's very kind of you to take the trouble, but Sylvana has already booked an American jazz band. Accommodation has been arranged for them in the village.'

'A jazz band?' Helen pressed her palms to her cheeks. 'Really, I don't think that would be at all suitable for our friends.' She laughed. 'Can you imagine Caroline Pierucci's expression? Why, it's not even real music with a proper tune.'

'I must beg to differ,' said Luca stiffly. 'And as it's my wife's birthday party, she should be allowed to choose the music. Besides,

214

more than half of the eighty guests will be made up of our friends, and they don't care for country music.'

'I warned you, Luca,' said Umberto, his bushy eyebrows drawn together. 'You must take control of your wife or she will embarrass us all. She must learn to become one of us. A jazz band would be abhorrent to our friends.'

'My wife is *not* out of control, Nonno,' said Luca sharply. 'Sylvana is a modern woman and I applaud that. She'll bring a breath of fresh air to Villa Marchese and blow away all the outmoded ideas. Don't you realise we're no longer living in the nineteenth century?'

'How dare you speak so disrespectfully to me?' thundered Umberto.

Helen glanced at her husband for support, but he only shrugged, and there was an awkward silence.

I glanced at Luca's unhappy face and cleared my throat. 'I wonder if I might venture a suggestion?'

'Please do,' said Helen. Her cheeks were flushed, and her eyes too bright. 'I do so hate discord.'

'Since you haven't yet sent out the invitations,' I said, 'perhaps you might invite your more mature friends and neighbours to the luncheon? Harp music would be the perfect accompaniment and also quiet enough to allow conversation. Afterwards, Sylvana might like to show your guests her new garden before they depart. In the evening, Sylvana's friends from Florence and Luca's local friends can get to know each other over a buffet supper and cocktails before dancing to the jazz band.'

There was a brief silence and then Luca said, 'That's a marvellous idea, Violet. What do you think, Mamma?'

The tension left Helen's face and she smiled at me. 'I think Violet may have saved the day.'

Chapter 22

August arrived with an apocalyptic rainstorm that blotted out the sun at midday. It swept across the lake and up the hillside to lash at Villa Marchese's windows, banging doors and rattling the glass frames. Lightning rent the sky apart and thunder exploded like a bombardment of cannon fire. Edmund buried his head under a pillow, and Lucrezia shrieked and retreated to the wine cellar. In the eerie silence that followed the storm, there was no birdsong, and I took stock of the damage to the sodden garden. Flowers, heavy with rain, hung their heads, plant pots had been overturned and a swathe of honeysuckle detached from a trellis panel. I nearly wept at the sight of several glorious dahlia blooms that had been on the point of perfection before the violent winds flattened them. I set to work to re-stake them before night fell.

Over the following days, Massimo and Edmund worked tirelessly alongside me to restore order. I'd tucked several pots of spare plants down behind the glasshouse as insurance against just such an event, so I was able to replace most of those that were beyond help. We swept, trimmed and weeded until, a week before Sylvana's birthday, we stopped and leaned on our rakes in satisfaction. No one could now detect the trail of destruction left by the storm; nevertheless, there was still plenty to do before the party.

Luca returned from Como after a day at the silk factory and came to find me in the rose garden. He was carrying a large parcel wrapped in brown paper.

'Look what I've brought,' he said. He beamed as he tore off the paper and revealed a plaque that read, *'Il giardino di Sylvana'*. The wording and twining stems of honeysuckle around the perimeter were of highly polished copper and stood out against the green patination of the background. It was a truly beautiful piece.

Jealousy, hot and raw, bloomed in my chest. I'd put my heart and soul into making the garden, and even though I'd always known it was for Sylvana, how I wished it was mine.

'Well,' prompted Luca, 'what do you think?'

'It's very handsome,' I said at last. 'I'm sure your wife will love it.' I could hear the lacklustre tone of my voice and tried to cover it by forcing a smile.

'But you don't like it,' said Luca, the pleasure draining from his expression. 'I wanted to add a decorative touch of my own to your garden and I thought the craftsman had made an excellent job of it.' He wrapped the paper over the plaque again.

'He did; it's beautiful, Luca,' I said. 'It's only that . . .' I couldn't bear his disappointment at my reaction and decided to be honest – nearly honest anyway, 'it makes me sad that my work here is almost done.'

Luca laughed. 'Is that all? But of course your work here isn't done!' Frowning, he said, 'Unless you want it to be? Was I wrong to assume that you and Edmund would stay on to manage the garden?'

'Surely that depends on whether your wife prefers to do it herself? Coming from Florence where she has a very busy social life, she'll want an absorbing hobby to keep her occupied.'

'I suppose you may be right,' said Luca. He scanned the nearest flowerbed, now humming with bees and packed with a glorious tapestry of blooms. His face brightened. 'But, as yet, Sylvana has no experience of the pleasure to be found in tending a flower garden, so she's bound to need your advice for some time to come. Later, of course, I hope she'll be occupied with our children, so you'll still be needed. You must stay; I simply can't imagine this garden without you.'

I abruptly bent to pull up a stray weed to hide the pain his words inflicted. I couldn't think about the prospect of leaving Villa Marchese or the babies Sylvana and Luca would make together. No matter whether I stayed or went, I would suffer heartache.

'Violet?'

I stood up, my expression now impassive. 'Time will tell,' I said, and glanced at Massimo who was busy deadheading the roses on the pergola.

He pursed his lips. 'I hoped you and Edmund were happy here?'

'We are. You've all been so kind to us and so understanding about Edmund's difficulties, but I don't want to outstay our welcome once the garden is finished.'

He took my hand and squeezed it. 'You won't. I would miss you terribly. Mamma is so fond of you, and my father takes a special interest in Edmund. Violet . . .' His gaze locked with mine and I looked into the depths of his pupils.

I saw Massimo put down his secateurs to watch us. Reluctantly, I slid my hand out of Luca's grip, my skin on fire from his touch. 'I'd better finish weeding the gravel,' I said.

Luca stepped away. 'I won't keep you, then. I'll ask Massimo to fix the sign over the garden door. I'll sit in the rose garden to write my book for a while, if you should have any time to sit and chat with me.' He picked up the copper plaque and walked away.

Later, I saw him on the bench absorbed in his writing, but I made sure to keep busy in the furthest corner of the garden and away from the dangerous allure of his company.

Caroline Pierucci came to see how the garden was developing, and I shone with pride at her fulsome praise. 'It's almost ready for the new Signora Marchese's birthday next week,' I said.

'Oh, how I wish Flora could see her garden bloom again!' Signora Pierucci clasped her hands to her breast and a shadow moved across her face. 'I know the despair she suffered – would have suffered – if she'd known what Umberto did to destroy her Eden. It would have marked her for life.'

'The desecration of the garden was an extreme reaction to his grief,' I said. 'He came into the garden one evening, and I saw him weeping. After all this time, he still mourns Flora.' I didn't mention that he'd thought I was either Flora's ghost or that I was Flora in the flesh, unchanged by age.

'Perhaps he loved her too much.'

I wondered what she meant by that. 'It's hard to imagine,' I said, 'that such destruction ever took place here. It's so peaceful now with only birdsong and the breeze to break the silence.' I smiled. 'Sometimes I fancy I can hear the echoes of happy children's voices.'

'My boys loved coming here. It was a paradise for them.' There was a smile in Signora Pierucci's eyes.

'And now the fig tree is smothered in nearly ripe fruit again. You know, Beppe showed me some letters Isabella had written to him from when she was away at school, and in one of them, she mentioned the fig tree and how they used to sit beneath it to gorge on the fruit.'

Signora Pierruci laughed. 'I had to scold the children more than once because they upset their stomachs by eating too many.'

'However, the first letter was heart-breaking because she was homesick and grieving for her mother. It's poignant that she died soon after she wrote the second note, when she was happy again.'

'Domenico and I were her godparents, so I came to see her after Flora died, only to discover Umberto and that terrible mother of his had bundled her off to boarding school.'

'Poor little Isabella,' I said. 'At least she was happy for the last few months of her life.'

Caroline Pierucci cupped a rose in her hand to breathe in its fragrance.

'I wonder if Luca knows anyone who might take a photograph of the garden for me?' she said. 'It wouldn't capture the glorious colours, but it would remind me of how it looks at the peak of perfection.'

'I have a better idea,' I said. 'Come with me.'

I led her over to where Edmund was raking the gravel. He wore a battered straw hat of Massimo's, his shirtsleeves were rolled up to the elbow and he looked strong and healthy again. He glanced up and smiled at our approach.

'Edmund,' I said, 'Signora Pierruci was asking for a photograph of the garden, but I wondered if she might have one of your water-colours. A photograph simply doesn't do justice to the colours.'

His face broke into a grin. 'I'd be delighted. There are several to choose from, if you'd like to come with me, Signora Pierruci?'

They set off together towards the house, and I continued my battle to free the roses from bindweed.

I'd never before known heat as fierce as it was that August in Bellagio. After dinner every day, I returned to the garden to water the plants in the comparative cool of the evening. It was a peaceful and contemplative task in the twilight. I loved the sound of water

220

splashing onto the parched ground where I imagined the roots of my plants eagerly reaching out to quench their thirst. Luca hadn't arrived back from Como in time for dinner, and I'd missed him. Every few minutes we spent together was precious to me.

The air was sweetly perfumed by the Mme Alfred Carrière roses that climbed over the rose tunnel, and I buried my nose in one of the ruffled blooms. Footsteps crunched on the gravel. I turned abruptly, in the hope and expectation that it was Luca, and snagged my hair on a thorny stem.

'There you are, Violet!'

Luca arrived at my side while I was still disentangling myself. 'Were you looking for me?' I asked.

'I came straight to find you once I arrived home.'

'Busy day?' I enquired. I twisted my hair into a knot and pinned it at the nape of my neck with the only hairpin I could find.

'The factory is always busy, but I've discovered I like that. The business has turned out to be far more interesting than I'd imagined.' He took a silk-wrapped package from his pocket and held it out to me. 'This is for you.'

I took it from him, noticing my hands bore smears of mud. I doubted Sylvana would ever have dirty hands. Carefully, I undid the ribbon and pulled aside the shimmering mauve silk to reveal a book of Shakespeare's sonnets. It was bound in green leather with exquisite gold tooling. 'How very beautiful!' I said.

'Open it!'

On the flyleaf, he'd written:

To Violet, who created our glorious garden with such passion
    With grateful thanks
    Luca
    'If you have a garden and a library, you have everything you need.' Marcus Tullius Cicero

My pleasure at such a special gift was only tempered by wondering if the words 'our garden' referred to Luca and me or to Luca and Sylvana. 'Thank you,' I whispered. 'I shall treasure it.' I slipped the book into my pinafore pocket.

'I'm so lucky to have found you, Violet,' he said. Even the dying light couldn't conceal the tide of colour that flooded his cheeks. 'I mean, I couldn't have found a better person to make this garden so perfect. You've given it your all.'

For you, Luca. For you. The words I could never say aloud reverberated in my mind, and I bowed my head so he wouldn't see the sudden tears in my eyes. Then the hairpin gave up it's uncertain grip, and my hair fell loose again.

He reached out and ran a curl between his fingers. 'It's like silk,' he murmured. He captured my face between his palms and pressed his lips to my forehead, my cheeks, my nose.

I froze, completely unable to move.

And then he kissed my lips. This was no gentle peck of friendship, but a kiss so full of heat and passion that a sharp arrow of desire ignited a fire within me. For one fevered second, I melted into his arms and my mouth sought his.

But in another heartbeat, reason and propriety returned and I pushed him away. '*No*, Luca!'

His eyes were glazed as he reached for me again. 'I've wanted this for so long, Violet. And I thought you—'

I stepped back, my palm held up to prevent him from coming closer. 'What have I ever said to encourage you to believe I'm the kind of woman who would come between a man and his wife?' I spoke sharply to cover my yearning to do exactly that. 'Have you forgotten that this garden is for Sylvana?'

He stared at me with an anguished expression. 'No,' he said so quietly I almost didn't hear him. 'I haven't forgotten that. It torments me. I apologise sincerely, Violet. It won't happen again.'

Desolation washed over me in an icy wave, and my throat grew tight with the effort of not weeping. I fixed my gaze on the ground, knowing that if I looked at him I'd weaken and throw myself into his embrace.

'I'm truly sorry, Violet.' He turned and walked away into the gathering gloom.

Chapter 23

The following morning, I went down to breakfast full of trepidation. I was anxious about facing Luca after what had happened the previous night, but the longer I delayed it, the more difficult it would be. After he'd left me in the garden, I'd sat on the bench in the grotto and wept for what might have been. If only we'd met before he'd married Sylvana. I wept for the loss of solid, sensible William and for all the devastation that the 'war to end all wars' had wreaked on countless lives. At last, I'd dried my tears and crept through the darkness back to my room in the tower.

Now, morning sunshine flooded the hall but raised voices came from within the dining room. I hesitated before entering. But I needn't have worried; Luca wasn't there. Helen looked up at me with a distracted smile as I said a subdued good morning and took my usual seat at the table, aware of the tension in the air. Umberto glared at Helen while Edmund ate his bread without lifting his eyes from his plate.

'It is not your place to complain because Luca is not here to assist you with the arrangements,' said Umberto. 'You should be grateful that your son has seen sense at last and has gone to assert authority over his wife.'

'I didn't *complain*,' protested Helen. 'I'm perfectly capable of arranging the birthday party next week. I merely said there were last minute decisions to be made and Luca had promised to discuss these with me today. He'd given me no indication he was going to rush off to Florence barely an hour after he arrived home last night. Whatever was he thinking of?'

I paused in the act of pouring myself a cup of coffee. So, Luca had gone to be with Sylvana straight after I'd spurned his advances.

'Besides,' continued Helen, 'I would have thought you'd be angry with Luca. Surely he's needed at the factory this week?'

Umberto shrugged. 'The factory manager knows his job. Luca's absence for a few days will not cause problems, and I have told him many times that he must insist his wife behaves in a proper manner. Now he has realised I am right. "A New Woman" he called her! It's against God's law and the proper order of life.' He drained his coffee cup and stood up. 'There will be continuing discord in this house unless he takes control of that girl.'

Bent and frail as he was, Umberto still managed to exude an air of authority as he stalked from the room.

Helen let out her breath in a sigh. 'Unfortunately, there's some truth in what my father-in-law says. Of course I want Sylvana to enjoy her party and to feel welcomed into the family, but her role as Luca's wife brings her obligations and responsibilities, too. It's time for her to cease kicking up her heels and settle down to her wifely duties.'

Edmund stood up. 'Excuse me, but I must return to my own duties in the garden.'

'I'll join you shortly,' I said.

'I apologise for that family disagreement over the breakfast table, Violet,' said Helen, after the door had closed behind

Edmund. 'Luca can be very impulsive, and the forthcoming party is important to our family.'

'It's more than a birthday party, isn't it?' I said. 'It's really a delayed wedding reception and an opportunity for Sylvana to meet your neighbours and friends.'

'Especially since she didn't stay as long as expected at Christmas. In time, she'll take over my role as mistress of Villa Marchese.' Helen looked down at her fingers twisting together on the tablecloth. 'I wish I had more confidence that she was suited to the role.'

'Once she's living here, you'll befriend and guide her.'

'I do hope so. I want to like her, but the question is, will she like me?'

'How could she not?' I said. 'You've made me feel so welcome here, and you'll do the same for Sylvana.'

Helen gripped my wrist. 'Sylvana is a very different kettle of fish. You and I had a good rapport from our first meeting. How I wish . . .' She shook her head. 'There's so much to do today, and I need to speak to Lucrezia about the tablecloths for the hired tables.'

Lost in thought, I walked through the garden doorway. Had Helen intimated that she thought I'd have made a better daughter-in-law for her than Sylvana? The idea was flattering, but even if it were so, it wasn't possible. It was imperative, if only for my own peace of mind, to put aside all thoughts of Luca. This was easier said than done; however, the garden, cool and fresh in the morning dew, distracted me from my unhappy ruminations.

I waved at Edmund, who was raking the gravel paths, then concentrated on the weeding and deadheading. It was our final week to bring the garden to its peak of perfection in time for Sylvana's birthday.

Several hours sped by, and the August heat grew oppressive again. I heard Massimo talking to Edmund and looked up to see him give my brother's arm a playful punch. Edmund laughed and set off towards the garden door, and Massimo, carrying a basket, walked towards me.

'I bring you Claudia's lemonade,' he said.

'How considerate.' I batted away a wasp that circled my head. 'Weeding is thirsty work today.'

'Come sit with me by the pond.' We sat on the stone wall that bordered the pond, and he took the bottle of lemonade from the basket and poured it into two glasses. The sweet-sour drink was wonderfully thirst quenching.

'You look tired, Violet,' he said.

'There's been a lot to do to finish the garden,' I said, 'and I'm not used to such hot weather.' I dipped my hand in the pond hoping to cool it, but the water was tepid.

'But that is not the only problem for you, is it?' His brown eyes were filled with concern. 'I saw you with Luca last night.'

Fiery heat seared my cheeks. 'What did you see?'

'He kissed you, and you pushed him away.'

'Of course I did! I made it perfectly clear I'm not the kind of woman to have a dalliance with a married man.'

'I know you are not,' said Massimo, 'but you *wanted* him to kiss you, didn't you?'

'How dare you!' I thrust myself to my feet.

He caught my hand. 'Please! Do not upset yourself.' He pulled me down to sit beside him again. 'You care for Luca,' he said, 'but you are an honourable lady. The war damaged your brother and killed your husband, cheating you of your future together. I understand some of the pain you feel. After my beloved wife died ...' He swallowed and looked away until he'd composed himself. 'My Claudia is the best daughter a man could have, but every day, I regret that with my wife's passing, I lost my chance to have a son.'

My own heart frequently ached because of my childlessness, and tears of sympathy welled up in my eyes. 'Life is cruel and lonely sometimes,' I murmured.

Massimo still held my hand, and he raised it briefly to his lips. 'Violet, can we not comfort each other? You are a beautiful woman still in her prime, but you should have a happy married life fruitful with little ones. I am older than you, but I am strong and healthy. We are friends, but with kindness and understanding, might we become more?'

A pulse throbbed in my throat, and I could not move or speak.

Massimo caressed my hand. 'Could you learn to love me, Violet? It would make me so happy if you would be my wife.'

My thoughts were in turmoil. I'd guessed he had some romantic feelings for me, but I'd never imagined he might propose. He was an attractive man and I enjoyed his company, but I didn't love him. How could I when my thoughts were so filled with Luca? But that had to stop. I'd been living in a dream world where Luca was free, and in one week, his wife was coming to live with him at Villa Marchese.

'Violet?' His voice was gentle.

'I don't know, Massimo,' I murmured. 'I hadn't expected . . .'

'And I've surprised you?'

My fingers shook, and I clasped them tightly together and nodded.

'I was going to wait until after Luca brought his bride to Villa Marchese, but it hurt me to see you so sad last night. Please, do not refuse me without some thought. It would be my honour to cherish you. I would make every effort to ensure your happiness, but I will never speak of this again if you wish it.'

'I need some time to think.'

'Will you let me know your decision in one month?'

I lifted my head to look at him. 'Yes, Massimo,' I said. 'I'll consider your proposal very carefully.'

He studied my face for a moment. 'Good,' he said, then collected the empty glasses and walked away.

My thoughts were in such turmoil that it was impossible for me to pay proper attention to my work. I walked briskly around the garden several times in an attempt to dispel my agitation. From my earliest years, the expectation had been that I would marry. It felt as if the ground had collapsed beneath me when William died and all at once, I faced a lonely future as a childless widow. Massimo's proposal was a not-to-be ignored second chance of companionship – and perhaps, a baby. How I longed for a child of my own!

It was too hot to rush about in the heat of the sun, so I stepped into the shade beneath the broad leaves of the fig tree. I stood under the leafy bower and cupped one of the figs in my palm, and it separated easily from the branch. The fruit had turned from green to gold, and it yielded when I pressed it with my finger. Tentatively, I bit through the skin and found that the amber flesh inside was sweet. It was delicious.

Later in the day, I was reliving Massimo's proposal while I tied some loose tendrils of honeysuckle to the trelliswork. His talk of wanting a son had moved me, but I was imagining that I had a small daughter. She might have copper curls just like Isabella and would trot along beside me as I worked. How cruel it was that Isabella had died at such a tender age. I remembered her letter to Beppe telling him that she was happy in her new home. She'd recalled the carefree times they'd had together, sitting under the fig tree cramming their mouths with ripe figs. Then she'd written that she wouldn't see him again. Had she had a premonition she was going to die or was it simply that she was reaching an age when the class difference would have made it hard for them to remain friends? I was still pondering on this when Edmund came to find me.

'That looks tidier,' he said, nodding at the trellis.

'Honeysuckle grows so quickly if you don't keep on top of it.' I collected up my tools with a yawn to put them away for the day.

'Tired?' asked Edmund.

'I didn't sleep well last night.' That was an understatement. I'd paced the floor for hours, reliving that brief kiss with Luca and wondering what might have happened if I hadn't pushed him away. Part of me wished I hadn't.

'Why don't you have an early to bed tonight or simply take the chance to sit down quietly and read for a while?'

'There's the watering to do after dinner.'

'Claudia has offered to come and help me, so you can have a night off for once.'

'But I—'

'No arguments, Violet.' Edmund frowned at me with mock severity. 'You have dark circles under your eyes. It's my turn to tell you to look after your health instead of the other way around.'

There was nothing I could say that would stop Edmund from spending time with Claudia and, in truth, he looked happier and more relaxed than I'd seen him for ages. I was exhausted, and perhaps it was time for me to loosen my grip on my little brother. 'Well, thank you,' I said. 'An early night is a good idea.'

He smiled and gave me a brief hug. 'Let's go in for dinner, then.'

At midnight, I was sitting by the open window of my tower room, listening to the sounds of the night; the breeze rustling in the trees, the bark of a vixen and the hoot of an owl. Sleep still eluded me despite my exhaustion. My head ached as the recent, disturbing conversations with both Luca and Massimo whirled through my mind and I agonised over what I should do – or should have done.

Hours later, I stumbled into bed and gradually sleep crept up on me, numbing my legs and then my torso. As I drifted off, something niggled in my mind again. 'Bastille Day,' I murmured. 'I must find out about Bastille Day.'

Chapter 24

Although I was short of sleep the next morning, my spirits lifted again on my return to the flower garden. The pink and white oleanders continued to flower prolifically and, massed together with the magenta and purple bougainvillea, they made a marvellously exuberant and exotic backdrop to the more restrained English cottage garden flowers.

During those last days before the party, Edmund and I walked around the garden and surveyed everything with a critical eye. We sprayed the roses with soapy water to see off any lingering greenfly and removed browning petals from the buds. The dahlia blooms were so heavy they risked snapping the stems, so we staked them again for safety. Edmund was in a good humour and whistled under his breath like Father used to before Mother died. He disappeared off somewhere before lunchtime saying he wasn't hungry, and I returned to Villa Marchese.

The loggia was filled with tables and chairs stacked shoulder high, and Helen was engaged in a voluble argument with two men in hessian aprons. As far as I could understand, the tables Helen had asked for had been sent to another venue. At last she sighed, and the men shrugged, then left.

'Why is nothing ever straightforward in this country?' said Helen. 'You wouldn't think it was too much to ask to receive the furniture I hired, would you? They've sent round tables instead of the square ones.'

'Does it make a difference?' I asked.

'I expected to be able to push the tables together to make one long one for the birthday lunch. It's more convivial, don't you think?'

'I'm not sure,' I said. 'It might feel more informal if people seated themselves with their friends?'

'Perhaps you're right,' she said. 'And for the evening, smaller tables will make it easier for people to talk over the music.' She shook her head. 'A jazz band! Honestly, what is the world coming to? How can guests dance to music like that?'

'I'm sure Sylvana and her friends will find a way.'

'I expect so.' Helen looked less than enthusiastic. 'One of her friends is driving her here tomorrow, and I expect he'll bring Luca, too. An advance party of another four friends will stay here, but the rest have booked into local hotels, thank goodness'

'You must be very busy. Is there something I can do to help?'

'Bless you for offering, but everything is under control. Claudia never complains about extra duties, and Lucrezia is in her element. She loves to remember the days when we held frequent house parties here, but since Teodore died and my husband had his stroke, we've quite fallen out of the habit.'

'That's hardly surprising.'

'Perhaps Sylvana will breathe new life into Villa Marchese.' She didn't sound convinced. 'I've been in such a whirlwind of activity that I haven't been to see the garden since it was damaged by the storm.'

'You won't see any obvious signs of damage now,' I said. 'Massimo and Beppe helped put everything to rights, and I'm pleased to say it all looks tip-top again.'

'What a relief!' She glanced at her watch. 'Time for lunch. The kitchen is so busy that I suggested we simply have some bread, cheese and cold meat today. Orlando and my father-in-law had a tray in their study while they went through the accounts.'

After we'd eaten, I mentioned that I was going to walk into Bellagio later that afternoon to collect my new evening dress from the dressmaker.

'How exciting! I shall look forward to seeing it later.' She hurried off, murmuring about guest soaps for the bathroom. I left the dining room and paused for a moment outside the library before pushing open the door. Inside, I lifted the Marchese family Bible down from the shelf and laid it carefully on the table. I ran my finger down the list of names until I found what I was looking for. Frowning while I thought about it, I closed the Bible and returned it to the shelf.

At the end of the afternoon, I packed up my tools and was emptying a barrow load of weeds onto the compost heap when Massimo walked out from behind the tool shed.

'You are finishing early today?' he said.

'I'll come back later to do the watering,' I said, 'but I have to walk into Bellagio to collect a dress and some shoes from the dressmaker.'

'Would you like me to take you there in the boat?' I hesitated, and he laughed. 'Don't worry! I promised I wouldn't press you for an answer to my question.'

'I would love the boat ride, if you have time.'

Massimo grinned. 'I always have time for you, *cara*.'

'I need to change first.'

'I will wait for you at the boathouse.'

Half an hour later, Massimo handed me into the boat and rowed away from the jetty with a strong and steady rhythm.

'It's so refreshing to be out on the lake after the oppressive heat of the garden,' I said. The breeze plucked wisps of hair out from under my straw hat, and I squinted my eyes against the glare of the sunlight reflected up from the intense blue of the water. Sailing boats tacked across the lake, and the wash from a ferry made the rowing boat rock from side to side. I was conscious of Massimo watching me, and a blush warmed my face.

He gave me a slow smile, but I turned my gaze to the mountains on the opposite shore. I couldn't help but think how attractive he was with his powerful physique and the sun glinting on his dark curls. I wondered again what it would be like if he became my husband. Even though I didn't love him, he was kind and full of energy.

We passed the Arabic temple in the grounds of Villa Melzi and soon arrived at the jetty where Massimo moored the boat.

'May I walk with you?' he asked.

'Of course.'

We strolled along the road that bordered the lake, sheltering from the sun in the shade of the grove of oleander trees. Heat radiated up from the cobbles, and the air smelled of hot dust mixed with the sweet fragrance of oleander.

'Aren't they lovely?' I said.

'Beautiful, but deadly,' said Massimo. 'Every part of the plant is poisonous, even the flowers. You must always wear gloves when pruning it. The sap is extremely toxic.'

'I'll remember that. It's too cold to grow oleander in England'

We came to the town and climbed one of the staircases to the upper town. Closely packed shops and houses lined either side of the steps, and I stopped when we came to the dressmaker's narrow door set between a cafe and an ironmonger's shop.

'I'll wait for you in the cafe,' said Massimo.

I'd had three fittings already, and Signora Greco greeted me like an old friend. It pleased me that my Italian was improving all the time, thanks to Signor Romano.

'You will love your dress,' said Signora Greco, 'and your satin shoes have returned from the dyer. They match the dress perfectly.' She led me into the spare bedroom she used as her sewing room and drew back the fitting room curtain with a flourish.

The finished dress hung on a hanger, and the sight of it made me catch my breath with pleasure. The dark green silk Helen had given me was shot through with teal blue, and it shimmered when I slipped it over my head. The sleeveless bodice crossed over my bust to form a deep vee neckline and then fell in soft folds to a dropped waistline caught at my left hip with a tulle rose. I put on the matching shoes and buttoned the delicate ankle straps. I had never owned such a daringly fashionable dress before, and I pirouetted before the mirror, thrilled to see how the silk moulded to my form and elongated my body.

'You like it?' asked Signora Greco.

'It is the most beautiful dress I have ever owned,' I said.

Smiling, she wrapped it in pink tissue paper, laid it reverently in a slim cardboard box and tied it with satin ribbon. 'Enjoy your party,' she said.

I stepped out of Signora Greco's house as if I were floating on air.

Massimo was sitting under the cafe's awning with a carafe of white wine and two glasses. 'A glass of wine, Violet?'

'Thank you.'

'You look happy,' he said. 'You like your new dress?'

I nodded. 'Signora Marchese gave me a length of beautiful green silk for her dressmaker to make one for me.'

'She is a good lady. I will always remember how kind she was to Claudia after my wife died. It has been very hard for her to lose her son and then for her husband to be struck down in such a way.'

I was intensely aware of Massimo while we sipped our wine and watched the people passing by: black-clad elderly ladies with shopping baskets of fruit and vegetables, a trio of lively children jumping down the steps and even a sprinkling of English tourists and men on their way home from work. A middle aged man called out to Massimo and smiled at me as he hurried past.

'There is always something to see here and someone you know to talk to,' said Massimo.

Maybe it was the languorous warmth, but Bellagio felt far friendlier and more full of life than the grey streets of London. 'I could sit here for the rest of the day watching the world go by,' I said, 'but I must go and do the watering. I can't risk any of the plants dying just before the party.'

'Stay a few more minutes,' said Massimo, 'and I will help you later. It's a pleasure to spend time with a beautiful woman.' He shared the last of the wine between our two glasses, and we lingered a little longer before returning through the town towards the jetty.

Once back in the boat, Massimo rowed along the lakeshore towards the villa. It was peaceful listening to the oars creak and feeling the sun and breeze on my face. A small kernel of calm began to unfold inside me. If only I could quash my inappropriate feelings for Luca, I could be content here in Bellagio. I had no desire to go back to London except to visit Father, and it felt entirely possible that Edmund and I might build a new life here. The question was: might Massimo also be part of my future?

I was roused from my musings when the boat changed course, and a moment later it nudged up to Villa Marchese's boathouse.

Massimo jumped onto the jetty, and I handed him my precious dress box and the package containing my new shoes before stepping ashore. We walked in companionable silence along the woodland path up the hill until we reached the house.

'I'll change back into my gardening clothes,' I said.

'And I will start to water the plants,' said Massimo.' He walked away, whistling as he went.

A short while later I found him in the garden, unrolling the rubber hoses that were fed from the pipe that supplied water to the pond.

The sun was low in the sky and cast a golden glow over the garden. I savoured the scent of warm earth as the water splashed onto it while I moved steadily amongst the snapdragons and marigolds. I kept a bucket beside me to collect faded blooms while I watered the roses. The intense heat had gone out of the sun now, and the air was as warm and perfumed as a luxurious bath. If Sylvana experienced even a fraction of the pleasure I found in the garden, then she would be a very happy woman indeed.

The branches of the fig tree were heavy with fruit, and I ate a few figs while the hose soaked its roots. I'd been too busy to think much about what I had confirmed in the library, but the figs reminded me that I wanted to talk to Beppe about it. I let my thoughts run free until Massimo called out to me from the flowerbeds on the other side of the pond.

'It's too dark to see anymore,' he said. 'I will turn off the taps.'

We left the hoses unrolled so that I could finish the watering in the early morning and then closed the garden door behind us.

Twigs snapped under our feet as we walked along the rhododendron walk, chatting about the garden. We came to the gardeners' cottages, and I said goodnight to Massimo.

'I will walk you back to the villa,' he said.

'Please don't trouble yourself,' I said. 'I've walked this way on my own in the dark many times.' He hesitated and I said, 'I'm going to call in on Beppe for a few moments. I can see his light is on.'

'If you change your mind afterwards, knock on my door.'

'Thank you.'

'I enjoyed our visit to Bellagio,' he said.

'So did I.' He took a small step towards me, and I wondered if he intended to kiss me. 'Goodnight, Massimo,' I said, lifting a hand in farewell. He moved back, and I went up the garden path to Beppe's cottage.

Chapter 25

That last day before the party flew by. Edmund and I trimmed and weeded, scrubbed the marble bench in the grotto, fished stray leaves from the surface of the pond and tidied away forgotten plant pots and tools. I didn't have much time to ponder on either Massimo's proposal or the other matter that had kept me awake last night.

It was late afternoon when we finished. Edmund stood with his hands on his hips while we surveyed the garden. Drifts of colourful herbaceous and annual plants merged together in glorious harmony, and bees and butterflies busied themselves on the lavender and roses. The pergolas and trelliswork were clothed in a mass of scented blooms, and the rich, dark earth was weed-free.

'Who could have imagined last November that it was remotely possible to turn a wilderness of brambles into such a beautiful place?' said Edmund. 'You should be extremely proud of what you've achieved here, Violet.'

I laughed. '*We* should be proud. I could never have done it on my own. After the party, we must ask Luca if we can invite Vincenzo, Raimondo and the rest of the men to see how it's turned out.'

'I'm sure he'll be happy to show it off.'

'The important thing is for Sylvana to love the garden.' I brushed soil off my crumpled pinafore. 'She'll be here before long, and I must have a bath before she arrives.'

A short while later, I unlaced my boots in the loggia. The sound of laughter and lively conversation drifted towards us.

'It sounds as if Sylvana and her friends are already here,' I said.

'I need to speak to Massimo before I come in,' said Edmund. 'He should have returned from collecting Sylvana's trunk from Varenna station by now.' He hurried outside again.

In stockinged feet, I crossed the hall towards the tower rooms, but Helen saw me through the open door of the drawing room. 'Come and join us, Violet!'

I hung back in the doorway. 'I've come straight from the garden, and I'm on my way to bath and change,' I said.

'Do have some tea first.' Her voice was unnaturally bright, so I guessed she felt out of place amongst Luca and Sylvana's Florentine friends.

In the drawing room, several elegantly dressed people stopped chattering and turned to look at me.

'It's Violet, isn't it?' Sylvana said, and frowned. 'Luca told me you were still here.'

I was embarrassed to compare my dishevelled gardening clothes against her immaculate, white linen dress and gleaming black hair forming perfect kiss curls against her cheeks. I couldn't think of a reasonable explanation without giving away Luca's surprise.

'I invited Violet and Edmund to extend their stay,' said Helen. 'I believe I mentioned before that Violet is a horticulturalist. She has been discussing future plans for the grounds with our garden staff. And I do so enjoy having visitors from my home country.'

The best lies always contain a grain of truth, but Helen's timely explanation was a pretty thin excuse for a stay lasting nine months.

I needn't have worried, however, since Sylvana had already turned to speak to one of her friends.

Luca rose to his feet from his seat beside his wife.

He looked tired, I thought – not that it was my business.

'Yes, come and meet everyone, Violet.' He didn't smile, and his gaze slid away from me.

A man lounging on a sofa looked me up and down with an amused smile.

Hesitantly, I stepped into the drawing room.

Luca introduced me to his friends: Rafaele, Francesca, Serafina and Emilio. The man with the amused smile was Leandro, and he made room for me on the sofa next to him.

Helen handed me a cup of tea, but I placed in on a side table and folded my hands so that my grimy nails were concealed. The conversation was in Italian, and while I did my best to follow, everyone seemed to be speaking at full volume at the same time, all underlined by flamboyant hand gestures. I soon lost the thread.

Leandro leaned towards me. 'You are the daughter of Signora Marchese's school friend?' he asked in heavily accented English. 'Luca spoke of you and your brother.'

'My mother died some years ago,' I said, not wishing to tell a direct lie. 'Did you have a good journey? You must have set off from Florence very early.'

Leandro shrugged. 'We stayed last night near Piacenza.'

His shoes were polished to a brilliant shine. I glanced at my own feet and was horribly embarrassed to see my big toe poking through the end of my snagged gardening stockings. I tucked my foot as far under the sofa as it would go while Leandro entered into a spirited and flirtatious exchange with Sylvana.

I drank my tea in agonising self-consciousness until I realised no one was looking at me.

Ten minutes later, Sylvana clapped her hands for attention and told her friends it was time they returned to Bellagio to meet the others, who would have arrived at their hotels by now.

'You will come with us?' asked Leandro.

Luca was looking at us with a tense expression.

I shook my head. 'As you can see, I've been gardening, and I need to change.'

'We will wait,' said Leandro.

I tried not to squirm in my seat as he studied me with heavily lidded eyes.

'No time!' interrupted Sylvana. 'What a relief you brought your motorcars, Leandro and Rafaele. It would be impossible to live here in the country without one. Hurry up! The others will be wondering where we are, and we mustn't be late for our *aperitivo*.'

There was a flurry of laughter and a gathering up of belongings, and then the chattering group blew kisses to Helen as they departed. Luca glanced back at me over his shoulder before he disappeared into the hall.

'Well!' said Helen. She sat down again and reached for the teapot.

The front door slammed, and we heard the motorcars start up and drive off with a blaring of horns.

'I'm afraid our dinner will be a very quiet affair,' said Helen. 'I'm sorry you missed the opportunity to spend an evening in livelier company than Orlando and I can offer you.'

'I would have felt like a fish out of water,' I said

'Have another cup of tea before you go for your bath.'

The following morning, I awoke at dawn and remembered it was Sylvana's birthday. I scrambled into my gardening clothes and hurried outside to check that everything was still perfect in the flower garden before Luca brought his wife to see it.

Dew drops glittered on the grass, and the air was cool and fresh when I pushed open the garden door. I wandered under the pergolas, inhaling the perfume of honeysuckle and sweet peas, before traversing the intersecting gravel paths leading to the grotto and the rose garden. I pinched the lavender and sniffed the resinous scent on my fingers, enjoying the last precious, bitter-sweet moments when the garden remained mine.

Sighing, I leaned over the wall that surrounded the pond and looked for the fish. They darted towards me in flashes of gold from beneath the waterlily leaves, no doubt in the hopeful expectation of being fed. My reflection rippled, and when the fish swam away and the pond grew still again, another face was mirrored in the water beside mine.

I turned around to find Luca close behind me. His hair was unbrushed, and his shirt was open at the neck, as if he'd dressed in a hurry. He held out a hand towards me.

It took every ounce of my willpower not to take it, but I knew that once I felt the touch of his skin on mine, I would be powerless to resist. Clenching my fists, I recoiled.

'Did I startle you?' His hand fell back to his side.

I shook my head, my thoughts too tumultuous to speak.

'I came to see if the garden was finished,' he said, 'and it's taken my breath away. In my wildest dreams, I never imagined it could be so lovely.' His gaze was fixed so intently on my face that I had to look away in case he read my feelings.

'I'm pleased you like it,' I said. 'And today is your wife's birthday. I hope she will be happy with her garden.' My voice was cool and formal, but my thoughts churned with all the forbidden things I longed to say to him and all the forbidden things I wished he'd say to me. It would be irresponsible for me to linger. 'I must go back to the villa,' I said and turned to leave.

'Violet?'

I glanced back over my shoulder.

'I'm sorry,' he said. His shoulders sagged. 'I never meant to distress you.'

I couldn't speak for the lump in my throat as I fled from the garden.

❧

I decided not to go downstairs for breakfast to avoid facing Luca, Sylvana and their friends and instead skulked in my tower bedroom. Edmund had gone to help Massimo trim the edges of the lawn at the front of the villa, and I sat by the open window where Helen's voice drifted up now and again as she directed operations. The caterers were swarming all over the place and setting up the tables under the loggia. A number of horse-drawn carts arrived bringing crates of china, cases of wine and hampers of food.

It was late morning when I changed into my dove grey dress and went downstairs to see if Helen needed any assistance. Two men, supervised by a lanky, middle-aged woman, were carrying a harp into a corner of the loggia. Several maids were laying the tables under Lucrezia's watchful eye. Helen was advising the florist on the placement of large vases of lilies and roses on pedestals.

'Is there anything I can do?' I asked, once she was alone again.

'The caterers have it all in hand, but I'm hovering nearby to make sure everything on my list happens.' She leaned towards me and murmured, 'I'm relieved that Luca and Sylvana's friends haven't stirred out of their rooms yet. Luca was up early and came to tell me they returned from the town very late and are sleeping in before going into Bellagio again. Luca's going to tell Sylvana about her garden during the luncheon party and then lead a procession of guests to look at it afterwards.'

'I like that idea,' I said, 'though I'd imagined he would have taken her there alone this morning.'

'That's what he'd intended, but she's still asleep.' Helen's face brightened. 'He's thrilled with the garden and has nothing but praise for you. In fact, he asked me to change plans for the evening party and hold it in Sylvana's garden instead of here in the loggia.'

'Won't it be too dark?'

'It was a full moon only two nights ago, and he's asked Massimo and Beppe to line the path to the garden with oil lamps and candles in jars. We have a great number of candles and storm lamps in store from garden parties in earlier years, and they'll look very pretty.'

'Will the guests return to the house for their supper?'

'I've instructed the catering staff to transport the tables down to the garden immediately the luncheon guests depart. We'd already decided on a cold buffet, so that won't be a problem. Luca will tell the jazz band to set up in front of the grotto. It's a fairy-tale location for a party, don't you think?'

'But if there's to be dancing,' I said, 'there's no dance floor, only gravel paths.'

Helen laughed. 'That was exactly my reaction, but as Luca said, dancing to a jazz band is very different from a demure waltz around a ballroom.' She shrugged. 'It's Sylvana's party, and Luca knows what she and her friends want. All I ask is that Luca remembers that the luncheon is specifically for his wife to meet our circle of friends and neighbours. I know many of them expected to be introduced to her soon after the wedding or at Christmas, and I'm tired of attempting to explain why that didn't happen.' Her expression became troubled. 'Orlando is upset because he simply cannot make a speech anymore. He has asked Luca to say a few words to welcome Sylvana to Villa Marchese on his behalf. We won't attend the evening party, either. Neither of us want to feel like a spectre at a wedding.'

'I'm sure everyone will understand,' I said. I thought it

diplomatic to change the subject. 'Is Signora Pierucci still coming to the luncheon today?'

'She told me she wouldn't miss seeing your garden in all its glory for the world,' said Helen.

'I know it reminds her of the happy days she spent with Flora.'

'After all these years,' said Helen, 'she still misses her friend.'

'Flora's diaries gave me some insight into her character,' I said, 'and I enjoy listening to Signora Pierucci's memories.'

The harp had been set up in a corner of the loggia and the harpist, her elongated form now swathed in ethereal drapes, began to tune her instrument.

Two of the catering staff collided, a tray of glasses crashed to the floor and Lucrezia joined in the ensuing noisy altercation.

'It's time for me to go and dress in my finery,' said Helen after the broken glasses had been cleared away. 'The guests will be here before long. By the way, there's no need for you or Edmund to join the receiving line.' She hurried away.

I went into the drawing room and found Orlando and Umberto chatting together. 'Am I disturbing you?' I asked.

Orlando looked up at me with his lopsided smile. 'Not at all. Have you come to escape the fuss of party preparations?'

'It seems there's nothing I can do to help. Helen has gone to change.'

'Luca tells me your garden is very beautiful. He's arranged for me to be transported in the *timonèlla* to see it along with my daughter-in-law.'

'I hope you like it,' I said. 'It wasn't possible to recreate all of your mother's garden in the time available, but there's scope for further development in the future.'

'I wish I had known my mother,' said Orlando, 'but the garden you have made will allow me to imagine her there.' He looked up at Flora and Isabella's portrait above the fireplace.

'Will you excuse me?' I said. 'I must fetch a handkerchief before the guests arrive.'

I returned to my room, where I smoothed my hair and dabbed a little perfume behind my ears. My reflection in the mirror was calm, despite the fluttering of unease and excitement in my stomach.

It was time for the luncheon party.

I tucked a clean handkerchief next to a folded piece of paper in my pocket and returned downstairs.

Chapter 26

Many of the guests had arrived by boat and walked up the woodland path from the boathouse, while others had come on foot or by pony and trap from neighbouring properties. In all cases, they were met by Lucrezia or Claudia and ushered into the hall. Helen and Orlando, who was seated on a carved hall chair as grand as a throne, greeted them. Luca was next in the receiving line and smiled as he introduced the guests to his wife.

My stomach lurched with jealousy. Sylvana looked enchanting again, this time in demure pink linen perfectly suited to the occasion. She gave Luca frequent coquettish glances from under her eyelashes and exchanged a brief word with each new arrival. The guests moved on, smiling in approval of Luca's bride.

Waiters hovered with trays of drinks, and the guests congregated in the drawing room. Caroline Pierucci waved discreetly at me from the other side of the room before turning back to speak to an elderly man. There was something I wanted to discuss with her, but I decided to wait until she was alone.

Edmund, a head taller than most of the Italian men, came through the doorway and made his way through the throng towards me. Dressed in his suit with a freshly ironed shirt, he looked handsome and at ease. I felt very proud of my brother for rising out of his former crippling pit of terror and despair. This was due in no small measure to the kindness of the Marchese family.

'At last the big day has arrived!' he said.

'I'm nervous,' I confessed. 'I hope Sylvana likes English cottage garden plants. The Italian taste is usually for a more formal style.'

'She can see that in any number of parks,' said Edmund, 'but the flower garden is so charming, she'll find it irresistible.'

'Luca is to present it to her after lunch.'

There was no more time to speculate since all the guests had arrived, and we were guided into the loggia to seat ourselves. The harpist was playing, and the melodious strains of her instrument were soft enough not to drown the guests' conversation. The sun was hot, and I was relieved we had decided to sit in the shade of the loggia. The summer breeze circulated through the colonnade, the garden beyond would be a perfect backdrop to our luncheon. The parterres had been neatly clipped, and there was an intriguing glimpse of Neptune's fountain through the archway in the yew hedge.

I'd hoped to sit next to Caroline Pierucci, but by the time Edmund and I had tagged onto the end of the group, she was already seated and there was no space at her table.

Happily, we found ourselves next to a charming married couple who lived a little further along the lakeshore. The husband was pleased to have the opportunity to practise his English, and Edmund and I practised our Italian. We laughed our way through the meal and promised to meet up in Bellagio for lunch another day.

We'd finished the apple tart and were sipping our coffee when Luca stood up and rapped a spoon against his wine glass. I sat up straight and watched Sylvana to see her expression when Luca told her about the garden. I followed his short speech as well as I could while he welcomed his wife to Villa Marchese on behalf of his family. Sylvana simpered and blew kisses to the guests.

'Today is my wife's birthday,' he said, 'and I have a surprise for her.' He turned and beckoned through the columns, and then Zizzo the mule clopped into view, led by Massimo. The *timonèlla* was decorated with red roses and white ribbons, as was Zizzo.

Laughter rippled through the company as Luca bowed to Sylvana and led her to the *timonèlla* before returning to escort his father to sit in the vehicle beside her. He climbed up beside them and took the reins, calling out to the guests to follow.

Umberto retreated into the house. Clearly, he didn't care to visit his wife's restored garden with the guests.

Helen appeared by my side. 'Come on, Violet, we'll lead the procession. You and Edmund must be near the front as I'm sure Luca will want to thank you both for making the garden.'

We fell into step beside the *timonèlla*, and I could hear Sylvana's merriment as she tried to tease Luca into disclosing her secret present. 'Where have you hidden it?' she asked.

'You will have to wait and see.'

'But why are we going through the garden? I thought it would be at the front of the house.'

'Patience! It's worth waiting for, I promise.'

A small frown gathered on Sylvana's forehead, but then it cleared as the stables came into view. 'It's here, isn't it?' She clapped her hands and squealed in excitement, craning her neck to peer into the stable yard. 'What colour is it?'

'All the colours of the rainbow!'

'But why aren't we stopping?' Her voice trailed away as Zizzo plodded on past the stables.

'What would you want with a horse,' asked Luca, 'when we have dear old Zizzo?'

'You know I don't like horses,' said Sylvana.

'That's lucky,' said Luca, 'because I haven't bought one for you.'

The *timonèlla* and its passengers entered the leafy tunnel of the rhododendron walk, and a buzz of curious conversation arose from the procession of guests.

Finally, we came to a halt outside the garden door, and Luca handed Sylvana down from the *timonèlla*. 'Look!' His eyes shone with anticipation as he pointed to the copper sign over the door.

Il giardino di Sylvana.

'I don't understand,' she said.

'But you will,' said Luca. He opened the door and guided her into the garden.

The crowd of guests behind me pressed forward, craning their necks to see through the doorway.

'Shall we go inside?' Helen said to Orlando. She assisted him from the open carriage, passed him his sticks and they led the way, closely followed by Edmund and myself.

The guests surged through after us, and I was gratified to hear one or two gasps of delight at the sight of the masses of colourful blooms.

Edmund beamed at me, and my heart swelled with pride.

Luca took his wife's hand and gave her a tour of the garden, stopping by the grotto and the pond, drawing her attention to the rose garden and pointing out the rainbow flowerbed and the sweet peas on the trellis.

All the while, I scrutinised her changing expressions, the flush on her cheeks and her increasingly fixed smile.

Helen glanced at me, a small crease of worry between her eyebrows.

'Well,' said Luca, kissing Sylvana's hand, 'what do you think of your present?'

'It's certainly a surprise.' She flashed him a brilliant smile. 'It's very . . . pretty.'

Luca's face was impassive when he turned to me. 'And we have Violet to thank for it all,' he said in English. 'She designed the garden in the English style and worked tirelessly with her brother Edmund to bring it to fruition.'

'So, you are gardeners?' said Sylvana. 'Now I understand why you have been at Villa Marchese for so long.' She turned away, pulling Luca to her side and drawing him away from us.

'Edmund,' I murmured. 'She doesn't like the garden.' I felt utterly sick.

'But she's smiling.'

'Only to be polite. Don't you see how stiff her posture is?'

His expression was bewildered. 'But how could she *not* love it?'

Helen laid a hand on my wrist. 'I doubt this is like any other gift she's ever had. Give her a little time to take it all in. I'd better circulate amongst the guests. Will you be all right?'

I nodded, holding back my tears.

Helen went to accompany some of the guests who were wandering along the paths, bending to sniff the flowers and look at the goldfish.

Caroline Pierucci came to speak to me, her eyes alight with pleasure. 'Your garden is an absolute triumph,' she said. 'It's so very beautiful, and dear Flora would have loved it.'

'Thank you,' I said. 'Unfortunately, I'm not sure Sylvana feels the same passion for it that Flora did – or that I do.' My disappointment and the anti-climax to months of work made my voice sound flat.

She regarded me with shrewd blue eyes. 'Perhaps not, but don't let that detract from your achievement. And you have pleased Luca. He's very proud of it.'

I couldn't bear to speak of it anymore. 'Signora Pierucci, there's something I'd like to discuss with you.' I reached into my pocket for the piece of folded paper, but before I could show it to her, three of her friends, came and swept her away in a cloud of excited chatter to look at the statue of Cupid in the grotto.

Sitting by the pond, I watched the guests enjoy the garden. Several of them came to congratulate me and to ask the names of some of the plants. At least I hadn't failed to bring pleasure to others, even if the garden hadn't thrilled Sylvana. I watched her covertly, and it wasn't long before she asked Luca to accompany her back to the villa. My heart felt as heavy as a boulder under my breastbone.

Later, once the luncheon guests had mostly left, I found Signora Pierucci sitting alone on the marble bench before the grotto. 'May I sit with you for a moment?' I asked.

'Please do. You can't imagine how much pleasure this garden brings me. It reminds me so much of the happy days I enjoyed here with Flora, surrounded by perfume and the beauty of the flowers.'

Carefully, I snapped off a pink rosebud and handed it to her. 'I know from Flora's diaries that the children loved it, too. She painted a vivid picture of Isabella, your sons and young Beppe playing here and eating ripe figs straight from the tree. I was so sad when I discovered Isabella died so young.'

Signor Pierruci nodded. 'Heart-breaking.'

'Except,' I said, 'that she *didn't* die, did she?'

She started and then gasped as the thorny stem of the rose pricked her finger. 'Whatever do you mean by that?'

I had only to see her shocked expression to know that my conjecture was correct. I retrieved the folded paper from my pocket and held it out to her. 'Beppe has kept this letter from Isabella for fifty-seven years.'

She took it from me with shaking fingers. 'I don't understand.'

'I think you do.' I spoke gently, concerned for her wellbeing. 'It was the figs that made me realise.'

'Figs?'

'The figs on the old tree in this garden aren't ripe until August, and Isabella's letter is dated August 1863. Unless this is a letter written from the grave, Isabella wrote this to Beppe in the month after she was supposed to have died.'

'What makes you think that?'

'The date of her death is written in the Marchese family Bible,' I said. 'I remembered it because it was a notable date. The fourteenth of July – Bastille Day in France.'

Helen waved from the garden doorway to catch our attention and walked towards us.

Caroline Pierucci gazed down at the letter on her lap. Blood seeped from her thumb and stained the paper. 'Please,' she whispered, 'don't tell the Marchese family about this. There are reasons . . .'

'Caroline,' called Helen, 'would you like a lift with Orlando in the *timonèlla* back to the house?'

'Thank you,' she called back, 'I am rather tired after all the excitement.' She thrust the letter into my hands and whispered, 'Come and see me tomorrow, Violet, and I'll explain.'

Chapter 27

At half-past eight, I was dressing for the party when Edmund knocked on my bedroom door. 'Are you decent, Violet?'

I was bending over to button the delicate ankle straps of my evening shoes. 'Perfectly. Come on in.' I stood up and smoothed down my skirt. 'What do you think?'

He let out his breath in a low whistle. 'What a dress! You look stunning.'

'Thank you. And you're very smart, too. I didn't know you'd brought evening dress with you.'

'I didn't. It was Teodore's. Orlando was kind enough to suggest I wore it tonight. It must be hard for him,' said Edmund, 'having me here when his son is not. I've come to realise how lucky I am to have returned from the war. It might have turned out so very different for me.'

Hugging him, I said, 'But you *are* here.'

'Yes.' His eyes shone with happiness. 'I certainly am. Shall we go down?'

In the hall, the front door was open wide to the evening air, and shiny motor cars were tooting their horns as they drew up outside and parked in a haphazard row on the gravel drive. Guests were sauntering up the front steps, the men in evening dress and the women in bright silk or satin dresses in the height of fashion with dropped waists, where they were welcomed by Luca and Sylvana. They spoke in loud, confident voices as they wished Sylvana a happy birthday and kissed their hosts.

My Italian was good enough to follow the gist of most of the conversation.

'How can you bear to live in such a place – charming though it is – so far from civilisation and with such execrable roads?' asked one of the men.

Sylvana, dazzling in a silver beaded dress and a feathered headband, kissed his cheeks. 'I'm keeping my apartment in Florence, Nico, and will retreat to the calm of the countryside whenever I need a rest cure from my dissolute friends.'

Nico snorted with laughter. 'You're as fast-living as any of us, Sylvana.'

'Do take a drink,' said Luca, 'and then go through the rear door in the hall to Sylvana's garden. Follow the illuminated path and the music. We'll join you once everyone is here.' As he indicated where the guests should go, he caught sight of Edmund and me standing by the foot of the stairs.

Our eyes met, and he came to kiss my cheek. His manner was formal, and I felt the rift between us grow a little deeper.

'You look very lovely tonight, Violet. I hope you enjoy the party.'

'I'm sure we will,' I said.

'Luca!' called Sylvana.

He turned towards her and saw more guests arriving. 'Please, excuse me.' He returned to his place at his wife's side.

Two maids carrying trays stepped forward offering cocktails and bruschetta, and the guests swooped down on the canapés with eager cries like a flock of seagulls.

Edmund and I stood back until they'd helped themselves and then took a Negroni. 'Aren't you going to have a bruschetta?' Edmund asked me. He took a bite and licked tomato from his lips. 'They're awfully good.'

I sipped my drink. 'I don't want to risk marking my dress.'

Rafaele, Francesca and Leandro came down the stairs, closely followed by Serafina and Emilio.

Leandro's eyes widened when he saw me, and he kissed me on both cheeks. Slipping his arm through mine, he pulled me towards his friends. 'Look at our little gardener,' he said. 'Would you believe the change? She is like a butterfly opening her wings in the sun.'

I knew enough Italian to understand his comments. I didn't need to know any Italian at all to see the admiration in Rafaele and Emilio's eyes and the surprise on Francesca and Serafina's faces.

More guests arrived, and the noise level doubled.

Leandro kept a tight hold on my arm and beckoned to the others. *'Avanti!'* he shouted over the hubbub. *'Diamo inizio alla festa!'* Let the party begin!

The group set off down the steps from the hall into the grounds. It was dusk, and the path through the parterre was lined with flaming torches as we trooped past Neptune cavorting with his nymphs in the fountain. I was swept along amongst the chattering group, and their excited anticipation was palpable. One of Leandro's hands was hot on my arm, but the other still grasped his Negroni. He pressed the glass to my lips as we walked, and I took a sip. Glancing over my shoulder, I saw Edmund laughing at something a girl in a jade green dress was saying. She hooked her arm through his and whispered in his ear.

Between the trees along the path, I glimpsed the lake shimmering silver beneath the setting sun. Above us, the sky was streaked with slate blue, saffron and marigold, but the party was oblivious to the spectacular sunset, intent only upon their pleasure-seeking. When we passed Massimo's cottage, I glimpsed his silhouette against the lighted window as he watched us stride past; however, I was caught up in the infectious high spirits and didn't want to think about his proposal at that moment.

Lanterns hanging from the trees illuminated our way as we entered the rhododendron tunnel. I hoped the oil would last long enough to light us home after the party.

Leandro drained his cocktail glass and tossed it into the bushes. 'Listen!' he said.

The sound of an instrument – a trumpet perhaps – wafted towards us on the breeze. Someone whooped, and the crowd surged forward, carrying me with it.

The door to Sylvana's garden was ajar, and as we pushed our way through, I caught my breath at the magical sight. Candles in glass jars were suspended from the pergolas and trelliswork, while also edging the paths and surrounding the pond. A large mirror had been fixed to the pergola behind the temporary bar and the reflected candlelight gleamed on the sparkling array of glasses and champagne bottles. I'd underestimated the powerful atmospheric effect of candles in a night garden.

The music was louder now. Blazing torches threw mysterious shadows into the craggy interior of the grotto where the jazz band, comprising half a dozen men in evening dress, were playing a bouncy tune that made me want to tap my feet. I wasn't the only one. Couples were already fox-trotting around the pond, and before I knew what was happening, I found myself caught up in Leandro's arms and whirled away.

I'd never taken part in such a dance before, but Leandro clearly knew what he was doing. He held me tightly, and after a few embarrassing missteps on my part, I got the hang of it and began to enjoy myself. It wasn't long before a girl in a cerise dress pulled Leandro away, and as they fox-trotted off together, he pulled a wry face at me before twirling his partner into the mass of other couples.

Slightly out of breath, I retreated to one of the supper tables set up under the pergola. A waiter brought me a drink, and I sipped it while watching the dancing. Cigarette smoke and gossipy conversation drifted towards me from nearby tables, but I was pleased to have a moment alone without the need to follow the fast-paced Italian conversation.

My thoughts returned to Caroline Pierucci and how I'd shaken her by my revelation that Isabella probably hadn't died when she was young, after all. Could it be possible that she was still be alive, and if so, why had she never returned to Villa Marchese? Caroline Pierucci was an old lady, and I would be careful not to distress her; however, my curiosity was aroused. I hoped she would be able to satisfy it the following morning when we met.

A cheer went up when Sylvana and Luca came into the garden, and I watched them walk hand-in-hand along the path, pausing to chat to their friends. Her silvery laugh rose above the music and pierced my heart. She was so lovely that it was no surprise she had captivated Luca.

I jumped when a hand touched my shoulder, but it was only Edmund.

'I saw you dancing with Leandro,' he said, sitting down beside me.

'And I saw a girl in a green dress whispering in your ear.'

'That didn't mean a thing,' he protested.

'Neither did my dance with Leandro. Besides, he abandoned me and went off with another woman.'

We watched the band and the dancing for a while. The band members seemed to be proficient at playing more than one instrument, exchanging the trumpet for a trombone, a banjo for a guitar or a clarinet for a saxophone. I marvelled that the musicians had no sheet music but improvised as they went along, like an animated musical conversation.

'I never imagined,' said Edmund, 'that a little over a year from when I was shipped back from France that I'd be sipping cocktails in an Italian garden I'd helped my sister to create.'

'And I never imagined you would be so well again.'

'But I am, aren't I?'

I touched his cheek. 'I couldn't be happier for you.' Beneath the table, I crossed the fingers of my other hand and prayed he wouldn't have a relapse. Out of the corner of my eye, I registered that Luca, Sylvana, Nico and Leandro were sitting down at the adjacent table.

Edmund took a gulp of his drink and then put the glass down very carefully. 'Violet, I hope you'll still be happy for me when I tell you that I've asked Claudia to be my wife and she has consented.'

I became very still, alarm bells ringing in my mind.

'Violet? *Will* you be happy for me?' asked Edmund. His voice was strained.

I blinked. 'I want to be but ...'

'Can't you *see*? I'm well again. I don't want you to hover over me anymore!'

'I hope with all my heart that you have recovered, but will you still be happy years from now? Do you want to live at Villa Marchese as an untrained gardener for the rest of your life?'

'That's a bit rich coming from you,' retorted Edmund, 'when I know Massimo proposed to you and you haven't actually turned him down.'

I gave an incredulous gasp. 'He told you?'

'Since Father isn't here, he asked my permission. He's a good man, Violet.'

'I know, and I'm still thinking about his offer.'

'Well, think carefully. I know you, and it's obvious to me that you're in love with Luca, but you should consider how empty your life will be if you refuse Massimo's proposal. Do you really want to end up as a bitter old woman remembering an unrequited love when you could have had the opportunity of happy companionship and children?'

I caught my breath as Edmund's comment struck home like a blow to my stomach. 'Of course I don't, but neither do I want to spend the rest of my life with a man I don't love.'

He covered my hand with his. 'I'm sorry if I spoke out of turn, Violet, but I want you to be happy. I've come to understand that life is never perfect but only as good as we make it.'

'I'm sure you're right.' I glanced at Luca at the nearby table. He was gazing at Sylvana while she laughed flirtatiously with Nico. Of course I knew my brother's observations were sensible.

'Look!' said Edmund. 'Isn't that Stefano and Rosa making a beeline for us? You remember, Luca's local friends who came to Villa Marchese at Christmas?'

'So it is.' I rearranged my unhappy expression into a welcoming smile.

'May we sit with you?' asked Stefano. 'I wanted to ask you a question.'

Edmund rose to his feet and pulled out a chair for Rosa. 'Of course,' he said.

'We haven't met any of Luca's friends from Florence,' said Rosa, 'except for Sylvana, of course.' She glanced at one of the nearby tables where two women were smoking cigarettes in ebony holders and whispered to me, 'I would be embarrassed to be seen smoking in public.'

'I do not know what to say to these people,' said Stefano. He shrugged. 'They make me feel like a clumsy old peasant.'

I laughed. 'I know exactly what you mean.'

'You said you have a question for us?' said Edmund.

Stefano nodded. 'What are those exquisite pink roses near the pond?' He raised his eyes to Heaven and kissed his fingers. 'That perfume! I must have one.' He threw his arms wide. 'Or a whole garden full of them! Luca's bride is fortunate to have a husband who imagined such a romantic present for her, and he is fortunate to have found you and Edmund to make this garden for her.'

'You're interested in horticulture?' I asked.

'It is my passion.' He glanced mischievously at Rosa. 'After my beautiful wife, of course. She is always my favourite rose in any garden.'

Happy to have found a fellow enthusiast, we fell into a deep conversation about the benefits and disadvantages of different rose cultivars.

It was a while later when I saw that Rosa was frowning with her head cocked towards a nearby table where Rafaele and his wife Francesca sat with and Emilio and Serafina.

'What is it?' I asked.

She fidgeted with her bracelet and didn't look directly at me. '*Niente*. It is nothing. I made a mistake.'

Stefano laughed. 'You do not make mistakes, *tesoro*. Did you hear some gossip?'

'Gossip.' Rosa nodded in agreement. 'Yes, only gossip.'

'And?' probed her husband.

'The one they call Rafaele, he said Sylvana wanted an *autovettura*, a motorcar, for her birthday. She was unhappy Luca had ignored her ... ' She rubbed her fingers together while she sought to remember the word. '*Suggerimento*.'

'Suggestion? Hint?' said Edmund.

'Yes, yes!'

'Now I understand,' I said. 'I heard her teasing Luca, trying to persuade him to tell her what her present was. She seemed

263

disappointed her mystery present wasn't at the front of the house, and then she was excited when we passed the stables.'

'I remember at Christmas,' said Edmund, 'she said it would be impossible to live here without one.'

'Sylvana seems like the kind of woman who can always persuade a man to give her what she wants,' said Rosa, making a wry grimace at me.

I looked briefly at Sylvana whose arms were wound around Luca's neck as she looked up at him with doe eyes. There was a half-smile on his lips that made me burn with jealousy. 'Yes,' I said. 'I daresay she'll have her motorcar by Christmas.'

We talked about rose varieties again, and then Stefano asked me to give him and his wife a tour of the garden. His enthusiasm was infectious, and he revived my pleasure in the project as I explained the work that had been carried out and why I had selected certain plants for particular locations.

Rosa sniffed the air. 'The perfume of the jasmine is sublime.'

'And the night-scented stock, too,' I said, 'but despite the moonlight and candles, it's too dark to see the colours of the flowers properly. Perhaps Luca will show you around in the daytime?'

Our attention was caught by a procession of white-coated waiters carrying platters of food to the buffet table, and we joined the queuing throng to collect a plate of delicacies. A cheer went up as corks popped, and a pyramid of glasses became a champagne fountain.

The four of us had a very jolly supper together, and Stefano raised his glass to us. 'To new friends!' Edmund and I echoed his toast.

The champagne flowed freely, and the waiters made frequent visits to the tables to top up the glasses. The band had a brief break and then began to play again with renewed vigour. The tempo of the music increased, and my eyes widened when several of the party-goers began to dance the Charleston. Shrieks of breathless laughter came from the girls, and the men shouted encouragement as they joined in. I hadn't experienced a scene of such frenzied gaiety since I'd stood outside Buckingham Palace on Armistice Day.

Edmund nudged me. 'Look! I see now why they're called flappers.'

Sylvana was dancing on a table, surrounded by admirers, her arms waving in the air and then flapping up and down. Her legs kicked furiously in time to the beat of the music, and her short skirt did nothing to preserve her modesty. She reached a hand out to Luca, who stood nearby, and called out to him to come and dance with her. He refused so she turned her back on him and kicked her toes even higher.

Leandro leaped up onto another table, a bottle of champagne in one hand while he danced like a mad thing, and the crowd clapped and yelled.

A girl in a cerise dress danced near our table, her eyes vacant as she concentrated on moving to the fast and furious beat of the music. A moment later, she put a hand to her head, wavered and then sank to the ground. Those near to her didn't seem to notice their friend's collapse and continued their frenetic dancing.

Edmund hurried to lift the girl up to remove her from the danger of being trampled underfoot, but then another man dragged her out of his arms. He draped her over his shoulder before carrying her away as if she were a sack of coal. A moment later, she was on all fours, vomiting into a flowerbed.

Rosa and I looked at each other. 'Why doesn't Luca control his friends?' she said. 'This is not like the other parties we have attended at Villa Marchese. I would like to go home now, Stefano.'

They kissed us, said their goodnights and left without thanking their hosts.

The music was so loud, and combined with a cocktail and glass or two of champagne, my head was throbbing. 'Edmund, do you think we might slip away, too?'

'It's not yet midnight. It would be polite to stay a while longer.'

An hour later, a number of guests had fallen asleep with their heads on their tables while the party continued unabated around them.

Luca was chatting with a group of his friends beside the fig tree, the air around them clouded by cigarette smoke. Sylvana was still talking intently to Nico over a bottle of champagne. I couldn't help noticing how he gazed into her eyes while he caressed her arm.

Leandro lurched up to our table, glassy-eyed from too much champagne, and caught my hand. 'Dance with me.'

His breath was sour, and I turned my head away. 'No thank you, Leandro. I'm sitting this one out.'

'Yes, yes. You must dance with me!' He pulled at my hand, and there was an undignified struggle as I tried to snatch it back.

Edmund rose to his feet and gripped Leandro's wrist.

Leandro looked up at Edmund's superior height and shook his hand free. He muttered under his breath as he walked away.

'Now is a good time to leave, don't you think?' said Edmund.

We made our way to the garden door, but as we reached it, a high-pitched scream rose above the lively beat of the music and mingled with the sparkling high notes of the trumpet.

Near the band, a man was tussling with Serafina. She screamed again, and Emilio ran to her aid. There was a scuffle and a warning shout. Emilio reeled back, blood running from his nose. Within seconds, fists were flying and men were grappling with each other, grunting and yelling as they wrestled each other to the ground. Furious, Luca shouted at them to behave. He separated several of the combatants and thrust them away.

'I'd better go and help him,' said Edmund.

I snatched at his sleeve. 'Don't get involved; you'll only add to the problem. Some of them are so drunk they can hardly stand, and surely they'll run out of steam soon—oh no!!' I breathed as an obelisk of sweet peas toppled over and flowerbeds were trampled in the brawl.

Two men heaved another up onto the wall that surrounded the pond and pushed him into the water. They howled in amusement at the almighty splash and moved on to look for more trouble, only to be confronted by Luca who gave them a dressing down.

'Edmund?' I said a moment later. 'Where's the man who fell in the pond? I haven't seen him climb out.'

'Stay here!' My brother sprinted off towards the melee, and I watched anxiously as he leaned over the pond, then tore off his jacket and waded into the water. He bent down to lift the man's head and shoulders above the surface.

There was a movement close behind me, and as I turned to see who it was, an arm gripped me around my waist and a hand clamped over my mouth. I screamed, but the sound was far too muffled for anybody to hear me over the urgent beat of the music and the general commotion. My feet were kicked away from beneath me, and I fell backwards against my attacker's chest. He took his hand off my mouth to keep me imprisoned in his arms.

'Let me go!' I yelled.

He dragged me, struggling and kicking, through garden door into the dark shadows of the rhododendron walk. He pulled me to the ground and trapped me beneath him. I tried frantically to push him off but his hands were all over my body. He grabbed the neckline of my dress and ripped the thin silk apart. I felt his hot, wet lips on my neck and breasts, and his knee was forcing my legs apart. I beat my fists on his back and screamed again when his fingers probed roughly between my inner thighs.

Suddenly, my assailant groaned and fell off me.

I rolled onto my side and scrambled to my feet, ready to run away, but then a figure loomed out of the shadows. My heart turned over in a new wave of fear.

'Violet? It's Luca. Are you all right?'

Relief made my knees tremble. 'I . . . I think so.' My teeth chattered from the shock.

Throwing down the branch, he gathered me into his arms and held me tightly while he murmured into my hair.

His heart thudded against my breast, and I wanted to stay in the safety of his arms forever. But that could never happen. Freeing myself from his embrace, I clutched the torn pieces of silk together over my breasts with shaking hands.

'I was on the other side of the garden when I saw him drag you away,' he said. 'I was frightened I'd be too late. I couldn't have borne it if he'd hurt you.'

'If you hadn't arrived when you did . . .' My voice was as shaky as my hands. I couldn't think about what might have happened.

'I'm desperately sorry you've been subjected to such an attack.' He slipped off his jacket and put it around my shoulders

'What about him?' I nodded at the recumbent form on the ground.

'I went blind with rage when I saw what he was trying to do, so I hit him. Hard.' Luca turned the unconscious man over with his foot. 'I hope to God I haven't killed him.'

'It's Leandro!' I said.

Luca cursed under his breath. '*Bastardo!* I've seen him get nasty before when he's drunk but never so much as this. How dare they all behave like animals in my parents' home? Let me escort you back to the villa, and I'll ask Mamma to look after you.'

'No!' I couldn't bear Helen to see me like this. 'Will you fetch Edmund?'

'I'm not leaving you alone here in case Leandro comes to his senses.' He took my hand and raised it to his lips.

'Luca?' Sylvana appeared out of the shadows. Her gaze rested on her husband's jacket around my shoulders and his hand holding mine. 'What are you doing?'

'Leandro attacked Violet.'

Sylvana shook her head. 'He'd never do that. Not unless she encouraged him.'

I pulled my fingers out of Luca's grip. 'Luca, please will you find Edmund for me?'

'Of course. Sylvana, stay with Violet until I return. And don't go near Leandro.' He hurried back to the garden.

'Well,' said Sylvana. 'Now I see the truth.'

'What truth?'

'You have finished making the garden for Luca,' said Sylvana, 'so it is no longer your concern. You will leave Villa Marchese tomorrow.'

I stared at her in disbelief. 'Tomorrow? But—'

'What reason do you have to stay?' Her voice was cold. 'Except perhaps, that you wish to steal my husband?'

'No!' But I'd hesitated a moment too long for her to believe me.

'Men are weak, and Luca speaks of you far too often.'

'He's asked me to stay on to manage your garden.'

'And I have told you to leave Villa Marchese. I cannot imagine what made Luca think I might want a garden, but I will employ a servant of my own in the unlikely event that I choose to keep it. And that servant will certainly not be you.' She turned away and walked through the door into her garden.

My fists clenched. I wanted to sprint after Sylvana and shake her until her teeth rattled. She had so much, but what had she ever done to deserve it, besides being beautiful and vivacious? In a few seconds, she'd deprived me – and probably Edmund, too – of our livelihood.

On the ground nearby, Leandro groaned and stirred.

In my terror to get away from him, I forgot Sylvana and darted through the door into the garden.

Edmund was sprinting towards me, and I ran into his arms. 'Leandro . . .' I sobbed.

'Luca told me. Shush now. You're safe with me and I won't let him hurt you.'

He was dripping wet and smelled of pond mud, but I clung to him and sobbed until I had no tears left.

Chapter 28

Edmund supported me back to our quarters in the tower and ran me a bath. I was desperate to remove every lingering trace of Leandro's touch and scrubbed my skin until it was burning. My brother tucked me into bed, but my nerves were still jangling and I was too jittery to sleep. Every time I closed my eyes, I relived Leandro's assault.

Outside, the sounds of revelry gradually faded away, and I heard cars crunching over the gravel, horns blaring, as they drove into the darkness. I kept the light on and stared at the ceiling for the rest of the night, wondering how I could avoid coming face to face with my attacker and his friends.

Edmund had said he'd speak to Luca to see if he would override Sylvana's orders, but in my heart of hearts, I knew she was right. I had to leave Villa Marchese, but the prospect of returning to my father and stepmother's home was intolerable. I trusted Helen wouldn't allow Sylvana to throw me out onto the street immediately with no notice and nowhere to go. After all, it was impossible that Sylvana had any proof I'd made any advances to Luca.

At first light, I could remain in bed no longer. Restless and anxious about the future, I decided to avoid Leandro by taking the early ferry to Lenno to visit Signor Cocci. He'd offered me work in his plant nursery a few months previously, but even if he hadn't been serious, he might know somewhere else I could try. Edmund was asleep, so I left him a note, put on my walking shoes and stuffed a cotton sunhat in my bag. Outside the house, I was surprised to see that all but one of the motor cars had gone. I'd imagined the guests would have slept late to recover from their excesses of the previous night.

A while later, I arrived in the town and made my way to the ferry ticket office. There was an hour to wait. It was then that I remembered I'd agreed to visit Caroline Pierucci. Although I no longer had a place at Villa Marchese, my curiosity was piqued to discover what had happened to young Isabella. Perhaps that would distract me from thoughts of the previous night's attack, and Caroline's calm and friendly presence would be comforting. I turned my back on the ferry station and climbed the steps to the upper town. It was still quite early but the aroma of baking bread drifted from the bakery and men were smoking and drinking coffee at the tables outside the cafes.

Halfway up the staircase, I came to the iron gate and pressed the brass bell push marked *Pierucci*. Scarlet geraniums spilled over the balconies, and a cat and her kittens sunned themselves on the steps nearby while I waited.

Eventually, Signora Pierucci's elderly housekeeper came to the gate, and I asked her if I was too early to visit. She shook her head. The gate creaked open and then clanged shut behind us. I followed her through the courtyard and we entered the house. A few minutes later, I was invited into the dining room where Caroline Pierucci was having her breakfast.

'Do join me, Violet,' she said. 'You must have left Villa Marchese before breakfast!'

'I'm on my way to Lenno,' I said, 'and intended to catch an early ferry, but then I wondered if you might be able to see me first.'

The housekeeper poured me some coffee and then left us alone.

'So, how was the party last night?' asked Signora Pierucci.

I chose my words carefully. 'More *exciting* than I'd expected. Luca's Florentine friends turned out to be a pretty fast set.'

Studying me over the rim of her coffee cup, she said, 'It doesn't sound as if you liked them very much.'

I hesitated. 'They drank a great deal, and a fight broke out after midnight. Luca tried to stop them, but it all became very unpleasant. I was relieved Luca's parents were safely tucked up in bed; they would have found it upsetting. I haven't been to look at the garden in daylight, but some of it was heavily trampled.'

She frowned. 'Oh, what savages! And now you're off to Lenno. What are you doing there?'

'I'm hoping to find a new situation,' I said, my voice tinged with bitterness.

Her eyebrows rose. 'But Helen told me she was delighted you'd agreed to stay on to maintain the new garden. Heaven knows, Massimo and Beppe are already doing the work of half a dozen men, and they won't have time for it.'

'Luca's wife wishes to employ her own staff to maintain the flower garden, and she's given me notice with immediate effect. I hope she won't ask my brother to leave, too. He's settled so well at Villa Marchese.'

'Well, really! I'm sure Helen and Luca won't stand for Sylvana's whims.'

'Perhaps not, but I'd rather not stay where my presence isn't wanted.' I drained my coffee cup. 'I didn't come to grumble about that. I'm hoping you'll tell me about Isabella. If she survived the diphtheria, as I believe, why did she never return to Villa Marchese?'

'You're very clever to have guessed the truth.' Caroline Pierucci sipped her coffee. 'In all these years, I've never told a soul, and I worried about it all night; however, I've decided to trust you with the truth. Will you promise never to discuss with anyone what I'm about to tell you? It might cause a great deal of harm.'

I put my hand on my heart. 'Of course. I promise to keep your secret.'

'It was so long ago, but I remember it as if it were yesterday. Isabella was utterly bereft when her mother died; poor little mite. Then, Umberto's mother sent her away to school and wouldn't allow me to visit her. Umberto said she'd settle better if I didn't fuss over her.'

'So, what happened?'

'Well, it happened like this . . .'

After my visit to Caroline Pierucci, I didn't go to Lenno after all but hurried back to Villa Marchese. I was relieved to discover that the last motor car had gone and I wouldn't have to face any of Luca's Florentine friends. The villa was silent, and before I returned to the tower, I went to look at the flower garden.

The catering staff had arrived to clear up the mess, but in the daylight, it was all a distressing sight. The ground was strewn with empty bottles, cigarette butts and overturned tables and chairs. I righted the obelisk that had been knocked over, but the sweet peas had been trodden underfoot and the roots torn from the ground. Plant pots lay on their side in a sea of spilled soil, the lovely rainbow bed was trampled and the stems of the glorious dahlias snapped. A dead fish and a champagne bottle bobbed about in the pond amongst the remains of the water lilies. I was too shocked by the wanton destruction of months of hard work to cry. All I wanted was to get away from it all as quickly as possible.

'Violet?'

I whirled around to see my brother with a pair of secateurs in his hand.

'How are you this morning?' he asked. 'I was worried when I found your note saying you'd gone out.'

'I had to get away in case Leandro—'

'Don't worry! He's gone. He was still drunk and argumentative last night, but Luca manhandled him to his room and stood over him while he packed his bag. Rafaele and Francesca drove him away in the early hours.'

'Thank God!'

'It was lucky for Leandro that he'd gone by the time I had you safely tucked up in bed or I'd have given him a couple of shiners and a fat lip. Come here!' Edmund hugged me. 'It's over now, and I won't let him near you again.'

I managed a small smile at my younger brother's protective reaction. I'd vowed to always look after him, but now the tables had turned.

'I was hoping to restore some of the damage in the garden before you came back from Lenno,' he said. 'I didn't want you to see it like this, so I've been cutting back the ruined plants.'

'How could those people be so irresponsible and selfish, Edmund?' Disappointment and despair drained away my energy. 'Much of our hard work has been wasted, and what's even worse is knowing Sylvana didn't appreciate any of it.'

'Umberto is right,' said Edmund. 'She's had too much of her own way. Her friends seem to be the same, seeking only selfish pleasure without thought for others. Did you notice that air of desperate gaiety about the party? The war has changed us. The survivors are determined to make the most of every moment, but nothing can ever take us back to those golden years before 1914.'

He rubbed a hand over his face. 'And what do we do now that

Sylvana has asked you to leave? I can't bear to be too far away from Claudia.'

I wanted to persuade Edmund to come away with me and leave Claudia behind, but then I pictured the joy in his eyes when he'd told me about their engagement. It would be more than selfish of me to come between them simply because I was lonely. It was time for me to set him free. 'If I'm not here, Sylvana may tolerate you at Villa Marchese,' I said. 'Besides, Beppe is getting older and the family needs another gardener.'

Edmund grimaced. 'Perhaps, but what about you? I can't leave you to fend for yourself.'

'I visited Signora Pierucci this morning,' I said. 'She's going to Turin to stay with her long-time friends, Adriano Conti and his wife Liliana. I was pleased to accept her invitation to travel with her as a paid companion. After what Sylvana said to me last night, I have no choice but to absent myself from Villa Marchese.'

'Perhaps it's for the best. A quiet week or two with Signora Pierucci and her friends will do you good and give you time to reflect on what needs to happen next.' He sighed. 'Sylvana and Luca weren't at breakfast, but Helen is hopping mad with them. Helen had to get up during the night to tend to the head wound of the chap I pulled out of the pond. He bled all over her sofa.'

'Does she know what Leandro did?'

'She knew he got roaring drunk and made a nuisance of himself but not the full story of his attack on you.'

'I'd hate her to think I'd encouraged Leandro in any way. Edmund, will you have a quiet word with her and explain that Sylvana has told me to find a new position? You see, Signora Pierucci thinks there's a chance the Conti family might find work for me in their garden. If that's possible, it will save me returning home to Father and Mildred with my tail between my legs.'

My brother shuddered. 'Heaven forbid! In any case, I'd better speak to Luca and his parents to let them know Claudia and I are engaged. I'm hoping to continue to work here, but I'm not sure what they'll think about that.'

'And you're absolutely sure Claudia is the right girl for you?'

'Completely.'

I hugged him. 'Then I wish you all the happiness in the world.'

He held me tight for a moment before letting me go. Reaching out to a rosebush with a broken stem, he snipped off a dangling bud. 'I shall paint this for you,' he said, stroking the velvety petals, 'to remind you of the beauty you created out of a bramble patch. Then our efforts won't have been for nothing.'

A lump rose in my throat. 'That's such a lovely thought, Edmund.'

'Violet, what will you say to Massimo?

I pressed my fingers to my lips. 'Massimo! I'm not sure what to say to him. If I'm not welcome here and if he and I were to marry, we'd have to live and work elsewhere. Villa Marchese has been his home all his life, and I don't want to be the cause of making him leave the place he loves'

'You're going to refuse his proposal? I had hoped ...' The corners of my brother's mouth turned down.

'I don't know. I still need time to think.'

'You won't find work elsewhere and then take the easy way out by writing to him to let him down, will you?'

I shook my head. 'He deserves more than that and I promised him my answer within a month. But for now, I'm going to pack my suitcase and return to Signora Pierucci's house. We travel to Turin early tomorrow.'

The journey to Turin by ferry and train was long and arduous for Caroline Pierucci. While she dozed on the train, I studied her marble-white face and blue-veined eyelids. I wondered how

277

long she would have the strength to continue these visits to her dearest friends.

It was early evening when the train steamed into the station, and I helped Signora Pierucci down to the platform.

'There's Adriano's coachman waiting for us!' she said.

A man in a dark green uniform greeted us deferentially and proceeded to organise a porter to carry our luggage.

A short while later, we were settled in the Contis' carriage and bowling along one of the city's wide boulevards. I enjoyed looking out of the window at the elegant baroque buildings, smart shops and cafes.

On the outskirts of the city, we turned in through a pair of wrought iron gates. The name incised on the stone gatepost was Villa Bellissimo. We drove along a gravelled drive and came to a halt outside an imposing primrose yellow villa with dark green shutters and a portico topped by an ironwork balcony.

We descended from the carriage, and I was interested to see that the grounds appeared to be extensive with clipped hedges, terraces and mature trees stretching into the distance.

The entrance door opened, and a steward ushered us into a hall with a highly polished parquet floor. He opened the drawing room door and announced us.

Two ladies sat on a sofa. Caroline Pierucci kissed them both and then drew me forward. 'Mrs Honeywell,' she said, 'this is my dear friend Signora Liliana Conti.'

I shook the hand of the elder of the two ladies.

'Caroline has told me all about you,' she said in lightly accented English.

'And this,' said Caroline Pierucci, 'is Signora Conti's daughter-in-law, Signora Roberto Conti.'

'I am delighted to meet you,' I said.

She seemed to be in her mid-sixties, and her slender figure was elegantly dressed in the latest fashion. Her green eyes regarded me with interest. 'We have been fascinated by Caroline's recount of your recreation of the flower garden at Villa Marchese.'

'Violet, Signora Roberto Conti is my goddaughter,' said Caroline Pierucci. 'Her name, before she married Roberto, was Isabella Marchese.'

Chapter 29

Three weeks later it was a Saturday morning in early September, and the trees were turning gold when Caroline Pierucci's carriage pulled up outside Villa Marchese. Her coachman assisted her and her elderly friend to descend, and then Isabella and I followed. I took my companions around the side of the house and let us in unobtrusively through the back door into the tower.

'If you will both wait on the bench here,' I said, 'Caroline and I will find Helen and briefly explain matters to her. She's the best person to judge how to break the news gently to Orlando and Umberto.'

'Don't be too long,' said Isabella. 'I'm in an agony of anticipation and nervous my brother won't want to see me after all these years.'

I squeezed her hand reassuringly. 'We'll be as quick as we can,' I said.

She nodded.

We went through the door into the hall, and I paused to listen. All was silent apart from the distant clatter of pans in the kitchen, and some of the tension in my shoulders drained away. I'd been worried Sylvana might accost me and demand that I leave the house. We crossed the hall, and I opened the door to the drawing room.

Helen, alone in the room, sat on the sofa sewing. I heaved a sigh of relief.

She glanced up and her face broke into a smile. 'Violet, my dear! I've been so worried for you.' She rose and embraced me. 'And you've brought Caroline with you. How lovely! Did you have an enjoyable trip to Turin?'

Caroline kissed Helen. 'We did, and the journey was made so much easier for me with Violet to assist.'

'Violet always gives of her best, no matter what she does.'

'Thank you,' I murmured.

'But I do wish you'd spoken to me before you went away. Luca was very upset when he discovered you'd gone without a word. I don't blame you, of course, not after I saw the state of the garden after the party. Sit down both of you, and tell me what has happened while you've been away.'

'A great deal,' I said. 'Signora Pierucci has something important to tell you.'

'Something interesting, I hope?'

'I believe you will find it so.' Signora Pierucci leaned towards Helen and began to speak.

Afterwards, Helen sat silently for a moment, absorbing the momentous news. 'It's an astonishing story,' she said. 'It will be a shock for Orlando, but I hope a pleasant one. As to Umberto's reaction . . .' She shook her head. 'If you bring the others to wait here in the drawing room, I'll fetch Orlando from his study. He's working with Luca, but I'll break the news and then bring them both here.'

'And your father-in-law?'

Helen's mouth tightened. 'Umberto can wait. I'd like Orlando to know about your discovery first.'

Fifteen minutes later, I waited with my new friends in tense silence, listening to the sonorous ticking of the drawing room's mantel clock.

Slow footsteps and the tapping of Orlando's sticks sounded in the hall. We sat up straighter as the door opened and he entered the room, closely followed by Helen and Luca.

Luca's gaze sought me out. I looked away but not before I noted his strained expression.

Isabella stood up and went tentatively towards Orlando. He reached out a hand to her, but dropped one of his sticks.

She picked it up it and handed it back to him. 'Shall we sit?'

'I don't know what to say to you,' he said once he was settled, 'and yet we share blood.'

'You won't remember me at all,' she said, 'and I'm trying to reconcile my memory of you as a baby with the man you are now. I used to sing to you when you wouldn't sleep. This is such a strange situation, isn't it?'

'Very,' said Orlando, his gaze fixed on Isabella's face. 'I hope we will be friends, but where do we begin?'

Isabella reached out and covered his hand with hers. 'If you wish it, we have the rest of our lives to get to know each other.'

Orlando's breath caught, and he gripped her wrist. 'I *do* wish it,' he said.

Isabella lifted their clasped hands to her cheek and Orlando, his mouth working with emotion, fumbled in his pocket to pass her a handkerchief.

Surreptitiously, I wiped away a tear from my own cheek.

'And this other Signora,' said Caroline Pierucci, gesturing to her other friend, 'is your mother. As Helen will have explained, Flora didn't drown all those years ago as everyone thought.'

Flora Marchese, straight-backed with silver hair framing her delicate features, gazed at the son she hadn't seen since he was a few months old some fifty-seven years before.

'I never imagined such a thing,' said Orlando. 'To have not only my sister but also my mother returned to me. This is one of the most extraordinary days in my life.'

Flora drew in a sobbing breath. 'I'm so sorry, Orlando. It was a terrible thing that I did, leaving you behind when I fled from Villa Marchese. I was not entirely in my right mind after your birth, and I was terrified that if I took you with me I wouldn't be able to look after you properly. Later on after I'd recovered, I was too frightened to come back for you. Besides, I thought my reappearance would cause you more turmoil than my continuing absence.'

'Please, don't distress yourself!' he said, 'I'm sure you had your reasons for not returning.'

'I did. I feared for my life and for Isabella's, but I knew your father doted on you and that you'd be safe with him.' She buried her face in her hands and wept.

'Please, don't cry!' Awkwardly, Orlando grabbed his sticks and pushed himself to his feet.

Luca hurried to support him and helped him to sit beside Flora.

Orlando placed his arm around his mother's shoulders. 'For all his faults, Papà has loved and cared for me all my life. And I had an excellent nurse who lives with us still. I was told you had drowned, but of course, I always wondered about you.'

'And I *never* stopped thinking about you,' sobbed Flora.

'Papà loved you so much that it was too painful for him to talk about you, so my curiosity grew. That led me to go to England to study, where I met Helen, the love of my life. She gave me my two wonderful sons. So, you see, my life has turned out very well.'

Flora looked up at her son, with tear-drenched green eyes. 'Caroline told me about poor Teodore and then your illness caused by the shock of his death. I grieve for you all and for the grandson I'll never know.'

'Teodore remains forever in our hearts,' said Orlando, 'but now you must meet Luca, your other grandson. And my Helen.'

Helen rose to kiss her mother-in-law's cheek. 'We're so delighted you came. You've never been forgotten, and as you see, your portrait still hangs in this very room.'

Flora looked up at the portrait above the fireplace, and a small smile hovered on her lips. 'My first husband, Gabriele, commissioned it.'

'It was this portrait,' said Luca, 'that inspired me to ask Violet to recreate your garden.'

'The garden that Umberto destroyed after I left Villa Marchese.' Flora studied her grandson gravely. 'When I heard about the new garden, I was honoured. Caroline brought me some of Edmund's paintings of it, and Violet has described it to me in great detail over the past three weeks. I would love you both to show it to me.'

'It will be our great pleasure.'

Flora smiled. 'Charming as well as handsome.' Turning to Orlando, she said, 'Will you ever find it in your heart to forgive me for deserting you?'

He kissed her cheek. 'There is nothing to forgive.'

'But there is a great deal for me to explain,' said Flora. She looked slowly around the drawing room. 'I never imagined I'd ever set foot in Villa Marchese again.'

'Why did you run away?' asked Orlando.

She hesitated. 'It's always difficult when two people don't love equally. My marriage to your father was not a success. It was made worse because he knew how happy I'd been with Gabriele, and he was painfully jealous. But he never understood that love has to be earned. You can't *force* someone love you.'

Orlando drew in his breath. 'Did he employ force when trying to persuade you to love him?'

Flora stared down at her tightly clasped hands and gave a small nod.

'Perhaps,' said Helen, 'we should call Umberto? He should know his wife has returned to us and be given the opportunity to defend himself.'

'I'll fetch him,' volunteered Luca.

'Umberto will be incandescent with rage,' said Flora after the door had closed behind Luca.

'Perhaps not,' I said. 'I was in the garden late one evening, and I saw him weeping. I tried to creep away without disturbing him, but he looked up and saw me. He thought that I was you. Or your ghost.'

'Once upon a time, my hair was the same colour as yours,' said Flora.

'And I had a trowel in my hand. He called your name, and his voice was so full of pain it nearly broke my heart.'

'Things aren't always as they seem. I suspect Umberto only sounded heartbroken because my supposed death deprived him of control. Despite his professed love, I was nothing more than a coveted possession to him. Once we were married and he discovered I didn't meet his expectations, he was determined to master me.'

'He's had strong opinions as long as I've known him,' said Helen, 'especially about a woman's place in the world.'

'And yet, his mother was anything but a submissive wife. I found her terrifying, but she doted on Umberto. At the beginning, he behaved like a love-sick puppy towards me, and although Madre Marchese disliked me, she wanted him to be happy. So, she presented me with a situation where I had no choice but to marry her son.'

'But how?' asked Orlando.

'She wanted a male heir of her own blood at Villa Marchese, but Umberto refused to look at any other girl while he fancied himself in love with me. I'd already told him I would never marry him because I still loved Gabriele.' Flora sighed. 'So, Madre Marchese took Isabella away from me and sent her to a convent school. I begged and pleaded with Umberto but he couldn't bear Isabella because she was Gabriele's child and he was happy to have her out of his sght. Then, Madre Marchese locked me in the tower until arrangements could be made to shut me up in an asylum. As long as I refused to marry Umberto, she wanted me out of the way so he'd forget me and marry a more suitable bride.'

'But that is barbaric!' said Helen

'She said my continuing grief for my husband two years after his death was unnatural and rendered me incapable of looking after my daughter.' Twisting her hands in her lap, Flora said, 'I knew she would carry out her threat. So, my choice was no choice at all, and I married Umberto. It was a disaster from the beginning.'

Footsteps and raised voices echoed in the hall, and then the door burst open.

'Where is this imposter?' Umberto's bushy eyebrows were drawn together in a frown as he scanned the room. His gaze fixed on me, and I fidgeted under the intensity of his scrutiny.

'Umberto,' said Flora. Her voice quavered, but she sat with her back poker-straight.

He walked towards her, shaking his head. Catching hold of her chin with his thumb and forefinger, he tipped her face up to the light and stared into her eyes. '*Madre di Dio!* So old! Is it really you, Flora?'

'None other.'

He shook his head in bewilderment, and his face crumpled. He sank to his knees before her, his arms around her waist and his head on her lap. His shoulders heaved as he sobbed.

Flora remained stiff and motionless while the rest of us sat in embarrassed silence.

At last Umberto drew a deep breath. 'I thought you were dead! What happened, Flora?'

'I could no longer endure your cruelty, so I ran away.'

'*Cruelty?* That's a lie!' He struggled to his feet and glared down at her. 'You know I adored you, even though you were so wilful.'

'And was it your *adoration* for me or merely your desire for control that made you beat me and force yourself on me, night after night?'

Orlando gasped. 'Papà? Is that true?'

'As my wife, it was her *duty* to give me sons!'

'As my husband, Umberto, you had a duty to allow me to recover from the birth of our child – a child conceived out of the savage attacks you inflicted upon me. Three days was not enough time for me to heal before you began to assault me again.'

'Papà, how could you?' Orlando shook his head. 'That was inhuman.'

'What else was I to do? Flora knew I adored her, but still she refused to love and obey me.'

'What did you ever do to earn Mamma's love?' said Isabella.

Umberto gave her a cold stare. 'I honoured her by making her my wife. That should be enough for her.'

'How can you say that? She never wanted you,' Isabella scoffed. 'Why would she? You were half the man my father was, and you never had any sympathy for her grief. And you were cruel to me simply because I was Gabriele's daughter.'

Flora laid a hand on her daughter's wrist to halt her impassioned outpouring. 'Isabella, don't waste your breath fighting with him. Umberto means absolutely nothing to me, and he cannot hurt either of us now. Quite the reverse, in fact.'

'What do you mean by that?' snapped Umberto.

Ignoring him, Flora turned to Luca. 'Recreating my garden was a wonderful idea,' she said, 'but it's lifted the lid on Pandora's box. Ever since Caroline wrote to tell me about a skeleton that might have been Gabriele's found in the pond, I've been plucking up courage to return to Villa Marchese.'

'I wish you hadn't waited so long,' said Orlando.

'For years I was too frightened of Umberto, but now that I see this pathetic old man before me, I wish that, too,' she said. 'It wasn't until I learned Gabriele might not have died on the battlefield at Solferino, after all, that a puzzling incident from the past spurred me into action.'

'A puzzling incident?'

Flora clasped her hands and leaned forward. 'On the day you were born Orlando, Isabella came to find me in a state of great excitement. She told me she'd seen her father walking through the gardens. To my shame, I didn't believe her, blaming grief and an overwrought imagination.'

'I always knew I'd seen Papà,' said Isabella, 'but until his skeleton and ring were found in the pond, there was no proof that he must have returned from the war.'

'But can the ring alone be proof Gabriele returned?' said Orlando.

'If Gabriele had been your father,' said Isabella, 'wouldn't you want to see justice done? I'm going to ask the police to reopen the case and discover the truth.'

'No!' barked Umberto. 'Do not meddle with the past!' He whirled around and pointed a finger at me. 'This is your fault, Violet Honeywell!'

I started. 'Whatever do you mean?'

'Why did you come here and interfere in our family business?'

'I wasn't aware of your family history when your grandson asked me to restore the garden,' I protested.

'I shut the garden, but you refused to listen to me when I told you to go away. *Dio mi salvi dagli idioti!*' He clutched his head and paced around the room, muttering to himself.

Luca took his grandfather's arm. 'Why was it so important that the garden door remained closed, Nonno?'

'No reason that concerns *you*,' snapped Umberto.

'On the day Orlando was born,' said Isabella, 'Gabriele came to my mother's garden, didn't he, Umberto? He'd promised he'd meet Mamma there when he returned from the war. But no one expected him to return alive, three years after Domenico Pierucci was so sure he'd seen him dead on the battlefield. It must have been a terrible shock for you.'

Umberto covered his eyes with his palms and rocked slowly back and forth.

'What happened, Papà?' murmured Orlando.

Umberto drew a shuddering breath. 'I don't want to remember.'

'I think you must, Papà.'

Umberto, eyes still covered, began to speak in a monotone, as if it were a story he'd told himself a myriad of times. 'It was almost sunset. Flora was hiding from me again. She was near her time, and I'd forbidden her to work in the garden for fear of miscarrying my child. I thought she'd disobeyed me, and I was angry. I went to her garden and saw someone sitting on the side of the pond. But it wasn't Flora.'

'My father?' whispered Isabella.

'At first, I didn't recognise him. He wore a filthy old coat and there was a terrible scar on his face running from his forehead down to his jaw.' A cruel smile played around Umberto's lips. 'He was no longer handsome.'

Flora gave a little cry and pressed her knuckles to her mouth.

Umberto ignored her. 'Gabriele stared at me, his eyes hollow and dark, as if he'd seen unholy happenings. I asked him where he'd been. His voice was slurred, but he told me he'd been ill for a long time. A farmer and his wife had found him in a ditch a week after the battle. His head was split open. They took him in, but he didn't know who he was or where he came from. After a long time, his wounds healed. He worked on the farm to earn his bread. Gradually, his memory returned, and he walked for weeks until he found his way home. When I saw him, he said he was waiting for Flora.'

'What happened then?' asked Isabella.

'I told him I was married to Flora now and that he must leave Villa Marchese, of course,' said Umberto.

'How *could* you?' Flora rose to her feet, her complexion milk-white.

'You were my wife, and that wreck of a man was no good for you. Gabriele's speech and movements were slow, as if he were half asleep. We'd believed he was gone, and I refused to let that wreck of a man come back from the dead and ruin our lives. You were on the point of giving birth, and no one was ever going to call my son a bastard.'

'But it was *you,* not he, who ruined our lives!' cried Flora. 'Gabriele was still my husband! We could have had manymore years of happiness together.'

Umberto continued, as if he hadn't heard her. 'I told him you were *my* wife now, and that he must leave Villa Marchese and never return. He roared like a wild animal and ran at me. I put my foot out and stepped sideways. He tripped over my ankle and smashed his head on the edge of the pond. And then he was quiet.' Umberto uncovered his eyes.

His recount of Gabriele's death was so vivid that I had to clasp my hands together in my lap to stop them trembling.

'What happened next, Papà?' whispered Orlando, white-faced.

'I put stones in his pockets and tied bricks to his feet, neck and waist with garden wire. Then, I pushed him into the deepest part of the pond and piled more bricks onto his body. After, I carried buckets of earth into the water to cover him until he was hidden beneath the waterlilies.' He looked at Orlando with a half-smile. 'There were a lot of flowers that year.'

There was a shocked silence broken only by Flora and Isabella's muffled weeping.

Umberto caught Flora by the wrist and yanked her arm. 'Stop that whimpering!' he commanded. 'Isabella, you will return to whatever place you came from. Flora, you are still my wife, and you will come with me.'

Her eyes blazed as she snatched her wrist away from him. 'You're out of your mind, Umberto! I was never your wife because my husband was still alive when I married you under duress. You *murdered* my husband and deprived me of a life with the man I loved – no matter how damaged he was. I'd rather die than spend a single second longer in your company.'

He raised his hand to slap her face.

'Stop!' shouted Orlando.

Umberto let his hand fall and rubbed his eyes as if he was beyond weary. 'Have you no pity, Flora? I grieved for you for nearly sixty years.'

'But what pity did you ever show to me or Gabriele or Isabella?'

'It was an accident.'

'Was it? We'll see what the police have to say about that. Now, get out of my sight!'

Umberto gave her a stricken look and stumbled from the room. A moment later, the front door slammed.

Orlando stared after his father while tears ran unchecked down his cheeks.

Luca drew a deep breath. 'Papà,' he said, 'I think I'd better speak to the police, don't you?'

Chapter 30

After Luca had returned with the news that the police were coming to question Umberto, I slipped away to look for Edmund and left Helen drinking tea with Caroline, Flora and Isabella.

Edmund wasn't in the tower, but Lucrezia told me he'd gone to Massimo's cottage, so I set off to find him. Melancholy enveloped me as I strolled through the grounds. I'd grown to love Villa Marchese, but it wasn't likely I'd ever return. I climbed the winding path behind the house up to the temple and sat there for a while, listening to the birdsong. Beyond the house, I glimpsed the lake through the trees. The view was breathtakingly beautiful. The water was navy blue today with the wooded mountains rising up steeply on the opposite shore. Down by the water's edge, Umberto stood motionless on the boathouse jetty, watching a ferry steam by. I couldn't help wondering if Gabriele's death had been a dreadful accident, as Umberto said, or if a moment of blind rage had pushed him along the path to damnation. But that wasn't for me to judge.

Sighing, I left the temple and went to the stables where Zizzo whickered at me over his stable door. I fondled his long ears while he regarded me gravely with great, liquid eyes. I said my goodbyes to him and made my way to Massimo's cottage.

Claudia was laughing over her shoulder as she opened the door. Her eyes widened when she saw me, and her smile faded.

Edmund was in the passage behind her, and he put his arms around her waist. 'Violet! Come and tell me all about your visit.'

'I hardly know where to begin,' I said, 'but first, I must congratulate you on your engagement.' I embraced Claudia. 'I'm so happy for you both.'

She beamed at me. 'Thank you,' she said, 'and I promise to always look after your brother – in sickness and in health.'

'I'm sure you will.' And I truly believed she would.

'Come into the garden with us for a while,' said Edmund.

I followed them into the kitchen and through the back door to find Massimo and Beppe sitting at the garden table in the shade of a mulberry tree. Massimo's face lit up when he saw me. He sprang to his feet, and I was reminded again of the seductive appeal of his physical strength. 'Please, sit with us, Violet. How was your visit?'

'Eventful,' I said. 'Beppe, I have some good news for you, but you might find it a shock.'

He looked at me warily. 'What is it?'

'You've told me about your childhood friend, Isabella, and of your sadness when she was sent away to school and subsequently died.' I reached out to take his calloused hand. 'I'm pleased to tell you that she isn't dead, after all.'

'But how can this be?' His weather-beaten face displayed both delight and confusion. I told him how I'd guessed Isabella hadn't died of diphtheria after reading her note to him written in the August of 1863, a month after she was supposed to have died. Her death was recorded in the family Bible on Bastille Day, the 14th July.

'What I hadn't even dreamed of,' I said, 'was that Flora hadn't perished either. In fact, she's very much alive and is drinking tea in the drawing room with Helen, Isabella and Caroline Pierucci.'

'But this is astonishing!' said Edmund. 'What happened?'

'Caroline knew Flora's marriage to Umberto was unhappy,' I said, 'and after Orlando was born, she became so worried about her friend that she and her husband Domenico planned to help her escape.'

Massimo frowned. 'But how did they do this?'

'The night before Flora disappeared, Caroline went to the boat in the Marchese's boathouse and hid some of her clothes At dawn the following morning, Flora left the house in her nightdress, with a small purse of gold that Gabriele had given her tied around her waist. She rowed to the middle of the lake, where she changed into Caroline's clothes. Domenico's boatman came to meet her and rowed her to Lenno. The Marchese's boat and Flora's nightdress were left drifting on the water. Domenico waited for Flora at Lenno and accompanied her on the steamer to Como. They continued their journey by train to Turin, where he took her to the house of his soldier comrade, Adriano Conti.'

'And Caroline Pierucci visits the Conti family to this day,' said Edmund.

I nodded. 'Adriano's sister Madolina was an invalid. Flora became her paid companion, and they lived together in a house that had been built for Madolina in the grounds of Villa Bellisimo. They became fast friends, and Madolina was so moved by Flora's grief at leaving Isabella behind that she offered a home to the little girl, too.'

'But how did Isabella escape from her convent school?' asked Beppe.

'Caroline, as Isabella's godmother, was allowed to visit her one Sunday afternoon. It was distressing to see the little girl so bereft and not to be able to risk telling her then that her mother was safe.'

294

I smiled at Beppe. 'But Caroline knew you had been good friends and offered to take a note to you from Flora and leave it on your doorstep.'

'So, that was how it happened!' Beppe's face wrinkled into a grin.

'Since Umberto had never visited Isabella at the school or brought her home for the holidays,' I said, 'Domenico wrote to Mother Superior, signing the letter as if he were Umberto. He requested – and received –permission for himself and Isabella's godmother to take the little girl out for a day during the Easter break. While they were waiting for Isabella to be brought to them, Domenico crept into the school office and stole a sheet of the convent's writing paper.'

Edmund laughed. 'That must have taken some nerve. Why did he want it?'

'I'm coming to that,' I said. 'The minute Isabella saw her god-mother, she threw herself into Caroline's arms. Caroline whispered that she must call Domenico "Papà".'

'And did she?' asked Massimo.

'She played her part perfectly, and the three of them went to a hotel for lunch, laughing at their adventure. Domenico told her it was a trial run before asking permission for her to come and stay with them for the summer holidays. But that isn't the end of the story,' I said. 'In the following months Domenico wrote to the school, under Umberto's name again, saying he wished to bring Isabella home for the summer. In July, once they'd collected Flora from school and she was safely in their carriage, Caroline told the little girl her mother was alive.'

'Can you imagine her happiness on discovering that Flora hadn't died after all?' said Edmund.

I continued, 'Before the end of the holidays, Domenico wrote to Mother Superior to say Isabella had perished from diphtheria so wouldn't be returning. Then, he wrote to Umberto on the writing paper he'd purloined from the school office to inform him Isabella had died and, due to the risk of infection, had already been buried. He knew Umberto would neither care nor wish to visit her grave.'

'What an incredible story,' said Edmund.

'It has a happy ending,' I said. 'Isabella grew up, secure in her mother's arms. She went to a local school but lived with Flora in Madolina's cottage, married Adriano Conti's son Roberto and they live at Villa Bellissimo, the Conti home near Turin. Flora looked after Madolina for forty years until she passed away. She was given the cottage for the remainder of her life in recognition of her devoted service.'

'Poor Flora,' said Massimo, 'but she was lucky to have such good friends.'

Claudia brought us coffee and biscuits while we discussed the news.

'Violet,' said Massimo, 'will you come with me to see the flower garden? Edmund and I have repaired some of the damage.'

My brother looked at me with a question in his eyes. 'I'll stay here with Claudia,' he said. 'We're planning our wedding.'

A month had passed, and it was time for me to answer Massimo's proposal.

We strolled along the rhododendron walk towards the flower garden. Sun filtered through the leaves and birds chirruped in the bushes. In the sunshine, it wasn't at all the dark place of terror it had been when Leandro assaulted me after the party.

Massimo opened the door to the garden, and we went inside. He took my arm, and we walked along the freshly raked paths, now free of cigarette butts and champagne bottles. The terracotta planters had been righted and most of the plants reinstated, albeit slightly battered. The plants in the rainbow bed were neatly trimmed so the damage wasn't too noticeable, and the waterlilies in the pond had turned their leaves up to the sun again. There were signs, however, that the garden was past its first bloom and fading into autumn.

I stopped to rub the lavender leaves between my fingers to release their resinous scent, delaying my inevitable conversation with Massimo.

'Shall we sit by the grotto?' he asked.

I felt as if Cupid's statue was watching me disapprovingly as we sat on the marble bench.

'You've worked miracles to bring the garden back to its former glory,' I said.

Massimo lifted my hand to his lips. 'I did it for you.'

There was an ache in my chest because he was good and kind man.

'Well?' said Massimo gently. 'A month has passed, and I hope you have an answer for me.'

I bowed my head. 'Yes, I do.'

He sighed. 'But it isn't the answer I hoped for?'

'I'm sorry, Massimo. I like you so much, and if things had been different, I think we would have made a marriage of friendship that might have grown into love.'

'You still love Luca?' His brown eyes looked into mine.

I dropped my gaze. 'The heart isn't always rational. I must leave Villa Marchese, but you'd be miserable if you left this place where your family have gardened for generations. Isabella and her husband have offered me the opportunity to work with Flora to design an English cottage garden for Villa Bellissimo. I shall be provided with two under-gardeners to do the heavy work.'

Massimo's strong brown hands gripped his knees, and he looked into the distance while he considered what I'd said. Then, he turned to face me. 'You are wise. Neither of us could be happy if your heart is with someone else, and it would tear me apart to leave Claudia and Villa Marchese.' He touched my cheek and managed a small smile. 'But Claudia and Edmund are a good match, and in time, perhaps they will provide me with a grandchild who will begin the next generation of the Bernardi family – albeit with a different name – to garden at Villa Marchese.' He leaned towards me and kissed my cheek. 'And I pray you will find serenity, Violet.'

I watched him walk towards the garden door and felt a deep pang of regret that I hadn't been able to accept his proposal. I was acutely aware my response had caused both of us to lose the chance of enjoying the security and comfort of married life again.

Closing my eyes and listening to the bees was calming, and I mentally relived how we'd restored the wilderness behind the walls to a beautiful garden once more. It was bitter-sweet knowledge that Luca had commissioned the garden out of love for his wife, while I had given it my all because of my forbidden love for him.

Someone called my name, and I opened my eyes to see Isabella and Flora approaching. I went to greet them, and the beatific smile on Flora's face told me everything I needed to know.

'I feel as if I have stepped back in time,' she said, her gaze sweeping around the garden. 'The planting is different from how it was, but it's more natural and in tune with the gardens I prefer these days. The pond and the grotto are almost the same.' She reached for my hand. 'We're going to have such fun, you and I, planning an English flower garden for Villa Bellisimo.'

'Since I used your diaries to guide me,' I said, 'in a way, we've already collaborated on this garden. Do come and look here. I planted a *Dicentra Spectabilis* on your behalf and in memory of your husband Gabriele. It's not in flower now, of course, but it will be beautiful again next spring.'

The three of us wandered around the garden together, and as every moment passed, I knew the connection I'd felt with Flora through her diaries was real.

Isabella glanced at her watch. 'We must hurry back,' she said. 'The police inspector will be there by now to question us.'

'I wonder if Umberto has stopped sulking yet,' said Flora. 'He's gone to earth somewhere and we left Luca searching for him.'

'I saw him down by the boathouse earlier,' I said, 'staring out over the lake.'

Isabella and Flora glanced at each other.

'Violet,' said Flora, 'I think you should run back to the house and tell the police that, don't you?'

Alarmed by her troubled expression, I sprinted back to Villa Marchese.

In the drawing room, Helen was sitting with her arms around Orlando while he blotted his eyes with a handkerchief.

I shivered with foreboding. 'What is it? Did Luca find Umberto?' I asked.

'I'm afraid so,' said Helen. 'He was in the lake. Luca pulled him out of the water but . . .'

I pressed my fingers to my lips. 'I saw him standing on the jetty by the boathouse soon after I left you. Oh, why didn't I persuade him to return to the villa?'

'Do not blame yourself,' said Orlando. 'It would have made no difference. He had tied his ankles together and his pockets were filled with stones.'

'That doesn't necessarily mean he's admitting—'

'He left a note under a stone on the jetty,' said Helen. 'He'd written that he didn't want to live in a world where his beloved wife despised him. He said he'd only done what he did to protect her from years of misery living with an invalid. Inspector Giuliano has gone with Luca to take a look.'

'I'm so very sorry, Orlando.' I sank down onto the sofa and wished I'd never come to Villa Marchese. Recreating Flora's garden had inadvertently caused heartache for so many.

Much later, after all the questions had been asked and Inspector Giuliano had taken our statements and left to write his report, Caroline took Flora and Isabella back to her house. Edmund and I would spend one last evening together before I joined Flora and Isabella on their return journey to Turin.

The villa was quiet again. Helen had gone upstairs to sit with Orlando, who was exhausted by grief and shock. Lucrezia bustled upstairs after them to take him a cup of herb tea.

There was no sign of Luca and Sylvana, for which I was grateful, so I returned to Flora's garden for one last time before beginning my new life.

I watched the fish darting about in the pond for a while, and then went to sit on the marble bench, my thoughts racing after the tumultuous events of the day.

Sometime later, the door to the garden opened.

Luca, his footsteps slow and heavy on the gravel, approached me. 'I thought I might find you here,' he said as he sat down beside me.

'I'm so very sorry for your loss,' I said.

He massaged his temples. 'Nonno has always been here, and it's hard to comprehend that in one day I've lost a grandfather but gained a grandmother.'

'It must have been a terrible shock to find Umberto like that.'

'The shock was discovering that he had mistreated my grandmother in such a terrible way. I knew he was authoritarian and had strong opinions on a woman's place; we quarrelled many times about that, but I never imagined . . .' His voice cracked and he shook his head.

I longed to comfort him but knew it was impossible.

'Violet, I wish you'd come to say goodbye to me the morning after the party.'

'I had to escape. Leandro's assault was terrifying and left me

300

feeling defiled. I was also very distressed your Florentine friends cared so little for the garden I'd worked so hard to bring it into being,' I told him. 'And while you went to find Edmund, your wife ordered me to leave immediately now my project was finished. She said you spoke of me too often, and *if* she wanted to maintain the garden, she'd choose her own gardener.'

Luca rubbed his eyes with his knuckles. 'I can't express strongly enough my anger for what happened on the night of the party. And Sylvana should never have spoken to you like that.' He bowed his head. 'She guessed I'd fallen in love with you.'

His words brought me mingled joy and anguish.

'What makes it all the worse,' he said, 'is that I knew from the first time I brought Sylvana to Villa Marchese that my impetuous marriage was a dreadful mistake. It was desperately painful to read the disappointment in Mamma's eyes because her daughter-in-law had so little interest in being a part of our family. I hoped the restoration of my grandmother's garden might make Sylvana feel at home here. What a fool I was!'

'I understand she'd expected a motorcar for her birthday present.'

'A motorcar would have given her the opportunity to run away from Villa Marchese whenever she wanted,' he said in bitter tones. 'We had a blazing row after the party. I was so angry about Leandro and how our friends had behaved. When she said she'd told you to leave, it was the final straw. I was sick of trying to appease her all the time, and I no longer cared a fig for my so-called friends from Florence.'

'I will not be the cause of discord between you and your wife,' I said. 'To that end, I've found alternative employment with the Conti family in Turin.'

'But you can't!' Luca gripped my arm.

'It's all decided.'

'Don't you see, there's no need for you to leave Villa Marchese

301

now! I told Sylvana our marriage was a mistake and I wanted a separation. She laughed and said I could have it because she intended to live with Nico in his palazzo in Florence. He could afford to give her whatever she wanted.'

I'd seen how she flirted with Nico, so I wasn't entirely surprised.

'Stay here with me, Violet. Please! My mother loves you, and I'm sure my father will accept the situation, in time.'

Shock and anger coursed through my veins. I brushed his hand off my arm. 'Are you asking me to remain here as your mistress, Luca? I can only assume grief over your grandfather's demise has turned your mind.'

'But I love you! Do you think I wouldn't marry you if I could?' There was desperation in his eyes.

'How could you possibly imagine I'd find such a proposition acceptable? Your mother and father would certainly have no respect for me if I became your mistress, and I would never insult them, or myself, in such a way. You've been so tainted by your Florentine friends you no longer know how to abide by a code of behaviour that is decent and honourable.'

He took a step closer to me. 'Violet—'

I yearned to fall into his arms, but one of us had to remain firm. So I turned my back on the man I loved and rushed out of the garden before I weakened and condemned us both to being shunned by our families forever.

302

Chapter 31

Villa Bellisimo, Turin

August 1922

It was late in the day but still hot when Edmund came to find me in the new flower garden that Flora and I had created together. I stuck my garden fork into the soil and squinted into the sunlight, wondering for a moment if too much time alone with my thoughts had made me imagine my brother's lanky figure.

He waved, and I ran towards him. 'But how wonderful and unexpected!' I said, kissing his cheek. It had been very nearly two years since I'd left Villa Marchese and six months since I'd seen Edmund. 'Why didn't you let me know you were coming?'

'Isabella wrote to me and told me how sad you were after Flora died. I hoped a visit from me might cheer you up.'

'It will. I miss Flora dreadfully. Somehow, the difference in our ages never seemed to matter; we shared our passion for horticulture and became such close friends when we made the garden together.'

I didn't say that I'd skulked behind a tomb in the cemetery while Luca and his parents had attended her burial. I wept as I watched them, half hoping Luca would turn and see me. He hadn't.

'You always said you felt an affinity for Flora after reading her diaries.'

'I did. And I was blessed to enjoy her friendship for two years.'

'At least she died peacefully in her sleep.'

'But tell me,' I said, 'how are Claudia and little Alfio?'

Edmund laughed. 'Blooming.' He took a photograph out of his wallet.

I studied the portrait of my nephew's chubby cheeks and curly hair. He had Massimo's dark eyes. 'Such a handsome little boy.'

'I would have brought Alfio and Claudia to see you, but she isn't quite well enough to travel at the moment.'

'Oh?'

He grinned. 'She told me a couple of weeks ago that we're expecting another happy event next summer.'

'How lovely! Congratulations!' I was delighted to hear his news and firmly repressed a tiny prick of envy. At least I could enjoy watching my brother's children growing up, even if I had none of my own.

'Massimo is so happy for us. He's such a doting grandfather, and Alfio adores him.'

I remembered how much Massimo had wanted a son and how he'd hoped for grandchildren. I was glad for him.

'He was utterly dejected after you left Villa Marchese,' said Edmund, 'but he's found companionship now with a widow in the village. I don't know if anything will come of it but it's good to see the twinkle in his eye again.'

I remembered that twinkle and experienced a pang of regret. I could almost hear the echo of the door to my happiness slamming shut, but it was a door of my own making.

'Did you know that Luca's book has been published?' asked Edmund.

'*Il Giardino Segreto*,' I said. '*The Secret Garden*.'

'Have you read it?'

I pictured the well-thumbed volume on my bedside table. 'I've dipped into it.'

'It's heart-breaking, isn't it? I found it fascinating that Luca was able to breathe such vitality and emotion into the star-crossed lovers, even though the story is set centuries in the past. When I was studying the classics at school, I never thought about how the fall of the Roman Empire might have affected the ordinary men and women of that time. Claudia cried for days after she read the part when the hero was dragged away by soldiers and killed.'

I hoped Helen and Orlando hadn't been too upset by that description. 'It's certainly a story that will resonate with many.'

'Of course, much of the action takes place in the secret garden.' Edmund laughed. 'No prizes for where he found the inspiration for that! Anyway, it's selling well, and his publisher has asked for a sequel.'

'I'm very pleased for him,' I said, but I didn't want to talk about Luca's book. I'd sat in bed night after night reading it and noting how many of the conversations between his hero and heroine reflected our own. 'Come with me, Edmund,' I said. 'I want to show you something.'

I linked my arm through his, and we strolled under a honeysuckle-clad pergola and then up a flight of steps through an arch to a raised terrace. The darkness of the enclosing yew hedges was softened by a foam of silver and white flowers and foliage. In the centre of the terrace was a fountain with a classical statue of a girl wearing a coronet of flowers and carrying a cornucopia. Water spilled in a gentle stream from the cornucopia into the pool at her feet.

'What a charming place!' said Edmund. 'It's a secret oasis hidden away from the rest of the garden.'

'But do you see the significance?'

'Of what?'

'The statue,' I said. 'She's the Roman goddess, Flora. I suggested it, and Isabella commissioned it. We can come here and remember Flora, even though her body is laid to rest alongside Gabriele's bones in the local cemetery. Come over here into the shade.' I led him to an arbour smothered in crimson roses.

We sat down, and Edmund drew a small package from his pocket. 'A present for you.'

I unwrapped the tissue paper and shook out a large silk square printed with exquisite paintings of pink roses, sweet peas and honeysuckle. 'What an enchanting scarf! It shows all my favourite flowers.'

'I know,' said Edmund. He smiled. 'I designed it myself, choosing the blooms from the flower garden at Villa Marchese. Do you see the pink rosebud? It's the painting of the rose I cut from a broken stem on the morning after Sylvana's fateful birthday party. Luca liked it, so I showed him some more of my work. The upshot is that I'm working part-time on a number of designs for silk scarves and dress fabrics, which are made in the Marchese factory. They're selling well, and my income from that is far greater than my salary as a gardener.'

Hugging him, I said, 'I'm so proud of you.'

'I couldn't have done it without you, Violet. After the war, my life was a living nightmare, but your stubborn determination to believe I could – and would – recover has come true.'

'Well, you were right to sense Villa Marchese was the place where you could heal.'

'I wish you'd come back.' He gave me a sideways look. 'Then you could take over Flora's garden again and give me more time to create textile designs. Perhaps you'll visit when the new baby comes?'

'Perhaps,' I said.

'Helen asked me to persuade you to come home. She misses you, especially since she's enjoying gardening so much now.'

'I miss her, too,' I said, 'but Villa Marchese isn't my home.' I wished that it were. I'd never told Edmund that Luca had asked me to be his mistress, and my pride forbade any return to Villa Marchese.

Edmund stood up. 'Isabella is waiting to give me a tour of Villa Bellisimo,' he said.

He kissed my cheek. 'I'll see you at dinner.'

I remained in the arbour after he'd left. It was so good to see Edmund, but his news, happy though it was, had left me melancholy. Yet, if I could turn back the clock to the day I first met Luca in Claridge's and make it never happen, would I? I wouldn't have enjoyed the rich life experiences Italy had brought me or the love that I still felt for Luca, despite his character flaws. Edmund was well, and however painful it was at times, I had no desire to return to my former drab and narrow life in London.

Something moved at the edge of my vision, and I turned towards the archway. My heart skipped a beat and then began to race.

Luca walked hesitantly towards me, coming to a halt six feet away. 'May I?' he said, gesturing to the seat beside me.

I gave a barely perceptible nod and made room for him.

He studied my face and a smile briefly curved his lips. 'You look exactly the same. Your complexion is glowing, and the sun has painted freckles on your nose. A curl has escaped your sunhat, and there's a smudge of earth on your cheek.' He raised a hand as if to wipe it away, but then thought better of it.

My mouth was unaccountably dry, and I licked my lips. 'What are you doing here?'

'I came to give you some news.'

My stomach clenched. 'Not your father?'

'No, no! Papà is well. His walking and speech improves every day. Mamma is well, too.'

'I'm relieved to hear that. What is your news then?'

He took a breath and looked into my eyes. 'My marriage to Sylvana has been annulled.'

'Annulled? But that's impossible. You were together for some time and ...'

I bowed my head so he wouldn't see my blush.

'Yes,' he said. 'I need to explain—'

'You don't have to explain anything.'

'Please! I want – need – you to know how it was.' The words tumbled out of him as if he half-expected me to refuse to listen.

'When I returned to Florence,' he said, 'after the agonies and hardships of the war, Sylvana seemed to me like a glittering jewel. She made me believe life was worth living after all. Beautiful and spirited, I let her draw me into her hedonistic way of life.' The muscles of his jaw tightened. 'I cannot blame her; I was a willing participant. At first, anyway. But I grew increasingly uneasy and hankered after a steadier existence. So, at the height of my passion for her, I persuaded her to marry me. Shortly afterwards, my father had his stroke.'

'And you needed to return to live at Villa Marchese and manage the family business?'

Luca nodded. 'We quarrelled, but eventually, she agreed to come with me on the condition that she could have some time with her friends first.'

'I'm surprised she agreed to that when clearly she wanted to be in Florence.'

'While I was under her spell, I lavished her with expensive presents, and she imagined I had more money than I did.'

He shrugged. 'When she discovered I'd depleted my savings, everything went sour between us. I tried to play the part of a loving husband but it was useless. She had affairs with other men, and she had no intention of changing her self-indulgent and unrestrained habits for me.'

A shudder ran through me at the thought of what he must have endured.

'I tried very hard to make her happy, but we had such different ideals that our marriage was never going to work. Restoring the garden,' he said, 'was a desperate attempt to get her away from the pernicious influence of her friends. Then, on the night of her party, when they showed such disrespect for the garden and everything and everyone that mattered to me, we had a savage and bitter argument. We both said things that could never be unsaid. She laughed in my face and said she'd no intention of ruining her figure, or her life, by having children. Especially mine. Finally, I realised any reconciliation was hopeless, and I told her so.'

'I still don't see how your marriage could have been annulled,' I said, 'simply because you tired of each other.'

'The Church moves slowly. It's taken time for the annulment to be granted on the grounds of "defect of contract",' said Luca.

'Defect of contract?'

'I had to prove there was a "defect of intent" on Sylvana's side to commit to a "lifelong and exclusive union, open to reproduction".'

'How could you prove that?'

'Sylvana provided me with a letter from a doctor in Switzerland attesting that he'd fitted her with a birth control device. And then Mamma remembered Sylvana had made a comment at Christmas during the children's nativity play about not wanting children.'

'I remember that! Helen was visibly upset.'

'She recalled that the school teacher, Signorina Lubrano, had heard it, too. My mother visited her, and shortly afterwards

Signorina Lubrano went to the Notary where he witnessed her statement confirming Sylvana's shocking comment.' He gave a half-smile. 'Motherhood is sacred here in Italy.'

'And was that enough to obtain an annulment?' Gripping the armrest of the bench I held my breath.

'Not quite. I had a few unpleasant encounters with my former friends in Florence, but in the end, obtained statements from some of the women whose husbands had betrayed them with Sylvana. With that, there was finally enough evidence for the Ecclesiastical court to pronounce a Sacra Rota annulment.'

I released my breath in a long sigh.

'To be clear,' said Luca, 'the marriage has been declared invalid from the beginning, and both Sylvana and I are released from any rights and obligations to each other.'

Every muscle in my body was tense. He stroked my hand, and this time I didn't stop him.

'I apologise unreservedly for any suggestions I made previously that you considered insulting. I admit, in my relief that Sylvana had left Villa Marchese, I was very wrong to suggest you live with me without the sanctity of marriage. You are the epitome of everything that is wholesome and good, and in my desperation not to lose you, I hadn't properly considered how distressing such a suggestion would be to you.'

'It was. It really was.' My mouth trembled, and I couldn't say anymore for fear of tears.

'You may consider me tarnished,' he said, 'but I've learned a hard lesson. You captured my heart that first time I met you in Claridge's, and my love for you grows every day – even while we've been apart for the last two interminable years. At last, I'm a free man and released from heavy chains of my own making; still, I can never be happy unless you are at my side. Violet, will you ever be able to forgive me?'

I made a small sound of assent. A pulse beat fiercely in my throat, and the melancholy and despair I'd carried in a tight knot in my chest for so long began to unravel.

Luca caressed my cheek, his eyes soft with love. 'Violet, if you will consent to be my wife, I will promise to be faithful to you and to love and cherish you forever.'

A sob of sheer joy escaped my lips. 'Oh, yes, Luca,' I said. 'I should like that very much.'

He caught me in his arms and crushed me in a tight embrace, his breath warm on my cheek as he whispered words of love.

We kissed and talked about the future, then kissed again.

The sun was setting by the time we left the arbour. We walked hand-in-hand through the garden, surrounded by the perfume of a thousand blooms, while we planned how to extend Flora's garden at Villa Marchese. And how one day, perhaps, a clutch of copper-haired children would climb up the fig tree there to gorge on its juicy fruit.

Acknowledgements

One of my favourite childhood books was *The Secret Garden* by Frances Hodgson Burnett. The idea of a lost garden intrigued me and, many years later, I've loved writing my own secret garden story.

Grateful thanks to my wonderfully supportive agent, Heather Holden-Brown and my lovely editor, Eleanor Russell, who has worked with me on several of my books. Eleanor has now handed over her role to Rebekah West, who has worked with enthusiasm on the final stages necessary to bring *The Italian Garden* into being. Thank you also to Grace Menary-Winefield for her careful copyediting of the manuscript, Charlotte Stroomer for the brilliant cover design, and all the team at Piatkus who made it possible for this book to be published.

Many thanks to my writing group, Wordwatchers, who read and critiqued my first draft of *The Italian Garden* and to fellow author Liz Harris, who was always willing to help me out when I fell into a 'plot hole'.

Thank you to my husband and family for their understanding when I creep away into my writing cave for hours at a time and, finally, a huge and heartfelt THANK YOU to those of you who have bought, enjoyed and reviewed my books.